BLOOD
ON THEIR
HANDS

Relax. Read. Repeat.

BLOOD ON THEIR HANDS
By Bob Brink
Published by TouchPoint Press
Brookland, AR 72417
www.touchpointpress.com

ISBN-13: 978-1-946920-96-6

Editor: Jenn Haskin
Cover Design: Colbie Myles
Front cover images: Blood Splattered Paper Background by Derek R. Audette, Adobe Stock; Burning wheel by misha, Adobe Stock

Visit the author's website at http://www.bobbrinkwriter.com

First Edition

Library of Congress Control Number: 2020935049

Printed in the United States of America.

To Kate Newton, an attorney and author, whose understanding of judicial practice was indispensable to an authentic rendering of courtroom interplay and legal procedures, and whose content suggestions were insightful. Also, Joseph Disser, aka Indiana Joe, whose extensive knowledge of automobile mechanics I depended on for a technical explanation of a car explosion.

CHAPTER ONE

A siren sliced through the drone of traffic, and Alec Monceau caught the glint from a flashing red light in his rearview mirror. The police car bore down hard, and he glanced at his speedometer.

His eyes widened. "I go only thirty-seven in forty zone," he muttered.

Checking his mirror for the cop car, he glimpsed his own face. "Police Shoot Young Black Man in Traffic Stop," the recent headline read. There had been others during his three years in the United States. But Alec was in his mid-forties. Still ... maybe that thing on his bumper was a mistake.

Fear pierced his calm demeanor, and he stiffened, his grip on the steering wheel tightening.

The squad car was on his bumper. Alec turned his head and saw, through the gloaming engulfing the prosaic suburban landscape like a rising tide, a line of cars traveling beside him.

He slowed to allow the cars to get ahead, then moved over and exited from Lake Worth Road onto Shelby Road, continuing for twenty-five yards before coming to a stop on the gravelly shoulder.

The cop car, bearing the insignia Granville Police, turned onto the road and pulled up behind Alec's Geo Prizm, a 1999 model that looked newer than nine years, its royal-blue exterior glistening in the fading daylight.

As it did so, a passenger in a gray, 2004 Mazda 3 sedan several cars back on Lake Worth Road, in the right lane, said to the driver, "Quick. Pull over into that vacant lot. I have to piss, and I can't wait."

1

Garbuncle's voice rang with urgency, and Brad Hitchens swerved the Mazda into the lot, just before the side road. He stopped the car and turned the lights off as Hiram Garbuncle stumbled out and stood beside the car so motorists couldn't see him urinating in the charcoal twilight. Hitchens gazed out the passenger-side windshield at the scene on Shelby where the red light flashed.

The cop on the passenger side of the squad car jumped out, pulled his sinewy six-foot-two frame upright, and marched toward Alec. The officer walked with knees turned outward, looking to Hitchens as though he had a stick up his rectum. The cop's muscled arms poked outward at the elbows.

"Why didn't you pull over sooner?" he shouted in mid-stride.

"I couldn't," Alec said in a plaintive tone. "There was cars next to me and ..."

The cop's billy club slammed into his head above and to the side of the right eye. A large gash opened, and blood spurted out. Alec staggered, almost falling.

"Holy crap," said Hitchens. "Did you see that?"

"Aw shit," said Garbuncle. "You made me jerk and piss on your car."

"Great," said Hitchens. "You got enough booze in your urine to take the paint off. Why didn't you piss at the end of the ballgame, before we left my place? Although I don't suppose it would have done a lot of good, after all the vodka you drank."

Garbuncle continued urinating while gawking at the police scene, his head angled right. The driver of the police car, somewhat older than his young partner, got out, revealing a modest paunch, and bounded up to Alec.

"So you like Obama, huh?" the cop shouted. "Maybe you oughta worry about gittin' that busted taillight fixed 'stead o' decorating your bumper."

"Taillight?" Alec sputtered. "Oh, yes, I forget. I have appointment at shop tomorrow and ..."

The thickset driver cop rammed one end of his billy club into Alec's solar plexus. He doubled up, gasping for air.

"Oh man," said Garbuncle, who had finished evacuating and was pulling his zipper up. He stood motionless and stared. "They're beating the crap out of that guy."

"That'll teach you to resist arrest," yelled the squad driver. The other cop smashed his club on the back of Alec's neck, pitching him forward. He fell face down. The older cop kicked him in the ribs and ripped his arms back and up, sending Alec's face grinding into the gravel. The partner kneeled and thrust his knee into the small of Alec's back, then jerked his wrists together and locked them in handcuffs. The officers grabbed his forearms and yanked him to a standing position. Alec screamed.

"Where you from, mother fuckin' darkie?" the younger cop demanded. "You got an accent."

"Trinidad," Alec mumbled.

"Where the fuck is that? Someplace in Africa?"

"By Venezuela," Alec croaked.

"That's what I said. Don't get smart with me." The cop swung his stick hard across Alec's shins. He cried out.

"Yer kinda light-skinned, like Obama. Prob'ly from the same place. Fuckin' monkeys tryin' to take over the country."

The cops shoved Alec into the back seat of the police car, and he gasped from the wrenching in his shoulder. The driving officer ambled to the back of the squad car with his arrest book and wrote the information on the faulty taillight. As he climbed behind the wheel, his partner in the passenger seat lowered his head and, without turning it, said out of the side of his mouth, "Maybe we oughta sit here for a little while and let this guy recover some before we haul him in. He don't look too good."

"Yeah," the driver agreed, and began writing in his arrest book:

Subject driving west on Lake Worth Road, aproksamatly 400 yards west of Military Trail at 7:45 p.m. Obzerved rite tail lite of subject's car not working. Terned on flashing lite, but subject kep going strate. Got on his bumper and he finely terned on to Shelby Road and pulled over about 100 yards north and got out. When officer Pickens aprocht him, subject began cersing and saying he didnt do nuthing rong. I insturkted subject to get in his car, and he swang at me with his rite fist. I dukt and he put his hed down and hed buted me, noking me to the gruond and kauzing abrashuns on my left forarm. Subject then charjed at me and I tript him and swang my billy and hit him in the hed. He fell hedfurst to the gruond and we kuft him.

He handed the arrest book to his partner, who read it. "You can't spell too good, can ya?" He smirked. "Looks good ta me."

Garbuncle got back in the Mazda.

"I don't want to detour, so don't turn your head when I drive past them," said Hitchens. "We don't want them to think we saw what happened or they might stop us and make trouble."

Hitchens drove back onto the thoroughfare and took an immediate right, heading north on Shelby. The Mazda passed the black-and-white squad car at medium speed. Hitchens and Garbuncle kept their heads pointed straight, though Hitchens couldn't resist looking out of the corner of his eye and seeing the despairing, slumped figure of Alec in the lighted interior.

A mile farther, just past the Granville city limits, another squad car loomed on the west side of the road. As the Mazda approached, the two men could make out **Hardinton Police** on the back. A little beyond the squad car was a burgundy colored Toyota and two officers standing in front of it with a woman. She walked a couple of yards with one foot in front of the other before losing her balance and stepping sideways to right herself.

"Is that ...?" Garbuncle said, leaning forward. "Yes, by golly, that's Donna. Pull over."

"What the hell for?" Hitchens said as he drove onto the right shoulder. "Who's Donna?"

"We rolled around in the hay a few times, maybe a year ago."

"That was before your divorce, wasn't it?"

"Uh ... no. Yes. Sexy gal. A little extra weight, but I like 'em with a lot o' meat on their bones. We shacked up a couple o' times since then, too."

"Oh yeah, I remember dropping you off at her apartment in Lake Worth one night after bowling. That old clunker of a tank you drive was in the shop again."

Garbuncle got out of the car and stood with the door open, looking at the scene across the road.

"What in blazes you got in mind?" asked Hitchens.

Without answering, Garbuncle closed the door and began walking around the back of the Mazda, halting to steady himself and then resuming with slow, steady steps. A chronic alcoholic, he'd long before learned how to affect sobriety when the situation demanded. A gentle breeze off the Atlantic tousled the thin dark hair combed back from where it began several inches beyond his forehead. His average-boned, short frame carried an ample paunch that hung over his belt, and he walked slightly hunched, feet slanted outward to complete the distorted effect. His face usually was solemn, Hitchens had observed, and during the brief periods when he went on crash diets, he closely resembled Richard Nixon in face and body, even in his walk.

He approached the officers, and Hitchens noted his air of nonchalance. Extending an open wallet, which displayed his driver license, he stared stone-faced at the cop and said, "Excuse me, officer. I'd like to confer with my client."

"Get back in your car," the policeman said, jerking his head toward the Mazda, "and mind your own business."

"Pardon me, sir, but this *is* my business. That lady is my client, and I need to assist her."

"Did she ask for your help?"

"No, but—"

"Then get back on your horse, Lone Ranger, and ride the hell out o' here, or I'm gonna arrest you for interfering with a police officer."

"With all due respect, officer, I have the right to speak with my client."

"That's it," said the cop, reaching to his left side and releasing a pair of handcuffs from his duty belt. "Turn around."

Garbuncle stood motionless, still staring at the officer.

"You gonna turn around, or am I gonna turn you around?" the cop said, his voice raised.

Garbuncle slowly turned one-hundred-eighty degrees.

"Put your hands behind your back," the cop ordered. "You're under arrest."

The attorney complied. The officer attached the cuffs, grasped Garbuncle on the shoulder, and marched him to the squad car, shoving him into the back seat. He grimaced as the cuffs dug into his wrists.

The other policeman finished putting Donna through the physical dexterity tests and turned to his partner. "What's up with that guy?"

"Says he's the woman's attorney and wants to talk to her. I ordered him to leave, but he wouldn't budge, so I slapped the cuffs on. I'll have to write him up."

"Okay. This gal's a DUI. Failed all the tests. Let's haul 'em in." He helped Donna into the squad car beside Garbuncle, and both officers boarded.

"I don't want you two talking to each other," said the driver, looking into the rearview mirror. "You got that?"

"Yesh," Donna slurred. Garbuncle glanced at her but said nothing.

The Palm Beach County Jail was several miles north, a large, imposing facility on Gun Club Road in West Palm Beach. The cops marched the pair up to the booking desk. Each was escorted to a separate section for males and females, where the cuffs were removed, and they were deposited.

After a half-hour, Donna was allowed to use her cellphone to call a girlfriend to pick her up. Garbuncle sat on the edge of the cot and rubbed his sore wrists. He slumped forward and dozed, jerking when his head dropped to his chest. Forty-five minutes later, a jail guard released him. The desk sergeant let him use a jail phone, and he called Hitchens at his apartment for transportation.

While making the call, Garbuncle watched as the two cops who'd beat up Alec brought him in and booked him. They turned right at the desk, almost brushing Garbuncle on the way to a cell. He turned his head to look at Alec as he passed, and noticed his puffed face and an eye swollen shut. The officers returned to the desk, and Garbuncle heard them tell the sergeant Alec resisted arrest and they had to subdue him. The sergeant smiled—sardonically, Garbuncle noticed—as the lawman stood behind the counter and read the report one of the officers handed him.

"Another uppity ni ... colored guy," he said.

Hitchens arrived, and Garbuncle turned his head to look down the hall at the cells as the sergeant escorted him to the exit.

"You curious about somethin'?" said the escorting officer. "The way you're lookin' around, you must like this place. Ya wanna stay awhile longer? I can arrange it."

"No, no. I was just stretching my neck. I got a kink in it when I ducked to get in the squad car."

Hitchens stood waiting by the entrance. The two got in the Mazda, and Hitchens stared at his passenger.

"Your eyes don't look glazed anymore. I take it that was a sobering experience."

Garbuncle looked straight ahead and said nothing as the car moved west to

Military Trail, then south to Forest Hill, and west on the way to his apartment. Finally, "Those cops are going to cause me a lot of trouble." He slowly turned his head toward the man behind the wheel. "They charged me with obstructing a police officer. They let me out on my own recognizance. But I'll have to fight this in court. If they win, I could lose my attorney's license."

"I don't know why the hell you did that," said Hitchens. "Did you think she'd reward you with another romp in the sack?"

Garbuncle looked at his friend with a faint, grim smile. "Yeah."

"Why didn't you wait till the cops did their thing and then call her and offer to represent her in court?"

"'Cause that would have been the smart thing to do. I wasn't thinking too clearly."

"Hell, I can see why. You were too damned drunk. I'm surprised the cops didn't charge you with public intoxication. Although I gotta say, you sure put on a good disguise. You were even walking straight." Hitchens paused. "Guess you've had a lot of practice."

Garbuncle didn't reply. His head hung, and his friend saw the glum look.

At Forest Hill Boulevard, Hitchens turned west for a quarter-mile, then south onto Sherwood and into Pine Tree Condominium, dimly illuminated with fuzzy orange light from fixtures in the hallways. He stopped in front of one of the cream-colored, brown-trimmed buildings.

"When's your car going to be ready?"

"Tomorrow. He works out of his garage."

"So I guess you'll want me to drive you there."

"Will you?"

"Yeah, I suppose so."

Garbuncle got out, stood for a moment looking down and away, and muttered, "Thanks."

"That Marlins game ended up costing you a lot," said Hitchens, leaning toward the open passenger door. "And they didn't even win."

"As usual," said Garbuncle as he closed the door. Feet splayed, he trudged to his first-floor apartment.

CHAPTER TWO

"I'm having a hard time understanding you," said Hitchens.

"Yeah, I been meanin' to call Bell South 'bout dat static," Hiram Garbuncle replied, sounding groggy to Hitchens.

"There, I understood that. You haven't been meaning to call anybody. You're too damned much of a tightwad to even get your phone line fixed. And you're too damned *tight* to talk right—as usual. What about your car?"

"Thass what I was tryin' to tell you," Garbuncle said. He sounded to Hitchens like a parent patiently lecturing a child. "The mechanic said iss ready. But he lives two miles away."

"So I guess I have to drive you there. Son-of-a-bitch. What time is it?" Hitchens glanced at his watch. "Four-fifteen. You're lucky. I just finished waxing the Mazda and you caught me before I headed to Publix. Okay, I'll see you in fifteen minutes."

Hitchens knocked, then pivoted to look without interest at the surroundings. He turned back as Garbuncle emerged and closed the door behind him, and was almost startled as his gaze squarely met his questionable friend. It was as if the man were unseeing. His eyes looked dead, like a fish's.

"Come on, let's go," said Hitchens. "Got your license?"

Garbuncle stood a moment, seeming to ponder, then jerked around, opened the door, and wobbled inside. He re-emerged stuffing his wallet into a back pocket of his loose-fitting jeans, which dropped below his belly. His shirt was open to the fourth button, revealing a flat chest sparsely layered with graying hair.

"With all the money you got," said Hitchens as the two men slid into his gray Mazda, Garbuncle bumping his head on the frame, "why the hell don't you get a new car?"

"I can't afford it," said Garbuncle, as Hitchens drove out of the condo complex.

"Horseshit, you can't afford it. You made a lot o' money keeping people out of jail. I gotta say, you were a hell of an attorney. Before the booze burned your brain, that is. And what about those four condos you rent out in this complex. You get a pretty good monthly income."

"Chicken feed," Garbuncle said. He turned his head slowly to his buddy, who caught the scornful smile.

"Chicken feed for you, maybe, but sure as hell not for me. Ham, you can't bullshit me. And you did damned good trading those gold and silver coins. Not to mention all those usurious loans you made to people down on their luck. You've got a lot of money sitting in the bank, I'm sure."

"I helped those people. They were in desper't circ'mstances, and I saved 'em. They had no place else to turn." Garbuncle's voice was softly pleading.

"I'm so touched, I think I'm gonna cry. But that's the way I am." Hitchens tightened his cheeks as if in pain. "I just want to kiss kidnappers—I love them so much—when they release their victims after getting their money. Only thing is, your victims will be in hock to you for the rest of their lives—or yours, whichever ends first. They may get lucky."

Hitchens was getting worked up. He knew he was being hard on his friend, but was so disdainful that he didn't care. No one was making Ham put up with it.

Hitchens glanced at Garbuncle with a look of disgust, wondering why he continued this friendship. He and Ham had met fifteen years before in a bar both frequented to watch Miami Dolphins games. He'd just divorced, and Garbuncle had separated. Companionship. That's what it was all about. For ten years, Hitchens owned houses with extra bedrooms that he rented to guys, and felt less lonely during those times. And he had a five-year, volatile relationship with a mercurial woman that mercifully ended. If he were going with a gal, he wouldn't need male friends, and probably wouldn't bother with Ham. It was Hitchens' own need. And Ham's. He needed a buddy, too. Still, he'd been eager lots of times to help Hitchens repair his car and stuff in his apartment. And he was pretty shrewd with advice sometimes.

"I pay a big alimony check."

Hitchens' face screwed up in a look of disdain. "Yeah yeah yeah."

"You are using a defense mechanism called projection," said Garbuncle.

"Oh no, not more psychobabble. How am I using projection? I forgot what the hell it is."

"It's when you project your own feelings of guilt or inadequacy onto someone else."

"What are you talkin' about?"

"You're stingy with your money, too," said Garbuncle.

"Sure, I'm careful with my money. But that's frugality—born of necessity."

"Now what you're doing is rationalizing," Garbuncle said with smug confidence. Before Hitchens could reply, his passenger thrust his arm toward the road and yelled, "Look out!"

Hitchens jerked his head left. He had crossed the center line toward an oncoming car, and swerved back to his own side, causing Garbuncle to fall toward him.

"I guess you're not as drunk as I thought. But if that'd been you behind the wheel, we'd both be plastered against the windshield. Your reflexes aren't good enough—especially in your altered state of consciousness."

Garbuncle looked ahead and said nothing.

"Ya know, Ham, all that psychology is really a way of avoiding being honest with your own shortcomings."

Silence.

"So you gonna be able to drive that junk heap back?" Hitchens asked.

"I won't have a problem." Garbuncle flipped a hand.

"I suppose not. You've done this enough times to know how to keep the cops away. That's what made you such a good attorney. You're wily as hell."

"Not *made* me. *Makes* me. I'm not finished yet."

"Keep at the booze and it won't be long."

In the mechanic's yard, bare ground with splotches of dead grass, the 1993 white Mercury Marquis was gray with a coat of dust. Hitchens conjured an alligator that just crawled out of a Florida phosphate pit. The car sat under a small tree to the right of a dirt driveway that led fifty yards off the road to a square frame house with a sagging porch. The white paint peeled into curls intermittently with bare spots where the wood had turned gray from exposure to the elements. On the car, deep orange rust splotches on the hood, top, and bumper peeked through the grime. Bird droppings dotted the roof, and mud clung to the lower side panels. The sprawling frame hung low over tires that were almost smooth, cords showing through the edge of the left-rear one.

"How 'bout we watch the Florida Marlins game?" said Garbuncle. His speech indicated he was sobering. "I'll pick up a frozen pizza and you can make the salad."

"I got a better idea. You can pick up a couple o' nice, juicy steaks—and a potato for you. I'll cook some broccoli for me."

"Steaks? Uh ... well ... okay, I guess I can do that."

"Yeah, I guess you can. The game starts at six today."

"Before we go to Publix," Garbuncle said, "can you follow me to the Computer Freak store on Lake Worth Road? My eMachines computer finally gave out and I've got to shop for another one, but I don't know anything about them."

"It just happens I'm in the market for one, too. But let's drop your car off at your place first, and then we'll go together. I don't want to take the chance your car will conk out again. I'm not up to dealing with it today. But don't drive so doggoned slow. I go crazy. You know how I drive. I'm impatient as hell.

"Suits me."

Garbuncle got out of Hitchens' car and trudged to the porch. He rapped on the torn screen door. A skinny guy with thinning hair and several days' stubble, wearing a white undershirt, opened the wood door and beckoned Garbuncle inside. The attorney withdrew his wallet, handed over some bills, and accepted the keys.

The car started, and Garbuncle drove off. Hitchens followed him on the narrow road, his stick-shift Mazda in third gear.

"Damn, that guy is slow," Hitchens muttered. Daydreaming, he pictured the long, low-slung Mercury as an alligator creeping along the banks of a river, Garbuncle seated on its back. His head barely rose above the car's seat. And then it hit him why a little guy would choose a vehicle so big it engulfed him. It gave him a feeling of power to be in charge of such a large machine.

At Garbuncle's apartment complex, the attorney joined Hitchens for the short trip south to the Computer Freak. They reached the warehouse-like store on 10th Avenue North, not far from where the police had stopped a car and beat up the driver. Entering through the automatically opening doors, they stood inside of the cavernous box and gazed around: office supplies to the far right, printing on the left, office furniture straight back, shelves with printers in the right-middle with adjacent rows of cartridges.

"Ah, right in front of us," Hitchens said, and headed for the computer section, waving over his shoulder for Garbuncle to follow.

Continuing past an assortment of Dells and Gateways, they stopped in front of a Hewlett-Packard desktop.

"I think the best deal all-around is an HP," said Hitchens. Both bent over a sticker attached to a low-priced model and read the product details.

Behind them, a softly accented voice said, "May I help you?"

Hitchens straightened and turned his head as the clerk moved beside him. "Oh, yeah, I was wondering whether the gigabytes or the RAM was more ..." He stopped for a second, staring at the clerk. "Hey, you look a little familiar. Where the heck do I know you from?" He paused, still staring, then snapped his fingers. "Now I know—I think. Aren't you the guy ...? Yeah, you must be, with that arm in a sling and the big shiner." He bent sideways to look at the clerk's head. "And that bandage on your head. Don't be offended if I've made a mistake, but ... didn't we see the cops beating the hell out of you off of Lake Worth Road? About ten days ago."

Garbuncle looked up from the computer he was inspecting. "You look familiar to me, too." A Eureka look lighted his scruffy face. "I saw what they did to you, and then ..." He was going to say he'd gotten a good look at him at the jail, but stopped.

"You see dat?" the clerk asked, his face brightening. "I see nobody. It almost dark."

12

"I'd pulled off the road 'cause my buddy Ham here—"

Garbuncle extended his hand. "I'm Hiram Garbuncle," he said with a broad smile that Hitchens knew was insincere.

Hitchens reached out a hand. "And I'm Brad Hitchens. What's your name?"

"Alec Monceau." He beamed, his white teeth glistening in a broad smile. "I please to meet."

"So anyway, we stopped, 'cause Ham had to take a leak."

"What dat mean—take leak?"

"Oh, sorry. He had to urinate."

The clerk chuckled.

"Yeah, I call him highbrow Ham."

Garbuncle smiled weakly, looking a little chagrined.

"You have a bit of an accent," said Hitchens. "Where you from?"

"I come to FlorEEda from Trinidad tree years past, in two-tousand-five. I never have trouble like dis."

"What in the hell happened, if you don't mind me asking?"

"I driving, see police car wid light flashing. I go on little road, stop. Two policemen come and beat me wid clubs."

"We saw them beating you," Hitchens said. "Didn't they give a reason?"

"One say I like Obama and my back light no work. He know I like Obama 'cause I have Obama bumper sticker. I tell him I know about light and get it fixed next day. Den he hit me wid club. Da two o' dem hit me and hit me and hit me."

"Ah, so that's it," said Hitchens, his face lighting up in a Eureka expression. "Couple o' racist pigs."

Garbuncle passed a hand over his face, covering a sarcastic expression.

"They use any racial epithets?" Hitchens asked.

"Ep ... I no understand."

"Oh, 'scuse me. Any bad names. They talk nasty to you?"

"Yes, yes. One call me monkey."

Garbuncle fought to suppress a smile.

"I figured so," said Hitchens. "They charge you with anything?"

"Yes. Dey say resis arres wid vi'lence. I never resis. I do what dey say."

"How did you get out of jail?"

"Police take me to judge next morning. He let me go—own recog …"

"On your own recognizance," Garbuncle said.

"Yes, dat it. He say I no have record, and I have job. He tell policeman take me to hospital."

"So you have to go to court," Hitchens said. "When's the court date?"

"July on seven."

"July the seventh?"

"Dat right."

"You got a lawyer?"

"No. I know nobody. And I have no much money. I like job, but I no paid much."

"You're in a tough predicament," said Hitchens. "You don't have much income, but probably enough to disqualify you from getting a public defender. Right, Ham?"

"Yeah, unless this place pays him minimum wage. What do they pay you, if you don't mind my asking?"

"Ten dollar hour. I am chief of computer department."

"That's probably just over the limit for getting a public defender," said Garbuncle. "But you don't make enough to pay a lawyer. What a messed up system we've got. Oh well, nothing we can do about it." He fidgeted. "Okay, let's get on with the computers," he said, mild impatience in his voice.

"Right," said Hitchens. "Alec, what do you think of that HP for $349? Is that a pretty good deal?"

"Oh yes, dat has much power for price."

"Yeah, it seems like a good buy to me. I think I'll take it. What about you, Ham?"

"I don't know. What about that one next it? It's only $334."

"Dat not so good deal," said Alec. "It not on sale. It have only one gigabyte memory—dat only half power—cost only fifteen dollar cheaper."

"Well," Garbuncle said slowly, "I don't really need all that power. I might as well save myself fifteen bucks."

14

"That's nuts," said Hitchens. "When you get better with the computer, you're going to want more power. What's fifteen bucks?"

"Four or five steaks," Garbuncle said with a wry smile, looking sideways at Hitchens without turning his head.

Hitchens rolled his eyes. "Whatever you want."

"Yeah, I'll take that one," said Garbuncle. "Alec, is it difficult to set up this computer? I'm an ignoramus when it comes to computers."

Alec moved close to the two men. "I not s'pose do dis, but ... you want me come your house, help you start? I take out stuff dat slow computer. I no charge you."

"Really?" said Garbuncle, his face brightening. "That would be great. Okay, let's do it. When can you come?"

"Today Sunday." He looked up, his forehead crinkled. "I finish work 5 o'clock Wednesday. Where you live?"

"You got a pen and slip of paper? I'll write down my address."

Alec hustled a few yards to his station and returned. Laying the paper on a shelf, Garbuncle printed his address and abbreviated directions.

"Think you can find that? It's not too far from here."

Alec studied the address. "Yes, I know main street here. I find."

Alec pulled the two computers from the storage space beneath the display shelf. The two men declined his offer to carry them to the check-out cash register in front, said thanks, and bade him goodbye.

"I can't believe you gave up such a good deal to save fifteen bucks," Hitchens said as the two men carried their new computers to Hitchens' car.

"I don't care about the deal," Garbuncle replied curtly. "I got what I wanted. Case closed."

Though perceiving that Garbuncle was getting angry, Hitchens wasn't in a combative mood. "Okay, whatever." He sighed.

They drove in silence, broken after a few minutes by Hitchens. "That poor guy is in a pickle. How the hell is he gonna defend himself against those lyin' bastards? They'll make up all kinds of crap. They just made a routine traffic stop and he fought and reached for their guns. They feared for their lives and managed to subdue him, but not before he kicked and punched them, causing contusions and abrasions that have since healed. Who is the jury going to believe, him or the cops? That's a foregone conclusion. Especially him being a black guy and a foreigner."

"Well," said Garbuncle, "if he didn't have that broken taillight, they wouldn't have stopped him. Those nig… colored guys don't give a damn about the law and drive around in beat-up old junk heaps that shouldn't even be on the road, and then they yell discrimination when they get pulled over."

"Are you shittin' me?" Indignation flared in Hitchens' face. "You drive around in that oversized hunk of scrap metal and knock the blacks for the cars they drive? Wow. You and I know damned well why those bullying bastards stopped him. The Obama bumper sticker. They probably wouldn't even have bothered about that burnt-out taillight if they hadn't seen that sticker. And another thing: You still have to use the N word, dontcha? What the fuck's wrong with you, man? You're like obsessed. I don't use the N word, but there are times when the H word is called for, and this is one of them."

Forehead wrinkled in bewilderment, Garbuncle turned his head slowly toward his companion, who looked him squarely in the eyes. "Hypocrite."

"I'm not prejudiced," Garbuncle said softly, feigning innocence. "My mama never talked bad about the n … the coloreds. I learned to ha … I was an adult when I started getting tired of blacks whining all the time about being mistreated instead of working to prove they weren't inferior and could stand on their own two feet. They weren't the only ones discriminated against. What about the Irish? When they came over to this country, the people here were awful to them. But they rose above it."

"Oh really? Ever hear of any Irish lynchings? Did they have to use separate public bathrooms and drinking fountains? Were they denied service in restaurants? Did they find it almost impossible to get a decent job?" Hitchens threw Garbuncle a contemptuous look. "You're full of it."

Garbuncle said nothing the rest of the way to his apartment.

"Can you stop in and set this thing up for me?" Garbuncle asked. "I won't know where to begin."

"I'm not much in the mood for it, but, yeah, I can help you with the basics.

But it's a little complicated because they stick a lot of stuff on the computer you don't need, and that slows it down. Alec said he'd come over and delete the junk."

Garbuncle had moved to this apartment eighteen months before, and Hitchens, aware of his friend's slovenliness, had made excuses not to enter. He carried the computer box to the door and stood inside, mouth open, stunned. Clothes and miscellaneous belongings covered the floor. Dirty, torn old jeans. Three towels and two washcloths. A plastic soap dish and, separately, a used bar of soap. Binoculars. A soiled, crumpled blanket. A pair of worn tennis shoes, one with the laces missing, and a beat-up pair of leather loafers. Coins of every denomination, mostly pennies. A faded blue T-shirt and a torn, long-sleeved flannel shirt. Several unmatched socks. A broken, small wooden bookcase. A note pad opened to a page of scribbles. Scattered pencils and ballpoint pens. A table lamp with the shade bent out of shape. A host of objects that Hitchens couldn't identify.

There was hardly any bare carpet.

"Come on in," said Garbuncle.

Hitchens set the box against the wall, next to the door, and appraised the route across the room to an overstuffed brown armchair. It partly blocked a spacious window looking onto a narrow strip of grass, yellowing in patches, that separated the condo building from an adjacent one. Playing a version of hop-scotch in a broken path, he reached the chair and plopped down, ignoring articles of clothing on the seat and one arm. His eyes roamed over three Kmart-quality paintings, each hanging askew on a different wall: a straw-hatted boy fishing with a bamboo pole at the edge of a pond, an alligator sunning on a river bank, a flock of blackbirds winging past two fluffy white clouds in a blue sky over undulating green hills. Smudges and scrapes besmirched the walls' faded, powder-blue paint. A ratty, light-brown couch rested against one of them, perpendicular to the armchair. A king-sized bed, its headboard marred with a plethora of scratches, abutted the wall across from the couch. The bedding was in such jumbled disarray that Hitchens imagined a wrestling match had occurred.

"Where's your head?" Hitchens asked.

"Next to the bedroom across the hallway."

Fearing the worst, Hitchens wasn't surprised. A wet, dirty towel lay crumpled on the floor next to a tub with a half-drawn shower curtain layered with a scum of mixed soap and dirt. The sink, beneath a cabinet with a cracked mirror and a ledge strewn with disheveled toiletries, was gray with gunk and streaked with white toothpaste. The toilet next to it, its bowl encrusted with brown lime, repulsed Hitchens. He urinated and hastily returned to the living room.

Through a rectangular opening in the kitchen wall, Hitchens spotted Garbuncle's back bending forward in front of a cabinet and quickly straightening. Head tilted back, he held a one-and-a-half-liter jug of clear liquid against his lips and guzzled for several seconds. Vodka, Hitchens knew, even without seeing the label.

Hitchens nimbly negotiated the route through the rubble to the chair. Garbuncle sprawled on the bed, reaching to the middle for a pillow to cushion his head against the headboard.

"The Marlins game begins in an hour and ten minutes," said Garbuncle. "They're playing the Cardinals."

Hitchens walked up to the bed, and sat on the edge, the only part of it uncluttered, and the two discussed baseball for nearly a half-hour.

"Les get 'at 'puter set up," Garbuncle said. Pulling himself off the bed, he stepped shakily toward a corner on the opposite side where a small computer desk and a rusty filing cabinet sat behind a rickety-looking, armless office chair.

Bam! Tripping on a tangled bedsheet, he pitched onto the floor as though shot, dropping so fast that his knees didn't bend to break the fall. It was as if a truck had slammed into him from behind. In an instant, he went from vertical to horizontal, hitting the floor so straight he could have been lying head down in a coffin. He landed nose-first, smack on a crumpled towel, which saved his face from injury. It struck Hitchens as so comical that he burst out laughing. He had stopped pitying his pathetic friend long before.

Garbuncle pushed himself up to a kneeling position, and stared down. Hitchens saw the look of wonderment at the motley cloth articles that had saved the inebriated man. He slowly climbed, one leg at a time, to a standing position, steadied himself as though preparing to walk a high wire, and resumed his journey to the small, wooden computer desk. He had removed the old computer and stashed it against the wall, next to the desk.

Hitchens retrieved the new computer from near the door, and headed for the cheap desk, deliberating every step, making his way among the rubbish like a soldier treading a mine field. He unpacked the carton and set the computer on the desk, briefly studied the start-up chart, and plugged in the cables and cords. Fifteen minutes later, he'd finished guiding Garbuncle through the registration process.

Hitchens Googled a couple of random subjects. "Seems to be a little slow. Would have been better if you'd bought the one with more power. Sit down and try it." He rose to let Garbuncle occupy the chair, and instructed him in Googling. He knew Garbuncle was woefully deficient in operating a computer, and realized it would be hopeless to help him in his drunken state.

Meandering through the junk to the armchair across the room, Hitchens left the besotted man sitting slumped in the desk chair, which looked as though it might collapse. Hitchens tossed several socks, a polo shirt, and a white underpants onto the floor, and sat back.

Garbuncle turned to the computer. "Lessee. Whaddo I wanna Google? I know. Cheap carpets."

"Cheap carpets? What for?"

"My tenant Earl's been complainin' the carpet is rotten."

"Why don't you just give him yours? You don't need it anyway, with all the junk covering it."

Garbuncle ignored the remark and painstakingly typed the words in the Google bar, erasing and starting over several times. "Now whaddo I do?"

"Hit enter."

"Oooh. I forgot 'at. Look at all 'at stuff came up."

"Okay, now you know how to do it. I'd advise you to forget it for now, and work at it again when you're sober—although I don't know when that might be."

Garbuncle rose with effort from the desk chair, paused, and wobbled to the bed. He crashed onto it and propped his head on a pillow.

The two men fell silent.

"You know, I was thinking," Hitchens said.

"I'm glad to hear it." Garbuncle didn't smile.

Hitchens was accustomed to his friend's brassiness when he was drunk.

"Alec is coming over here to help you without charging anything. Why don't you think of how he could defend himself in court? You know those cops are going to lie their asses off."

"Nothin' I can do for 'im. He should'na been drivin' with 'at burnt out headlight.'"

"Taillight. Man, did you forget already the excuse they used to stop him?"

"I thought it was 'is bumper sticker." Garbuncle sat with his head in his chest, his eyelids drooping.

"Now you're talkin'. That was the real reason. Look, we both saw what happened, and we need to help him. Otherwise, the jury will believe the cops, and throw him in the slammer maybe six months or more for resisting arrest."

"So?"

Hitchens waited.

"I'll think aboudit," the attorney said without raising his head. His eyelids flitted up and then back down, as if they were too heavy to hold in place. "I gotta worry 'bout my own case. I could lose my law license." He half-lay, half-sat with eyes closed. Finally, they popped open. "I'm gonna call you as my only witness."

Chapter Three

"Alec get here yet?" Hitchens asked when Garbuncle opened the door. "I left the paper a few minutes early so the traffic wouldn't be so bad."

"No, he's not here yet. I had to break away from a client early. She was yammering on and on about what a rotten bastard her husband was. This gave me an excuse to get away from her."

"Not that you couldn't have invented one, I'm sure." Hitchens stood just inside the door, surveying the room. "Not much has changed in three days—except, I didn't notice that red polo shirt on the floor before. Is that a complement to the collage?" He added, "Or should I say, the garbage?" pronouncing the word to rhyme.

"Yes. I'm always trying to be creative," Garbuncle deadpanned.

Hitchens tip-toed through the clutter to the armchair, while Garbuncle plopped down on the bed. A rap on the door.

"He's punctual," said Garbuncle, sounding surprised.

"Hallooo," he greeted the light-brown-skinned man. "I wasn't sure you'd make it, but here you are. Thanks for coming."

"Oh yes," Alec said with a gentle smile. "I try keep promise." He glanced around. "You have lot of tings." Hitchens saw his smile tighten into a strained look.

"Yeah, Alec, I'm not the most organized person on the planet. Why don't you follow me to the computer?" They stepped in a circuitous route over small patches of bare carpet to the corner. Alec planted himself in the decrepit chair and pressed the power button. He clicked on Control Panel, then Programs, and did a quick check of the items.

21

"What you use it for?" he asked.

"I just need to write letters and stuff, and do emails, and Google to find answers to things I need to know, or just to satisfy my curiosity."

"You no want play video games, listen music?"

"Oh, hell no. I'm not interested in that stuff."

"Okay. I delete dose programs from computer. It run faster."

"Sounds good to me. Have at it."

Alec hunkered over the keyboard and worked in silence. Garbuncle returned to his favorite spot on the bed, resting in a supine position with his head lifted onto a fat pillow shoved against the headboard.

"You know," he said, facing Hitchens, "I was just reading about that clunker program Obama is thinking about."

"Cash for Clunkers?" said Hitchens.

"Now, I'm gonna tell you what I think of that program, and I don't want to discuss it."

"There you go again. I'm supposed to listen to your opinion, but aren't allowed to differ with you. Huh-uh. I don't play that game. I've told you that before."

"The government gives rebates to buyers of new cars who turn in their old ones that use a lot of gas, and they destroy them. What a dumb idea. The oldest cars, the ones causing the most pollution, don't even qualify. This thing will cost us a hell of a lot of money and it's not going to do any good."

"I'm not so sure," said Hitchens. "It ought to make the environment cleaner, and anytime the government puts more money in the hands of people to spend, it stimulates the economy."

"Horse shit," Garbuncle retorted. "It's just adding to the debt."

"You just don't like it because you don't want to give up that sprawling, gas-guzzling piece of crap that looks more like a battleship than a car. It makes you feel powerful."

"I like my car, and if that's what I want to drive, nobody's going to tell me I can't."

Hitchens heard the irritation. "Have it your way."

"You damned right I'll have it my way."

Hitchens divined that his friend's pique would turn to anger if he said anything more, so he fell silent. The ire in Garbuncle's face evaporated, and he dropped his head onto his chest. Neither man spoke for several minutes.

"Okay," Alec piped up, turning to face the two men. "I make it—how you say—streamline. Dat right?"

"So you took all the junk out of it?" Hitchens said.

"Yes. I try it. It faster now."

"That's great, Alec," said Garbuncle. "I really appreciate your doing that."

"I think you said your court appearance is July seven," Hitchens said. "Is that right?"

"Yes, yes." He looked upward while counting on his fingers. "Sixty and one day."

"How are you going to defend yourself?" Hitchens asked.

"I no know. I tink I just tell trut. I say what police do to me. I tell dem I do nuting wrong, and dey hit me on head wid stick, injure my shoulder." Hitchens and Garbuncle both saw and heard Alec's helpless feeling.

"What makes you think the judge will believe you?" Hitchens asked. "Are you going to ask for a jury, or let the judge decide the case?"

"Jury? Dey let me choose? I no know which better."

Garbuncle sat listening. His eyes, looking up from his lowered head, were bright and alert as they shifted from Hitchens to Alec, but his face was impassive.

"You don't ask for a jury," Garbuncle said.

Hitchens knew his disinterested look was genuine as he stared at the wall between the computer where Alec sat and the chair occupied by Hitchens on the far side. "A jury of six is automatic in a felony case unless it's a capital crime. Or you can ask for a judge."

"Ah," said Hitchens, "I didn't know that. Okay, what do you think he ought to do?"

"That's up to him." Garbuncle let his chin drop to his chest again.

"Wait a minute, Ham. You're a criminal lawyer. You must have an idea which is better."

Garbuncle twisted his body a little, waved his right hand in a dismissive gesture, and raised his eyes without lifting his head. "I don't know what to tell him. I've been doing divorce cases lately. Haven't had a criminal trial for a while."

"Aw, come on. You saying you've already forgotten how to handle a criminal case? That booze must be taking an even bigger toll than I thought."

Garbuncle pulled his body to more of a sitting position and adjusted the pillow higher against the headboard. Hitchens saw his expression turn ponderous and authoritative. "In my experience, judges rarely find fault with cops. I don't know why this case would be any different. Alec might be wise to go with a jury. In pitting a cop against a defendant, they tend to give greater credence to the defendant. On the other hand, juries sometimes are biased against, uh, minority defendants. There could be a mistrial. A new trial would be held. That might be better or worse for the defendant. It's a tough call. But all in all, I think your best chance is with a jury."

"There you have it, Alec," said Hitchens. "Let the judge call a jury." He paused. "But it's still going to be hard to convince the jury to believe your word over the cops' word. Because there were no witnesses. Except ..." Hitchens looked at Garbuncle out of the corner of his eye,

"You're going to need a lawyer." He turned his gaze back on Alec.

"Lawyer cost lot of money. I no have money. I send to fam'ly and kids in Trinidad."

"Oh, you have a family?" said Hitchens.

"Yes. I no can get dem to United States. I come alone. Very hard to get job in Trinidad. I make much more money here, help family."

"You probably wouldn't be able to afford an attorney even if you weren't supporting a family," said Hitchens. "Not on your salary from that computer store. Trouble is, you probably make too much money to qualify for a public defender."

"What dat is?"

"That's an attorney the court appoints to represent poor people who can't pay for one."

Hitchens looked at Garbuncle, whose head had again dropped to his chest, as though he were dozing. "Well, at least we'll be there to testify for you. We saw the whole thing. Right Ham?"

"Huh?" Garbuncle raised his head, pretending he hadn't heard. He lifted his arm to look at his watch and sat erect. "Well, it's getting late and I need to see if I can operate this computer. I shouldn't have any trouble with that contraption now. You've been a tremendous help, Alec. Thanks a lot. Let me walk you to your car. I'm sure you have other things you need to do."

He rose from the bed and toddled the few steps to the door.

"Happy to help," said Alec as he rose. His head down at the floor, he took small steps in a twisted route through the debris on the way to the door.

Garbuncle opened the door for him.

"You no need go car wid me," Alec said. "Tank you."

"Okay. I'll be seeing you sometime at the Computer Freak."

"Yeah, see you later, Alec," Hitchens called.

Garbuncle shut the door and planted himself back on the bed.

"I thought you were going to go to work on the computer," said Hitchens.

"I'll get to it. I'm in no hurry."

Silence.

"Ya know, he's gonna need us to testify. He was too polite to correct me when I said there were no witnesses. Doing this favor for you, he certainly could have asked you and me to testify for him."

"I got my own case to worry about."

"Look, we saw what happened. We can't let him get convicted of something he didn't do. We have to testify for him."

Garbuncle didn't reply. Then, "If we get on the witness stand and contradict the cops' account of what happened, we are calling them liars. And regardless of the outcome of the trial, they will never forget that. They'll keep our license tag numbers with them and pass the word to other cops, and they'll hound the hell out of us. Rear light out, headlight out, switching lanes without signaling, five miles an hour over the limit, rear stoplight not—"

"Okay, I get the picture," Hitchens interrupted. "I know what you're worried about. It's not about getting a ticket for some little infraction. You're worried you'll get hit with a DUI, 'cause you seldom drive sober."

"Listen buddy. You're not exactly a teetotaler." Garbuncle's baritone voice was sharp. "I've been riding with you when you've had a lot to drink plenty of times."

"Sure. That's usually after we've been watching a ballgame on TV and I've had several glasses of wine, and then I had to drive you home because that gas guzzler you drive was in some cheapo mechanic's driveway where he's trying to fix the broken down hunk of junk. That sorry excuse for a car should have been in an automobile graveyard long ago. In fact, you should've donated it to automobile research so they could examine the parts to determine why they kept breaking down. They'd prob'ly find out it was because the owner drove so slow the car didn't get enough exercise and the parts froze up."

Hitchens realized he was being defensive. There were plenty of times when he'd driven after drinking too much in situations that had nothing to do with Garbuncle.

Garbuncle looked off into space, and Hitchens knew he was pretending not to listen. "Let's talk about what you're going to testify in court for me," he said. "We need to go over that—what I'm going to ask you and what you're going to say. I got a court date a week from Tuesday."

"Aren't you hiring an attorney?"

Garbuncle's lips widened in a faint smile. "I don't need anybody."

"I've always wondered if attorneys advised people to hire an attorney just to make people think they were indispensable, so they could charge unaffordable prices."

"People don't know all the tricks in either defending themselves or suing somebody else. It takes experience to learn the ins and outs of effective representation—how to get the jury to side with you, whether to ask a question you know the other side will object to, things like that."

"Right. And in your case, won't another attorney be able to see things that you don't because you're too emotionally involved in the case?"

Hitchens divined the self-confidence oozing in Garbuncle's smile. "I'm savvy enough to control my emotions when I have to. I can handle it."

"You sure it's not because you're too stingy to hire somebody?"

Garbuncle looked at the ceiling. "I don't want to pay somebody to defend me on something I'm not guilty of. But if I didn't think I could do the job myself, I wouldn't be penny-wise and pound-foolish." His gaze settled on Hitchens. "Don't worry about me. I'll be all right as long as you follow my instructions and testify the way I tell you to. Think you can do that?"

"Of course. There's just one problem." Hitchens looked his friend in the eyes.

"What are you talking about?"

Hitchens hesitated. "You have to help Alec."

Garbuncle's right arm swept up and away, as though he were getting rid of something. "I can't help that ni … that Neantherthal," he retorted. "How am I going to help him? He can't even speak English."

"You were going to use the N word, weren'tcha? You can call him a Neanderthal all you want, but he knew how to set up your computer and you didn't. And as far as his English, he speaks perfectly well. Almost, anyway. He just drops a preposition here and there and gets the verb forms a little wrong. But he's easy for anybody to understand."

"So how do you think I can help him?"

"Same way as I can—and will. I'm going to testify about what I saw. I'll tell the metro editor at the *Hawk* I need to recuse myself from any reporting on the case."

"We've already been over this. If you want to have the cops harassing you forevermore, go ahead. I don't need them giving me a hard time. I've got enough problems."

"I'm sure you do, and they're all like tentacles of an octopus, branching out from the mouth. That liquid you pour into your mouth with abandon sprouts those tentacles."

"All right, all right, you don't need to call me an alcoholic. I already know it. Looks like you're hell-bent on getting us both into everlasting trouble."

"Does that mean you're going to do it?"

"Hell, looks like I don't have any choice."

"Look, Ham, it's the least you can do for a guy who helped you without asking for anything in return."

"He may not have asked for it, but I'll wager that's what he was thinking of when he volunteered to help with the computer. That office supplies store doesn't allow employees to do work for people on their off hours and make money that the store should be getting."

"What are you talking about? He didn't charge you anything."

"Sure, but he wasn't doing it for nothing. He figured we'd help him in court."

Hitchens stared at Garbuncle, saying nothing. Finally, "You know, Ham, I realize this is beyond your comprehension, but there are people in this world who do things for others simply because it's in their hearts to do so. They're not always calculating what they can get out of it. Their lives are about more than just money."

Garbuncle looked at his watch. "Oh shoot. The car guys are on WXEL in five minutes. My radio doesn't pick up the public radio station, so I go out to the car and listen. It's not really clear, but it works good enough."

"You talking about *Car Talk*? Click and clack, the tappet brothers?"

"Yeah. I love those guys."

"I can understand why. That junker you drive could provide them with three years of problems to solve."

"I learn a lot from them."

"Yeah, well, don't ever call them, 'cause they're likely to tell you something you don't want to hear."

"Huh?"

"Get a new car."

Chapter Four

Just beyond the urban reaches of West Palm Beach, twilight wrapped around a stretch of wooded grounds like a harem dancer's diaphanous skirt.

Brad Hitchens meandered among the few tables laden with wares, attended by women in frumpy attire. They gazed out at the sparse gathering of people walking about the grounds. Now and then someone inspected the trinkets, costume jewelry, hunting paraphernalia, decorative wood carvings, and other unremarkable items offered for sale. Few purchased.

At scattered picnic tables, persons of both sexes and wide-ranging ages, including children, munched on American comfort food: fried chicken, potato salad, cole slaw, green-bean and macaroni-and-cheese casseroles, apple pie, potato chips, washing it all down with assorted sodas. They chatted in tones ranging from subdued to boisterous, sprinkling their conversation with laughter.

Hitchens carried a notepad and pen, occasionally jotting something on the pad. After one entry, he looked up, and felt a presence behind him. Turning his head sideways, he was startled to find a strapping, six-foot-two fellow around age twenty, with dirty-blond hair, following him only inches away. The reporter whirled and faced the handsome guy, who stood staring. Hitchens returned the stare for several seconds, chilled by the cold eyes, clenched jaw, and stony expression. The reporter walked on.

Sauntering up to a table near the entrance to the grounds, where a man and a woman checked visitors as they arrived, he asked to be shown to the Exalted Cyclops.

"Do you mean the Imperial Wizard, Ronald Stanton?" asked the beer-bellied man, who looked hostile to Hitchens. The man wore a white T-shirt and baggy pants held up by an outdoorsy belt that had a metal buckle engraved with two crossed rifles. He'd allowed Hitchens in when the reporter said he'd never been to a Klan meeting, and was curious.

Hitchens fought to suppress a laugh, and smiled instead. "I'm sorry. I get the nomenclature a little mixed up."

"Nom ...?" the man said, looking bemused.

"I mean the titles," Hitchens said. "I'm looking for the chief Klansman."

"Whaddya wanna see 'im fer?"

"I'm a newspaper reporter, and I'm supposed to interview him."

"I thought ya said you was just curious."

"Well ... yes, I am. But I'm on an assignment, too."

The man regarded him momentarily, as if debating how to respond. "So yer one o' them pinko *lib*rals, huh?"

Hitchens saw the contempt in the man's face. "Well, I don't know if—"

"Never mind. Y'all wanna go straight back through them pines 'n' turn left. Yull see a trailer hooked to a truck. He's in the trailer."

"Okay, thanks."

Hitchens headed toward the pines, disquiet rising inside him at the same pace that the last remnant of dusk was settling over the grounds. He walked briskly while straining to see the occasional fallen limb, stumbling now and then on a piece of deadwood. A clearing opened at the end of the pines, and he spotted the trailer on the far side.

Darkness had turned the muggy early-autumn air balmy, a gentle breeze carrying its dampness toward the ocean, like a restaurant waiter gliding into the kitchen with plates of food scraps. As Hitchens approached the clearing, light from the trailer glowed ever brighter, just as a setting sun's fading luminescence is sharper toward the horizon. He fought to suppress a growing apprehension, but his pulse quickened as his gait slowed.

"Halt!" The baritone bark came from his left, out of the woods. Shocked with fear, he whirled to face the voice. A bear of a man entered the clearing, pointing a double-barreled shotgun at Hitchens.

"Where the hell ya think yer goin', mister?" He walked in a slow, deliberate manner toward Hitchens, who raised his hands even with his head, palms outward.

"I'm a newspaper reporter," Hitchens said, his voice trembling. "Your public relations person granted me permission to interview Mister Stanton."

"Whatsis name?"

"Stanton. Ronald Stanton."

"I ain't deaf. I heard ya the first time. I'm talkin' 'bout the guy ya talked to."

"Oh, sorry, you mean the PR person. Uh ..." Hitchens panicked as he fought to remember the guy's name. "Sykes. Jerry, I think."

The bear was ten feet away now, and Hitchens could make out his ruddy complexion with a nose made bulbous from rosacea, under a straw hat. He had lowered the gun to Hitchens' feet.

"Empty yer pockets—real slow-like."

Hitchens removed his wallet from one back pocket of his casual pants, his notepad from the other, and his set of keys and a pen from a front pocket, dropping them to the ground while he turned his other pocket inside out. "That's all I have."

"Step back," the man ordered. He picked the wallet off the ground and inspected it. "Okay, that's you. Reporter with the Hanoi *Hawk*. Figgers that's what ya'd call it. Jes like you commies ta insult a noble fowl."

He handed the wallet to Hitchens, who picked his other items off the ground. "Go on. When ya git through, ya might wanna stick 'round a bit ta watch the cer'mony over yonder"—he pointed west—"on ta other side o' the woods."

"Thanks," said Hitchens, adding under his breath, "dipshit," as he walked the short remaining distance to the trailer. The door was open. He slowed, then rapped on the door frame. A burly man with a crew cut, wearing soiled jeans and a black tee-shirt emblazoned with a white skull-and-crossbones, approached from one side. Hitchens perceived hostility in the man's face and figured he was the Imperial Wizard's bodyguard.

"Whaddya want?" he demanded

"Hi. I'm Brad Hitchens with the *Palm Beach Hawk*, and I'm here to interview Mister Stanton."

The man walked away without answering, and Hitchens heard him talking in an undertone.

He returned. "All right. Come in and sit down on this here chair."

Hitchens extended his hand to the man sitting in a leather recliner, who remained motionless. Ronald Stanton was gaunt, his deep-brown hair flecked with gray, and he peered out of horn-rimmed glasses. Without raising his head, he looked upward, scrutinizing his guest, then motioned silently with a flip of the hand to the armless green occasional chair. Hitchens pulled out his pad and pen, and sat.

"What do you want to ask me?" Stanton's face was expressionless.

"Well, to begin with, I wonder if you can tell me a little about yourself."

"Ain't much to tell. I'm from Baton Rouge, Louisiana. Born and raised there. Worked in a cotton mill, got to be a foreman. Quit seven years ago to head up the Klan in this part of the country."

Hitchens scribbled notes. "What brings you to West Palm Beach?"

"Well, the local Klavern is trying to recruit new members, so they invited me to speak."

"The Klan's popularity has waned, hasn't it?"

"A little." Hitchens saw anger creep into Stanton's face. "That's why we've got to get the word out about what we do, so people will join and help us take our country back from the people trying to tear it apart. We've got to stand up for the white man who came here first and founded the United States of America."

"I believe the first people here were the Indians."

"You don't have to get technical. I'm talking about the people who made this country great, not a bunch of illiterate savages."

Hitchens stared at Stanton, saying nothing. *And what are these Klansmen?* he thought.

"And who might those people be?"

"Well, Andy Jackson, for one. Robert E. Lee. Jefferson Davis."

"What about Abraham Lincoln?"

"That's when the country started going to hell." Stanton talked about the supposed inferiority of the "lazy coloreds"—he didn't use the N word—and how their "moral turpitude" in producing babies out of wedlock was causing the country to deteriorate. Hitchens decided to keep quiet and let him drone on with the all-too-familiar rhetoric.

Stanton held his arm up and looked at his watch. "Uh-oh. It's gettin' close to when I have to deliver a speech to the crowd. I have to get goin'. Stick around if you want to. We're just gettin' started. The stage is farther west. You can get there on foot. Just walk down the narrow road back of this trailer."

"I may just do that." Hitchens extended his hand again, and this time Stanton reciprocated.

The reporter headed down the arcing dirt road through the woods, keeping to the grassy edge to prevent the sandy dirt from getting in his shoes. A quarter moon had risen, casting a pale glow that seeped through the tree branches, affording a view of the road's outline. After a hundred yards or so, he saw the clearing ahead. Getting closer, he noticed the stage Stanton had mentioned, on the right side of the clearing. He heard construction sounds to his left, and caught sight of amorphous forms that were animal or human, perhaps a dozen. Slowing his pace so as to take in the scene, he soon saw that they were men plying axes and wood saws to large pieces of lumber. They'd apparently transported the wood on a low-slung, open trailer hooked to a pick-up truck parked off the path, he deduced.

Fearing a confrontation if they noticed him, he slunk by, looking straight ahead. Finally, the woods thinned, and he noticed that he'd gone almost full circle, and was back at the grounds where attendees of the event had gathered. The area was dimly lit by a light pole on the side of two-lane Southern Boulevard and the headlights from passing cars. He ambled about aimlessly, observing picnickers finishing their desserts: pies, cakes, cookies, and ice cream kept frozen in styrofoam coolers situated next to the tables. Women were clearing the tables and packing their wares in baskets.

"Attention ev'body," a voice boomed. Hitchens could make out the man at the check-in desk, maybe 125 feet to the east, speaking into a bullhorn. "The main events are 'bout ta happen on the north end of the woods. Y'all need to put yer stuff away in yer cars 'n trucks, and head on down the road to the back. It ain't fer, so leave yer vee hicles behind, cuz there ain't enough room ta park 'em."

"Jimmy Lee, you can finish that apple pie later," Hitchens heard a mother admonish her young son. "We've got ta go." He watched the families pack away their picnic paraphernalia and begin the trek to the small stage to hear their leader expound.

Hitchens brought up the rear, keeping his distance from the hundred or so men, women, and children until they arrived at the clearing. The adults milled about the grass in front of the stage, while children scampered about playing impromptu games.

Hitchens jotted down a few notes on the scene, then became conscious of someone behind him. He snapped his head around to see the same buff young fellow who'd tailed him coming up to his right side. Their eyes met, and the guy sneered as he kept walking.

Hitchens' gaze followed him to where he stopped near the stage. *Scary character*, the reporter thought.

Then a floodlight popped on, and a short, thin man who could have passed as a banker or attorney strolled up to the microphone. "Folks," he said in a clear tenor voice, "let's welcome to our esteemed Klavern ..." he paused and swept his hand out to the right rear corner of the stage ..."his highness, Grand Imperial Wizard Ronald Stanton." The audience applauded.

Stanton climbed the few steps to the platform and strode briskly to the podium. "Good evening ladies and gentlemen. I don't s'pose the children are going to pay much attention to what I have to say, but I might get the older ones' attention later." Parents looked at each other, bemused, Hitchens noticed, as he, too, puzzled over the import of the greeting.

"We're gathered here this evening because we're concerned that our once-great country is being taken over by people who are different from the ones who made it what it is. I'm talking about people with low morals, people of wrong religions or no religion." Stanton's voice grew louder.

"These people are trespassers who are trying to corrupt our children and rob us of our values." He slapped the podium. "They came to this country to take advantage of the sacrifices in blood, sweat, and tears made by those who started from the eastern shores and spread west to unknown territories, fighting savage

Indians and facing vicious wild animals. Those brave pioneers overcame scorching heat, freezing cold, floods and tornadoes. They made the country safe for millions who followed after them to live as God's son Jesus Christ would have us live, raising families, working hard, and going to church."

He held up clenched fists, and shouted, "They were white folks, just like you and me."

The adults applauded, and the children stopped their rompings, staring open-mouthed at the speaker.

Hitchens eye caught a dark form off to the right, moving closer. As it passed in the grass off the road, he saw that it was the pickup truck with the trailer attached, bearing some long, angular apparatus.

Stanton continued unabated. "It was the white man who came across the ocean and risked his life, and sometimes lost it, so he wouldn't be held back by a government that didn't allow him to worship the true God and own land and live free. And what has happened since then?" He was reaching a crescendo. "The communists have infiltrated our government and passed laws that take away our liberties. Used to be, you wanted to build yerself a house, you bought the lumber and tools, and you got somebody to help you, and you built it. Now you have to get permission from the government, which tells you just where you can put it, what kind of materials you can use, how thick the foundation has to be, and on and on. It's the commies doing this, folks. They keep making the government bigger and bigger, taking more and more control over yer lives."

Stanton spoke extemporaneously, using no notes. He's probably given pretty much the same speech many times, Hitchens mused as he jotted notes.

"Once upon a time, you needed a loan to build that house, you went to your bank, and you and the banker made an agreement and sealed it with a handshake. Now the kikes control the banks, and make you sign so many forms you get writer's cramp." A few laughs erupted.

"And you know all about the Mexicans. Those wetbacks'll stab you in the back and steal you blind." He waited for the audience to absorb his remarks so he'd have their full attention for his next remarks.

"The niggers is the worst of them all," he thundered.

Children who had resumed skittering halted in their tracks and stared at the speaker, their mouths open and eyes fixed in wonderment, Hitchens noted. The image of a boy fifty-odd years earlier, playing with a neighbor child on the sidewalk in front of their homes, popped before his mind's eye. *"Eeny meenie miny mo, catch a nigger by the toe. If he hollers, let him go. Eeny meenie miny mo,"* the boy chanted.

He was that boy. Though he repeated the rhyme frequently around the house, his parents never remonstrated him. He became confused after his mother warned against eating unwashed fruit because "it's been handled by niggers," but his educated father later spoke favorably of black co-workers at the factory where he was a purchasing agent in a mid-sized Midwestern city.

For several years, he'd heard the N word tossed around casually, and didn't think much about it. Then the family moved to another, rural Midwestern city, where there was only one black family, and he never heard anyone speak badly of them or witnessed any ill treatment. But, sorting copies for his newspaper delivery route, he saw the photos of Governor George Wallace standing in a doorway at the University of Alabama. Another photo showed National Guard troops standing amid a crowd of white students, some carrying hateful signs about blacks, appearing to be yelling. He didn't share those feelings, and saw how wrong it was. And he felt shame at the chant he'd innocently recited as a child.

It was the 1960s, and the Civil Rights Movement continued—the march from Selma, Alabama, to Montgomery; the Voting Rights Act; and finally the assassination of the movement's leader, Dr. Martin Luther King, Jr. After those and other events, he noticed a decline in use of the N word, and thought racism had diminished. And it had—on the surface. Fewer people voiced their bigoted feelings openly. Regardless of one's feelings, his nuanced ex-wife once remarked, "It certainly isn't fashionable."

But two events in his early newspaper reporting days made Hitchens realize racism lay dormant. It remained intact, but had evolved from overt to insidious expression.

He was checking on a record in the jail of the medium-sized city, and a guard was relating a past incident to two police officers. "This colored prisoner tells me he's got a right to make a phone call. So I says, 'Sure, just step this way.' And I hauled off and smashed him in the face. He goes down with a thud, and I says, 'You still wanna make that phone call?'" The guard roared with laughter, and the cops chuckled.

A year later, he was stunned to read personal remarks typed underneath a crime story written by a sixty-five-year-old reporter at the news wire service where Hitchens had begun working. A young black man was charged with going on a violent spree on Chicago's Michigan Avenue, smashing windows of high-end stores.

"Give that motherfucker 10 years of hard labor," the veteran reporter wrote.

And then there are the people at this rally. They make no attempts to cover up their hatred—at least not amongst themselves. He wondered how discreet they were in their employment environment and public gathering places.

Stanton's voice snapped Hitchens out of his reverie. "Way back when, more'n a century ago, that black mark on American history, Abraham Lincoln, told them they was as good as the white man. And they've caused us nothin' but trouble ever since. The whites took care of them for more than two hundred years, and then they got real uppity, and took jobs that rightfully belonged to us. That is, the ones who actually wanted to work, which wasn't many. We pay taxes to support the lazy ones. And their good-fer-nothin' children, too. Yet they think they should have the right to eat at the same restaurants with us white folks, use the same bathrooms, take up seats on buses and make whites stand. And some of the young bucks even have the nerve to date our daughters.

"I'm telling you tonight," he shouted, pounding the lectern and stabbing his forefinger at the audience, "if my teenage daughter ever went out with a nigger, I'd kill her." Murmurs and a few "Yeah"s swept through the crowd.

Stanton ranted for several more minutes. Apparently noticing the crowd was becoming restless, he said, "I see a lot of young children here and it's past their bedtime, so I'm going to close. The rest of you probably will want to stay and watch the ceremony. Just remember that all of us have to do whatever we can to help take this country back for the white man. Goodnight to you all."

Everybody began trudging back along the dirt road to the front of the woods where their vehicles were parked, and Hitchens joined them. At the edge of the parking area stood a fifteen-foot-high wooden cross, made of four-by-four lumber. Past the cross, a short distance into the woods, a group of people in white garb huddled. Hitchens stared, agape.

Ah, that's what those guys were making back there off the road, he mused. They obviously hauled it on the trailer through the woods to the front.

Families with young children piled into their cars and pickups, and headed out the entrance onto Southern Boulevard. The remaining one-third, adults and teenagers, moved their cars to the far side of the parking area, away from the woods. Watching them, Hitchens realized they had been through this routine before, and knew just what to do. They gathered on the now-vacant grassy stretch, chatting.

"'At was a durned good speech," Hitchens heard a man tell his wife. "He made me want ta go out and put them jigaboos in their place—show 'em there ain't no room for their kind in a Christian country like ours." The wife nodded her head in vigorous agreement.

In eerie silence, the dozen or so men wearing white robes and hoods, only their eyes showing, strode with purpose in their gait around the cross, forming a circle. They stood, legs apart, wielding what appeared to Hitchens to be torches. The man directly behind the cross came to the front. He lit his torch and flung it at the foot of the cross, which was wrapped in a burlap sack.

The base erupted in flames, which climbed all the way to the cross arm and the top, setting the whole thing ablaze. Hitchens figured the entire cross had been doused in gasoline.

For a few seconds, the men stood at attention, then began lighting their own torches and hurling them onto the grass at the foot of the cross.

Hitchens glanced down at his watch, which read almost 9 p.m. He caught a peripheral view of someone approaching, and looked up as the strapping young man he'd encountered twice before sauntered by, casting the same smirk. Their eyes met again, before Hitchens turned and scurried past him down the path to his Mazda.

The reporter drove the short distance to busy Southern Boulevard, where cars streamed in both directions. After waiting a couple of minutes for spaces to open in both lanes, he tromped on the accelerator, sending dirt flying from under the tires, and pulled onto the grass-patched shoulder on the other side. In the semi-darkness of his car, he began writing in his note pad. A half-hour later, he took his pad and the radio provided by the newspaper photo department to the front of the car, where he called the paper.

"Hold on a minute while I get Sally over here," a photographer answered.

Oh no, he thought, *not Sally*. Underhanded snake. She'd stolen a story from him two years before, after both had been assigned to check out the cause of a sudden outbreak of respiratory illness among thirty-two children at an elementary school in Boynton Beach. All of the children had been sent home, and only a few teachers and administrative personnel were on the premises. He'd found the principal and asked several questions of him in an empty classroom when Sally barged in, plopped down in a chair opposite them, and began peppering him with questions. The man was obviously irked by her brusqueness, and told her he'd already answered those questions for Hitchens. That hadn't deterred her, and the principal answered a couple of her questions between his responses to Hitchens, which she scribbled in her notepad. Back in the newsroom, she'd quickly approached the city editor, who told her to write the story.

"Brad, I have to use a typewriter for this because there's no computer in the photo room. It's sitting on an empty ink drum, and I have to stand up to type."

Hitchens said nothing. He heard her tap out the story tag line.

"Okay, I'm ready."

"The serenity of a bucolic roadside park just outside West Palm Beach was riven Saturday night ...," Hitchens began reading slowly as he bent into the headlights of the cars streaming by on Southern. Over the buzz of traffic, he heard her mumble the words' consonants with the clackety-clack of the typewriter. "Okay, go ahead."

"... by the venomous language of racial hatred in a speech by Ronald Stanton, Imperial Wizard of the Ku Klux Klan's southeast division." The reporter paused to let his colleague catch up. "The Klansman held nothing back, labeling the country's blacks as 'lazy,' 'good for nothing' and 'uppity.' He shouted to the modest-sized audience that if his teenage daughter 'ever went out with the N word, I'd kill her.' Put 'the N word' in parentheses."

He paused. "You got that?"

"Yup. Keep going."

Hitchens narrated how Stanton covered the gamut of political and ethnic enemies, berating supposed Communists in the government, Jews in the banks, and Mexicans, besides blacks, for which he held a special hatred. The reporter described the "sinister cross-burning that glowed against the dark night like flames in a furnace lapping at the black coals."

It took a half-hour for him to wend his way through the traffic to the newspaper office, where he saw Sally conferring at the city desk with an assistant city editor. He shot her a malevolent glance, which, he was certain, she pretended not to see.

The next day was Sunday, and both Hitchens and Sally were part of a skeleton staff on duty. He picked up the paper off the stack on a small table just inside the newsroom, and leafed through to the local section. The headline at the top read: "KKK Head Spews Hatred at Local Rally." His eyes fell on the first paragraph. It was indecipherable, the words garbled with typographical symbols and mistakes so flagrant as to render the meaning unknowable.

He stalked up to Sally's desk, his face red, and slapped the paper on her desk. "What the hell is this? It's not readable. How did it happen?"

"Well, gee, it was hard balancing the typewriter on top of that barrel."

Hitchens glared at her. "That wasn't a balancing act. It was sabotage."

She didn't reply.

He walked to his desk and sat down hard on his swivel chair. *I faced despicable hatred last night,* he thought, *but this mean-spirited jealousy is almost as venomous.*

CHAPTER FIVE

"The trial is set for the seventeenth, 1:30 p.m."

"Of this month?" Hitchens asked. "That's only a couple weeks away."

"I know," said Garbuncle. "I got the notice last month. That's all right. There's not much preparation I need to do. Like I told you before, you're the only witness I'm calling."

They sat in early evening at the bar in the Night Owl, a watering hole on South Dixie, across the street from the *Hawk*. Hitchens visited it occasionally, and Garbuncle frequented it during lunch time,

"What about Donna—wasn't that her name? The gal you went to help and got yourself arrested instead?"

"Yeah. Donna Malone. She's ..." He lowered his head a little, a smile of what Hitchens perceived as disdain crossing his face. "Let's just forget about her."

"What's the matter? Doesn't she want to testify?"

"She's got her own problems. The DUI charge."

"Are you going to represent her?"

"I offered, but she ..." Hitchens noticed a tinge of sad resignation. "She's getting her own lawyer. I guess she's over me."

"Ah, you had something going, huh? Probably would have been complicated, anyway—both of you involved in the same incident."

"Yeah." Garbuncle clenched his jaw and stared into space. "So we need to sit down and rehearse this thing to make sure we've got it right. Let's go to Publix and I'll buy a pizza."

"One of those cheapo frozen pieces of cardboard?"

"I'll cut up some onions and peppers, and throw on a can of mushrooms. It'll be better'n the kind from a pizza parlor."

Hitchens uttered a sardonic little laugh. "Yeah, sure. We've seen this picture show before." He tossed his hands up in resignation. "Okay, okay, let's go."

They drove to the Publix on Southern, picked up the items, and headed for Hitchens' small apartment in a complex in northwest Lake Worth. They cut the veggies, and spread them over the hard, shredded-cheese-topped pie. Hitchens set the oven at 350 degrees, then walked across the blue-gray carpet, soiled from his own traffic, and plopped down on the fraying couch of interwoven brown, red, and blue hues. Garbuncle sat in the yellow suede armchair opposite the antique-ish coffee table, both of which Hitchens had picked up from Goodwill.

"Okay," said Garbuncle, leaning forward, we need to be on the same page as to what happened. My car was in the shop for repairs, and you were driving me back to my apartment, on Shelby Road, heading north. Right?" He looked up at Hitchens.

"So far, so good."

"I spotted Donna on the west side of the road, with two police officers. I told you to pull over to the shoulder."

"Not so good."

"Geez, I know it wasn't so good. Will ya let me continue?"

"Sorry. Go ahead."

"We parked slightly north of the scene, and I told you that was a client of mine."

"If you say she was your client, that's your business. I didn't know her."

"Good. Go ahead and answer my question like that. It'll give you credibility—like we hadn't rehearsed and made something up."

"I could add something like, 'She was Ham's paramour.'"

Garbuncle jerked upright, his face intense. "You want to get me disbarred?"

Hitchens cackled. "Lighten up. I'm pullin' your leg," he said, glancing at the TV. He lurched forward. "Oh shit, look. The Pirates outfielder just robbed Cody Ross of a homer. Helluva leaping catch." He paused and gawked open-mouthed. "Yikes. Dan Uggla almost got doubled off second."

"Look, it was a short fling. Come on, we've got to get serious. I could lose my law license."

42

"All right, all right. She was your client."

"What happened next?" Garbuncle asked.

"I was driving and you were on the passenger side—"

"You're right about that. I'd never have let you sit on my lap." Garbuncle looked as though he were trying to repress a smile. "Can I continue?"

"Sorry. The devil made me say it."

"So I got out," Garbuncle said, "and crossed to the other side of the road. The one officer was having Donna do a roadside sobriety test, and the other one was watching."

"Kinky cops like to watch." Hitchens said, chuckling at Garbuncle's sign of frustration.

"I went up to him, pulled my wallet out of my back pocket, and showed him my card. I said she was my client, and I wanted to talk to her."

"I remember it well, but I couldn't hear what you were saying."

"That doesn't matter. Tell me what you saw next."

"It appeared you and the cop were exchanging words, and then he raised his voice and told you to leave."

"Good."

"Not good. You should've left. Anyway, you—"

"By the way, don't call him a cop. Call him a police officer."

"I'd like to call him something else, but—so anyway, you stood your ground. And you weren't shouting or acting angry or making any gestures. You looked pretty calm."

"That's good. Try to remember what you just told me."

"I think you should be preaching to the mirror."

Garbuncle lowered his head, his mouth twisted in a wry look.

"And then the cop—the police officer pulled his handcuffs off his belt, and I heard him order you to turn around. You complied, and he cuffed you. Then he led you to the squad car, and the rest is history."

***

"We're friends, aren't we?"

Hitchens heard it as a rhetorical question. He looked over the heads of the two police officers sitting on the front courtroom bench and a formally dressed, slight black man positioned at the prosecutor's table. "Yeah, yeah," the defense's witness said wearily, turning his head away.

"Good friends, right?"

"Oh, come on now. Let's not overdo it." Hitchens glanced at the tall, slender female judge to his right, plain-faced, leaning back in a leather swivel chair behind the podium, and noticed her quizzical expression. "Yes, we're good friends." His tone revealed the distaste he felt at having to answer the question, and he raised his hands in a gesture of resignation.

Ham is a shrewd operator—preempting the certain cross-examination of me by the prosecutor to learn about our relationship and show I was heavily biased and not a credible witness.

"Okay. Now I want you to tell me: Do you recall when you pulled your car off the road across from where those two police officers were giving my client Donna a sobriety test?" He turned sideways and pointed at them. "That's Hank on your left and Art on the right."

"Of course."

"Had we come from Hap's?"

Hitchens stared at Garbuncle with a crinkled brow. "What's Hap's?" He paused for a second. "Oh, wait a minute, you mean that bar on Congress, just north of 10th Avenue? I go past it when I jog. Never been in it."

"Okay, good. Can you describe exactly what happened after we stopped the car and I went to help Donna?"

"Well, we were heading north on Shelby Road from Lake Worth Road after watching the Florida Marlins game at my place. It was a late afternoon game, and we had dinner at the same time. I was driving you home because your car was in the shop. You told me to pull over to the east shoulder when you saw two policemen with your client Donna on the west side." Hitchens continued describing what he witnessed.

"That's all, Your Honor. I have no further questions."

The prosecutor declined when the judge asked him if he wanted to cross-examine Hitchens, and they proceeded to closing arguments.

"What the heck was that Hap's business all about?" Hitchens asked as they walked down the courthouse hallway on the way to the parking garage.

"One of the cops said we had come from there."

"You mean he flat-out lied?"

"I'm sure they were trying to imply I'd been drinking. They never asked me about it when they took me to jail. I was able to act sober."

"Yeah. You've had a lot of practice. So what's going to happen? You think the judge is going to find you guilty?"

"I don't think so. I had a right to do what I did. And your testimony was pretty convincing. She probably will have doubts about those cops' truthfulness. But maybe not, because the judges almost always side with the police. And it's not like these two cops are rookies and don't know what they're doing. Hank and Art. Hank's the one who put me in cuffs. They've been with the force for a few years. If she does find me guilty, I'm out of a job. I'll then wish I hadn't waived the right to a jury."

***

"The judge had us in session for the verdict today." Garbuncle swirled the ice in his glass of vodka, took a swig, set the glass on the cardboard coaster, and rested his arms on the rectangular, mahogany bar top at the Big Daddy's in Lake Worth. Football, basketball and hockey games, college and professional, played on an array of screens in front, back, and both sides of the bar as patrons watched with expressions that Hitchens judged as ranging from mild interest to disinterest to glum. Garbuncle looked serious.

"Uh-oh," said Hitchens.

Garbuncle broke into a sly smile. "Not guilty."

"Hallelujah!" Hitchens shouted. A few folks on the other side of the rectangular bar looked his way, then returned to their conversations. "You know what? I think you ought to file a charge of perjury against those cops."

"Nah. I'm going to let it go. Better not to stir anything up."

"Yeah, they'd probably dig into your drinking habits. What about Donna?"

"I'm not going to get involved in that case, either—not that she'd want me to. The whole thing about my arrest would get rehashed. No thanks."

"Well, now that that's out of the way, we can start thinking about the other case."

Garbuncle cocked his head. "What are you talkin' about?"

"You know what I'm talkin' about. Alec."

"Oh come on." The vexation in Garbuncle's face and annoyance in his voice were on full display. "I've forgotten all about that. I've got too much to worry about to get involved in that jigab … his problems."

"Just what I figured would happen. But you're not going to get away with it. We made a deal. I testified for you, and you promised to help Alec. And you're not going to weasel out of it."

"If he hadn't a been driving around with a burnt-out taillight, he wouldn't a gotten into trouble."

"You've come back with that more times than I can count. And by the way, if you hadn't been drunk, you wouldn't have had me stop so you could score points with that sexpot."

"Oh, so you've never let your dick lead you astray?"

"I never said that. I've been guilty of more sexual indiscretions than I want to remember. But that's not the point. If you're gonna point fingers, you'd better look at yourself. Besides, that hunk o' junk you drive has more things wrong with it than Alec's Geo."

"My car's taillights and headlights work just fine."

"What about those nearly bald tires, and brakes that barely work?"

"Maybe the cops'll drop the charges. Let's just wait and see what happens."

CHAPTER SIX

"Hi Alec," Hitchens said, smiling. "How's it going? I just dropped by to pick up some printer paper."

Alec Monceau looked up from the store-dedicated computer mounted on an elevated desk at the end of the computer section of the Computer Freak. A look of surprise transformed into a big grin. "Oh, hello Mister Brad. Good to see you."

"You can drop the Mister." Hitchens waved a hand. "So how's everything? Your court date is July seven, right?"

"I get letter again ..." he looked away in thought "... about ten days ago. It tell me dress good and be on time. Yes, July on seven."

"So, less than a month from now. How are you going to prepare?"

"I no know. I go dere and tell trut."

"Look, I'm going to talk to Ham—you remember, the guy you helped with his computer."

"Oh yes, I visit in his 'partment."

"Let's the three of us get together. Maybe we can help you. Today is Monday. How about you come to my place on Wednesday—say, 8 o'clock, after dinner? Are you working then?"

"No, I no workin'. Dat very nice of you. I 'preciate. Yes, I come."

"Give me a pad and pencil, and I'll write down the directions. And give me your phone number. I might have misplaced it."

The two jotted down the information on a note pad on the desk, and exchanged notes.

"See you then."

***

"That's the last time I'm gonna eat one o' those cardboard discs you call pizza. A *dog* wouldn't eat that frozen grocery store junk." Hitchens wiped his mouth with a paper towel that he used as a napkin.

"You're prob'ly right. Are you saying you have better taste?" A sly smile opened on Garbuncle's face.

"I sure as hell do, and I want a real pizza next time."

"But I supplied the mushrooms."

"Wow. And I supplied the extra hamburger and the salad—and made it besides."

"Can we go to your computer? I need to see about getting a good deal on a fishing rod, and you know how to look that stuff up."

"Yeah. Come on." They rose from the table positioned under a cheap chandelier in a corner of the living room that served as the dining room. The table rested atop a Home Depot oriental rug of mostly blue and red colors.

The computer sat on a desk next to Hitchens' bed in the next room. Garbuncle sat on the edge of the bed while Hitchens Googled "fishing rods," then began clicking on the menu options and checking out the offerings.

"What do you want to spend?"

"No more'n a hundred bucks."

"You're not gonna get much quality for that." Hitchens kept clicking. "Ah, here's one. Looks pretty good. At least it's got a lot o' specs. Seventy bucks."

"Is it strong enough to handle bass fishing?"

"Hell, I don't know. Read it yourself. I don't know anything about fishing."

They exchanged places. "By golly, that's a pretty good rod for the money," said Garbuncle.

Hitchens got off the bed and leaned into the monitor. "Click on the customer service tab. Maybe you can give them a call, although it's a little late."

"Oh, good, here's the number." Garbuncle dialed. "Hello ma'am. How are you tonight?"

"Just ask the damn question," Hitchens muttered.

Garbuncle turned his head sideways with a questioning look. "Yes, I'm here ma'am. I have a question about one of your fishing rods. The product number? I'm sorry, I don't see any."

Hitchens returned to the monitor, scanned it for a few seconds, and pointed to a number. "There. It's at the bottom of the specs."

"Oh, I found it ma'am. Thank you for your patience."

"Look, she's being paid to do this," Hitchens said in a low tone. "Just get on with it, will you?"

"Okay, are you ready? It's YA3923."

A pause. "Okay, I found it," the woman said, loud enough for Hitchens to hear. "What is it you want to know?"

"I was wondering if this rod is strong enough for bass fishing. Sure, I can wait." Garbuncle turned to Hitchens. "She's asking the supervisor."

They waited. About three minutes later: "Yes, I'm still here. No, I didn't mind waiting. I can bass-fish with it? Oh, that's great. I'm going to go ahead and buy it then. Credit card? Oh, sure, just a minute." He fumbled for his wallet in a back pants pocket. "Okay, I have it."

He read the numbers and the expiration date, and gave the woman his address.

"Within ten days? Yes, that will be fine. Thank you so much, ma'am." In a gentle tone, "You were very professional."

"Oh, cut the crap," Hitchens said, rising off the bed as Garbuncle cradled the receiver. "That woman doesn't need to hear that. You sound so damned condescending—like you're the teacher talking to a pupil."

"I wanted to let her know she did a good job," Garbuncle protested softly, wearing a sheepish grin.

"Hell, you sound as phony as a three-dollar bill."

"I didn't know three-dollar bills could talk," Garbuncle deadpanned.

Hitchens turned toward the living room, Garbuncle following.

"What time does the Marlins game start?" Garbuncle asked.

"In fifteen minutes. But we're not watching the game. We're going to have company."

Garbuncle's face brightened as he slumped onto the couch. "You found a couple o' women?"

"Not exactly. Alec is coming."

"Huh? Who's ... you mean the computer guy? What's wrong with your computer?"

"Nothing's wrong with it."

"Then what's he ...?" Hitchens saw Garbuncle's look click from puzzlement to comprehension. "Oh, come on, don't tell me we're going to talk about his problem with the law."

"That's exactly what we're gonna do, and we're gonna try to help him solve it."

"I told you. I can't help—"

A rap on the door of the ground-floor condo interrupted Garbuncle.

"Hey there, Alec," Hitchens said, stepping aside from the entrance to allow the man in. He wore a New York Yankees baseball cap.

"So you're a baseball fan?"

"Oh yes. I play second base. Team in Trinidad. Just guys in my town. Play for fun. No professional team in Trinidad."

"What brought you to the U.S.?"

"My wife die since four years. I so sad, and I want go someplace, forget. I come here one year after. My son and daughter grown up. Dey stay. I send money. My son clerk in hotel and daughter clean motel rooms. Her husband fix houses. Dey have baby girl. Dey all poor."

"Gee, I'm sorry to hear that. Come in and sit down. Take that chair."

Hitchens pointed to the nearest of twin yellow armchairs that he'd picked up at Goodwill for twenty bucks apiece after his divorce. They were on either corner of a real Oriental rug he'd bought at a traveling show in a hotel to complement the one under the table. A worn couch of finely interwoven reds, blues, and browns that he'd gotten on the cheap from a newspaper ad sat next to the rug. Atop it was an antique-ish marble-and-wood coffee table he'd acquired for twenty-five dollars from a college teacher who was moving from his apartment. Reproductions of Renaissance and French impressionist paintings he'd bought after writing a newspaper story about the producer hung on the walls. He'd been offered a discount but paid the full price to avoid a conflict of interest.

"How about a beer, or a glass of red wine. I don't drink white—too much sugar."

"Thank you, Mister Brad. I like—"

"Alec, just skip the Mister and call me Brad." He felt slight irritation, perceiving a hint of obsequiousness.

"Oh, sure. I like red, too, but 'fraid to spill, cause stain."

"Not to worry. I know a great way to get it out. Equal parts dish soap and hydrogen peroxide. Let it sit, and rinse. Works like a charm. I'll get you a glass of the cheap but good Chianti I drink every day."

Hitchens brought glasses of wine for Alec and himself.

"You drink alcohol, Mister Hiram?"

"No, Ham doesn't like wine. Just vodka. And I'm out of that. He'll just have to suffer."

Garbuncle, sitting on the other side of the couch from Hitchens, looked blankly at the frayed carpet, saying nothing.

"You speak English pretty good for being here only three years," said Hitchens.

"I study English a little in school. Many people in Trinidad speak English. But it no da same in dis country, as I learn."

"No, we've got so many strange ways of saying things that you can't know from English classes. Okay, look, we have to figure out how we're going to get you cleared of this resisting arrest charge. Ham and I both saw what happened. We are eyewitnesses. And Ham is a lawyer—a good one. He will defend you."

"Now just a minute here," said Garbuncle. "I'd love to help you, Alec, but how in the hell am I supposed to be the defense attorney and a witness at the same time?"

"Oh, I'm sure there's a way," said Hitchens. "I already said you were a good attorney. What're you gonna do, disappoint us?"

"The law is the law. It would be a conflict of interest."

"There must be a way around it. I'll bet you can find something in the statutes that allows it—probably something obscure, because this is a very unusual situation."

"It sure is. I've never run across it before."

"Mister Hiram," said Alec, "it okay. I no want make problem. I be all right."

"Look Alec, if worse comes to worst, we'll at least be there as witnesses for you," said Hitchens. "But we're going to check the law on this and see if Ham can be your attorney."

"I can't ..." Garbuncle began, then cut himself off with a sigh. "Let's watch the baseball game. I think they're playing the Braves tonight. You like watching Major League baseball? I see by your cap you must be a Yankees fan."

"Oh yes, I like watch."

Hitchens turned on the TV. "It's already the third inning. What's the score? Show us the score, dammit. Oh, there it is. Why did I bother? Six to three, Atlanta. Not too bad, I guess. At least the Marlins have a chance to come back. I hate to lose."

"So do I," said Garbuncle with a meaningful look at Hitchens.

***

"Okay, Ham, I went to the library and did a little research," Hitchens said on the phone. "According to the American Bar Association rules, a defense attorney can also be a witness for his client, on one condition. Not representing the client would impose a hardship on him."

"Aw c'mon. Look, I had a rough day today. A guy who was gonna repair the rot in a corner of my bedroom ceiling made up with his wife and doesn't need me anymore. We'd agreed to a trade. I would handle his divorce and he'd fix the ceiling—and replace a couple of broken screens and a few other things. So now I have to find somebody else and pay him."

"You need to notify the court that you will be representing Alec, and also will be a witness in his behalf."

"I can't do that. It's not allowed."

"As I just told you, it is if Alec can't afford to pay for a lawyer. And we know he can't afford one. You can inform the judge that you'll be his lawyer in return for work he did for you on your computer. By the way, his daughter's child came down with diphtheria, and they've been quarantined, so she can't go to work. Alec is trying to save even more money to send her."

Garbuncle said nothing.

"You still there?"

"Yeah, I'm here." Garbuncle sighed. "Okay, I'm going to the clerk of court's office tomorrow to file a motion for a client. I'll file another one asking permission to be Alec's lawyer and witness at the same time. Do we know what judge is assigned?"

"Alec said said it was Jonathan Crabtree," Hitchens said.

"Oh hell, we don't have a chance. He's a hard ass. Follows the law meticulously. Doesn't bend an inch."

"Really? Shit." Hitchens went silent. "Hey, wait a minute," he said, almost yelling. "I think I know him."

"Yeah?"

"Hold on. I'm trying to remember—yes, I know who he is. A while back, maybe three or so years ago, we had a story in the *Hawk* about a judge. I'm fairly certain Crabtree was the name. The profile was really interesting and stuck in my mind. I don't remember who wrote it—most likely one of the women in the features department. The story said he was a tough judge, but he also was known to make unpredictable rulings on occasion. But here's the part that stood out for me: His daughter married a black man, and the judge opposed the marriage. But then he got to know the guy, and did a turn-around. He came to like his son-in-law, and it had an impact on his feelings about race relations."

Garbuncle was silent.

"On the other hand," Hitchens continued, "he's come down hard on a lot of black defendants in recent years, according to some research I did in the *Hawk* library. So who knows? Look, give it a try. We've got nothing to lose."

"Okay, I'll file a motion requesting permission to testify on behalf of my client. But I can tell you right now, he'll turn me down. It's just never done. I've been a criminal defense attorney for decades, and I've never heard of it happening."

CHAPTER SEVEN

Garbuncle sat in his apartment, mulling over the argument for permission to testify he'd make in a hearing before the judge. He began to rut. He craved a woman. He wasn't desperate enough to call his ex-wife, even though they were on good terms.

Last time he talked to Donna, his occasional paramour, she gave him the cold shoulder—didn't want him defending her against the DUI charge. But she was probably upset at the time. Maybe enough time had passed, and she'd be more friendly to him now. No harm in trying. He dialed.

"Haven't talked to you since your encounter with the cops, and I've been wondering how that turned out."

"It turned out better than I expected."

"Hold it. I want to hear all about it. If you're not doing anything, how about I come over tonight and you can give me the lowdown over a couple of drinks?"

"I guess that would be all right. Don't get any ideas, though."

"No, no. We'll just have a nice chat." He understood that women always worried about being seen as sluts, and felt compelled to go through this ritual of pretending to be chaste. He wished he could just come out with what both knew they were after, and pop the question: "Wanna fuck?" No matter, he'd play the game, since that's what it took.

***

54

Donna was a handsome woman, the same height as Garbuncle, with a little extra girth diminishing her sex appeal. But he carried a bigger spare tire, and had long realized that he couldn't be too choosy. He never admitted that to his friend Hitchens, telling him instead that he preferred fat women. Hitchens knew he was rationalizing.

"It's been a while since I've been here. You keep everything so clean and tidy."

"I'd ask you what you want to drink, but I already know. Vodka on the rocks." Her voice was deeper than most women's, and Garbuncle found it sexy.

"So what happened in your case?" He accepted the drink, and she sat on the couch next to him with a scotch and soda. Her tight skirt, several inches above the knee, rode half-way up her thighs, revealing sculpted legs that filled Garbuncle with lust.

"I'd just started dating Ernie—he's a lieutenant with the Hardinton police— and he got the chief to drop the DUI charge."

Garbuncle felt his passion plummet, but tried not to let the disappointment show on his face. Maybe she'd been honest, after all, about her admonition against "getting any ideas."

"Ernie told the chief that it was rumored the two Hardinton cops who put you in jail had lied in court about where you and your friend had been before you stopped to help me. Hap's, I think it was?"

"Yes, Hap's."

"Ernie said the case might boomerang on them, so they'd better not bring me to trial."

"That's great. You got a break. Are you still seeing this Ernie?"

"Sort of. But he doesn't seem very enthusiastic, and I'm not either. It's really more of a friendship than anything else. We had sex once, but ..."

Garbuncle noticed her sheepish look. "But what?"

"It was pretty forgettable."

Garbuncle's heart quickened. She'd been demure with him, after all. He set his glass on the coffee table, put his arm around her shoulders and gently pulled her closer while sliding his hand under her skirt. She didn't resist, and soon they were in a passionate embrace. She rose and led him to her master bedroom, and pulled the covers back. His fingers worked like a virtuoso violinist's as he unbuttoned her blouse and unclasped her brassiere, while she wiggled out of her skirt. He went to work on his shirt buttons, and she pulled his belt loose. They rolled on the bed, devouring each other with wet kisses, sucking, licking, nibbling, and finally consummating their carnality.

"Oh wow, that was sensational—or should I say *sin*sational?" Garbuncle said, beaming with pride over his pun.

Donna chuckled. "It was awesome."

He rolled onto his back, his arm still under her neck, and went silent. After several seconds, Donna said, "Ernie had a lot to drink one night and told me about this friend Jake, who's got a tiny trucking business. Ernie said Jake belonged to the Ku Klux Klan, and he mentioned to Ernie that a couple of cops were Klan members."

Garbuncle jerked his head toward Donna. "He say what police department?"

"No. He didn't tell me, and I didn't ask."

Garbuncle said nothing. "There's thirty-eight cities and towns in Palm Beach County, most of them with their own departments. And the rest use the sheriff's department, which has a few thousand deputies. We're talking a total of thousands of police officers in the county."

"Ernie also told me he suspected a couple o' cops in his Hardinton police force gambled at dog fights, and maybe were part of a dog fighting ring."

"I don't have a very high opinion of these guys," Garbuncle said. "Too damn many of them are like the bad guys they go after."

"Oh, I don't know about that," Donna protested. "They do dangerous work, and they keep us safe."

"I'm not saying most are bad. But too many are on the opposite side of the same coin with the criminals. Maybe I'm just pissed about things that have happened lately. Those two bastards with the Hardinton department had no business hauling me to jail. But I'm going to tell you about something a lot worse."

He related the story about the beating he and Brad Hitchens had witnessed.

"The two cops who beat him charged him with resisting arrest with violence, and Brad pushed me into representing him in court pro bono. His name is Alec Monceau, and he's a computer expert at Computer Freaks. Came to my place and helped me with my new computer, so Brad said I owed him a favor, especially since the guy hardly has any money."

"Oh, I know who Alec is," Donna said, propping herself up on one elbow. "I've been to that store several times. I ask him questions about my computer, and he's always so kind and helpful."

"Yeah, I suppose so. But I sure as hell don't want to be defending a jigaboo. It's against my religion." He shot her a wry smile. "Not only that, but Brad's been pushing me to be a witness as well as the defense attorney. Highly irregular. I told him I'd try, but the judge wasn't going to allow it."

"I hope you can help him. He's a very good person."

Garbuncle sighed. He got up and dressed. "I'll see what I can do."

***

"Your Honor, I know it is highly unusual for a defense attorney to testify on behalf of his client—almost unprecedented, in fact. However, there actually is precedent, and the law does not forbid it."

"That's the craziest thing I've ever heard," said Judge Jonathan Crabtree. "Have you taken leave of your senses?"

Assistant State Attorney Darrell Seward, sitting in an armchair next to Garbuncle in the judge's chambers, threw his hands in the air. His disdainful, screwed up smile of disbelief registered with both the judge and Garbuncle.

"I completely understand how you feel about it, Your Honor," said Garbuncle. "But I implore you to hear me out."

"Okay, give me the background," Crabtree said. "What does the ABA say about this?"

"The American Bar Association's rule covering such a situation is this." Garbuncle withdrew a paper from his briefcase on the table. "Model Rule 3.7(a) establishes that an attorney"—he looked up—"and I'm quoting here, 'shall not act as advocate at a trial in which the lawyer is likely to be a necessary witness.' But then it provides for three exceptions, the third one of which is relevant to this case: if prohibiting the attorney from testifying, and this is from the rule, 'would work substantial hardship on the client.'"

The judge leaned forward on his arms folded across his desk and peered over the top of his glasses. "Can you cite the precedent for me—or precedents?" Garbuncle saw the defiant look on Crabtree's face, and knew the judge thought he'd won.

"In McElroy versus New Hampshire, the state supreme court decided that the issue was up to the discretion of the trial judge, and his decision could not be overturned unless there was error of law or abuse of the discretion."

Garbuncle saw the look of surprise on the judge's face. "Hmmm," Crabtree mused. "Anything else?"

"Yes. Texas law holds that the lawyer may be a witness for his client if the lawyer has promptly notified the opposing attorney of intention by said lawyer to so testify, giving as the reason the substantial hardship that disqualification of the lawyer would cause his client. In the New Hampshire decision, the state court even reduced the need to show hardship by substituting the word *reasonable* for *substantial*."

Judge Crabtree paused. "Is that it?"

Garbuncle withdrew another paper from his briefcase. "I conducted further research and discovered that a scholar with the University of Alabama Law School concluded"—he lowered his head to the paper—"'In the great majority of courts attorneys are competent to testify and are allowed to remain in the case as advocates even though the court deems the attorney's actions improper and unethical. This is because, in most jurisdictions, the rule against an attorney being a witness for his client is a rule of ethics and not of law. Under the law of evidence, the attorney is a competent witness and his testimony is admissible regardless of whether he is breaching his professional ethics.'"

Garbuncle looked up at the judge. The lawyer was almost frightened by the stern expression, which bordered on fierceness, he felt. He glanced sideways and saw the contemptuous look on Seward's face.

"What you want to do is a blatant violation of ethical standards," said Crabtree. "There is an obvious conflict of interest. As counsel for the defendant, you are working to exonerate him. Therefore, what you testify in his behalf is inherently suspect. It takes a lot of gall, counselor, for you to ask me to deviate so radically from accepted practice and violate a primary principle of law. It's wholly unorthodox."

Seward broke into a broad smile.

"Your Honor," said Garbuncle, "I cannot disagree with you, and I have debated this point with myself. However, I have concluded that the interest of justice is so critical in this case that it supersedes any ethical consideration."

"Counselor, please explain to me why you find it so compelling that you be allowed to testify in this case," the judge interjected.

"Certainly. My client earns a low wage as a sales clerk in a computer store. From that wage, he sends money to help support his two grown children in Trinidad. Their mother died. The son and daughter have children themselves and get by on the meager salaries of service workers. The son suffered a severe back injury in a car accident several years ago, and requires weekly physical therapy sessions, part of which my client has to pay for. So Mister Monceau can't afford an attorney. I witnessed the entire episode in which he was arrested. I believe that my eyewitness testimony would have a profound impact on the jury. I need to tell the court what I saw in my effort to prevent a gross miscarriage of justice."

Crabtree caught Seward's smirk.

"Why did you decide to represent him?"

"I am almost illiterate with the computer. Mister Monceau came to my home and set up my new computer, then instructed me in its use, without charging me anything. I owe it to him to defend him, as well as to provide crucial eyewitness testimony. Further, I have come to know him, and he is a kind, selfless, and thoroughly honest person. I need to let the jury know that I am motivated far beyond the attorney-client relationship in my defense of him. I need to be allowed to testify not just to what I witnessed with my own eyes, but to the man's character as I know it."

The judge half covered his mouth with his hand and rested his elbow on the desk. A wrinkle formed between his eyes.

"Your Honor," said Seward, "counsel for the defendant speaks of a miscarriage of justice, but I submit that a far greater travesty would occur if he were allowed to breach the ethical principle that clearly applies here, to wit, that it would be a flagrant conflict of interest for him to serve as a witness for the person he represents."

Crabtree stared at Garbuncle for several seconds, then announced brusquely, "I'll ponder it and get back to you. Please leave the documentation you cited with me so that I can review it."

"Thank you, Your Honor. I appreciate your consideration on this." He handed the envelope with the results of his research to Crabtree.

The two attorneys rose, and Seward shot Garbuncle what he saw was a malevolent look. They left the judge's chambers.

Two weeks later, Garbuncle's secretary called his attention to an email from Judge Crabtree. The attorney called it up on his own computer, and saw that it was the judge's order on the motion: "I have decided to grant your motion to testify on behalf of your client, Alec Monceau, in his trial on a charge of resisting arrest with violence. Precluding your testimony would, I believe, defeat the ends of justice."

The lawyer punched buttons on his phone. "Hey, buddy, wanna have a drink after work at Big Daddy's?"

"Well, I'm working on a story and can't get out o' here till about six, if that's all right," Hitchens answered.

"Yeah, I could stay a little late and get some work done myself."

"See ya there."

***

"So—anything new on Alec's case?" Hitchens wondered, fingering his beer coaster.

"Not much. I did get a notice from the judge today. Nothing important."

"What was it?"

Garbuncle took a swig of his vodka on the rocks. "Oh, just something about his giving me permission to testify for Alec," he deadpanned.

"What?!" Hitchens almost shouted, spilling beer on the counter, as bar patrons glanced at the pair. "Holy crap. That's great."

"What'd you expect? I ain't no slouch."

"You be da man. The drinks are on me."

CHAPTER EIGHT

"Let's just have one more," Ernie said.

"Nope," said Donna. "We've had three already. I can't have a hangover tomorrow. The office staff depends on me to keep things running smoothly. Besides, I just got off of a DUI, and it won't look good if we get stopped."

"Nothing to worry about. I'm driving, and the cop would just wave me on." They sat at a table with Ernie's friend Jake Schmidt at Johnny's in Granville. "Oh hell, okay, let's just have another one at my place. Jake, you can follow us."

The three drove in two cars to the police lieutenant's unremarkable, wood-frame house in a lower-middle-class neighborhood west of Lake Worth. Ernie made drinks for them, and put a vinyl record on his stereo turntable. Sarah Vaughan sang *Lover Man*, and Jake asked Donna to dance. He drew her up against him and they moved to the slow music. She could feel his erection. The song over, he led her to the couch, and pulled her onto his lap.

"Hey, buster, what are you doing?" she protested.

"It's okay," said Ernie. "Jake is just having fun." He went to the kitchen for another drink, and returned to find Jake kissing Donna and running his hand under her skirt.

"Go to it," said Ernie. "I'll just watch."

Donna pulled away and sat apart from Jake on the couch.

"Anybody up for a hand of poker?" said Ernie. "I'm talking about strip poker."

"No no no," Donna objected. "It's time for me to get home."

"That's okay," said Jake. "I'm going to take off. I don't mean my clothes." He and Ernie laughed. "Got a load to haul in the morning."

"How's the business going?" Ernie asked.

"Pretty good lately. I'm keeping all three trucks operating. Lot of trash and dirt hauling with all of the new construction going on."

When he left, Donna asked, "Didn't you even care that Jake was making out with me?"

"No, Donna. I don't mind sharing you, as long as it's with a friend of mine."

"That's pretty kinky. I don't know if I'm up to that. I have to get going."

Several days later, Jake called Donna and asked for a date that Saturday night.

"How'd you get my number?"

"Ernie gave it to me."

She did find him attractive: chiseled features, a full head of dark-brown hair, a thin mustache, trim, and muscular. She was tall and he only medium height, compared to Ernie, who was several inches taller than she, but he also had an ample belly. Jake was debonair—in an unpolished way. She accepted.

Jake asked her to pack a picnic lunch, saying he'd pay her for the food and beer, but wouldn't tell her where they were going. "It's a little surprise."

He picked her up at 6 p.m. in his red Dodge Charger, and they drove west on Southern Boulevard for miles until only an isolated business dotted the landscape intermittently: Dan's Welding shop, a shanty fronted by a Madame Clare Voyant Palm Readings sign, a dog kennel, a Mexican food shack, a two-pump gas station and tiny convenience store. They came upon a woods on the north side of the road, with an entrance.

Jake drove his car parallel with Southern along a path with dried grass beaten down by vehicle traffic. He passed a row of pickup trucks and old-model cars, most with faded paint and rusting fenders, and found a spot amid a smattering of newer ones. He and Donna walked a short distance to an area with a few pines that lent a bucolic feel. They found an empty picnic table among several occupied by mostly late-middle-aged folks and three younger couples with children. Most of the men wore loose denims, and the women were clad in dowdy dresses and skirts, their faces devoid of makeup. Jake wore Bermuda shorts, and Donna was clad in snug-fitting slacks that revealed a moderate midriff roll, which was offset by ample cleavage showing in a low-cut, gossamer blouse, and by a well-rounded derriere.

They unpacked the basket, and Jake popped open two cans of Pabst Blue Ribbon. Two men approached, one young and the other somewhat older.

"Hey Pete, Larry," Jake greeted them. He stood and shook their hands. "This is my friend Donna. Ain't she a sight for sore eyes?"

"Sure is," said Pete, the older one. Donna smiled.

"Howdy ma'am," Larry said without smiling.

"Nice to meet you gentlemen."

"Ever been to one of these?" Pete asked. Donna detected a wary tone and look in his face.

"Nope," Jake answered for her. "She doesn't know what a great show is comin' up. You guys need somethin' to drink?"

"We've got a twelve-pack over yonder at our table," said Pete. "I'll go over and get a few cans."

"Oh hell no," said Jake. "We've got plenty. Sit down."

They talked about Jake's trucking business, which he said was "picking up—no pun intended." The men were on their fourth can of beer, and were feeling good. They laughed uproariously. Donna, on her second can, chuckled.

"So what's happenin' in cop country these days?" Jake asked.

Pete shrugged. "Not much excitement. The usual DUIs, burglaries, domestic fights—"

"What about that nigger with the white girlfriend?" Larry interrupted.

"Oh yeah, that was a lot o' fun—at least for Larry. Tell 'em what happened, Larry."

"We get a call from a woman who says her neighbors are yellin' bloody murder, and she's scared somebody's gonna get hurt. Pete and me knock on the door, and this dude yells at us to leave. I break the door open with my foot, and he's standin' there with no shirt on—big muscle-bound buck—and the white bitch is backed up against a wall. He tells us they're just havin' a argument, and we ain't needed. I walk up to him and say what makes him think he's got the right to have a white woman, and he tells me it's a free country and he can have anybody he wants. I haul off and knock two teeth out, and he goes down. Pete kicks him in the ribs, and he doubles up in a curl. I ask him if he's gonna behave now and treat his woman right, and he moans and nods in the affirmative. 'Just to make sure,' I says, and kick him in the kidney. The woman begs us not to hurt him anymore, and Pete asks her if she's gonna be all right. Yes, she says, no problem. Pete tells her she needs to get a white guy who knows how to treat her. So we leave. We get called back, I'll kill 'im."

Donna's mouth hung open and her eyes were big. She said nothing.

"You guys have all the fun," said Jake. "And you got perks, too. You know Lieutenant Ernie with Hardinton?" Pete and Larry said they knew who he was, though neither knew him personally.

"Ernie and me are friends. A couple o' guys in the Hardinton force stopped Donna on a DUI, and Ernie got his chief to drop it. Ernie'd helped the chief move when he bought a new house. Donna's got this friend who's an attorney, and this guy and his buddy are driving by and see Donna doing the roadside test. They pull over, and the lawyer butts in, thinkin' he's gonna help Donna." Jake interspersed his narration with laughter as he talked. "So they cuff him and lock him up for a few hours. Donna says he went to court and got the interference charge dismissed. Now if that happened to me, I'd prob'ly still be in the slammer."

"Not if it happened in Granville," said Pete. "We got your back."

"Hey, it's nice to have friends in high places." All except Donna laughed.

"It's got dark," said Larry. "Time for the show to begin."

"Yep, it is," said Jake. "Let's pack up, Donna."

"What're ya gonna do with that basket," Pete asked.

"Tell you what. We'll take it to the car, and then walk over and meet you guys up by the show."

When they were out of earshot of the two policemen, Donna said, "I don't think too much of your friends. That story they told about beating up on the black man—how awful. Do you think they really did that?"

"Aw shucks, they're just good ol' boys. Maybe they was just braggin'."

"Not much to brag about. How could anybody be so mean?"

"I'll put the basket in the back seat and roll the windows down just a little to let air in so's the food won't spoil," said Jake. "Nobody here's gonna steal nothin'."

They trudged up a narrow path through the woods to a clearing, where fifty to sixty picnickers had gathered. They stood huddled in the dark, half a football field back from a wooden cross that reached toward a half-moon casting a pale illumination over the scene.

In a few minutes, a semicircle of nine men clad in white robes and hoods formed in front of the structure. They carried torches. An owl in the woods broke the eerie silence with a plaintive coo.

That seemed to be the cue for the man in the middle, who lit his torch with a cigarette lighter and flung the burlap-wrapped stick at the base of the cross. One by one, the others copied the ritual. As the flame grew beneath the kerosene-soaked cross, it ignited, and climbed the post to the cross-arms. No one spoke as flames engulfed the cross. The red glow radiated into the night sky, ebbing until it dissipated in the blackness.

After several minutes of mute observance, the group of gazers, led by Jake and Donna, began to break up and trek toward their cars.

"Did you like it?" he asked.

Donna didn't respond, and Jake said, "I enjoy it every time. It's kind o' like a religion to me. Like we're worshipping."

"Strange religion," Donna said.

"Well, I don't cotton much to regular religion."

"I don't either, but this is weird."

He looked at her, and she could tell he was annoyed.

"Let's change the subject," she said. "I could use a stiff drink."

"Good. We'll head over to my place."

At Jake's spare apartment, she sat on a brown leather couch while Jake made rum-and-Cokes for both of them in the untidy kitchen.

"I'm sorry you didn't enjoy it, but I think I can get you in a better mood." He sat beside her, took a long swig, and began kissing her on the forehead, ears, neck, and finally the lips, gently at first and becoming more passionate as her breathing deepened. All the while, he caressed her body with firm strokes. He rose, pulled her up, and walked her to his bedroom.

"You didn't like the show tonight, and I'll bet you can put on a much better one," he said, falling onto the bed and propping his head on the pillow.

"I'll be right back." She retrieved her handbag from the couch and sashayed to the adjoining bathroom. Several minutes later, she emerged, wearing bejeweled, spike heels, her lips a bright red and eyelids cobalt beneath dark lashes. She stood unmoving in front of the bed, where Jake lay in his jockey briefs. Slowly she unbuttoned her low-cut blouse and flung it to a chair in the corner. The brassiere came next, and Jake grew erect as he drank in her rounded, firm breasts with perky nipples that stood out beyond her waist. Then she reached down and removed the heels. She wiggled out of her tight slacks, kicked them aside, and sauntered to the bedside, wearing only a black thong.

"Put your heels back on," Jake said.

"You guys are so kinky," Donna replied, with a coy smile. She picked up the shoes and returned to the bathroom. Balancing without effort on the five-inch spikes, she sashayed up to the bed.

"Turn around," said Jake, and she made a languorous turn, looking back at him over her shoulder. He sat up and reached for her abundant derriere, sliding his middle finger up her crack. She slipped out of the thong, and reclined into his arms. They rolled, clawed, and pecked each other like fighting dogs, sweating and gasping until they consummated in ecstatic moans.

CHAPTER NINE

Garbuncle hoped to get this trial done and over with in a hurry, and didn't want to spend the time and bother of picking a jury, even though he'd advised Alec to go that route. But Hitchens pressured his attorney friend for a jury, figuring the members would be more compassionate than the hard-nosed Judge Crabtree.

Prosecutor Darrell Seward quizzed fifteen prospects, his full head of silvery hair glinting in the ceiling lights as he rested his chin on a curled hand. He asked if they'd had any bad experiences with the police. A young black man with an Afro hairstyle said he'd been stopped twice while driving through white neighborhoods, and was frisked, though he wasn't told the reason for the police action either time.

Did he harbor resentment toward police because of those incidents? Yes, he told Seward, it put a "bad taste" in his mouth that lingered. The short-statured prosecutor peered up at the man, and dismissed him.

A pretty, middle-aged white blonde said a policeman had pulled her over for failure to use her turn signal, and made lewd remarks about her breasts and thighs. The experience had made her wary of law officers. Seward rejected her.

The prosecutor found nothing objectionable in the answers of six others to his questioning. They were four men and two women, all but two of them whites ranging in age from thirties to about seventy. A Hispanic man and an elderly black woman were the minority members.

Garbuncle knew his indifference would be obvious if he didn't go through the motions of questioning the prospects. He asked them a few perfunctory questions.

Did they harbor any prejudices against mixed-race people? None would admit to any.

How did they feel about immigration? The four white men and white woman thought the government should deport illegal immigrants regardless of whether their children were born in the United States, and that stronger anti-immigration laws were needed.

Without commenting, Garbuncle posed the next question: Did they have any relatives or friends who were policemen? The white woman had a brother-in-law who was a police officer up north.

Did she and the brother-in-law have a positive relationship? They'd met only a few times and her feelings toward him were neutral, she said.

The process was moving along smoothly, and Garbuncle did not want to cause a delay. He went along with the prosecutor's preferences.

"I have no objections to placing these persons on the jury, Your Honor," the attorney said.

"Let's all be ready at nine a.m. tomorrow for the trial in this courtroom," the judge announced.

***

"All rise," the bailiff instructed. Everyone stood. "Court is now in session. The Honorable Jonathan Crabtree presiding. All please sit down."

Garbuncle saw Alec crinkle his nose, and realized that he could smell alcohol on the attorney's breath.

The judge looked up from the bench, where he'd been shuffling papers.

"State of Florida," he called.

Assistant State Attorney Seward rose from the prosecution table.

"On the evening of April eighteenth, Sergeant Peter Bullard and officer Lawrence Pickens stopped a car driven by the defendant, Alec Monceau, for an inoperable taillight. It was a routine stop, and would have remained that way. However, Mister Monceau, upon being approached by the officers, cursed them and denied any wrongdoing. Instructed to get back inside his car, he attacked

Sergeant Bullard, who fell to the ground but managed to overcome the assailant and, with officer Pickens's help, handcuff him. They arrested Mister Monceau and charged him with resisting arrest with violence. The testimony of these two honorable police officers will show conclusively that Alec Monceau violently resisted when officers Bullard and Monceau attempted to fulfill their duty of upholding the law. Thank you."

"Counsel for the defendant," Judge Crabtree announced.

Garbuncle rose slowly, as if with effort. The alcohol was beginning to take effect. "In the weeks and months since I first met Alec Monceau, I have come to know him as a gentleman and a scholar." The attorney smiled broadly. "Well, maybe the scholar part is a bit of an exaggeration. But he certainly is a gentleman, and if you knew him, you would be amazed that anyone could accuse him of violence. He is the epit … the epim … the epitome of gentleness. I know that because I, along with my friend Brad Hitchens, witnessed the encounter with officers Bullard and Pickens. They were the ones who were violent as they brutally beat Alec, who never even lifted a finger to resist their attack. Screams of pain could be heard as the policemen smashed Alec in the head and on the shins, and jerked him up from the ground by his handcuffs … his cuffed … his handcuffed arms, causing dislocation of a shoulder. Mister Hitchens and I will testify to what we witnessed, and I will introduce a hospital report showing the medical treatment that Alec Monceau required as much as fourteen hours after the attack. The evidence that we present will clearly prove not only that Mister Monceau did not resist, but that officers Bullard and Pickens were in fact the perps … perpors … the perpetrators of violence."

Garbuncle fell silent for fifteen seconds as he looked the jurors in the eyes, his gaze moving down the row in the jury box to focus on each one. Finally, "I trust that you, the members of the jury, will be fair and open-minded enough to render a just verdict of not guilty, thereby exonerating Alec Monceau. Thank you."

Garbuncle dropped into his seat. He noticed Alec's wide-eyed look, and said almost in a whisper, "Don't be bothered about what you're about to hear. It will be all lies."

"The state may present its first witness," Judge Crabtree said in a monotone while peering above his wire-rimmed glasses.

"I would like to bring Sergeant Peter Bullard to the witness stand," Seward announced. The bailiff summoned Bullard from the waiting room. He walked heavily to the stand.

"Please tell the court who you are."

"I am Sergeant Peter Bullard of the Granville Police Department."

"Were you the driver of the squad car that pulled Alec Monceau over on the evening of April eighteen, two-thousand-eight?"

"I was."

"Why did you pull Mister Monceau over?"

"My partner and I observed that a taillight on his Geo Prizm was not working?" The attorney removed his glasses and held them by one stem.

"After you stopped Mister Monceau's car, what happened?"

"I walked up to him and told him to get out of his car. He cursed me, and then got out and took a swing at me. I grabbed him and ordered him to get back in the car, but he swang again."

"Where was Officer Pickens when this was happening?" Seward asked, inserting a stem of his glasses in his mouth.

"He was on the passenger side, and came over to help me. Mister Monceau head-butted him and knocked him down. Officer Pickens got back up, and we rassled Mister Monceau to the ground and put cuffs on him."

"Thank you. That will be all."

The judge asked Garbuncle if he would like to cross examine Bullard.

"Yes, I would, sir ... 'scuse me, your honordom. I mean ... uh, Your Honor." Garbuncle smirked, and a deep furrow formed in Judge Crabtree's brow.

Garbuncle could have been mistaken for a homeless person. Two days of stubble covered his face. He wore a badly wrinkled light-blue shirt, an unmatched green tie, a ratty, blue-gray sport coat, frayed gray slacks, and worn, scuffed loafers. His left leg rested perpendicularly atop his right leg, exposing a thread-worn, faded pale-green sock too short to cover a white, hairy leg. He dropped the leg, leaned forward, and grasped the arms of the chair to push himself to the front of the seat. He rose like a cripple climbing out of a wheelchair.

"Would you rather remain seated?" the judge asked.

"No no, that's all right. I'll make it. I'm—I'm just fine."

Garbuncle walked gingerly toward the witness stand.

"Sergeant, will you please tell the court ..." Garbuncle hesitated, and the judge noticed he looked perplexed. He spun around, stood for a second, then walked back to the table, grabbing it for support as he tripped on an untied shoelace.

"'Scuse me for a moment, Your Honor. My shoe is untied." He fell into the chair, sitting on the side, and bent down to tie the lace. Rising, he reached for an off-white folder from the table. A tall, slim young man with a mop of chestnut hair, sitting at the table, handed it to him. He walked with much deliberation back to the witness stand.

"Sergeant, will you identify yourself?"

"Peter Bullard."

"Oh yes, you already told us." Garbuncle broke into a broad smile. "That's all right, Sergeant. Can you tell us what your job is?"

"I am a police officer with the Granville Police Department."

"What kind of an officer with the police department?" Garbuncle peered over the top of his glasses. Bullard wondered why he wore a cocky smile.

"A police officer."

"Oh, really?" Garbuncle said in mock amazement. "A police officer with the police department. Thank you. I never would have guessed that."

The judge stared open-mouthed at Garbuncle.

"Sergeant, did you write the report about the arrest of Alec Monceau?"

"Yes sir, I did."

"I have a copy of that report, which I would like for you to look at." Garbuncle handed the report over the stand to Bullard. "I'll give you a little time, in case you have as much difficulty figuring out the spelling of words as I did," the lawyer said with a sardonic smile.

Bullard looked down at the report and read, silently mouthing the words, his forehead wrinkled. After a few minutes, he said, "Okay, I read it."

"Sergeant, did you notice any discrepancies ...?" Garbuncle hiccupped. "'Scuse me. My breakfast didn't digest very well." The judge frowned. "Any discrepancies in what's in that report compared to what you testified?"

"Any discapan ...?"

"Discrepancies. It means differences. Did your testimony agree with the report?"

Garbuncle noticed the sergeant's befuddled expression. "I mean—I think so."

"Sergeant Bullard, did you just testify that, after you had stopped Mister Monceau, you walked up to him and told him to get out of his car?"

Bullard hesitated. "Uh—yes, I guess so."

"Is that what you testified?"

"Well, no. I said my partner approached him."

Garbuncle turned toward Judge Crabtree. "Your Honor, I would like to request that the stenographer read Sergeant Bullard's testimony beginning when the prosecutor asked what happened after the sergeant stopped Mister Monceau's car."

The frumpy court reporter drew the paper strip back from her stenotype, scanned upward, then back down, and finally read, "'I walked up to him and told him to get out of his car. He cursed me, and then got out and took a swing at me. I grabbed him and ordered him to get back in the car, but he swang again.'"

"That's enough. Thank you, ma'am."

Garbuncle smiled at Bullard. "Sergeant Bullard, you are either lying, or you have a very short memory. Are you still maintaining that you testified that your partner approached Mister Monceau?"

"I mean—I don't know what I said. I'm kind o' confused."

"Is that because you couldn't understand your own writing?"

"I admit I can't spell too good."

Garbuncle didn't respond. *Better not overdo this, or the jury will sympathize with him.*

"So which is it, Sergeant Bullard? Did you approach Mister Monceau, or did Officer Pickens approach him?"

Bullard shifted in his seat. He looked toward the jury, then at prosecutor Seward. Garbuncle noticed the attorney's grim expression.

"I guess I'm not sure."

"Sergeant, did you write in the report that Alec Monceau cursed at officer Pickens and attempted to strike you with his fist, then attacked you and knocked you to the ground?"

Bullard looked down at the report for several seconds. "I guess so."

"What do you guess?"

"I wrote that in the report."

"Did you also write that, while you were on the ground, you tripped Mister Monceau and hit him with your billy club, and he fell, and you and your partner put handcuffs on him?"

"Yes, sir."

"Sir? I'm not a sir, sir. I'm just a dumb-ass lawyer who got roped into—who's doing his job defending this col … this gentleman."

"Counselor," the judge barked, "I must warn you that you are not permitted to use such inappropriate language in this courtroom. You are making a mockery of its dignity, and that will not be tolerated. Do you understand?"

"Oh, certainly, Your Honor. I don't know what got into me. I apologize, and it won't happen again."

"See that it doesn't."

"Yes, Your Honor."

"You may proceed."

"Sergeant Bullard, did you and your partner handcuff Mister Monceau with his hands in back of his body?"

"Yes."

"And was he was lying on the ground face down?"

"Yes."

"Sergeant, did Mister Monceau, lying face-down with his hands cuffed behind him, rise to a standing position?"

"Sort of. We assisted him. Officer Pickens held one shoulder, and I held the other, and we helped him get up."

"Did he seem to be in pain when you helped him, as you put it?"

"No. He seemed a little groggy from the cut on his head where I had to hit him with my billy."

Garbuncle delved into the folder he carried, withdrew a sheet of paper, and displayed it to the judge and the jury. He reached up and handed it to Bullard. "Now, Sergeant Bullard, this is the JFK Hospital report on its patient, Alec Monceau, who was treated after his release from the Granville jail. Will you please read that report?"

Bullard looked down at the paper. Garbuncle gloated as he saw the witness' face grow sober.

"What does the report say, Officer Pickens?" Bullard stared at Garbuncle.

"Whatsa matter, Sergeant ... Officer ... ? Who ... ? Oh, 'scuse me. Sergeant Bullard.

Will you please read it aloud for the court?"

Bullard looked at the judge, then at Garbuncle, then at the report.

"Patient's right shoulder was dis ... dis ..."

"Does it say dislocated?"

"Oh, yeah, that's the word."

"Continue."

"He appeared to be in great pain," Bullard read in halting fashion. "X-rays revealed damage to surrounding nerves and soft tissue. Morphine was admin ... administered, and the bone was rine ... I don't know what that word is."

"Is it reinserted?"

"Oh yeah, that must be it. Reinserted into the socket."

"What else does the report say?"

"Deep lac ... lacer ..."

"Is the word lacerations?"

"Oh yeah ... I mean ... okay. Deep laceration above and to the right of right eye, approx ... approximately one inch long. Another deep laceration, three-quarters inch, to the back of the skull. Severe bruising of the ... the corral in both legs, especially the left one."

"Can you spell corral for us?"

"C-r-u-r-a-l."

"Do you know what that is?"

"No."

"Do you think it might be pronounced cur ..." Garbuncle smiled. "Guess I have a little trouble with that one too. Crural?"

"Yeah, yeah ... I mean, I don't know."

"What does it mean?"

Bullard shrugged. "Don't know."

"It means shin. Sergeant Bullard, I have a copy of the docket at the Granville Police Department showing when a police officer took Alec Monceau to the hospital after his release by the judge. Would you please read it and tell me what time Mister Monceau arrived at the hospital?"

Bullard reached forward to accept the paper, sat, and looked at the docket. "It says here 11:15 a.m."

"Fine. Now would you please read in the JFK Hospital record the part about what time he checked in there?"

"Fifteen minutes after 11 a.m."

"So the police and hospital records agree on what time he arrived at the hospital, is that right?"

"Well, yes, I s'pose so."

"What time was Mister Monceau taken from the Granville jail to see the judge?"

Bullard looked up and beyond Garbuncle, and said nothing.

"Officer Bullard, please answer the question."

"At 9 a.m."

"Approximately what time the night before was Mister Monceau placed in the Granville jail?"

"Oh, I'd say about 8 o'clock."

"So how long did he remain in his jail cell before he was taken to the judge?"

"Uh—I guess that that would be thirteen hours."

"How many hours elapsed from the time of his arrest to when he arrived at the hospital?"

"Well—let me see." Bullard began counting off the hours on his fingers.

"Sergeant Bullard, is 8 p.m. to 9 a.m. thirteen hours, and 9 a.m. to 11:15 a.m. two-and-a-quarter hours?"

"Uh, yes, that sounds about right."

"And does thirteen plus two-and-a-quarter equal fifteen-and-a-quarter?"

"Yes."

"Sergeant, will you please read again what the hospital report says about the pain Mister Monceau was in?"

Bullard looked at the paper on the table for a few seconds: "He appeared to be in great pain."

"Does it say anything about morphine?"

The policeman picked up the paper. "Morphine was administered."

"Sergeant, were Mister Monceau's injuries so severe that the doctor felt morphine should be administered more than fifteen hours after you and your partner arrested him?"

"Objection," Seward interrupted. "Sergeant Bullard is not a physician and is therefore unqualified to testify as to the seriousness of the injuries."

"Sustained."

"Your Honor, I have no further questions."

Seward sat in his chair with head lowered, glowering at Sergeant Bullard.

"It's 12:30," Judge Crabtree said. "Let's recess for lunch and return at 2 p.m."

Garbuncle and Alec decided to have lunch at the McDonald's at Dixie and Palm Beach Lakes Boulevard. Alec offered to drive, but the attorney insisted they walk the seven blocks. He didn't tell Alec that he'd become groggy from the alcohol and needed the exercise to get the blood coursing in his veins. They munched on burgers and fries, and headed back. Garbuncle told Alec he'd join him shortly in the courtroom, and stopped at the courtyard café, where he bought a pack of menthol mints to combat his alcohol breath. He walked to the elevator, hesitated, and backtracked to the restroom, where he entered a stall and took a couple swigs of vodka from the flask in his coat pocket.

***

"Order in the court." Judge Crabtree rapped his gavel.

"Would the prosecution like to question Officer Pickens?" the judge asked.

"Yes, I would," Seward responded. The bailiff walked to the waiting room in the right of the courtroom. The muscled Pickens emerged and strode to the stand, his bowed legs and inward-pointing feet forcing a back-and-forth motion of his torso. Garbuncle studied him, and perceived an air of confidence, with no trace of nervousness.

Pickens identified himself, and prosecutor Seward asked, "Officer Pickens, what happened after you and your partner, Sergeant Bullard, stopped Alec Monceau's car on the night of April eighteen?"

"I walked up to the car, and the subject got out." Pickens' voice was a low baritone, almost bass. "He took a swing at me, and I ducked, but not fast enough 'cause he caught me in the face.

"Did Mister Monceau curse at you and Officer Bullard?"

"I don't remember that he said anything."

The prosecutor frowned. "Are you sure he didn't curse?"

"Huh? Well, maybe. I don't recollect for sure."

"Did he become violent?"

"Yes, he charged at us and we subdued him."

"Did he knock either of you to the ground?"

"Well, uh, yes—I'm not sure—I mean, I almost went down, but I'm good on my feet, and it takes a lot to put me away. My partner and me put handcuffs on the defendant."

"No more questions, Your Honor."

The judge invited the defense counsel to cross-examine Pickens.

Garbuncle walked up to the witness stand.

"Officer Pickens, who wrote the police report on the incident with Alec Monceau that occurred on the evening of April eighteen?"

"My partner, Sergeant Bullard, wrote the report."

"Did you read it?"

"Yes."

"And did you find it accurate?"

"Well ..." Pickens hesitated. "I don't mean to say anything wrong about my partner, but to tell the truth, he can't spell too good. I tried to read it, but had to give up."

"I listened to the prosecution's account of what happened, and read the report," Garbuncle said. "After much parsing"—he turned a corner of his mouth down—"I discerned that it was written in the English language. Officer Pickens, is it your opinion that Sergeant Bullard intended to convey that Mister Monceau kept driving after the sergeant turned on the squad car's emergency light?"

"Yeah, that's what happened."

"Officer Pickens, which lane was Mister Monceau driving in?"

"The center lane."

"Uh-huh. And were there any cars in the right lane?"

"Yeah, it was a nice night. There was a lot o' cars on the road."

"So when Sergeant Bullard wrote"— Garbuncle fumbled in his breast pocket for his glasses—'subject kept going straight,' what did you and your partner think Mister Monceau should have done?"

"Well, he could have—I mean, yeah, there was cars, but ..." He hesitated.

"But what, Officer Pickens? What did you two officers expect Mister Monceau to do? Did you think he should have crashed into a car in the right lane?"

"No, of course not."

"Did Mister Monceau have any other choice but to continue driving straight until cars cleared so he had room to move to the right?"

"Well, that depends on how you look at it."

"And how do you look at it, sir?"

"I just, I mean, I think ..." Pickens sighed. "Okay, he couldn't move over."

"Were you two officers trying to make it appear in the report, sir, that Mister Monceau tried to avoid pulling over?"

"No, I mean, uh, my partner just wrote it the way we saw it."

"Officer Pickens, after Sergeant Bullard stopped Mister Monceau's car, what happened?"

"Mister Monceau got out of his car, and I came up to him. He right away swung his fist at me, and grazed my jaw while I was backing away."

"He grazed your jaw?"

"Yes."

"Why did you testify that he struck you in the face?"

Pickens shifted in his seat. "Well, I mean, he meant to, and he would have if I hadn't ducked."

"But didn't you just testify that you backed away?"

"Well, I could have—I mean, I guess I did both."

"Officer Pickens, would you like to come forward and demonstrate how you managed to duck and back away at the same time?"

The officer bent his knees and simultaneously leaned backward, losing his balance and falling on his rear.

Garbuncle covered his broad grin with a hand. "You may get up now, Officer Pickens."

The witness rose and returned to the stand.

"Is it almost impossible to both duck and back away at the time, Officer Pickens?" Pickens said nothing, and Garbuncle didn't press him.

"Now, officer, did Mister Monceau say anything before he swung?"

"No, he didn't say anything. That's why I was so surprised. I didn't expect him to swing, or I'da ducked. I mean—well, you know what I meant."

"No, sir, I don't know what you meant. Would you like to explain?"

"I just—I'm not sure what happened."

"Officer Pickens, are you not aware that the report says you ducked Mister Monceau's fist, and mentions nothing about the fist grazing your face?"

"Is that what it says?"

"Would you like to see it?"

"No, I don't need to."

Pickens leaned back in his chair and looked up at the ceiling. "Pete prob'ly was checking a message on his radio and didn't see it happen."

"Are you saying Sergeant Bullard invented that assertion in the report? Are you accusing him of making it up?"

"No, of course not. Everything happened so fast, maybe he wasn't concentrating when he wrote that."

"Officer Pickens, you said that you approached Alec Monceau after he stopped his car and got out. Is that correct?"

"Yeah, I walked up to him."

"Did you know, officer, that your partner testified that he, not you, first approached Mister Monceau?"

"Well—I can't help what my partner said."

"So are you saying that your version is the correct one?"

"No, I'm not saying anything. You're putting words in my mouth." Pickens raised his voice, and a light red seeped through the tan in his face.

"Did you also testify that Mister Monceau didn't say anything when you approached?"

"I guess so."

"Officer Pickens, would you please read this report written by Sergeant Bullard?' Garbuncle handed Pickens the copy. "I know it almost reads as though it's in a foreign language, but can you try to read what the report says about the subject's having cursed?"

"'When officer Pickens approached him,'" Pickens read slowly, "'subject began cursing and saying he didn't do nothing wrong. I instructed—'"

"That's enough. Did you testify, officer, that Mister Monceau didn't say anything?"

Pickens looked around the room, and Garbuncle sensed that the policeman felt like a caged animal looking for a way out. "I prob'ly couldn't hear cuz of all the traffic."

"Where were the squad car and Mister Monceau's Geo Prizm parked?"

"On Shelby Road, maybe fifty feet north of Lake Worth Road."

"Hmmm," Garbuncle mused, looking at the report. "Would you please read what the report says about where Mister Monceau pulled off the road?"

"'Subject driving'—wait, that's not it. Here it is. 'Got on his bumper and he finely—finally turned onto Shelby Road and pulled over about one hundred yards north and got out.'"

"Officer, how many feet are there in one hundred yards?"

"That's easy. Three hundred."

"Did you just say that Mister Monceau stopped his car about fifty feet north of Lake Worth Road?"

"Did I say that?"

"You did, officer Pickens. Would you like to have the court reporter read the transcript?"

"Naw, don't bother."

"So how do you explain the huge difference in the distance from Lake Worth Road that you and Sergeant Bullard estimated?"

Well—I'm not very good at judging distances."

"Are you saying that Sergeant Bullard is right?"

"Yeah, prob'ly so."

"One hundred yards. That's the length of a football field. Does it make sense to you that the traffic on Lake Worth Road must have been pretty loud if it prevented you from hearing Mister Monceau cursing?"

"I—I don't know."

"Wouldn't there had to have been a whole armada of eighteen-wheel semis on the road to make that kind of noise, officer Pickens?"

"I said I don't know." Pickens put his clenched fists on the stand and raised his voice, his face reddening.

"Why did Sergeant Bullard testify that Alec Monceau cursed and proclaimed his innocence if, as you say, Mister Monceau didn't say anything? Is it possible that Sergeant Bullard lied?"

"I don't know, I don't know," Pickens bellowed, the veins in his neck protruding. "What do you want me to say?"

"Your Honor, I have no further questions."

Pickens stalked back to the waiting room, and Garbuncle noticed with amusement that the swagger was gone.

"I'm going to call an end to today's proceedings, and allow emotions to cool down," the judge announced. "The weekend is upon us. Let's resume at 9 a.m. Monday. Members of the jury may return to your homes. However, you are strictly forbidden from discussing any aspect of this case with anyone, including family members. You are all free to leave—except for Mister Garbuncle."

Crabtree scowled at the attorney and said, "I'd like to have a word with you before you go."

Garbuncle walked up to the railing in front of the bench as though he were approaching a snarling dog.

"Counselor, in fifteen years as a criminal court judge, I don't recall ever having to admonish an attorney for his appearance. But I am about to for the first time. Your disheveled condition shows a lack of respect for this court. Please return Monday clean-shaven and wearing attire that conforms with the sobriety of this august institution."

***

Hitchens put his beer glass down on the bar and waved at Garbuncle entering Big Daddy's.

"Pretty good day today," the attorney said, pulling the bar stool under him. "I thought I'd get to you, but I'm sure you'll be able to testify Monday. And then this thing will wrap up."

"That cop, the young one, Pickens—something about that guy is vaguely familiar," Hitchens said. "That cocky look, and the way he walks—you know, when he walked up to the witness stand."

"Maybe you've seen him in a bar. Some of the cops hang out at Johnny's."

"Yeah, that might be it. I got a look at the jury, too."

"We got a black woman, three white men and one Hispanic man, and one white woman."

"I didn't scrutinize them. How old are they?"

"A couple of them in their upper thirties, I'd guess, and the others older."

"That doesn't sound good. There ought to be more than one black in the mix. And older people tend to be conservative and pro-cop. There's a lot of racism, especially among folks who grew up in the old South. I think you know what I'm talking about." Hitchens looked down at his beer with a sarcastic smile.

"I'm not racist," Garbuncle said, his tone oozing what Hitchens heard as innocence. "My momma taught us kids to not hate anybody."

"Yeah yeah," said Hitchens. "I've heard that before."

Garbuncle didn't respond.

"You should've tried to get more blacks."

"The pool was pretty homogeneous. A lot of them were dismissed for one thing or another. I did the best I could."

"I'm not so sure your heart was in it," Hitchens needled. "I know you hate to lose. I hope you get fired up."

"It's going good, I think. Those two cops are a couple of dunderheads. And the younger one really pisses me off. Acts like he's Mister America."

"That's what I want to hear."

"I have to do some shopping tomorrow. The judge told me he didn't like the way I looked."

"I don't blame him. You look sloppy."

"That's what my wife always nagged me about. I don't like being formal. I hate having to conform to somebody else's standard of decorum."

CHAPTER TEN

"Hey Donna, what are you doing here?" said Garbuncle. He'd left Alec Monceau at the defense table in Courtroom Seven to use the hallway bathroom before the trial resumed.

"Hi Ham. Wow, that's quite an outfit you're wearing."

"You like it?"

"Well, it's not something I would recommend for a courtroom, but I'm not going to badger you. It looks good."

"Hmmm. Yeah, well, my other duds were sort o' shabby, and the judge wanted me to spruce up."

"I work Saturday mornings inputting data from the week's business, so I have Monday morning off. Thought I'd stop over and see you in action." She'd realized after her romp in the sack with Jake that her attraction to him was purely physical. While she didn't have any special feelings for Garbuncle, she did grow to like him better after the effort he'd made to help when the police stopped her for her DUI.

"Really? That's awfully nice of you. I'm glad to see you. I'm headed to the john and have to hurry, because the trial is about to continue where we left off Friday. So I'll see you when we recess for lunch."

"No, that's okay. I have to leave before noon to get to work in time. Be in touch."

"Yeah, I sure will. I'll talk to you later."

Both stalls were occupied, and Garbuncle stood at the urinal. Looking around and seeing no one, he withdrew a flask from his coat pocket and took a long swig.

He'd stopped at his favorite bar on the way to the courthouse, but needed further fortification. He returned to the courtroom, nodding with a smile at Donna in a rear row as he passed.

Judge Crabtree rapped his gavel. "Order in the court."

The motley courtroom attendees hushed.

"Would counsel for the defendant like ..." Judge Crabtree hesitated, staring at Garbuncle in a way that the attorney perceived as disapproving. In a sober tone, "Counsel for the defendant may call his first witness."

The overhead lighting bounced off Garbuncle's face, which glowed with after-shave lotion. His straight, graying hair was slicked back from a receding hairline. He wore a bright yellow leisure suit a la the nineteen-seventies, pressed and neat except for a small red wine stain on a lapel. A fire-engine-red shirt and royal-blue tie completed his ensemble. Glistening black patent leather shoes competed with his face for reflection of the ceiling lighting.

Garbuncle motioned for Alec to rise, and pointed to the witness stand. Alec walked with a hesitant gait, glancing to his right at the six-member jury.

"Now, Alec, I want you to tell the court what happened on the evening of April eighteen that led to your arrest." Alec wore an anxious look, and Garbuncle said, "Go ahead, Alec. You may speak."

"I drive west on Lake Worth Road, go home from Computer Freak. I work dere."

"Excuse me, Alec. What time of day was it?"

"About forty-five minutes after 7 o'clock."

"Was it beginning to get dark?"

"Yes, but not all da way."

"So it was about as dark as you? Never mind, that was a joke." A broad smirk.

Judge Crabtree jerked his head back, staring with eyes wide. Alec had a blank look.

"Tell us what happened next," said Garbuncle.

"I see red light in back mirror, den I hear police car."

"You mean you heard a siren?"

"Yes, dat it. I forgot what it called. I know should drive right side of road, but no can move. Cars in dat lane. I go slow, and when cars past, drive to right lane.

Police car come behind me. I turn onto road at corner, go past water on side, den park. I get out. Police park car behind. One walk to me. He ask me why I no move over quick. I say no can, cars dere. He hit me on head wid stick."

"Do you mean his billy club?"

"Dat what it called? Yes, club—long, narrow."

"Tell me which of those two men sitting at that table"—Garbuncle turned back toward the defense table and pointed—"which one struck you."

Alec pulled his shoulders in and hesitated. Garbuncle could see the fear in his client's face.

"It's all right. He can't hurt you now. You need to tell us which one struck you."

"Dat strong man, tall. Young."

Garbuncle pointed to him. "You mean that one? Larry Pickens?"

"Yes."

The cop's face was impassive.

"Did Officer Pickens say anything to you?

"Yes. He yell at me I resis' arres', and he teach me lesson."

"What happened next?"

"Den oder policeman come from police car, say I need fix back light, no put Obama sticker on bumper. I try tell him get light fixed tomorrow. He hit me in stomach wid club. I no can breat'. Oder policeman hit me wid club back of neck." He placed his hand just above his shirt collar.

"I fall on ground. Dey put handcuffs on me, pull me up. Hurt very bad. Dey injure my shoulder. I wear ting for arm two weeks."

"Do you mean a sling?"

"Yes, yes. Doctor call it sling."

"Then what happened?"

"Strong policeman ask where I from. I say Trinidad. He hit me wid club low on legs. He say I look like Obama. He say monkeys take over country. I tink he mean Obama and me monkeys."

The judge, his dome shiny through strands of white hair, noticed Garbuncle trying to squelch a laugh, but allowing a smile to open. "Counselor, do you think that's funny?"

Garbuncle saw, peering over the top of wire-rimmed glasses, a stern face. His grin vanished like a rabbit disappearing at a magician's snap of the fingers. "Oh, no, Your Honor. A joke I heard last night popped into my head for some reason. I apologize."

In a soft tone, "What happened next, Alec?"

"Dey push me in back seat. My shoulder hurt very much. Dey take me jail, make me stay all night. I no sleep. Head hurt. I see doctor next day, he say my shoulder dis … dis …"

"Did he use the word dislocated?" Garbuncle asked.

"Yes, yes, he say dat word."

"Your Honor, I have no further questions."

The judge asked if the prosecution would like to question the accused man.

Assistant State Attorney Seward stepped to the witness stand. "Mister Monceau, you testified that your car had an Obama bumper sticker. Is that right?"

"Yes, I say dat."

"When did you affix that bumper sticker, Mister Monceau?"

"You mean put sticker on bumper?"

"Yes."

"Oh, before about tree monts. Maybe four monts. I no sure."

"The July seven trial date was set ten, eleven weeks ago. So are you not sure if that sticker was on your bumper when officers Pickens and Bullard stopped you?"

Garbuncle saw the confusion in Alec's face.

"You ask sticker on bumper?"

"Yes."

"Oh yes. Policeman tell me I like Obama. I get sticker …" Alec looked up and away. "… I tink two, tree weeks before policemen stop me."

"Where did you get that bumper sticker?"

"I get email saying it free. I reply to email, say I want."

"Why did you want that sticker, Mister Monceau?"

Garbuncle's hand shot up. "Objection, Your Honor. That is irrelevant."

"Objection sustained," the judge declared. "You don't have to answer the question, Mister Monceau."

"Mister Monceau, are you not in fact lying about when you applied that bumper sticker in order to make it appear that officers Pickens and Bullard are racist?"

Alec turned his head slowly from side to side. "No, sir. Sticker on bumper before policemen stop me."

"Mister Monceau, your computer will show the date when you bought that sticker, is that right?"

"Yes. I tink."

The prosecuting attorney looked hard at Alec for several seconds, and saw that Alec's innocent expression didn't change.

The prosecutor looked away. Then, "You invented that comment about Obama that officer Bullard supposedly made, didn't you?"

Alec looked at Garbuncle, seated at the defense table, who understood the nonplussed look. The attorney turned his head from side to side.

Alec hesitated, then looked as though a light bulb came on. "No. I tell trut."

"Had you been drinking?"

"No. I go home from work, Computer Freak."

"Did you have a rough day? Were you angry?"

"No. I like job. I help people buy computer."

"Then why did you curse the officers when they approached you?"

"I no curse dem. I no use bad words. I no say nutin."

"Why did you take a swing at officer Bullard?"

Alec looked bemused.

"I'll rephrase the question. Why did you try to hit officer Bullard with your fist?"

"I no try hit nobody," Alec said.

Garbuncle heard impatience in Alec's voice and raised his arms in front of his body, palms down, then slowly lowered them.

The prosecutor raised the volume. "You were so angry that you head-butted Officer Bullard and knocked him to the ground, didn't you?"

Alec looked at Garbuncle. He tilted his head back and sucked in air with his mouth open in a pucker. Alec got the cue, and took a deep breath.

"I no angry. I no knock officer down," he said with calm deliberation.

"And then you charged at him, am I right?" The attorney crescendoed. "You were so angry that you charged at the officer and knocked him down."

"No, I no charge," Alec replied in the same even tone.

"I'm through questioning the defendant, Your Honor."

"Uh, Your Honor, may I use the restroom for a minute?" Garbuncle asked.

"You may."

"Thank you. I'll just use the one in the hallway, around the corner. I'll be right back."

Garbuncle waddled down the aisle and found the rest room. He looked around to see if anyone were there, and entered a stall, closing the door. He pulled a pint flask out of the inside pocket of his sport jacket, twisted the cap off, and guzzled a third of the contents. His eyes clamped shut and his face screwed up as the liquor burned. He replaced the flask, urinated, and returned to the courtroom in six minutes.

"My apologies, Your Honor."

"Do you wish to call another witness, counselor?"

"Yes. I would like to summon Brad Hitchens."

The bailiff escorted Hitchens to the stand.

"Is it true that you and I are friends?"

"That depends on my mood that day." A few muffled chuckles from the jury. "Okay, yes, I guess we're friends, although you often try my patience—as I'm sure I do yours."

Garbuncle ignored the remark. "Were we together on the evening of April eighteen?"

"Yes. The Florida Marlins were playing the New York Mets, and you were at my place to watch the game while we had dinner that I cooked. I had picked you up because your clunker of a car was in the shop—as usual."

"Where did we go after the game?"

"I was driving you home. You'd eaten too much, and had an upset stomach. On Lake Worth Road, you told me to pull off the road because you were going to be sick."

"Where exactly was this?"

"Just east of Shelby Road, on the north side."

"How far east, would you say?"

"Oh, maybe fifty yards."

"What happened next?"

"You got out of the car and began to retch. When you raised your head, I called your attention to a police car that had stopped a vehicle on Shelby Road."

"How far north on Shelby were the squad car and the other car?"

"Probably—I'd say about the length of a football field, a hundred yards or so, give or take five or ten yards."

"What did you see?"

"Two police officers were attacking a man by the parked car. Both of them hit him with their billy clubs and knocked him to the grass. One of them kicked the guy while he was face-down. They put handcuffs on him and yanked him up, and he screamed. They hauled him to the squad car."

"Did you see the man do anything physically to the two officers?"

"No. He didn't do anything before the beating started, and he didn't try to stop it. He just stood there and took it."

"Did you see the man do anything to instigate the attack by the officers?"

"No. I saw the first police officer approach him and hit him with his billy club, and then the other did the same thing. I heard the two officers talking to him in loud voices, but I couldn't hear anything the victim said."

"Did anything else happen."

"No, that's all I saw. You got back in the car, and we drove back onto Lake Worth Road and then turned onto Shelby. We drove past the scene of the incident, and saw the two officers in the police car and the man they'd beaten up in the back seat."

"That's all, Your Honor."

"Would the prosecutor like to cross-examine the witness?"

"Yes, I would," Seward said as he walked to the stand.

"Mister Hitchens, what time of day was it when you pulled off of Lake Worth road and witnessed the arrest of Mister Monceau?"

"I remember that it was about 7:45 p.m., because we left my apartment after the fourth inning of the Florida Marlins game."

"That was in mid-to-late April, so it was getting dark, isn't that correct?"

"It had been a beautiful day, sunny all day, and no clouds were blocking the setting sun. So yes, it was twilight, but there still was ample light for me to see what was going on."

"Could you tell what Mister Monceau was wearing?"

"What the two officers were doing to him was pretty shocking, and I wasn't focused on his sartorial make-up. As far as I can recall, he was just wearing a normal shirt and pants."

"Was he wearing a tie?"

"I don't remember that he was."

"He has testified that he was heading home from work at the computer store. Don't you think he'd have been wearing a tie?"

"I've been at that store since the incident and spoken with him, and neither he nor any of the other employees was wearing a tie."

Seward inserted a stem of his glasses into his mouth and looked down, as though consumed in thought. "You testified that the officers struck Mister Monceau with their billy clubs, and he fell to the grass. Are you sure there is grass on the side of that road?"

"Maybe it was gravel. There's grass beyond the gravel, and I just remember the grass."

"But it was getting dark, which is probably why you couldn't distinguish the grass from the gravel, wouldn't you agree?"

"No. I was fixated on the brutality that was occurring, and wasn't assessing whether the spot where Mister Monceau fell was grassy or gravelly. The violence took precedence in my mind, and I wasn't heeding such details."

"If it was dark enough that you couldn't tell what kind of surface the arrest occurred on, isn't it reasonable to assume that your ability to correctly ascertain the action underway also was impaired?"

"I could see clearly, and remember vividly, that the two officers struck Mister Monceau, one on the head, and the other on the back of the neck. And then the one who hit him on the head also hit him on his shins after they raised him from the—the ground."

"No further questions."

"Does the defense counsel have any other witnesses?"

"Yes, Your Honor. I would like to testify on behalf of my client," Garbuncle responded.

Seward raised his hand.

"Do you wish to say something, counselor?"

"Yes, Your Honor. May I speak with you?"

"You may."

Seward strode to the bench, leaned forward, and said he objected to Garbuncle's testifying. The judge beckoned Garbuncle, and led the two attorneys to his chambers.

"Your request is highly irregular," Judge Crabtree said, looking at Garbuncle, "and presents a conflict of interest. However, it is not without precedent, and I believe that your testimony is critical to a fair disposition of the case. I am convinced that barring your testimony would be contrary to the interests of justice. Further, the financial circumstances of Mister Monceau prevent him from securing the paid services of another attorney, and you agreed to represent him in this court in return for services he has rendered you. Am I correct?"

"Yes, Your Honor, your understanding of the situation is correct."

"Counselor, may I ask what those services were?" said Seward.

"I'm technologically challenged, and he helped me with my computer without charging me. I owe it to him."

"But you're spending far more professional time on his case than he did on your computer, isn't that true?"

Garbuncle shrugged. "Yes, I suppose so."

"Why are you doing it?"

Garbuncle looked at the ceiling. "I ... I don't know. I guess ... it was just pretty rotten what happened."

Judge Crabtree continued, "I have decided that refusal to allow your representation would impose a severe hardship on Mister Monceau, and that such consideration supersedes the obvious breach of ethics. Further, such breach of ethics is less egregious when committed on behalf of the defense rather than the prosecution.

"In fact," the judge continued, "that is the key here. Ethics are morals. And justice also is a moral issue. If an ethic functions to the detriment of justice, the ethic is neutralized. Inherent in the legal principle of innocent until proven guilty is the presumption that protection from an unjust finding of guilt takes precedence over an inaccurate finding of innocence. If the situation were reversed, with the prosecutor petitioning to serve in the dual role of witness, that conflict of interest, constituting a violation of ethics, would require a denial of the petition. But that is not the situation we have here."

"Thank you, Your Honor," said Garbuncle.

The two attorneys returned to their stations.

"With the permission of the court, my assistant, Ronald Brownstein, will question me," Garbuncle announced.

"You may proceed."

The tall, lean young man who had been sitting at the defense table rose and strode to the stand.

"Mister Garbuncle," he said in a voice Garbuncle heard as tentative, "did you witness the arrest of Alec Monceau on Shelby Road in Granville on the evening of April eighteen?"

"I did."

"Where were you at the time?"

"I was standing by the side of Brad Hitchens's car, in which I was a passenger. I had asked Mister Hitchens to pull off of Lake Worth Road, just east of Shelby Road, because I was sick and needed to regurgitate."

"What did you observe?" Garbuncle heard increasing confidence in his young assistant's voice.

"My friend Brad Hitchens called my attention to what was going on after he saw the officer hit Mister Monceau on the head with his billy club, according to his testimony. But I was too busy spilling my cookies to see that. After I retched, I looked up and saw the driver of the squad car shove his billy club into Mister

Monceau's midsection. He doubled up. Then the younger policeman slammed his club onto the back of Mister Monceau's neck, and he fell down, face-first. The first officer, the driver, kicked him in the side and jerked his arms up behind him. His partner put his knee in the defendant's back, and slapped the handcuffs on. Then the two officers yanked him up to a standing position, which caused him to scream in obvious pain."

"Was that the end of the violence?"

"No. The younger officer yelled something at Mister Monceau, then slammed his club into his shins. He yelled in pain again. They finally pushed him into the back of the squad car."

"Did you at any time see Mister Monceau do anything physical to the officers."

"No. He didn't do anything. He just stood there while they beat him up."

"That's all the questions I have, Your Honor."

"Would the prosecutor like to cross-examine Mister Garbuncle?"

Seward stared at his opponent, and didn't respond for several seconds. "Yes, I would."

"Very well. You may begin."

"Mister Garbuncle, were you born in the United States?"

"Yes. I grew up in a rural area west of Fort Lauderdale."

"And where did your parents come from?"

"My mother came to this country from Honduras when she was a child, and my father came here from Panama as a young man."

"Panama. That's not far from Trinidad, is it?"

"Well, Panama runs into Colombia, and Venezuela is on the other side of Colombia. Trinidad is off the coast of Venezuela, way to the east."

"Uh-huh." Seward planted a stem of his glasses in his mouth. "Is Trinidad anywhere in your background?"

"Not that I'm aware of."

"But your parents came from countries down in the Caribbean. Does that give you a feeling of connection with people from that part of the world?"

"I don't feel one way or the other about them."

Garbuncle was surprised at Seward's insight. He was on the right track, just the wrong direction. But Garbuncle wasn't afraid the prosecutor would question him about his feelings toward blacks, because the attorney never would find anything in Garbuncle's past showing favoritism toward them. He knew the opposite was true.

"No further questions, Your Honor."

"At this time, let's take a one-hour recess. When we return, the prosecution and defense may make their closing arguments to the jury."

***

"Ladies and Gentlemen of the jury," prosecutor Seward began, "what we have here is a case of a man who escalated a routine traffic stop for a burnt-out taillight into a major confrontation with the officers who stopped him. All Alec Monceau needed to do was accept the ticket, and the officers would have been on their way. Instead, he became belligerent and attacked those two policemen, who managed to subdue him and put him in restraints even after he had charged Sergeant Bullard and knocked him over, and struck officer Pickens in the face with his fist. Then he came up with this cockamamie story that they asked him about his Obama bumper sticker and used racial epithets in the hopes of eliciting sympathy from you jury members. It's the old story of playing the race card, but it won't work. These two fine, upstanding officers fulfilled their obligations as protectors of law-abiding citizens, and now they are being forced to defend their actions, and their reputations, against the fantastical accusations of a man trying to use the American system of justice for all to his subversive advantage.

"The defense counsel will make much of the minor variance in the testimony of the two officers. I adjure you to consider that, with the officers struggling to defend themselves against Mister Monceau's violent attacks, details were apt to become confused in the heat of the moment. I urge you to keep your minds open and resist the temptation to accept the testimony of Mister Monceau and his two supporters at face value. The interests of justice demand that you question their motives.

"Brad Hitchens and Hiram Garbuncle knew Alec Monceau before this incident occurred, and are not disinterested parties. Their testimony in his behalf is a conflict of interest. It is tainted, and thus flimsy, and you must not allow it to move you toward rendering an unfair verdict. It is your duty to convict Alec Monceau of the felony of resisting arrest with violence. Thank you."

"The counsel for the defendant may now make his closing argument," Judge Crabtree said.

Garbuncle walked with measured steps to the podium, and stood gazing around the courtroom—first at prosecutor Seward and the two police officers, then turning his head to fix his eyes on the judge, and finally staring at the jury. "Ladies and gentlemen of the jury, I have been an attorney for thirty years, defending a host of persons accused of crimes. Never have I encountered a case of miscarriage of justice that reached this magnitude. I know beyond the shadow of a doubt what happened on the evening of April eighteen. I know with equal certainty that the gentleman sitting over there"—Garbuncle stopped and thrust his arm in a semicircle toward Monceau at the defense table—"is one hundred percent innocent of the charge of resisting arrest with violence. In fact, Alec Monceau is totally innocent of resisting arrest, period.

"On the other hand, those two police officers"—his arm shot out at the two sitting at the prosecution table, his finger stabbing at them—"are guilty of fabricating stories condemning Mister Monceau to cover their despicably violent actions after they stopped his car on Shelby Road in Granville. And they didn't even do a credible job of it, each providing testimony that conflicted with that of the other. The violence that night was initiated by the policemen, without a shred of provocation from the defendant. He never protested, not in the slightest, the vicious physical beating that he underwent at the hands, and feet, of those two men paid and sworn to protect, not abuse, the residents and passersby in the community of Granville.

"I heard the testimony of Mister Monceau, and that of Mister Hitchens. But I didn't need to hear it. I saw with my own eyes exactly what Mister Hitchens saw and Mister Monceau experienced. We have three persons, ladies and gentlemen, whose testimony was in complete agreement as to what transpired. This was a case of two police officers physically venting their racial hatred on a man who did nothing to deserve it. We cannot allow this to happen in our society. The witnesses at the prosecution and defense tables should be seated reversely. Lawmen Pete Bullard and Larry Pickens belong at the defense table, and Alec Monceau at the prosecution table. Regardless of the jury's verdict, I aim to have them at those respective tables in the future to see that justice is realized to the fullest extent. Thank you."

"State of Florida may give its rebuttal," Judge Crabtree announced.

"Thank you, Your Honor," said Seward. He stood and walked to within ten feet of the jury.

"Ladies and gentlemen, what we have witnessed here is a violation of ethics so outrageous as to render the testimony of the two primary witnesses to the arrest of Alec Monceau devoid of any semblance of credibility. By testifying on behalf of his own client, Hiram Garbuncle has sacrificed the right to be taken seriously. His testimony was totally self-serving, and simply cannot be believed. And what of Brad Hitchens? He and Garbuncle are, by their own admission, friends, a relationship that compromises the testimony of Mister Hitchens, as well. The entire effort to turn the case against Mister Monceau on its head by shifting the blame for the violence that occurred on two respected police officers was a shameless maneuver to pull the wool over the eyes of you, the members of the jury."

Seward's eyes roved over the jury members. "In the interest of justice, your duty is obvious. You must place the blame for this unfortunate incident where it belongs, squarely on the shoulders of Alec Monceau."

Judge Crabtree, his head leaning forward, kept his gaze riveted on Seward for several seconds after he'd finished. Finally, the judge pulled back. "Ladies and gentlemen, that will conclude today's session. In the morning, the jury will begin deliberating in an effort to render a verdict in this case. Please be here and ready to resume at 9 a.m. Uh, Mister Garbuncle, can I see you for a minute?"

"Yes, Your Honor?" The attorney strode to the rail.

"Go back to your former attire. You're blinding everybody in the courtroom."

"Huh?" Garbuncle looked down at his leisure suit. "You don't like it?"

"Do you suppose you can just wear a regular suit and tie?"

"Yes, certainly. No problem."

Hitchens and Garbuncle sauntered down the courthouse hallway together. "Where in the devil's hell did you come up with that outfit?" Hitchens exclaimed, turning sideways as they walked to gawk at his friend. "The judge and whole damned jury are gonna have vision impairment. That get-up is loud enough to break the sound barrier. Holy macaroni."

"Whatsa matter, you don't like it? I think it's pretty sharp."

"Yeah, maybe for a Halloween costume party. Who are you supposed to be, Bozo the Clown? Maybe Doc Severinsen?"

"Who?"

"Don't you remember? Johnny Carson's band leader. Used to wear the gaudiest outfits on television."

"Nah, I never liked those talk shows. I think they're dumb."

"Well, at least Severinsen dressed outlandish on purpose. You've got the sartorial sense of a llama."

"Buddy, I went to four different thrift shops Saturday before I found this suit. A little outdated, I realize. But I think it looks great. Got the snazzy shirt and tie at another shop. Saved me a lot of money. The judge didn't like it either. Wants me to wear a plain suit. I'm changing clothes so much I'm starting to feel like a model."

"Man, you're clueless. Just do what he says."

"Hell yes, of course. I'm not gonna piss him off."

"I gotta tell you something. That outfit of yours had me fixated, but something drew my attention away from it. The cop—Pickens. Every time he turned his head sideways, I couldn't keep my eyes off of him. Something about that face."

"I hope you're not falling in love with him," Garbuncle deadpanned.

"I've seen him before, and if it was at Johnny's, I think I'd remember."

"Well, maybe it'll hit you in the middle of the night. Don't wake me up if it does."

***

The next morning, Garbuncle left Alec Monceau sitting at the defense table to await the jury's verdict, and walked back through the courtroom, motioning Hitchens to follow him out to the hallway.

"Let's go to the coffee shop down in the courtyard," Garbuncle said. "It's going to be awhile before the jury comes back."

They went to the counter, where Hitchens ordered a decaf coffee and sat at a table. He watched while Garbuncle ordered an iced tea, then went to the condiment stand. The attorney looked around surreptitiously, then removed a flask from his jacket side pocket, spiked the tea, and strolled to the table.

"I hope you're not drunk when the verdict comes in. I saw your little maneuver. At least you look a lot more presentable. Except—something's wrong with your suit."

"Damn, I was hoping nobody would notice. I've had that suit for a long time, and it was in bad shape. I got out my old flat iron to press it, and it didn't come out very well. The suit is supposed to be a light-blue-gray color, but it doesn't look quite like that now."

"Yeah, it's got a tan tint. Sort of like it's been burnt."

"That's exactly what happened. You can't put water in that flat iron, so there's no steam. I burned the hell out of the suit. Had the iron too hot."

"And what happened to the tie?"

"Yeah, it's supposed to be a dull gray, but the iron made it shiny. Guess I need a new iron."

"I got a better idea. Why don't you send your clothes to a dry cleaner?"

"That's expensive."

Hitchens shook his head and said nothing.

"This should be a slam dunk," said Garbuncle. "Those two cops blew it, contradicting each other all over the place. You and me were right on target. How couldn't we be? We saw the same thing."

"You know, I'll say it again. The cop, the muscle guy, Pickens. Something about that face is vaguely familiar. I could swear I've seen him somewhere."

"Maybe you saw him in a bar? If I'm alone, I tend to study people, 'cause there's nothing else to do. They stick in my mind."

"Yeah, that might be it."

"Wait a minute. Don't you go to the gym to work out once in a while? This guy's biceps—he has to work out a lot."

"I used to go, but it's a waste of time and money. I can get the same results with my hundred-pound barbell in my apartment. I have to be frugal – unlike John D. MacArthur. Remember? That old billionaire dressed like a bum and lived in a shabby condo building in Palm Beach Shores. His only concession was that it was on the beach. He loved the ocean. He sure as hell didn't have to live like a miser, but money can rob people of their reason."

"We'd better get back," said Garbuncle. "I don't want to miss the jury call."

***

Garbuncle took the seat next to his client, who looked anxious. "Don't worry about anything. There's no way they're going to find you guilty."

"I no want go jail. And I no have money pay fine."

"It's not gonna happen. Relax."

The attorney took a folded newspaper out of the breast pocket of his jacket, and began working a crossword puzzle.

"What's a four-letter word that begins with the letter g and means attire?" he wondered aloud.

"I know only Goodyear."

"Huh? That's not ... Oh, you mean ... No, something you wear. Never mind." Garbuncle filled in a word, then said, "Going across, the last letter is b. Grab. Glib. Gelb—is that a word? I'm just thinking out loud, Alec. Gurb. Gorb. Ah ha! I've got it. Garb."

"I learn new word today."

"I'd like to learn what that jury… Oh, what's the bailiff doing?"

The judge accepted the note, and looked down. Garbuncle saw him gaze thoughtfully into space, then say something to the bailiff. He returned with the jury foreman, a portly, late-middle-aged man with a ruddy complexion. The judge spoke to him briefly, and the foreman returned to the jury room.

"Uh oh. Looks like the jury was not unanimous," Garbuncle muttered.

"What happen?" Alec asked, his eyes big.

"It's just going to take a little more time," said Garbuncle.

"Oh, Mister Ham, I so scared."

"It's okay. I can't believe that after what the jury heard, they could do anything but exonerate you. This jury is totally prej … Don't worry, we'll get through this. Just try to relax. We'll need to wait here while the jury deliberates."

Garbuncle pulled his crossword puzzle page and pencil out of his pocket, and began jotting down letters. "You want to learn some more words? Watch what I'm doing here, and I'll explain how this works."

The attorney managed to engage his client in the process and noticed that his mood was improving. They finished one puzzle, and Alec asked to use the restroom. He returned in minutes, and Garbuncle handed him another puzzle to try his hand at while the attorney used the restroom. In a stall, he took a quick swig, deciding he needed to stay mostly sober for persuading the judge to allow Alec to remain free pending a retrial or an appeal, in case the jury's decision made either necessary. He popped a breath mint.

"I no understand much about da crossword," Alec said when Garbuncle was seated beside him. "No know many word."

"That's okay. It's a learning process—a good way for you to increase your vocabulary."

"Yes, I try crossword at home."

After almost two hours, the bailiff brought another note to the judge.

Crabtree shifted in his seat and drummed on the podium. He leaned back, stared at the ceiling, and said something to the bailiff. He returned with the jury foreman.

Garbuncle leaned forward in his seat, and saw the man gesticulate while talking to the judge. "Go back and give it one more try," Garbuncle heard him say.

"That's not good," the lawyer said.

He turned to survey the gallery out of curiosity and because he wanted a diversion from the crossword puzzles. He saw Brad Hitchens enter. The reporter had returned to the *Hawk* after he testified to check whether the metro editor had any assignment for him. Hitchens gave the excuse that he needed to meet with a source for another story, and went back to the courthouse.

"Stay right here, Alec. Brad just walked in. I'm going to go talk with him."

"How's it going?" Hitchens asked.

"We're still awaiting the verdict. I can't believe this jury. They can't come to a unanimous decision. I'm going down to the coffee shop and grab a snack. I've got my cellphone. Give me a call if the jury returns, will you? I'll rush back. Go sit with Alec and help him pass the time. It probably won't be long. I'll return in a half-hour."

Garbuncle took the elevator down to the first floor, and ordered a sweet roll and a cup of coffee. A copy of *USA Today* was sitting on the table, and he became engrossed in a story about the presidential election campaign. He'd turned against the Republican Party because it favored the ultrarich, but hated the idea of voting for a black man. He hadn't decided yet.

His cellphone rang. "The jury is filing back in," said Hitchens. "Get up here."

"Oh damn, I forgot the time. I'll be there fast." He half-trotted down the hall to the elevator, rocked from one foot to the other inside, and did another scurry to the courtroom.

Garbuncle took his place next to Alec at the defense table just as the jury foreman began to address the judge. The attorney noticed Crabtree's grim expression as the judge looked down, his eyes fixed on the podium. He leaned forward in his chair. "Ladies and gentlemen, we have a hung jury. I hereby declare a mistrial."

A slumping Alec straightened with a jerk, and clasped the sides of his head with both hands, his face screwed up in pain, his white teeth showing. Flashing through Garbuncle's mind was the image of Ed as the mechanic, working on the attorney's car, was shocked by a wire as he stood at the edge of a puddle.

"Dey hang me?"

"Are you all right, Mister Monceau?" the judge asked, peering up from the podium over bifocal glasses.

"Excuse me, your honor. Do you mind if I have a word with my client?"

"Go right ahead."

Garbuncle turned to Alec, and spoke in a lowered voice. "Alec, just take it easy. That's not what it means. A hung jury is one where the vote isn't totally guilty or totally not guilty. There's going to be a new trial, but I think I can get the judge to let you remain free until then. I doubt very much you'll spend any time in jail. And I think we'll win next time. So compose yourself. Right now, this is just a formality. You're going to be all right. Okay?"

"I try be brave, Mister Hiram." But Garbuncle could see the anxiety on his client's face, and felt an urge to help him, an emotion the attorney had rarely experienced toward a client. Not only did he feel for Alec, whose kindness seemed extraordinary, but the injustice meted out to him made the lawyer indignant.

The two turned back to face Judge Crabtree.

"Would the prosecuting attorney and the defense counsel please come forward?" he called.

Seward and Garbuncle strode to the bench. "Counselors," Crabtree said, "we need to schedule a retrial. Would you like to do that now?"

"I'm okay with that," said Garbuncle.

Seward walked back to the prosecution table, opened his briefcase, and studied his calendar book as he returned. "I'm open all of November."

"I doubt that I have anything on my calendar that far in advance," said Garbuncle. "I'm fine with November."

"I can schedule it for November nine," Crabtree said. "Will that work for both of you?" They assented, and the judge said, "Let's make it for that date, 9 a.m."

"Your Honor," Garbuncle said, "considering that my client has a sterling record, with no arrest for anything as minor as a traffic offense, not even any parking tickets. He has a solid reputation as an employee at the Computer Freak store. I'm going to request that you extend his release pending the new trial. He lacks the resources to post bond and there is no danger that he will flee."

Crabtree looked over at the defense table, where Alec waited. "You have never been in trouble with the law before, Mister Monceau, and are gainfully employed. You have shown up on time for court appearances, and have an attorney to make sure you arrive for the next court date. I have no reason to doubt your attorney's contention that you have led an exemplary life prior to this event, and you do not pose a danger to the community. You are not a flight risk, and I am going to allow you to remain free on your own recognizance. However, you are not allowed to leave Palm Beach County until final adjudication is rendered. In case you are tempted to return to your home in Trinidad or escape to any other location, I must warn you that the court would seek extradition to have you brought back, and a harsher sentence then would be imposed. Do you understand?"

Alec looked at Garbuncle, who saw the quizzical expression. "His English is not perfect, your honor, and he doesn't comprehend terms such as recognizance and extradition and adjudication. Rest assured that I will explain the meaning to him, and I'm sure he will comply with your restrictions."

"Very well," said Judge Crabtree. "You are dismissed."

Garbuncle returned to the defense table.

"I lose job." Alec's brown skin lightened.

"No you won't," Garbuncle said. "I'm going to explain everything to your boss. I'm sure I can convince him you didn't do anything wrong. This jury was rac... Tell me your boss's name. I'll go to the Computer Freak tomorrow."

"Mister Edward Hampton. Ev'body call him Ed."

"The prosecution probably will move for a new trial. This isn't over. Just keep your chin up."

Alec bent his head back, and chuckled.

"Now that's more like it," said Gunbuncle. "You've got a sense of humor. Keep that attitude."

They left together, joined by Hitchens.

"Try to get some sleep tonight, and don't worry," Garbuncle said. "Okay?"

Alec nodded, but Hitchens knew he would.

***

"I have to say—this jury worried me from the beginning, but I'm still shocked at what they did," said Hitchens. He and Garbuncle stood in the city parking garage. "I was getting more comfortable as the trial moved ahead. It was such a clear-cut case that I couldn't see how even a prejudiced person could vote guilty. This is fricking outrageous."

Garbuncle shook his head. "I'm flabbergasted. And I'm pissed as hell. I've got to admit though—I screwed up. Never should have agreed to that jury composition."

"Well, nothing we can do about it now."

"Not now, but on the retrial, I'm gonna make damn sure we've got a jury that can see beyond the color of a man's skin. I'm royally pissed. I've never seen such a travesty of justice."

"How do you plan to argue the next time?"

"Simple. There was insufficient evidence to convict. Not only was there insufficient evidence in this case; there was ample evidence in favor of the defendant. I think we stand an excellent chance here if I can get a fair jury."

"Good. But Alec concerns me a little bit. He's pretty upset."

"Yeah, he was scared to death. But I think he'll be okay."

"I have to get back to the paper. We'll talk later."

Garbuncle returned to his office, charged with a newfound sense of purpose.

CHAPTER ELEVEN

"Hi—let's see, what is it? Larry?" Hank walked up to his acquaintance, fellow officer Larry Pickens, at the coffee dispensary. They were among hundreds who had gathered in the police union hall on Belevedere Road east of I-95 in West Palm Beach.

"Yeah. And you're Hank, with Hardinton. Right?"

"Yup," Hank said, holding a paper cup under the coffee machine spigot. He tore the top off of a packet of sugar, poured it in the coffee, and added a plastic spoonful of powdered creamer. He mixed them with a wooden stirrer.

"So what d'ya think about the contract?" Hank asked. "You plan to vote for it?"

"This is only my second union vote," said Pickens. "How do you feel about it?"

"It looks like a pretty good deal to me. I think we oughta go for it. Get it over with. I don't like these long, drawn-out contract fights. We never end up gittin' much more'n we had at the start. Sometimes we break even. I'm votin' for it."

"Well, you've had more experience at this than I have. I didn't know which way to go, so I'll just go along with what you're doin'."

"Hey," said Hank, "I wanted to tell you somethin'. Last week, I was headin' to court for a couple o' crappy traffic tickets I had to defend, and I see this lawyer me 'n' my partner Art jailed for buttin' in on a DUI arrest on the side of the road. He's talkin' in the hall with the broad we arrested. Ain't he the 'torney for the guy you and your partner Pete Bullard stopped for a broken taillight and got into a fight with?"

"Yeah, that's him. Wonder what she was doin' there."

"Who knows? She went into Courtroom Seven. Ain't that where you and Pete's trial was?"

"Yeah."

"I seen her enter, and then at the recess I see the two o' them talkin'. She left and he walked down the hall. I watched 'im head into the bathroom. He ain't young—prob'ly can't hold it too long during the trial. He claimed she was a client of his when he stuck his nose into the arrest. Maybe there's more to it. He's prob'ly hosed 'er down."

"I gotta get goin'," said Larry. "How long d'ya s'pose this is gonna take?"

"You can go up and tell the cop at the table that you have to leave and see if you can vote before the union president's speech. I think he'll let ya."

"Thanks."

Larry went to the ballot table and was allowed to cast his vote. He wasn't in a hurry, but was unsettled by what Hank told him about seeing the woman at the courtroom. He left the room, head down, deep in thought.

This Donna gal Pete and I met at the Klan meeting now knows we're the cops who beat up that black dude. She saw us at the trial, and heard the testimony about the beating. It was a mistrial. It's going to trial again?

***

"I need some TLC, Donna."

"What's wrong?" Donna cradled the phone on her shoulder while putting the dinner dishes into the dishwasher.

"The trial turned out bad."

"I heard about it on the news. There's something I've got to tell you."

"Okay. How 'bout we meet at Johnny's. You busy tonight?"

"The trial ended Friday, didn't it?"

"Yeah, and I've just been lyin' around the apartment, feeling crappy and thinking about how I can convince the jury of what bastards those two cops are in the retrial."

"Well, Sunday's the night I go out with the girls for our get-together, but I can see you first for just a little while. Is 6:30 okay?"

***

Garbuncle had already downed his first vodka on the rocks when Donna walked in and took the bar stool next to him. He stared at her ample cleavage. "You're just what a depressed attorney needs to look at to cheer him up. What are you drinking?"

"You mean you're actually buying?"

"I didn't say I was buying. I was just gonna order for you." He cackled. "I have my generous moments."

"Well, you won't be out much tonight. I'm being careful from now on. Just one drink when I'm driving. And since I'm going out with the girls later, I'll just have an iced tea."

"I can't believe two-thirds of that jury voted to convict Alec Monceau. Four out of six. And the fifth on the second try made it an even worse travesty of justice. I guess it's my fault. I shoulda objected to most of those jurors. They were clearly biased from the outset, but I didn't want to believe it. I just wanted to get the thing over with."

"If anybody can understand race prejudice, it ought to be you," Donna said with a wry look.

Garbuncle jerked his head to stare at her, and said nothing.

"I shouldn't have said that. You're feeling blue as it is."

He looked down at his drink, then took a swig.

"But maybe I can make you feel better."

Garbuncle spun his head to face her.

"Don't look at me like that. That's not what I meant. I'm going out with the girls tonight. I have to be to work early tomorrow. I'm backed up with the record-keeping. I've got some news that could be helpful to the case."

"All right. What is it?"

"Let's talk about it another night. I can't keep the girls waiting. I knew you'd be down in the dumps, so I didn't want to turn you away."

Garbuncle didn't mind, because this would give him an opportunity to see her again soon.

"Unless you need to get to work on the new trial right away."

"No, no, there's no urgency. What about Monday night?"

"That ought to work. Give me a call after work tomorrow.

***

The girls were having a lot of fun, and Donna stayed out late. She dozed after the alarm went off. She woke and looked. It was 7:15. She'd planned to be to work by 7:30. Jumping out of bed, she used the restroom, brushed her teeth, and wiggled into the dress she'd pulled out of the closet the night before and hung over the top of the door. She slipped her heels on, grabbed her purse with the makeup kit, and hurried out the door. She wouldn't get to work early at the Overholser Insurance Agency in the Northwood section of West Palm Beach, eight miles away, but she couldn't be late, either. The phone often started ringing early, and she had to be there to answer it.

The parking spot for her 2005 Toyota was at the far end of her condo building and around the corner, under a huge, low-hanging tree in a nook that was hidden from view of units in the complex. Donna's heels clicked on the asphalt as she half-walked, half-ran to the car. She sped to the exit, made a semistop, and whirled left onto the narrow road leading to Congress Avenue. The light was green, but she knew it would last only about fifteen seconds, and tromped on the accelerator. The light was yellow when she arrived, and she slowed only a little, the tires screeching in protest as she made the right-angle turn.

She felt play in the steering wheel as the car moved onto Forest Avenue, but was in too much of a hurry to worry about it. Heading down the center of the three lanes, she pulled the makeup kit out of her purse and, looking back and forth at the small mirror and the road, applied lipstick. Ignoring the thirty-five miles per hour speed limit, she glanced at the surroundings for police cars, and decided to move into the right lane, where her car would be less visible.

She turned the steering wheel, but nothing happened. Then it lurched to the left. She twisted the wheel hard to the right, but the car didn't respond, and was headed toward the median. It hit the median curb, and veered the other direction. Donna went for the brake, but her heel caught on the bottom of the accelerator, and the car hurtled over the curb and straight for a light pole. She screamed.

The crash snapped the metal pole, leaving it bent at a thirty-degree angle in the middle, hanging from the overhead wires. Donna had been in such a hurry that she hadn't bothered to fasten her seat belt. She hurtled into the dashboard, her head smashing against the windshield, which cracked in a ragged spider web design, but didn't shatter.

***

Garbuncle stopped at Johnny's after work, but planned to have only one drink. He was meeting Donna tonight, and wanted to be ready for what he knew was to come. A lurid smile crossed his face as he looked down at the ice in the vodka and swirled it with his finger. *Yeah, I need to be ready to come.*

"A Hardinton woman was critically injured this morning in a one-car crash on Forest Hill Boulevard in West Palm Beach." The television above the bar jerked Garbuncle out of his reverie. He looked up and stared.

"Police said a car driven by Donna Malone swerved off the roadway and crashed into a light pole. The accident happened at 7:45 a.m., and officers speculated the woman was on her way to work. The cause of the crash was unknown, but investigators found Ms. Malone's makeup kit on the floor of the heavily damaged vehicle, and believed she may have been distracted while applying makeup."

Garbuncle slapped four one-dollar bills on the bar, slugged his vodka in one gulp, and hustled out the door. He didn't have his cellphone, but his apartment was not far away. He drove much faster than usual, rushed inside, and grabbed the phone book. He dialed JFK Hospital, the closest one to the crash site. He asked if Donna Malone was a patient there, and the answer came quickly. The receptionist wanted to know who he was, and he told her he was her attorney and needed to see her. He would be allowed only fifteen minutes, she said.

Tubes, one of them connected to an apparatus with a transparent bag of clear liquid, hung from Donna's arms, and her head was swathed in bandages. Her eyes were closed. Garbuncle's mouth dropped open. He took a deep breath to calm himself.

"Donna, it's Ham," he said, almost whispering.

Her eyes opened part-way, and a small area of her face without bandages was expressionless. "Zeer," she muttered.

Seer? Garbuncle thought. "Did you say beer, Donna?" he asked.

Her eyes closed, and she didn't respond.

Garbuncle stared, thinking.

"Steer?" he said.

Donna's eyes opened.

"Steering? Steering wheel?" Garbuncle said, louder this time.

Her head nodded slightly.

"I'm going to let you rest now, Donna," he murmured. "I'll be back later." He lightly kissed the part of her cheek not swathed in white, and left.

What was she trying to tell him? Police told reporters they found her makeup kit on the floor, and she apparently lost control of the car while she was applying it. Sure makes sense.

***

After a night of fitful sleeping permeated with phantasmagorical dreams, Garbuncle drove to the West Palm Beach police headquarters downtown.

"I'm the attorney for Donna Malone, the woman injured yesterday in the accident on Forest Hill," he told the clerk. "May I see the police report, please?"

"Yep, got it right here," the matronly woman said. "Four news reporters were in yesterday checking it over."

Garbuncle stood at the desk and read. "*Appeers subject's Toyota Corolla vehicle ran over curb onto sidewalk, and then hit a light pole, causing it to snap. Subject wasn't waring seat belt, and probly was putting on make up found under the dashboard.*"

"Ma'am, could you tell me where the car was impounded?"

"Just a minute." The clerk walked to a glass-enclosed office, and Garbuncle saw her conversing with the man at the desk.

She returned. "The sergeant said he needs proof that you're her attorney."

"But I'm ... okay," Garbuncle said. He walked to his car and sat behind the wheel, thinking, before driving to his nearby office in downtown West Palm Beach. At 3 p.m., he headed for Johnny's.

"Were you working last night?" he asked the barmaid. She was middle-aged, on the pretty side but overweight, with straight, dyed-blond hair and a heavy layer of makeup that didn't hide the bags under her eyes.

"Sure was. Yer Ham, aintcha?"

"Yup."

"Whatcha need?"

"A gal named Donna comes in here once in a while. She and her girlfriends were here last night."

"Yeah, I know Donna."

"Do you know any of the gals who she was with?"

"Sure. Let's see, there's Gracie. I see her with Donna now and then. Don't know her last name. Works for some kind o' fancy stone business, west o' Lake Worth. I can't remember the name."

"Thanks. I might be back, but that'll do it for now."

Garbuncle was near his apartment, and drove there. He riffled through the Yellow pages, and found two listings under Stone Cast. One was in West Palm Beach, and the other had a street address, but no city. He dialed the first.

"'Scuse me, but do you have a woman named Gracie who works there?"

"That's me."

"Oh, great. I think you're a friend of Donna Malone, aren't you?"

"Who wants to know?"

"I'm Ham Garbuncle. Does my name ring a bell?"

"Oh yeah, you're the attorney. Donna 'n' me go way back.

"You sound pretty cheerful. I'm guessing that you haven't been in contact with Donna the last couple o' days."

"Well, I was with her just Sunday night, if that's what you mean."

"Yes, I know that. I meant yesterday or today."

"No, I haven't talked to her. This doesn't sound good. What's the matter?"

"Donna was in a serious accident on her way to work yesterday. She's in critical condition at JFK."

"Oh my God!" Gracie shouted. "What happened? Where'd it happen?"

"She was on Forest Hill, probably headed to I-95, when she ran off the road and hit a light pole."

"Oh mercy! Why'd she go off the road?"

"The cops found her makeup kit on the floor under the dashboard, and they think she was putting her makeup on and wasn't watching where she was going."

"I'll bet she was running late. I feel awful. We prob'ly kept her out too late Sunday night. She only had one drink though. She's being very careful after that DUI. No doubt she overslept and was in a hurry. I'm heading out right now to see her."

"You'd better call first. I went last evening, and could only see her for fifteen minutes. She could barely mumble when I talked to her."

"Oh my God, she's that bad? Okay, I'll call the hospital."

"Would you like me to go with you?"

"Oh yes. Would you?"

"Let me call the hospital, and I'll call you back."

The hospital desk nurse told him they could see her.

***

Garbuncle found the stone business.

"I have to leave a little early," she called to her boss, who was conferring with a customer. "My best friend had a bad accident and is in the hospital."

"So you know Donna well?" Garbuncle said on the way.

"She was my bridesmaid for my second wedding. The first one was when I was a teenager. Lasted only three years. We're like sisters. Confide everything with each other."

"Has she told you about the trial where I'm defending this guy who the cops beat up?"

"Yes. She told me all about it. She said you were really upset that most of the jury members didn't see through the lies those cops told."

"Yeah, it was a travesty of justice. But I'm not through."

They entered Donna's room, and stood. Gracie covered her mouth with her hands. Donna's head was sideways on the pillow, only part of her face showing.

"Donna, it's me, Gracie. Are you awake?" Her voice was soft and caressing.

Gracie detected movement in her friend's head. A muffled "Hi."

"I'm so sorry we made you late for work, hon. You must have been putting your makeup on while you drove."

"Seer wuhl."

Gracie gave Garbuncle a puzzled look. He whispered, "She muttered something similar last night." His face lit up.

"Donna," Garbuncle said in hushed tone, "did you say steering wheel?"

"Ya."

"Was something wrong with the steering wheel?'

In a bare whisper, "Ya."

Gracie looked at Garbuncle, her mouth open.

"We're going to let you rest now, Donna," he said. "We'll be back later."

"Bye Donna," said Gracie. "I love you." Garbuncle saw her eyes glisten.

"Uh," Donna grunted.

The pair walked down the hospital corridor. "I'm wondering if something went wrong with her car," Garbuncle said. "When you talked about her makeup, she tried to say steering wheel. I think she's trying to tell us it wasn't the makeup that caused the crash. I doubt the cops will charge her with a traffic offense, but in case they do, I want to try to clear her. It would be her second one in a short time."

"Is Donna more than a friend to you?"

"Huh?" Garbuncle said, whipping his head to stare at Gracie. "I mean ... I just ... no, I'm just trying to help her."

"Have you done much pro bono work before?"

"Well—to tell the truth, no. And all of a sudden I'm doing pro bono for two people. I guess the law of averages is catching up with me. Anyway, look, I went to the police station to find out where her car was impounded, but they needed verification I'm her attorney. That's why I got ahold of you. I need you and my buddy Brad to go with me to the station and vouch for me."

"Sure. Just let me know. My boss won't mind, as long as I get my work done."

Garbuncle dropped Gracie off at her home. At his apartment, he called Hitchens at the newspaper. "Did you hear what happened to Donna?"

"Yeah, I saw it in the *Hawk*. I was gonna call you about it tonight."

"I'm really worried about her. She's in bad shape—can hardly talk. But I got her to say enough that shows she thinks the steering wheel went haywire and she didn't crash because of putting on her makeup, like the cops think. They'll probably hit her with a traffic charge, and that'll drive her insurance cost up, especially since it happened so soon after the DUI. So I'm gonna fight the charge. I need you to come to the West Palm Beach police station with me and tell the sergeant you know me and that I'm Donna's attorney. Her friend Gracie is coming too."

"When? I can do it tomorrow morning before I go into the office."

"Yeah. Say, around 8:30."

***

Next morning, the three walked up to the police desk, and Garbuncle asked to speak to the desk sergeant.

"I was here yesterday, remember? I'm the attorney for Donna Malone, the woman injured in the crash on Forest Hill."

"Yup, I remember."

"I've brought two people who can vouch for me. They know I represent Donna."

"I'm Brad Hitchens. I'm a reporter for the *Palm Beach Hawk*. I've known Ham for years, and know that he's represented Donna in the past."

"Hello Lieutenant. I'm Gracie Sloan, Donna's best friend. We go way back. She has told me about how Mister Garbuncle has helped her with legal situations."

"Let me see your identification—both of you."

Hitchens and Gracie handed over their driver licenses, and Hitchens his press ID. The sergeant looked at the photos, then up at the two individuals.

"Okay, that's good enough for me. Now how can I help you, Mister Garbuncle."

"As I mentioned yesterday, I'd like to take a look at Donna's car and need to know where it's impounded."

"Mack's Towing, west of Lake Worth. You need the address?"

"Actually, I know where that is. Thanks Sergeant."

"Good luck."

CHAPTER TWELVE

A bulldozer sat on a patch of empty ground to the right of a ramshackle shack that greeted Garbuncle at the end of a long, wide dirt path leading from Lake Worth Road. A besmirched metal sign attached to the building read, Mack's Towing & A-Plus Auto Salvage. Row upon row of junk cars filled an expanse of what he guessed was about twenty acres. Some were wrecked, others partly dismantled for their parts, and still others both wrecked and dismantled. At the front of the sea of twisted metal was a fenced-off segment. Garbuncle surmised that the cars in this part of the automobile cemetery were in purgatory, some having been towed there for parking violations, and others incapacitated but not declared dead.

He and Ed, the mechanic who worked on his car, sauntered up to the desk in the office. Garbuncle handed his attorney's card to the tattooed, clerical-looking man. "I represent Donna Malone, whose car is here. I might have spotted it—the dark red Toyota, about two-thousand-four, over there almost at the end of the first row."

"Yes," the clerk said, "I think that's it. Came in a couple o' days ago. Front end banged up bad. Let me check to make sure." He grabbed a spiral notebook from a corner of his desk and thumbed through it. "Uh-huh, here it is. Donna Malone, burgundy two-thousand-five Toyota."

"Good," said Garbuncle. "We'd like to inspect it."

"Have at it."

The pair walked through the entrance, the wide, swinging gate of which was held open with a clasp. They followed the car tracks in the dead grass to the next to last car in a row of about twenty.

"Pretty bad shape," Ed said. "Grill and radiator bashed in, right headlight smashed."

"And the hood looks like a piece of abstract art."

"So you want me to check the steering?"

"Yes, but I don't know how you're gonna get to it. I think we need a jack."

"Nah. I'll just crawl under. I'm use ta that." He got down on his knees on the ground, which was bare except for patches of browned grass, and rolled over onto his back. Using his bent legs for leverage, he shoved himself under the car's front end.

Silence for several seconds. "Oh, wow, look what we got here." Ed's voice was raised. "'At 'er tie rod ain't connected. The ball's come out o' the socket."

Using his elbows, he pushed himself forward until his head showed. "What year did that guy say this car was?"

"Two-thousand-five."

"That's what I thought he said. Hell, that's only 'bout three years old."

He paused. "Ya think you could get a flashlight from the guy in the office? It's too dark under here to see very good."

"Yeah, let me see if I can borrow one. Just stay there. I'll be right back."

The clerk pulled a flashlight out of a drawer in his desk. Garbuncle hustled back to the car and handed it to the mechanic, who shoved himself back underneath. After a few minutes, he slid back out, and stood.

"Now I cain't be sure 'bout this, so I don't wantcha ta quote me. But it looks to me like 'at tie rod didn't come loose by itself."

"What makes you think so?"

"The car is too new fer that ta happen, even with that crash. And I couldn't find nothin' that looked worn. We need a real high-powered bright light. I couldn't tell if there was any marks from a wrench on the bolt that holds the ball in the socket."

"Do you think if anybody loosened that bolt, they would have had their hands on it?"

"Yeah, they prob'ly woulda put their hand around it, cuz just like me, they couldn't see good under the car. They mighta had a light, but they still had to fix the wrench in place."

"Did you put your hands on the ball and the socket?"

"Nope. I didn't need to. It was already loose."

Garbuncle drove Ed back to his house.

"I ain't gonna charge ya, cuz I messed up on fixin' yer car once."

"I appreciate that, Ed. I'll need you real soon to take the tie rod assembly off."

Garbuncle returned to the police station and asked for the name of Donna's auto insurance company.

"Hang on," the lieutenant said. "We've got her purse and makeup kit in storage for evidence." He left through a rear door, and emerged a few minutes later. "Save-A-Lot Auto Insurance. Never heard of it. Sounds like a fly-by-night operation."

"She might have been looking for cheap coverage after that DUI she got," said Garbuncle. "Her rate no doubt went up."

"Ya get whatcha pay for," the lieutenant said. "She better hope they cover her medical expenses."

Garbuncle returned to his office. He dialed the number that the lieutenant had jotted down.

"Ma'am, I represent a client of yours, Donna Malone, and I need to discuss the case with a claims agent." While he waited, Garbuncle read a note on his desk from his secretary to call Gracie.

"Uh, yes, my name's Hiram Garbuncle. I'm Donna Malone's attorney. Yes, that's the one. Donna's in awful shape, but I got her to mumble something that made me wonder about the police assessment of what caused the crash. I had a mechanic crawl under the car, and he found something very fishy. I think you'd better meet with me, so we can get to the bottom of what happened here. It might save you a lot of money." Garbuncle recited his office address, and said, "Tomorrow at 4 p.m. See you then."

He dialed Gracie.

"Donna's improved a little," her friend said. "She said a few words. She wants to see you."

Garbuncle hopped in his car and drove at an uncharacteristically fast speed to JFK Hospital, changing lanes on I-95 several times to get in the fastest one.

"Feeling any better, babe?" He planted a soft kiss on her cheek, just below the white gauze.

"Li'l," she murmured, lying on her back.

"I know now what you were trying to tell me—that the steering wheel didn't work and that's what caused the crash."

Donna's head bobbed a little.

"I know why it didn't work. Something called the tie rod came loose. It's connected to the steering. We're trying to figure out how it came loose. It doesn't look worn."

Donna's eyes opened wider. She fixed her gaze on the ceiling, but said nothing.

"Lar. Pede.

"Huh?" Garbuncle stared at her. "Wait a minute. Larry, Pete?"

She nodded.

"You mean Larry Pickens and Pete Bullard?"

She flickered her eyelids.

"Erna."

"Ernie?"

Her eyes opened wider.

"What about Ernie?"

She closed her eyes, and Garbuncle could tell from her breathing that she had fallen asleep. He kissed her cheek, and swiped a tear from his face.

***

Garbuncle helped Ed carry the tie rod assembly from the trunk of the grimy Mercury into the attorney's office.

"Be careful not to touch the area around the ball and socket," Garbuncle admonished as they laid it against the wall next to his desk. Ed washed his hands in the restroom, and Garbuncle followed. He had his secretary bring Ed a cup of coffee, and they chatted about the Miami Dolphins' prospects for the next season.

"Hello there," Garbuncle called to the man entering his office. "Come on back."

He pointed to the metal contraption. "This is what Ed here managed to remove from Donna Malone's car. It's the tie rod assembly. We took care not to handle the ball and socket, in case the technicians can lift fingerprints."

"I think you screwed up," the agent said. "A defense attorney will argue that you could have disassembled it yourself after removing it from the car."

Garbuncle reached into a desk drawer and withdrew five black-and-white photographs. He handed them to the agent. "I borrowed a camera from Donna's friend, and Ed took the pictures. I held the flashlight so there was plenty of light. I'll be submitting a dry-cleaning bill for my suit pants. The knees got smudged when I got on my haunches to hold the light. And Ed'll need to be compensated for the time he's taken to help out."

"Taking pictures was smart. I need to take this tie rod mechanism with me so I can have a forensic print analyst see if there are any prints," the agent said. "And I'll get a certified automobile mechanic to determine whether there are signs that a wrench was used to loosen the bolt holding the ball and socket."

The agent, Ed, and Garbuncle carried the auto part to the agent's car, and deposited it in his trunk.

"I don't want to demean you, Ed, but we'll need to present a professional opinion in court," the agent said.

"No problem," said Ed. "But I can tell you, it looks like that bolt is just a tiny bit rounded. That's what a wrench would do to it if the bolt was tight, which it prob'ly was. They don't make them things so's they can come loose easy."

***

"May I speak to Lieutenant Ernie Kowalski, please? Yes, Hiram Garbuncle. No, this is personal. Sure, I'll wait."

"Kowalski here."

"Lieutenant Kowalski, my name is Hiram Garbuncle. I'm Donna Malone's attorney."

"Oh yeah. I heard about that bad accident she was in. How's she doing?"

"She's in pretty bad shape at JFK Hospital. Haven't you been to see her? I understand you're a friend of hers."

"Well, yeah, we saw each other a couple o' times. I saw the news that she was critical. I figured she wouldn't be allowed to have visitors."

"I wonder if we could get together. I'd like to discuss something with you."

"What do you want to talk about? I don't know anything about that accident."

"I understand that. Donna could barely speak, but she mumbled your name."

"Why would she mention my name? I haven't talked to her in awhile."

"I'm not sure myself. But she muttered two other names too, and that's why I want to meet with you."

"Who are you talking about?"

"If you don't mind, I think we should discuss this in person."

"Well, okay. When? I'm working the day shift, get off at 4. Any time after that would work. How about Johnny's. Know where that is?"

***

"You must be Lieutenant Kowalski. Ham Garbuncle." He extended a hand. "Let's take a booth, where we can have a little privacy."

The waitress took their drink orders. While waiting, they chatted about the weather and how traffic was getting heavier with The Season just beginning.

"Thanks ma'am," Garbuncle said, accepting his drink.

"Maybe I shouldn't say this, but I happen to know you helped Donna with that DUI she got. I appreciate that."

"I hope you'll keep that to yourself, for obvious reasons. I know you got in trouble trying to help her."

"I guess we're both members of the Donna Malone mutual admiration society," Garbuncle said, smiling. He figured that would put Ernie at ease. "Like I said, Donna could hardly say anything. But she uttered two names. I'm not one hundred percent positive, but I'm pretty sure she said Larry Pickens and Pete Bullard. Do you know them?"

"I don't know them personally, but I've seen them at police union meetings. I read in the paper they were in the trial of that guy who resisted arrest, and you were his attorney."

"That's them. And for the record, he didn't resist arrest. But that's another story."

"I haven't got any opinion about that."

"So you don't know Pickens and Bullard. Do you know anybody who does know them? I'm just trying to figure out why Donna would have muttered their names, and then yours. It sounded to me like she was making a connection." Garbuncle stared hard into Ernie's eyes.

Ernie shifted in his seat and looked down. The attorney thought his face was tense.

"This is between you and me. Okay?"

"Mum's the word."

"It's possible my friend Jake knows them. He tries to be friendly with the Granville cops 'cause he's got a business in the town. I told you Donna and me were friends, but it was only casual. I could tell Jake had the hots for Donna when the three of us went out one night, so I told him I didn't mind if he hit on her. He told me later that he took her to a ... a kind of outdoor party west of town."

"Private party?"

"Well—uh—no. It was open to the public."

"What are you telling me? Somebody with a lot o' money threw an open party?"

Ernie sighed. "A certain organization held it. And when I say it was open—you wouldn't find any coloreds there. I'm not sure they'd be allowed, and they sure wouldn't want to be there anyway."

Garbuncle stared at Ernie with a quizzical expression. It flipped to a eureka look. "You telling me this was a Ku Klux Klan affair?"

Ernie looked down, and didn't say anything.

"Is Jake a member of the Klan?"

Ernie kept his head down.

"Okay. So Jake is a member of the Klan, and he takes Donna to a Klan meeting. Now where do Pickens and Bullard come in?" Garbuncle hesitated. "You telling me she met them at the meeting?"

"I didn't say that. All I'm saying is that Jake knows the cops in Granville. It's a small town. There's not many of them. Now again, I've got to swear you to secrecy."

"Sure. Go ahead."

"I've heard rumors for awhile that some Granville cops are Klan members."

Garbuncle remained silent for several long seconds. "That's a pretty small police force."

"I'm not going to speculate about anything," Ernie said. He pulled his tall frame straight. "Look, I'm having dinner with a buddy, and then we're goin' bowling. Can we wrap this up?"

"Yeah, you've given me some valuable information to chew on."

"Now remember, what I told you is strictly confidential. If you repeat it to anybody, I'll deny it. I don't know you. Okay?"

"My mouth is taped shut. Don't worry. I'm going to investigate, but I won't get you involved or mention our conversation."

***

"Hey buddy, what're you doin' tonight? We gotta talk."

"What about?" Hitchens detected, on the other end of the phone, that familiar air of brassiness in his friend's tone when he'd been drinking. But there was no slurring.

"I'll tell you when you get here."

"Are you thinking about dinner?"

"Yeah. You can bring a couple o' pork chops."

"No way. I'm not eating at your place. No offense, but all of that grunge is not conducive to a good appetite." Hitchens pictured the pile of dirty dishes in the kitchen sink and spilling onto the cabinet, scraps of food lying around, a rusty refrigerator, a small table with a food-stained oil cloth.

"Okay, I'll come to your place. Go get the meat, and I'll be there about 7:30."

"What? You get the meat."

"Hey, you're the one who got me into this case. That's what we've got to talk about." Ham was being brash, Hitchens knew, but there was humor in his voice. He seemed to be in a good mood.

"Don't arrive drunk."

"No problem. I did my drinkin' earlier."

***

Coconut oil sizzled in the nonstick frying pan with two large, lean pork chops as Hitchens chopped up a tomato, cucumber, and red pepper. He spread the vegetables atop two plates laden with mixed lettuces, and added Kalamata olives, walnuts, and crumbled blue cheese, then sprinkled the concoction with salad dressing made of a dry Good Seasons herbal mix and olive oil. He cut the ends off of a dozen or so asparagus spears, sliced them in two, and slid them into a steamer heating up on the stove.

Garbuncle walked into the kitchen and began picking pieces from the salad.

"What the hell are you doin'?" said Hitchens. "Stay the hell away from the food till I'm ready to serve it. Man, you got no self-control. Go watch TV."

"Nothin' worth watchin'. No football, and the Heat aren't in the basketball playoffs. Baseball goin' strong, but I get tired of daily baseball. It's not fast enough."

"That's 'cause you need instant gratification, which is also why you can't wait till the food is served to eat. Baseball requires patience, which I have a lot more of than I used to. I enjoy baseball now. Why don't you watch one of the political talk shows and learn something?"

"Those people are a bunch of blowhards. They can't tell me anything I can't figure out myself."

"Yeah, I know. You've got all the answers. You know more than anybody else." Garbuncle's picking at the salad had irritated Hitchens, and he still remembered all the times when his friend was criticizing him for his views on human behavior and politics. He had no reservations about coming down on his buddy now.

Garbuncle plopped down on the sofa, lowered his head, and closed his eyes. Hitchens saw that he was dozing.

"Okay, it's ready," Hitchens exclaimed. Garbuncle's head snapped up. He waddled to the table as Hitchens put a plate of salad before him.

"Mmmm," Garbuncle mumbled. "You make the best salad I've ever had."

"Well, I don't know if it's the tastiest, but it's gotta be one of the healthiest. So what's happening with the case that you wanted to tell me?"

"Okay. I found out some stuff that's a little scary. But it might be what we need to win this case. That is, if we can tie some ends together. And the key word is tie—as in rods. Tie rods."

"Huh? You lost me."

"Donna Malone—you know, the one who got me landed in jail. She's in real bad shape in the hospital. Had a bad car crash."

"Is she the one we had a story about in the *Hawk*? I didn't know that was the same person."

"Yeah. The cops said she lost control of her car when she was putting makeup on. She can barely mumble, but I got enough out of her to make me think the steering wheel malfunctioned. I had my mechanic check the car, and he said the tie rod came loose, which of course means she wouldn't have been able to steer the car."

"Gosh, I'm sorry to hear it. You think she'll make it?"

"I don't know. I'm a little worried."

"So what does this have to do with Alec's case?"

"I'm not sure. But Donna muttered a couple o' names that make me think there might be a connection. I'm almost sure she said Larry and Pete."

"Who's Larry and ... Oh, wait. Larry Pickens and Pete Bullard. But how did she—?"

"She was at the trial one day."

"Hang on," said Hitchens. He carried both empty plates to the kitchen, and emerged with a pork chop and asparagus on each.

"Oh my. Does that look good." Garbuncle cut into the chop. "Just a little bit of pink. Perfect. "

"Yeah. It's okay to eat pork a little undercooked these days, 'cause it comes from these big producers. The small farmers used to feed the pigs garbage, and they'd get trichinosis." Hitchens sliced a piece off and chewed. "Ah, tender."

He sipped his glass of cheap red wine. "So what happened with Donna?"

"This is where it gets interesting. She mentioned another name. I didn't know this guy, but I already knew that she knew him."

"Who?"

"I can't tell you. I met with him, and he told me some stuff in confidence. Get this: He said it was rumored the Granville Police Department had cops who were Ku Klux Klan members. He didn't know who they were. But he also told me a friend of his took Donna to a Klan meeting, and that friend is a Klan member and knows most of the Granville cops. We've gotta figure—"

"Holy crap," Hitchens shouted, his face lighting up as he dropped the fork with a morsel of pork on the plate. "It just hit me. I know—remember when I told you there was something familiar about Larry Pickens?"

"You did?" Garbuncle's forehead wrinkled. His expression switched to a knowing look. "Oh yeah. I remember you mentioned it a couple o' times while the trial was going on."

"Eight or ten years ago, I had to cover a meeting of the Ku Klux Klan out west off Southern Boulevard one Saturday night. I was walking around the grounds, taking notes about the picnickers, and just the setting, for my story in the paper. I sensed something behind me, and turned to find this big, strapping young guy, prob'ly nineteen or twenty, following me inches from my back. I stared at him, and he sneered and walked away. That was before dark. Then the grand imperial cyclops, or whatever ridiculous name he was called, gave his speech. When he was done, the Klansmen threw torches at a cross and it lit up the area. People started heading back to their cars, and that same muscular young guy passed close to me and gave me another sneer. Our eyes met, and I remember the cold malevolence in them.

"Guess who that guy was. Larry Pickens. It took awhile for his mean face to register with me. But I know for certain the guy at that meeting was the same one who beat up Alec."

"So that's what Donna was trying to tell me: Larry Pickens and Pete Bullard were the guys she was introduced to at the Klan meeting. We were going to see each other the night she had the accident, 'cause she had something to tell me that she thought could be helpful in the case. She must've wanted to tell me she'd met Pickens and Bullard."

"Yup. It all comes together," said Hitchens.

"But we still don't know if there's any connection between the loose tie rod and her knowing who Pickens and Bullard were. If they knew she was aware of the trial, they prob'ly would worry she could testify at the retrial that they're Klansmen. But how would they know she'd even be aware of the trial?"

"Wait a minute. Didn't you tell me Donna was at the trial one day?"

"Yeah, but that was just one morning, and I didn't even see her until the recess, when we bumped into each other in the hallway. After I got back from the rest room, I noticed her sitting way in the back. So if I hadn't seen her before, Pickens and Bullard sure wouldn't have."

"Hmmm. Yeah, and if they did know that she knew about the trial, and that she knew you, how would we find that out?" Hitchens said.

"I don't know," said Garbuncle, "But if they did know this stuff, it explains how that tie rod came loose."

***

Garbuncle slept fitfully, tossing and turning in the midst of disturbing dreams. At 6 a.m., he woke with a start, sat staring into space for a moment, and leaped out of bed. He urinated, then threw on trousers and a shirt, and slipped into his loafers, not bothering with socks. He half-ran, half-walked out of his condo building to the parking lot. He was driving faster lately, and raced down the streets to the Sheriff's Office south of Palm Beach International Airport.

"I need to see the lieutenant." The desk sergeant heard the urgency in his voice as he pulled out his attorney's identification.

"Whoa. What's up?

"I have reason to believe that a client of mine in the hospital may be in danger."

"Yeah? Hold on." The sergeant went to the back of the office, and returned with another police official.

"I'm Lieutenant Ricker. What can I do for you?"

"I have uncovered information that makes me think my client at JFK Hospital could be in imminent danger for her life. Some people could be out to kill her."

"So it's your client who's in danger, not you? Good thing. Otherwise I'd think you were paranoid. In fact, I'm not so sure you're not."

"Look, her car crashed when a tie rod came loose. I found out it didn't come loose by itself. She knows something that could get several guys in deep trouble. And I think they know she knows it."

"Hmmm. Can I see your card again?"

Garbuncle still had his ID out, and the hefty lieutenant inspected it. "Yeah, you're a criminal attorney, aren'tcha? Been around a long time?"

"Yes, I've practiced decades in this county."

"Come into my office and let's talk about it."

Garbuncle mapped out in greater detail his reasons for concern about Donna Malone's safety, carefully avoiding any mention of his suspicion that two police officers were involved. It required some crafty maneuvering around the probing questions the lieutenant asked, but the attorney had proven his mastery of the art of the dodge on countless occasions.

"I don't mean to rush you, Lieutenant," Garbuncle said after twenty minutes of conversation between the two, "but something could happen to Ms. Malone at any moment."

The lawman went silent, and Garbuncle saw the pensive look. Finally, he rose.

"Okay, you convinced me. I'll assign a guard outside your client's room."

"I much appreciate that, Lieutenant. I may be overreacting, but better to be safe than sorry."

"It's all right. I think you did the right thing. I'll get on it right away."

***

"So what did you learn?" Garbuncle asked the insurance agent, who sat across from the attorney's desk in an old, light-green, vinyl-covered chair. He rested his elbows on arms that were frayed, and worn in one spot to the foam underneath.

"The crime lab did find prints. They belong to a guy who was charged with a misdemeanor for belonging to a dog fighting ring. But the desk sergeant said it appeared the name on the file had been whited out and a name typed over the white-out. As for the wrench marks, I found a guy in Fort Lauderdale who's got an ASE Masters Certification. That stands for Automobile Service Excellence. He's been called to testify in a lot of trials. He said the bolt holding the ball and socket in place definitely had the marks of a wrench applied to it. And he said it's the original mechanism, so those marks weren't caused by replacing it."

"In other words, it looks like somebody loosened it?" Garbuncle asked.

"That's what he's willing to testify in court."

"Wow. All right, I'll be in contact with you as this thing unfolds." They shook hands, and the agent left.

Garbuncle called Hitchens. "Look, somebody was out to do Donna in. That tie rod was tampered with."

"What about the fingerprints?"

"The agent found who they belong to—somebody who was in a dog fighting ring, but the misdemeanor charge was dropped later and there's something fishy about the name on file. Mighta been tampered with. They're not Pickens's or Bullard's, which would be easy to know, 'cause cops' prints are on file. They prob'ly got this guy to do the dirty work for them. They may not even've known how to do it themselves."

Garbuncle paused. His face brightened. "Wait a minute. Donna said Ernie ... oops, I let the cat out of the bag. Okay, her friend's name is Ernie, and he's a cop. Don't breathe a word about that."

"Hell no. It means nothing to me, anyway."

"Oh yeah, sure. You guys would sacrifice your mother for a story."

"Uh, believe it or not, we keep our promises."

"Okay then. Ernie suspected a couple o' guys on the Hardinton force belonged to a dog fighting ring. At least they bet on dog fights."

"We need to find the guy with the prints," said Hitchens.

"Yeah, but how?"

CHAPTER THIRTEEN

"I will glue dee board to dee frame. Jou hold dees, and I pound dee nails," the Mexican instructed Garbuncle. "Dees wood eess bery rotten."

"Yeah, I know, Diego. I let it go too long. I'm glad you could do this on the weekend while my tenants are away, and I can keep the cost down by helping you. I need to thank Juan for recommending you."

"Juan make a beeg meestake stealing dat car. He eess not a bad man. He need dee car for heess jobss and to lay tile so he can support heess wife and four keeds."

"He doesn't seem like the criminal type to me, either, Diego, and I've seen a lot of them. I'm going to do my best to get probation for him so he can work. One of my apartments needs a new carpet, but I'll let Juan pay me for defending him by putting in tile."

"You have a rag? I put too much glue on."

Garbuncle hurried to the kitchen and returned with a roll of paper towels. "I knew just where my tenants kept them because I was here once when their cat threw up a hairball. I don't normally allow animals, but this cat was so damned cute, I made an exception."

"I don' like cats. My daughter Marie—shess fifteen—she don' like cats too. But she love dogss, so I buy her a pequeña Mexicano dog—Chihuahua. It cost forty dollarss, and I pay dee shop ten dollarss and tell heem I pay sirty dollarss later. I get dee money from dees job."

"Glad I could help you, Diego. And glad I found you."

"Meester Ham, I have a friend who goess to dog fights and bets. Heess a construction worker. He takes me to a fight, and I get seeck. Deess dogss hurt each oder bery bad. Eben kill. Dere eess so much blood. I am angry, and I tell my friend to neber take me again. But when he bets, he gib heess money to two men. He tellss me dey are police."

Garbuncle had pulled a flask of vodka from a pants pocket, and started to take a swig. He stopped with the flask at his lips. "Did you say the two guys taking the bets were cops?"

"Dees eess what my friend tellss me."

"Did your friend tell you which police department they were from?"

"He deed not say."

***

"Earl, I got a favor to ask of you." Garbuncle stood in the doorway of his tenant's apartment in a shabby complex farther south and east. The apartment was only a little less junky than his own.

"Come on in," said the broad, portly, but muscular man. He had a shock of black hair near the front of an otherwise bald, shiny head. "I ain't doin' no favors till you get me a new mattress you been promisin'. It's hurtin' my back. I told you I banged it up gettin' slammed around in the rasslin' ring. I hafta do a lot o' standin' at that security job at Walmart, and it ain't fun."

"Yeah, other stuff keeps popping up, and I never get around to it. Tell you what: I'll get you that mattress pronto if you'll do something for me."

"That depends on what it is."

"I know you're no friend of the police."

"Ya got that right. Ever since them three cops tried ta beat me up when I resisted—"

"I know all about it. You don't have to tell me again. I believe you. Here's your chance to nail a couple of 'em."

"Run it by me."

"There's a dog-fighting ring operating out in the boonies, somewhere in

134

Loxahatchee. There's two cops who take the bets. I need to find out who they are and what city they work for."

"Holy crap. Them guys is mean hombres. Dangerous as hell."

"Come on, Earl. I remember seeing you in a match at the old West Palm Beach Auditorium maybe six, seven years ago. Damned few people you can't handle."

"Yeah, with my hands. But these guys carry guns and knives. Lot of 'em's done time in the big house. What's this for?"

"I got a client who got beat up by the cops just like you. Except he got stopped just for a broken taillight. You had that, and a burnt-out headlight, and no brake lights. And he didn't try to fight them like you did. They just knocked the shit out of him."

"Prob'ly was a n... oh, 'scuse me, a black guy who deserved it."

"You know I'm no bleeding heart when it comes to coloreds. I told you why I had the room for rent, didn't I? Kicked the previous tenant out after he told me he'd fucked a black woman just a few days before."

"Oh yeah, I remember."

"That is just about the most perverted, depraved thing I can think of. But this guy's different. He's likable, and I want to help him. I think you'd like him too if you knew him."

"I don't think so. Whatever."

"You sound like you need a little motivating. I've told you this much; I might as well tell you the rest. Helping Alec—that's his name—helping him is only indirectly what I'm trying to do. There's a woman involved. A friend of mine. She dated a cop, and learned too much. It's tied to Alec's case. Now she's in the hospital. Real bad shape."

"What happened?"

"Tie rod on her car came loose. It didn't happen by itself."

"I'm gettin' the picture. This sounds even more dangerous than I thought."

"For me more than you. So will you do it?"

Earl sighed, and stretched his arms above his head, revealing sweaty, matted hair in armpits left exposed by his white undershirt. He clasped his hands together, then dropped them to his side. "What the hell? Life's not worth livin' if ya can't have a little fun. Besides, I hafta have that mattress. Tell me what I need to do."

"Okay. I've got to find out who those two cops are—the ones who belong to the dog fighting ring. I know two cops with the Granville department who are Ku Klux Klan members, but I don't know if they're the same guys."

"Oh, good for them. Maybe some cops ain't so bad."

Earl saw Garbuncle's teeth clench and his jaw tighten. "These two assholes beat up my client," he said, his raised voice fierce, "and he did nothing to deserve it. They obviously didn't like him just because he was black."

Earl shrugged.

"The two cops who arrested me when I tried to help my friend Donna after they pulled her over for drinking were from Hardinton. I think the two Granville cops who beat up Alec and the two Hardinton cops know each other. And I think either the Granville or Hardinton cops are responsible for that tie rod assembly on Donna's car coming apart. It gets kind o' complicated. The Hardinton cops obviously know that I know Donna. And Donna found out that the two Granville cops are KKK members. Did they learn that Donna is aware of that? If so, how did they find out? That's where you come in."

"Me? What the hell do you want me to do?"

"I remember you told me you did a little acting at the Lake Worth Playhouse. Were you any good?"

"Damn right I was good. The *Hawk* theater gal wrote me up good every play I was in. But that's been quite a few years ago. I'm pretty rusty."

"Well then, I think it's time for you to scrape the rust off and oil up your thespian talent. You'll need to wear a cellphone."

"Oh shit. If they find out, I'm toast."

"You do security work, so you must have a concealed gun permit."

"Yeah."

"Maybe you can fasten the phone underneath the shoulder holster. Masking tape oughta hold it."

"I'll need a small one."

"Yeah, and it has to be high quality to pick up conversation. They're not cheap, and I'm gonna get a good one. But I'll bill the *in*surance company. I'll give you a hundred dollars to bet with."

"You? Your money?"

"Hell no. *In*surance'll pay that too."

"You was raised down here in the South, wasn't ya," said Earl.

"What makes you think so?"

"'Cause you say *in*surance. Like the coloreds say *po*lice. Up north, people say in*sur*ance."

"Hmmm. Thank you for that lesson in proper English." Garbuncle looked down to hide a disdainful smile.

"Whose car do I drive to get out there?" Earl asked, Garbuncle's sarcasm not registering. "That's even past Wellington. I don't know if my junk heap can make it."

"Mine's not much better, but you can drive it. Just keep track of the mileage. When you place a bet, you need to get friendly with the cops. You could introduce yourself, just giving your first name, and they'll likely tell you their first names. You'll have to wing it from there."

***

Earl drove west on Okeechobee Boulevard past sprawled housing developments, their little man-made lakes barely visible in the dusk. Windows rolled down, he leaned back in his seat and sang with abandon as country music blared from WIRK-FM radio. Several miles past the big intersection with Royal Palm Beach Boulevard, he followed the road on the southern perimeter of Lion Country Safari, turned south for a mile, and finally west onto a narrow dirt road. He pulled over to check the map drawn by Diego, and continued to a path through pine scrub into a woods.

A quarter-mile farther, he came upon a steel mesh fence, beyond which was a small clearing with an assemblage of about thirty older model cars, mixed with pickups displaying confederate flags on the cabin windows, long guns on the racks, and bumper stickers with the usual messages defending the utility and nobility of guns. At the fence, a man with a long beard stood at an open gate, holding a shotgun at his side.

"What can I do fer ya, mister?" the man asked.

"I heard there's some dog fightin' out here I can bet on."

"Where'd ya hear that?"

"My landlord's handyman went to one and told us about it. I like to gamble."

"How much you plannin' ta put up?"

"Not much now—about a hundred dollars. I gotta learn how it works first."

"All right. Go on in."

Earl found a space among the vehicles, parked, and walked down a path with an agility that belied his bulk, but was appropriate for an athlete.

The first fight was just under way—a pit bull terrier versus an Argentine mastiff. Earl ambled up to a circle of men, several deep, gathered at the edge of a flimsy, three-foot-high wire fence. Clad mostly in denims, they leaned forward with intent expressions, pumping their fists for the animal they'd bet on. The mastiff was larger, and seemed to Earl to be in control, having opened long, deep gashes in the neck of the pit bull, whose snout was smeared with blood that flowed from a cut above one eye. The bull was slowing, and its handler threw in the towel. The two men entered the hard-clay arena and coaxed their canines to cages on either end of the fighting ground. The bull wobbled, and the mastiff marched, its head high in triumph, one side of the head caked with blood from an ear that the bull had ripped.

Earl made his way to a table on a small rise that had been landscaped back of the arena. One man sat on a wicker chair and entered names of bettors and amounts under headings of dogs and their owners. Another stood and accepted money from the gamblers.

"Ready to place your bet?" the man standing asked.

"Nah, not yet," said Earl. "I'm new at this. Think I'll just watch this next match before I dive in."

"Suit yerself."

"Is 'ere one o' them Porta Pottys around? Had two beers just before I came."

"Yeah. There's two of 'em right over there, next to them two big trees." He swung an arm in that direction."

"Thanks."

Earl locked the door. He didn't feel an urge to urinate, but needed to take up a little time to make it appear he did. After peeing, he reached under his shirt, covered with a zipper jacket, and pressed the cellphone record button. He rebuttoned the shirt, and returned to the desk.

"Lemme ask ya somethin'. You guys ever need somebody to keep order here? I'm a security guard and could use some extra work. I got a concealed gun permit"—he patted his chest where his shirt covered the holstered weapon—"and I was a pro rassler, so I can handle just about anybody. You prob'ly can't get any cops to do the job. Name's Earl." He thrust his hand out, and the man looked hard at Earl before grasping it.

"Hank. We haven't had hardly any trouble here, but my partner and I'll consider it."

"This here's a lot o' fun. Them fightin' dogs make me think of my days in the ring. Plenty o' times I took a beating."

"Where'd you rassle?"

"Just around here in the county. I did some matches in the old Leakey Teepee. Remember the auditorium in West Palm?"

"Oh yeah, I went to a few of those."

"Well hell, you prob'ly saw me. I got too old to take that kind o' punishment. But still ain't no pushover."

"'Scuse me. We gotta get the next match goin'." Hank stepped in front of the desk with a bullhorn, and announced, "Last call for placing your bets. The fight's about to start. Anybody else want in?" He paused. "Okay, get it underway. May the best dog win."

Hank resumed his position back of the desk.

"You guys ... what's your pardner's name?" Earl asked.

"Art."

"You 'n' Art look like you ain't to be messed with yerselfs."

"We ... uh ..." Hank lowered his voice. "We're cops."

"Well damn, then you don't need no security. You don't work in Hardinton, do ya? I live there, and I been stopped a couple o' times for a headlight out and shit like that. You wouldn't stop me, would ya?" He faked a hearty laugh.

"Nah. You don't need to worry. We look out for our friends."

"I got an excuse for driving such a junk heap. I ain't got any money. My landlord's car is just about as bad, but that stingy son-of-a-bitch don't need to drive that clunker. He's a lawyer and a fuckin' slumlord. Only reason I stay there is 'cause I can't find anyplace else. Got a little felony on my record. Beat up a guy once. He had it comin'. My asshole landlord has it comin' too, and if I ever got a chance to leave, I'd work 'im over if I thought I could get by with it. But I couldn't. He's a criminal defense attorney."

"What's his name?"

"Hiram Garbuncle. He goes by Ham. You guys might o' been in court together at some time."

"As a matter of fact, we were. He stuck his nose in when we stopped a woman on a DUI. We hauled him to jail, let him sit for a few hours. He went to court, and the judge let him off."

"Yeah, he said somethin' about that. So that was you guys? He wasn't too happy."

"I think he was more than her attorney. He defended a black guy from a resisting arrest charge two Granville cops slapped the guy with. I know one o' those cops. Just before the trial started one day, I saw the woman go into the courtroom. I ran into the cop in the union hall, and told him she was the one me and my partner Art ticketed for a DUI."

Earl's heart jumped, but he suppressed his excitement and maintained a nonchalant attitude. "Yeah, I saw somethin' on TV 'bout that trial. What a dumb fuck. Defendin' a nigger." Earl wasn't acting.

He turned to view the arena. "Guess I'll get closer and see how them dogs make out." He thrust a hand at Hank, who shook it. "Good talkin' to ya. Think I'll pass on puttin' any bets down tonight. When's the next fight? I wanna come again and try my hand at it."

Hank said the next scheduled fight was three weeks away.

"That long? Oh well, I guess I can wait. This here's somethin' I wanna do. Good entertainment, good company." Earl moseyed up to the edge of the crowd, and soon was joining some in shooting his fist in the air and cheering. He didn't relish the canine blood-letting like the others apparently did, but figured he needed to seem genuine to Hank. The fight was drawing to a close, with a mastiff torn and limping this time. He waved goodbye to Hank, and headed for his car.

Earl got behind the wheel, peered over his shoulder to make sure no one was around, and unclasped two buttons of his shirt. He reached under, and stopped the phone recorder. He ripped the masking tape from the holster, pulled the phone out, and laid it on the passenger seat. "Mission accomplished," he muttered.

Approaching the gate, he saw the guard walk toward his car with a rifle, waving him down. Fear gripped Earl. He glanced at the recorder and noticed a paper napkin he'd left on the seat after eating a McDonald's burger on the way to the dog fight. Without moving his upper body, he pulled it over the device.

The guard motioned for him to roll his window down, and bent to look inside. "I see ya got yer inside light on. Thought I'd check 'n' see if ever'thing's all right. Ya might run yer battery down."

"Oh, yeah. I went to light a cigarette, and remembered I left the pack at home. Forgot to turn the light back off."

"What's 'at metal thing stickin' out from under 'at napkin?"

"Huh? Oh, that's my lighter," said Earl, reaching down and patting it. "I got one o' them big fancy ones, 'cause I smoke cigars sometimes, and ya need a blow torch to start them suckers." He reared his head back and laughed.

"Okay, podner. Jes don't set yersef on fire now. And watch where yer drivin'. It's dark as a cave in this here woods."

"Good advice," Earl said as he reached up and turned off the light. "See ya later."

***

"I think I got whatcha need." Earl stood in the doorway of Garbuncle's apartment, and handed over the cellphone.

"Really? Let's see." Garbuncle weaved through the junk on the floor to the armchair, followed by Earl, who plopped down on the couch.

"It's ready to play," Earl said.

Garbuncle pushed the button. "It's a little muffled." He raised it to his ear. "Okay, I can hear it clearly now." He listened without speaking. Then, "This is good stuff."

His mouth opened wide as he listened a couple more minutes. He turned off the device.

"Wow, this is great. You did a fantastic job. You sure as hell haven't lost your thespian talent. Now I know how Larry and Pete found out Donna and I were friends.

"When do I get the mattress?"

"I'll shop around on the weekend."

"I don't want no piece o' junk that sags. I'm heavy and need somethin' firm for my back. It'll cost ya a little more, but I earned it."

"I'll see what I can do."

***

Garbuncle filed a motion for a hearing before Judge Jonathan Crabtree to ask for the judge's blessing on his intention to issue a subpoena to the Hardinton Police Department. The attorney wanted to inspect the file of the man whose fingerprints were found on the tie rod assembly. Garbuncle knew the file was crucial to his defense of Alec Monceau in his new trial. The name on the file that held the tie rod prints had been typed on top of a two-inch space that was whited out. He needed to find out if the name covered by the white-out fluid were the same as the name typed over it.

"You certainly come up with some unusual ideas, counselor," the judge said, peering above the eyeglasses resting on his nose, his forehead wrinkled in a frown. "First you asked for permission to testify as an eyewitness on behalf of the man you were defending. Now this. Don't you think you're pushing it a little too far?"

"Judge," the man facing him from a chair on the other side of his desk said, "I concede that my maneuvers have been less than orthodox. However, I have discovered new information that is critical in the new trial, and for winning that trial. I cannot sit idly by and allow what I consider to be a grave injustice wreaked upon my client to go unchallenged."

Garbuncle presented the evidence of the loose tie rod that he had uncovered. "This revelation shows that a criminal act of the gravest nature may have been committed."

Judge Crabtree's elbow rested on an arm of the swivel chair, his fist buried in his face. He stared unblinking for what seemed to Garbuncle like minutes, but was really about ten seconds. The attorney could sense the deliberations traveling through the judge's mind.

Crabtree leaned back, his head elevated. "This is not a frivolous plan of action you've come up with, and I cannot discourage you from pursuing every possibility in the interest of your client. You didn't have to apprise me of your plan to issue a subpoena, and I appreciate the courtesy you have extended. Bring it to me and I'll sign it. Good luck with the case."

CHAPTER FOURTEEN

The swarthy man with luxuriant, dark hair rested his thick forearms on Garbuncle's desk and lowered his head to a few inches above a sheet of paper with the name Harold McCann headlining a set of fingerprints.

"What do you think, Johnny?" Garbuncle asked. He stood next to his desk, watching the man seated in front of it.

"Giovanni," the man corrected, dragging out the a. He smiled.

"Ohhh, sorry Jo ... what is it?"

"Giovanni. Jo *von* nee," he repeated, sounding out the syllables. "It mean gift of God in Italian."

"Yeah? Well you're sure gonna be a godsend if you can find out what's been whited out under that name. You must be really good at this kind of thing if Donald Trump would hire you. I'll bet you're walking a tight rope, though: The gift of God working for a guy who thinks *he's* the gift of God." The attorney chuckled.

Garbuncle noticed Giovanni's blank look. "That's all right. Nobody else understands it either. So how's that restoration project at Mar-a-Lago going?"

"Mister Trump not easy to work for. I say dat in ... how you say ... in secret?"

"Sure, sure, you mean in confidence. No problem. The Donald and I aren't likely to be crossing paths."

"He's no liking to pay people." Giovanni scowled. "Somebooody painting in fresco on art tiles. Dat is crime. Not easy to taking off and making look like before."

144

"Well, somebody committed a crime with this white-out too. Do you think you can get that white-out off?"

"I em not sure. White-out is no paint. But I'm trying to maybe get some off."

"We prob'ly don't need all of it off—just enough to make out what's underneath."

"Dis paper tick, not tin. Dat good."

Garbuncle's brow crinkled, and he looked at the insurance agent standing on the other side of Giovanni.

"I think he means the paper is thick," the agent said.

"Si," Giovanni said, holding up a hand with finger and thumb close together. "Tick."

"Ah, yes," said Garbuncle, covering his mouth to hide his amusement.

Giovanni took an instrument that resembled a scalpel from the tool kit strapped to his waist. He scraped with refined, delicate movements. The dim appearance of black letters came to the fore.

"I stop now. No wanting to hurt da paper." He placed the tool back in his kit, and withdrew a vial of clear liquid.

"What's that?" Garbuncle asked.

"Chemee-cal. Ac-ee-tone."

"Acetone," the agent said.

"Yes, dat's right."

He pulled a Q-tip from the tool kit, dipped it in the vial, and meticulously rubbed it on the white-out. "We wait."

After fifteen seconds, he dipped the other end of the Q-tip and rolled it over the white-out. Now the lettering was a little more clear, but still undecipherable. Giovanni breathed over the treated area, and raised the paper to the dim fluorescent ceiling light.

"You see?" he said.

Garbuncle squinted at the name. "A little hard to put the letters together, with the other name typed over it. But I can make out a capital J. Can't tell the second letter, but the third looks like a c. Another letter, and I think that last one is a b. Geez, this is like those crossword puzzles I do every day."

"J-c-b," the insurance agent pronounced. "I think I've got it. Jacob."

"Damn if I don't think you're right," Garbuncle blurted. "Look at the second and fourth letters. Looks like they're an a and an o. Holy crap. Now for the last name."

They peered at the paper. "That first letter is a capital S, I'm sure," Garbuncle said. "And the second looks just like the c in the first name. The next one is either an n or an h."

"Probably an h, because n wouldn't work there," the agent said. "But h would combine for a sh sound. Oh, yes, because I'm sure the next one is an m. Next is an i or an l, likely an i because a vowel would have to follow those four consonants—unless it's some Slavic name. Let's see ... schmi ..."

"Beats me," said Garbuncle. "I can hardly spell my own name. Not that I want to. I never was very fond of it." He drew closer to the paper. "Looks like a b ... no, it's going the other way, a d. And that last one is a t. Growing up Catholic, I've seen so many crosses I can spot every one of 'em in a bowl of alphabet soup."

Giovanni looked up at him, frowning.

"Oh, sorry Jo... uh, Jovaaanni. Didn't mean to be sacrilegious. So what does that spell?"

"Schmidt," the agent said.

"Holy Schmidts ... I mean smokes," Garbuncle almost shouted. "Wow. I know who this is. It's that Jake guy."

"You see better wiz flashlight," said Giovanni. "I sorry, I forget to take. Light in room not enough bright."

"You did a great job, uh ... I won't try to pronounce your name again. I'll just call you God's gift to art. Somehow, you managed to do it without smudging or tearing the paper."

Giovanni smiled from ear to ear.

"Send the bill to this address," the agent said, handing him a card.

***

"Hi Donna. Glad to see you're out of intensive care. You're obviously doing better. You look better. No tubes sticking out all over. You reminded me of a Rube Goldberg contraption."

Donna managed a wan smile.

"And that bandage around your head made you look like a nun without her hood. That's some nasty bruising. But it'll heal okay, and you'll look just as gorgeous as ever." He leaned over and kissed her on the temple, watching as a look of peace come over her.

"Donna, I think we're getting to the bottom of what happened. That tie rod didn't come loose by itself. I don't want to scare you, but we have to be careful."

He pressed the On button of his tape recorder. "I've got a tape recorder, and I'm going to ask you some questions. Is that okay?"

Donna nodded.

"Can you say yes or no?"

"Yes."

"Okay. Has anybody come to your room who you don't know? I mean, other than the cop who's standing there now."

"Tall man. Big baseball cap. Cap too big. Stood in doorway. Looked around. Nurse come down hall. Man left."

"Oh my God. I knew I shoulda gotten that deputy here sooner. Do you remember what his cap looked like?"

"Royal blue. All Cranes Inc. Picture of pink crane. Long neck."

"Did you get any idea of what the guy looked like?

"Young. Strong. Can't see face much, but jaw like made of wood. I see him somewhere."

"You were at the trial one day. Was he one of the defendants?"

Donna's neck stiffened, and her eyes opened wider. "Yes."

"Do you know if it was Larry Pickens?"

Her face brightened. "Yes. That name. I know it. Before crash, I said I c-could help with trial." The words came slowly, and she winced between them.

"Yes, and you were meeting your girlfriends, so we were going to get together later. Take your time, Donna. I can tell it hurts to talk."

"Jake took me to Ku Klu Kux—

"A Ku Klux Klan meeting?"

"Yes. I met Lar and Pede."

"Larry and Pete? Pete Bullard?"

"Yes. I ruh-member."

Garbuncle turned the tape recorder off.

"Oh wow. Everything's falling into place. I'm going to let you rest now, Donna. I can see you're tired. You need to sleep. Okay?"

She moved her head and her eyelids lowered. Garbuncle kissed her tenderly on the lips.

"I'll be back soon."

CHAPTER FIFTEEN

Garbuncle waddled out of his condo toward his car. It was only 7:30 a.m., but he planned to stop at Johnny's before heading to his office. He climbed in the clunker and turned the ignition. Nothing. He turned it twice more, with the same result.

He pulled the lever under the dashboard to release the hood latch, and lifted the hood. Nothing wrong with the battery connections, he mused, tugging on the tight cables.

"Son-of-a-bitch," he muttered. Returning to his apartment, he called Hitchens, who answered after several rings.

"Dammit, man, you woke me up."

"It's after seven-thirty. Shouldn't you be up by now?"

"I don't have to be at the paper till ten. You know I go to bed around one in the morning, and I need a lot of sleep to function right. What the hell do you want?"

"Oh geez, I didn't mean to wake you. I'm in a pickle. My car won't start."

"No shit. Will wonders never cease? How can that be, a fine, modern piece of automotive engineering like that fifteen-year-old behemoth? Why on earth would it malfunction?"

"I need you to pick up Ed and bring him over to see what's wrong."

"Oh, great. What a wonderful way to start my day." Hitchens issued a deep sigh. "Okay, call him and tell him I'll be there in twenty minutes."

"Brad, I really appreciate this."

"Yeah yeah. Do it now and call me back.'

Ed was agreeable to checking out the problem with the car, and Garbuncle began telling Hitchens how to get there. Hitchens cut his friend off.

"Are you forgetting that I've transported you to this guy's place twice already? I could drive there in my sleep. In fact, that's just about what I'll be doing."

***

Ed wore several days' growth of stubble, and his denim shirt was smudged with grease. He exuded the smell of dried sweat, a pungent, rancid odor that made Hitchens' empty stomach queasy. The mechanic loaded his scratched and scraped, green metal toolbox into the trunk of the Mazda.

"Must be the starter switch," Ed volunteered on the way to Garbuncle's condo. "I just replaced it awhile ago. I wanted to put a new one in, but Ham made me get a used one from a junk yard. Ya never know how long them parts is gonna last."

"He doesn't mind taking a chance," said Hitchens. "He knows he can find a sucker like me to rescue him if his car breaks down."

Ed didn't seem to have heard the remark. Either that, Hitchens thought, or he felt uncomfortable joining in disparagement of the person who was a good source of business.

"Or it could be the solenoid," Ed said. "I ain't got any idea how old it is. Could be the 'riginal one."

"I doubt it. That junk heap should be in a museum. The world's first bionic car. Just about every part's been replaced. And it just keeps rolling—like old man river."

Hitchens turned from Hardinton Road west onto Forest Hill, and a half-mile later south on Sherwood. He pulled up at Pine Tree Condominium. It consisted of only a few buildings, and Garbuncle lived in the first one, facing the road. Parking at a guest spot near Garbuncle's apartment, Hitchens honked.

Garbuncle came stumbling out. "My car's way around on the side," he said, pointing. "I park it in a guest spot under a big tree so the sun doesn't hit it. It's kind of secluded there. When I get home late, I look around before I head to my apartment to make sure nobody's waiting to pounce. We had a couple o' strong-arm robberies here at night. Wasn't too long ago."

Ed asked Hitchens to open the Mazda's trunk, and lifted his toolbox out. With Garbuncle leading, the three trudged around to the attorney's car on the side.

"I hope you can get it started," he told Ed. "The battery seems to be okay." He handed Ed the keys.

Ed turned the key, and heard a click. He walked to the front of the car, and turned on a flashlight he'd pulled out of his toolbox.

"What's 'at water underneath?" He got on his knees, stretched an arm under the grill, and stood. "You've got a leak in 'at 'ere radiator. That ain't why it ain't startin', but it's gotta be fixed. I'll have to take it to my place and see if I can solder the leak. That's if I can get it started. I'm gonna see if I can hot-wire it."

He opened the hood, bent his head into the motor, and pointed the light to the back of the engine. "Ah, that's what I'm lookin' for, 'at 'ere coil," he said, his voice muffled. He reached back to check it.

Straightening, he bumped his graying, thin-haired head on the underside of the hood, and rubbed the bruised spot momentarily. He withdrew a set of jumper cables and an insulated, flat screwdriver from his toolbox. He ran a cable from the positive battery terminal to the red coil wire, and felt for the solenoid on the starter, under the steering wheel. Wedging the screwdriver between the steering wheel and the column, he pushed the locking pin away from the wheel with rough jerks. Removing the ignition switch wire from the top of the solenoid, he used the screwdriver to short the solenoid's positive post to the terminal where the ignition switch was connected. The engine ground, and hummed to life.

Ed put his tools back in the box, which he deposited on the passenger-side floor of the Mercury Marquis. "I should have it fixed today," he called out the window to Garbuncle. "I'll give ya a holler."

The mechanic drove down Sherwood to Forest Hill, east to Hardinton, and north. He pulled onto a side road leading to his home. He had another car repair that he'd promised to finish that day, and was in a hurry, driving forty-five miles an hour in a thirty zone. A few blocks farther, he heard a clunk.

"What the hell was that?" he said. Rolling down the window, he poked his head out to listen, and heard a grating noise, as though something in the rear of the car were scraping the pavement.

"I wonder if the muffler came loose," he muttered. Then he remembered replacing it recently.

He slowed and continued thirty yards, his ear cocked as he strained to ascertain the source of the foreign sound. He turned the wheel to the right and headed off the road.

The explosion blew the doors off and engulfed the car in flames. It rolled to a stop on the wide, grass-and-gravel shoulder, yards from a small, wooden frame house. A middle-aged man with a pot belly protruding from a white undershirt, his hair rumpled, came out of the house. He dashed back inside, and re-emerged with a cellphone. A fire truck arrived in minutes, and a fireman doused the flames. He looked inside the skeletal remains of the car, and saw the charred body of Ed.

***

"Ham, you're gonna have to get a new car. Or at least a newer car." Hitchens looked out the driver's side window after he spoke so as not to seem too confrontational. Garbuncle didn't respond for several seconds.

"You like your Mazda? It rides pretty well."

"I love it. I've had a few things go wrong, though. I'm getting a Toyota next. I've read *Consumer Reports*. Very few repair problems with a Toyota Corolla."

They arrived at Garbuncle's office on the southwest corner of downtown West Palm Beach, in a three-story, decades-old, cream-colored commercial building he owned.

"Guess I'll just go on in to the *Hawk*," Hitchens said as Garbuncle got out of the car. "It won't hurt to get there early. I have to wrap up a feature on some guy who had testicular cancer four years ago and refused radiation or chemotherapy."

"And he's still around? Takes a lot o' balls to do that." Garbuncle cackled.

"He went to a clinic in southern California that a friend said the Amish go to. Some off-beat treatment. Guy is in great shape today, but his wife said he shoulda had the radiation to slow him down, 'cause he's always in heat. She's worn out."

"Ed'll drive here tonight with the car if he's fixed it. Can you pick me up if he didn't get it fixed?"

Hitchens threw his head back against the headrest, rolled his eyes to the roof, and sighed. "Yeah, I s'pose so."

"I'll give you a call," Garbuncle hollered as Hitchens closed the door.

***

A photographer raced past Hitchens as he entered the newsroom. "What was that?" he asked the assistant editor at the city desk.

"Bad accident. Car blew up. Burned to smithereens. Driver dead."

"Where?"

"Someplace west of town, off Hardinton Road. You gonna have that cancer story done by this afternoon?"

"Yeah, that's why I'm in a little early." Hitchens started for his desk, and stopped. *Where did he say?*

He turned back to the city desk. "They know who the victim was?"

"Nah. The guy's charcoal. Or gal. They can't tell. Why?"

"Oh, nothin'. I just know a guy who lives near there."

"There's almost nothing left of the car, but they did manage to salvage the license plate. Checked out to a guy named Garbuncle. Hiram."

"Holy shit," Hitchens exclaimed.

The assistant city editor shot upright in his chair. "What's the matter?"

"I know whose car that is—and who was in it. I'll be back. Don't worry about the feature. I'm almost done."

Hitchens jumped in his Mazda and raced the two miles to Garbuncle's office. "Get off the phone. Come on."

Garbuncle said a few words into the phone and hung up. "Where are we going?"

"I'll tell you on the way."

Hitchens sped out of the downtown, and headed down a myriad of main streets that would lead to the area where Ed lived. Hitchens told the attorney what he'd learned.

"Oh. My. God." Garbuncle spaced each word, his mouth open wide. "That means Ed is dead."

"You got it."

They drove in silence for several minutes,

"Is this a strong enough message for you?" Hitchens said. He kept his eyes straight ahead on the road. "Have you learned your lesson? Are you finally gonna get a newer car that's not dangerous to drive?"

Garbuncle said nothing, his eyes wide, jaw tense.

The side street where Ed lived was lined with small, shabby houses, the driveways teeming with old-model pickups and beat-up cars. Two firetrucks and three sheriff's cars had the street blocked off, their red lights flashing. Hitchens drove as close as possible, and parked on the narrow dirt shoulder that was parallel to a crack-filled, uneven sidewalk. The two walked past the barricades.

Two deputies stopped them, and Hitchens pulled his press pass out of his wallet. Garbuncle told them the destroyed car was his. He saw the look of incredulity on the cops' faces.

"What?" one barked. "Listen mister, you better be tellin' the truth, or you're gonna be in big trouble. Wait here and I'll get the sergeant." He walked to the wreckage, said something to an officer who was directing emergency personnel, and pointed in Garbuncle and Hitchens' direction. The officer in charge turned to look, and headed toward them.

"Something I can do for you gentlemen?"

"The burned-up car is mine," said Garbuncle. "And the driver was my mechanic. He was taking it to his property up the street here to work on it. I couldn't start it this morning."

"How do you know this?" the sergeant asked. "That car is not recognizable."

Hitchens showed his pass from the *Hawk* again. "An editor told me you guys were able to read the license plate. The numbers are for Garbuncle's car."

"Yeah. We found it in that yard, with the bumper," the sergeant said. He pointed two houses back of the car.

He carried a note pad, and pulled a pen from his shirt pocket. He demanded Garbuncle's name, address, and phone number.

"I need you to go to the sheriff's office. You know where that is?"

"Yes, on Gun Club Road."

"Okay, you need to meet with the detective division. Now. I can't leave till we get everything cleared up."

"Can I take a look first, Sergeant?" Hitchens asked. "I'm covering this for the *Hawk*."

"Yeah, I don't suppose it would hurt. You got a strong stomach? The body is still behind the wheel. We have to handle it with care, and everything is still too hot to touch. Go on ahead."

The pair approached the car without conviction, apprehensive about what they would see. They stopped, and looked in at the charred, skeletal remains of Ed, white brains oozing from his skull. Garbuncle stumbled backward, caught himself, and stood looking away. He retched. Hitchens winced, and lowered his head, his stomach queasy. It was the most gruesome thing he'd seen since the county medical examiner in Milwaukee, where he'd been a reporter twenty-two years earlier, had shown him the severed body of a railroad brakeman. The man had been cut in half at the midsection when a freight car lurched backward after he'd uncoupled it from another car. The overweight man's eyes bulged and his face reflected horror.

"Come on," Hitchens said, trying to erase the memory. "Nothing we can do. Let's get out of here."

"Wait a minute," Garbuncle said. He walked up to the officer in charge. "Can you tell me where they're going to haul my car, Lieutenant?"

"Yeah. A-Plus."

"The auto salvage place west of Lake Worth?"

"Right. But why do you want to know? There's nothing left of that car to salvage."

"Yeah, I guess so. I was just curious."

Garbuncle and Hitchens began walking back to Hitchens car. Garbuncle looked down, feeling morose. He stopped, staring at the black asphalt. The pungent odor it gave off indicated it had been laid no more than a few days previously. It looked almost new, bearing hardly any traffic marks. Except for one long, heavy scratch.

"What's the matter?" asked Hitchens, who had continued walking several feet before noticing his partner wasn't beside him.

Garbuncle's eyes followed the gouge in the road, which began perhaps a hundred feet ahead. He turned, and saw that it continued another twenty feet back of him before veering to the right until it left the road. At that point, a furrow formed in the dirt and continued to a grassy stretch where the car had blown up.

"How'd we miss that before?" said Hitchens.

"I guess we were focused on the scene ahead."

Hitchens scanned the accident scene. "Ah, there he is."

"Who?"

"The *Hawk* photographer. Looks like he's walking around looking for stuff to shoot. Stay here."

He walked briskly up to the sergeant, who waved him on after Hitchens said he needed to talk to the paper's photographer. He and the cameraman came to where Garbuncle was waiting.

Hitchens looked toward the sergeant out of the corner of his eye, and saw that he had gone ahead to confer with the lieutenant.

"We need shots of the long mark in the asphalt and the groove in the dirt. It's obvious the car made these marks before it blew up. Be as discreet as you can, 'cause the cops must have missed this, and I don't want to call their attention to it."

The photographer took pictures from both ends of the indentation, and walked with Garbuncle and Hitchens back to the cameraman's car, which was parked near Hitchens' Mazda.

Hitchens and Garbunle drove away. The reporter glanced sideways, and noticed that Garbuncle looked glum.

"He was a good man," the attorney said, his head turned down and away.

"What are you going to tell the detective?" Hitchens said.

"There's not much I can tell him. I have no idea what could have made that car explode—although those gouges might give us a clue."

Garbuncle handed Detective Lieutenant Roy Casey his card, and summarized events leading to the accident. Casey asked, "You got any idea how this happened?"

"Not the faintest," said Garbuncle. "But it was an old car, so maybe there was something wrong I didn't know about. Still, Ed—that's the mechanic who was driving the car—Ed worked on it pretty recently, and he likely would have seen something serious. 'Cause he's worked on it a lot."

Hitchens drew his hand across his face to wipe away a sarcastic smile.

"Well, it sure wasn't spontaneous combustion," the detective said, his eyes lowered as he watched Garbuncle. "You have any problem with this Ed? You owe him money?"

"Not at all. He worked on my car so many times that we got to be friends. Like I told the officer at the scene, he came to my place 'cause I couldn't get it started. He hot-wired it. Maybe there was an electric spark, or something."

"That's a possibility, I suppose. I'm not a mechanic."

"Yeah. I guess we'll never know for sure."

"You're a lucky guy. Ed was unlucky. Maybe you oughta own a car that's in better shape."

"I keep telling him that," Hitchens said. "But at least he needs Triple A or better car insurance coverage if he's going to drive a wreck. This probably wouldn't have happened if the car had been towed to a shop. They sure as hell wouldn't have hot-wired it."

"Woulda coulda shoulda," said Garbuncle.

"So what's your name again?" the lieutenant asked Hitchens.

"Oh, yeah," Hitchens said, pulling out his wallet and handing the lieutenant his press ID. "Ham and I are friends."

"Here's my card, too," Garbuncle said. "I'll think about your advice, Lieutenant. Well, you know where to reach me if you need anything else."

"I'm gonna drop you off at your office so you can make some phone calls," Hitchens said as they climbed into his Mazda. "When you find a rental car, call me and I'll take you there."

"Rental?" Garbuncle looked at Hitchens, his mouth open.

"Geez, you look amazed. What did you think I was gonna do, be your transportation until you buy another clunker?"

"Uh ... well ... okay."

Hitchens pulled up in front of the attorney's office. "Give me a call when you find a rental. Make sure they're open into the evening, though, 'cause I'm gonna have some catching up to do at the paper."

Hitchens got the call from Garbuncle at 5:30 p.m. "Man, I got lucky."

"You work fast. A client of yours?"

"Huh?" Garbuncle paused. "Oh, you had me there for a second. No, I found a rental for ten bucks a day. Lease-A-Lemon. It's out on Hardinton Road, just north of Forest Hill. They rent used cars."

Hitchens groaned. "They probably buy cars with problems on the cheap. Look, if this piece of junk stalls on you, you're on your own. I'm not picking you up."

"That's all right. They guarantee it'll work, or they'll give me another one. They're open till eight."

"I'll get you at 7:30."

CHAPTER SIXTEEN

"So, neighbor, I see you got another car. Looks a lot nicer than the other one you had. And smaller." The short, bushy-haired retiree lived a few doors away from Garbuncle, who regarded the fellow as quixotic, always scampering about in different pairs of backless, bright-colored, feminine loafers. They'd exchanged pleasantries now and then ("I see they raised the homeowner association dues again." "When is this rain gonna stop?" "Wish they'd put those dumpsters out of my view.")

"You must mean that Ford Focus. The blue one. It's not my car. It's a rental. My old Mercury caught fire and burned up. It's a sad story. I'll tell you about it some time."

"Oh, sorry to hear that. I figured something was wrong with the car when I saw you working on it at 2 a.m. the other night. I have insomnia a lot, and was walking to the clubhouse to sit by the pool and get some fresh air."

Garbuncle stared at the man. "I wasn't working on my car. You say 2 in the morning?"

"Well, yes, I assumed it was you. That parking area is dark, you know. I couldn't make out who it was. Whoever it was didn't say anything to me, and I just kept walking. I probably should have said something to him. Did the car get broken into?"

Garbuncle was lost in thought. "Huh? Broken ... no, no, I didn't notice anything wrong with the car. Where exactly was the guy standing?"

"When I first saw him, he was crawling out from underneath, and he had some kind of lantern or flashlight. He stood up as I walked by, and I saw he had something in his other hand. Must have been a tool. He had to have seen me, but didn't hurry away or anything. I thought it was kind of strange you'd be working on your car at that hour of the night, but I figured maybe you didn't have time to work on it during the day, or you might be like me and have insomnia. Needed to do something to take your mind off things."

Garbuncle looked into the distance. "Hey, I appreciate your telling me that, uh ... I'm sorry, I keep forgetting your name."

"No problem. Joe. And you're ..." The man's eys widened, and Garbuncle could tell a light had popped on in his head.

"I just happened to think," Joe said. "That parking space next to yours is empty most of the year, right?"

"Yeah, those people are snowbirds."

"That's what I thought. But there was a black pickup truck there. Or maybe some other dark color. It was night, so I'm not sure. And it was parked facing out. I could see some kind of insignia on the door, but it was too dark out, and I couldn't read it."

"Really strange. I'll prob'ly want to talk to you again about this, Joe. Thanks for the information."

"Glad I ran into you, or I might not have thought to mention it."

Garbuncle was heading to the grocery store to pick up something for dinner, but turned back to his apartment instead. He'd lost his appetite for food. But not for booze. He pulled a one-and-three-quarter liter of cheap vodka from a cabinet beneath the kitchen counter, put it to his lips, leaned his head back, and guzzled five ounces. He walked to the living room, and plopped down on the couch. The alcohol worked like a surgeon's anesthesia, Garbuncle's eyelids drooping, head falling back on the cushion, legs spreading wide at the knees.

A pit bull terrier held the leg of a skeleton like a vise as it screamed silently while trying to flee. A distant ringing grew closer. Garbuncle woke with a start, scrambled to his feet, and fell back. He lurched off the couch again and stumbled to the phone in the kitchen.

"Where were you, in the can?" Hitchens sounded impatient. "I was about to hang up."

"Oh ... no ... where ... what time is it? Hold on." Garbuncle put the phone down and leaned forward on the counter, resting on his elbows. He staggered the few feet to the sink, and splashed cold water on his face.

"Whas goin' on?" Water dripped onto the counter and down the front of his blue, short-sleeved shirt, turning it darker.

"I take it the rental is working okay, or you would have called me."

"Iss not ass comforble ass my Mercry, but iss okay for now. Iss a li'l Ford Focus. Shiny blue."

"You're slurring. You remind me of that old cowboy song: Back in, the saddle, again. Back on, the bottle, again. Now that you've got wheels, we need to get together and strategize."

"Yeah. There's a new devep ... hic ... develpmint, and I don't think we should talk about it on the phone."

"Oooh. Sounds ominous."

"Yup."

"All right, get sobered up, and let's meet after work tomorrow."

"Yup."

***

Hitchens and Garbuncle took a table in an unpopulated part of the room at Johnny's so no one could make out their conversation. Garbuncle related the conversation with his neighbor.

"First they tried to kill Donna, then me," said Garbuncle. "I obviously was the intended target of that explosion."

"You gonna report what your neighbor told you to the cops?"

"I don't think I can trust them. Some of these cops know each other. Word gets around. We need to keep our suspicions under our hats."

"I agree. We don't need the cops investigating and finding out their compatriots were behind this. Wow. It's getting dicey."

"That's an understatement." Garbuncle twirled the ice in his glass of vodka with his finger, saying nothing for several seconds.

"Look, I can't continue investigating this thing. It's just too dangerous. These guys are gonna get me eventually if I do. I hate to let Alec down, but I think in this case, discretion is the better part of valor." A corner of his mouth twisted downward. "Bad cliché, I know. But true."

"Well, I can't tell you what to do. It's your decision. But Alec's not the only one who'll be disappointed. You're going to have to tell Donna."

Hitchens saw that Garbuncle was on the verge of crying.

"Yeah."

***

"Hi Donna. How are you doing, sweetheart?" Garbuncle kissed her softly on the lips.

"Sweetheart? You never called me that before." She spoke slowly, but was perkier than the last time Garbuncle had seen her, only two days before.

"Well, I just ... I guess I lost my head. You're looking better. And you sound better, too."

"Yes, I'm starting to feel better." Her pace of speech was still measured, but faster than before.

"They've got your bed raised. So the doctors must think you're on the mend. I'm really glad about that."

"How are you doing? How is the case going?"

Garbuncle's face darkened as he looked down.

"What's the matter? What's going on?"

"Honey ..."

"Honey? Mmmm. You're being very sweet."

"I care a lot about you." His eyes glistened. "That's why it pains me to tell you this."

"What? What are you talking about?"

"I think I'm going to have to drop the case. For your sake and mine. It's too dangerous."

Donna stared at him with lips parted.

"Some things have happened lately." He told her about his car exploding with Ed inside, and the story his neighbor related about someone climbing from under the car the night before.

"It's just too coincidental that both your car and mine had major problems that caused accidents. We found out yours was tampered with, and I strongly suspect mine was too. I may not be able to prove it, but these things wouldn't have happened so close together by accident—to use a bad pun. There's people out to get us, because they know we could get them in trouble."

Donna said nothing, staring into space.

"I'm very sorry about your mechanic. I know it's dangerous, but ..." She looked Garbuncle in the eyes. "I don't want to let these people run free because they scared us. Besides, we don't know what else they might do."

"I think if we just leave them alone, they'll leave us alone. Look, there are too many cops involved—maybe more than we're aware of. I already talked to the sheriff's office, because they're separate from the city police departments. I'm not sure it was wise to do even that. I just don't feel comfortable trusting any of them. They're too likely to protect their own."

Donna looked down, and Garbuncle could see she was disappointed.

"I just can't put you in such a dangerous situation."

She looked up at him from lowered eyes. "Are you sure you're not worried about yourself?"

"Yes, Donna. Yes, I'm scared for both of us. I'm no hero. And I care too much about you to risk your life."

She saw that his eyes had grown moist again, and reached out with her left arm. He bent close, and kissed her.

She placed her hand on the back of his neck and caressed. "It's okay."

A smiling nurse appeared at the door. "It's time for your meds," Ms. Malone. "I don't want to chase your visitor away, but you need to rest. And then you need some nourishment."

"No problem," said Garbuncle. To Donna, "Bye sweetheart. I'll see you soon."

He squeezed her hand, kissed it, and left.

***

Garbuncle dialed the insurance agent, and told him about the car explosion.

"I don't think it was an accident," the attorney said. "I'm pretty sure it was meant for me. This has gotten too dangerous. I'm going to have to back away from this investigation."

Silence on the other end. "I'm disappointed. I need your help on this."

"I know, but it's not worth getting killed over." Garbuncle paused. "But I'll give you some information my friend and I learned, and you can run with it."

"Whatever you can give me."

"Okay. But I don't want you to share it with the state attorney's office, because they'll want to talk to me, and then my life is in even more danger. I can't risk it."

"Let's have it."

"My buddy and I got to the scene of the explosion shortly after it happened. I identified the car as mine to the sheriff's deputy. On the way back to my buddy's car, I noticed a groove in the asphalt. It was laid only a few days ago. The mark in the road led onto the shoulder, and then it became a furrow in the dirt. My buddy is with the *Hawk*, and he had the photographer on the scene take some shots. I can get those to you after they're developed. You'll probably have to pay for them, though."

"This sounds like good stuff."

"I think you ought to have that hotshot car mechanic with the ... what was that expertise he had?

"ASE certification—Automobile Service Excellence."

"Yeah, that was it. He ought to be able to figure out what made that big scratch in the asphalt."

"It might have just been the muffler."

"Huh-uh. Ed put a new one on just a few weeks ago. Probably the only new part I ever put on that car. I wanted it to be quiet."

"I'll be in touch."

***

The distant, muffled sound of a siren. On the way to quench the fire and save Donna, trapped inside the car. Getting louder. No, not a siren, a ringing.

Garbuncle jerked awake, and looked around. He saw the large bottle of cheap vodka on the nightstand, next to the phone. He shot his hand toward the receiver, and knocked the partly empty bottle onto the floor, vodka flowing onto the dirty carpet. Lunging for the bottle, he fell onto the floor, his hand catching the cord and pulling the phone down with him, the receiver flying off the base. He quickly righted the bottle and stared. Still half full.

"Hello," he yelled into the receiver, lying on his stomach.

"Hello. Something wrong, Mister Hiram?"

"Huh? Who's this? Oh, hi Alec. Just a second." Garbuncle pulled himself onto the bed and placed the bottle and phone back onto the stand. "I'm all right. I was dreaming."

"I no see you long time. I call see if you okay. How your computer work?"

"Well, as a matter of fact, my email is ... uh, everything's fine. How are you doing?"

"I worry a little about trial."

"Yeah, well ... I'm not sure ... I mean, something's ..." He paused.

"What wrong, Mister Hiram?"

Garbuncle took a deep breath. "Alec, there's been a complication."

"Com... what you say?"

"A difficult situation has arisen. I'm not sure how to tell you this."

"Oh, this no sound good."

"Looks like the cops who beat you up are trying to get me and my girlfriend killed."

Garbuncle heard Alec gasp. "Somebody tinkered with our cars."

"What you mean, tinker?"

"Uh ... worked on them. Did something mechanically to them. My car exploded, but somebody else was driving it. Donna's car crashed, and she's in the hospital."

"Oh, Mister Hiram, dis awful."

"And I'm afraid whoever is doing this isn't going to stop until I'm dead—

unless I stop what I'm doing. Those cops know that Donna and I know some awful things about them, and they're afraid of what we'll say in court."

Silence on the other end. A drawn-out sigh.

"I'm sorry, Alec, but I can't continue representing you in court. But don't give up hope. I'll try to get an attorney to handle your case pro bono, like I've been doing. Maybe I'll find a lawyer who needs his computer fixed, and you can do a trade with him."

"Tank you, Mister Hiram. I try hope."

But Garbuncle could hear the fear in Alec's voice. The attorney's heart sank, and he said goodbye.

CHAPTER SEVENTEEN

Garbuncle sat back in his ratty office chair, gazing at a faded-mauve wall, but not seeing it. Who could he get to represent Alec in his court battle to show he was innocent of resisting arrest, and officers Pete Bullard and Larry Pickens beat him up without provocation? He couldn't come up with anyone, but he was having trouble concentrating. Donna competed for his mind's attention.

He checked his schedule with his frumpy, late-middle-aged secretary. Garbuncle was shrewd enough to hire someone for whom he felt no sexual attraction—to avoid complications, he told Hitchens. She informed him nothing was on his docket for the afternoon, though he needed to prepare for the deposition in two days of a client charged with battery against his wife.

He strode to the city parking garage where he left his Ford subcompact rental car, on the second floor. A muscular man in a white T-shirt, with a ponytail falling from a full head of hair, was heading down the aisle away from his car. As the two passed each other, Garbuncle caught the man glancing at him. Reaching his car, the attorney looked back toward the elevator in time to see the man board it.

Garbuncle stopped beside the car and stooped to inspect the underside. Detecting nothing amiss, he rose and peered into the interior. All okay. He turned the key in the lock, and stood back as he opened the door. He leaned in, pulled the lever for the hood, and walked to the front. Bending to look through the crack into the motor, he saw nothing out of the ordinary, and raised the hood. After lowering it, he climbed into the driver's seat, inserted the key, hesitated, and with his heart beating rapidly, turned the ignition. The car started, and the tension escaped him in a deep sigh, like rainwater gushing from a drain spout.

"I'm getting paranoid," he muttered. His mood became ebullient as he contemplated seeing Donna.

The desk clerk told him Donna could not see visitors.

"What?" Garbuncle asked, taken aback. "It's only 3:30—too early for dinner. Is she having some test, or something?"

"What is your relationship with Ms. Malone, Mister Garbuncle?"

"Oh, I understand. Security. That's good. Probably police instructions. It's okay. I'm her attorney and friend." He withdrew his wallet and showed the clerk his identification.

"That's not it," she said. "Donna is in ICU."

"Huh?" Garbuncle gaped. "How can that be? I just saw her two days ago, and she was doing well. In good spirits."

"It came on her quickly. The nurse said she seemed depressed yesterday, and wouldn't talk much. She caught an infection, and went downhill really fast. The doctor rushed her into the Intensive Care Unit, and put her on an IV. She's fading in and out of consciousness."

Garbuncle gawked, his face ashen.

"What can I do?" he pleaded. "How can I help her?

"Are you her partner?"

"No. I mean yes. She's ... we're ... ." His voice cracked. "I love her."

"I'm so sorry, Mister Garbuncle. Why don't you check back tomorrow? Maybe she'll be recovering by then. She's in good hands."

***

He sat propped in his bed, a pillow cushioning his back against the backboard. Charlie Rose interviewed a politician on the TV, but what they said didn't register with Garbuncle, who only stared as he drank from a glass with ice, filling it occasionally from a jug of vodka on the side table. Drowsiness overcame him, and he set the glass on the table. At 4 a.m., he awoke, and staggered to the light switch on the wall before climbing under the covers.

Arriving late to the office, he checked in with his secretary and asked her to postpone for several days the deposition set for the next day. "I might not be back today," he called over his shoulder while walking out the door.

The desk clerk asked him to wait while she paged the doctor. They walked to the waiting room. Garbuncle's years as an attorney had taught him to assess a person's character from his or her face. He perceived gentleness in this doctor.

"How well do you know Ms. Malone?" he asked.

"For several years. She's a client, and I dated her now and then. We've gotten close in the last six months or so. I'm ..." He choked.

"It's okay, Mister Garbuncle. But I don't have good news for you." The doctor stared at Garbuncle for a second. "Her condition is grave." He hesitated. "I'm not sure ... I don't think she's going to make it."

Garbuncle squelched a sob, and lowered his head. Tears slid down his face. After a quarter-minute, he looked up into space.

"I can make an exception and let you see her very briefly, if you'd like. We can wheel her into a private room."

"Yes," Garbuncle croaked. He followed the doctor to the elevator, and they got off on the second floor. The doctor escorted him to an empty patient room. In a few minutes, a nurse and an attendant wheeled Donna into the room.

Garbuncle took a deep breath. He didn't want her to see him crying, because that might worry her. But when he saw her, he realized he needn't worry. She was barely awake.

"Donna, it's Ham." Her eyes opened and closed. He took her hand in his, and kissed it. "Sweetheart, I've changed my mind. I'm going to pursue this case, and let it take me wherever it leads. I'll do everything I can to defend Alec, and to bring these guys who tried to kill you and me to justice."

Donna's eyelids opened into a thin crack, and a faint smile widened her closed lips.

He looked up at the nurse, who motioned it was time to go.

He leaned across Donna's torso, and softly kissed her forehead and cheek.

"Bye," he squeaked. His voice breaking, he added, "I love you."

A rose tint colored Donna's face, and her eyes opened.

Then they wheeled her away.

***

Garbuncle set about preparing the deposition for his wife-beating client. The guy accused his wife of attacking him when he arrived home three hours late and hadn't called to tell her he had to work overtime. She accused him of seeing another woman, a charge Garbuncle found credible when he saw the wife in a brief meeting with her attorney. The client seemed evasive about the real reason for his tardiness, but insisted he was only defending himself when she swung an ice bucket at him. She slipped on a melted ice cube and fell to the floor, bruising a hip, when he blocked the bucket with his arms.

The next day, the woman and the opposing attorneys met. Garbuncle just wanted to mope, but was relieved that the deposition took his mind off of Donna. When it was over, he called the hospital from his office.

"She seems to be just a little bit better today," the nurse said. "But nobody can see her yet. Try calling back tomorrow."

Garbuncle was elated. He called Hitchens, and they met at Johnny's.

"I think she'll make it," Garbuncle said, and they clinked glasses. "I have to tell you something. I had decided to quit this case with Alec. Too damned dangerous. I told Donna, and I think that's why she suddenly went downhill. She got real depressed. And I felt awful. I changed my mind, and I'm going after those cops with everything I've got. I already told Donna, but she was barely conscious. I'm going to be more emphatic about it tomorrow, if I can see her. Sounds like they'll let me. Then I've got to tell Alec, because I could hear the devastation in his voice when I called and said I was dropping the case. He'll be really relieved."

"Well, I agree this is dicey as hell. I can't tell you what to do. But you'd better be damned careful. I'll help you any way I can."

Garbuncle felt chipper the next day, and took only a couple of swigs from the bottle. At 4:30, he called the hospital.

"Mister Garbuncle, you'd better sit down," the nurse said. His heart plummeted, and he couldn't respond.

"Are you still there, Mister Garbuncle?"

"Yes," he mumbled.

"Donna didn't make it. She died an hour ago."

Garbuncle dropped the phone, stared into space for several seconds, and put his head on the desk as wracking sobs overcame him. Finally, he heard the nurse in the distance. "Mister Garbuncle, Mister Garbuncle, are you all right?"

He picked up the phone. "Yes, thank you. I'll be okay." He replaced the phone in its cradle. He pulled open the desk drawer with the bottle of vodka, stared at it for almost a half-minute, and slowly closed the drawer.

***

Donna had attended Unity Church in West Palm Beach on an irregular basis. Besides serving as a home for people turned off by the exhortations about sin and its consequences from the pulpits of conventional churches, Unity was a refuge for recovering alcoholics, people going through divorce, unemployed folks, and those down on their luck in sundry other ways.

Garbuncle and Hitchens sat in the fourth pew back from the altar, where a woman pastor spoke of the kindness and compassion that Donna's friends credited her with. Gracie, her close friend who worked at the stone ornament firm, sat with head bowed, dabbing her eyes with a handkerchief. Several other woman friends sat adjacent to her in the second row. A woman, her husband, and their pre-teen daughter and young son occupied the front row, along with a few other men and women. Gracie had pointed them out to Garbuncle as Donna's family.

His shoulders convulsed as the minister spoke. Afterward, he and Gracie hugged before everyone drove to a modest cemetery on the south end of West Palm Beach.

The service over, Garbuncle drove back to his office.

"Are you free to talk, Alec?"

"Yes. No many customer today. But I no can be on phone long."

"Okay. I'll be brief. I'm staying on the case. You don't need to worry. I'm not abandoning you. I'm going to get you cleared. Those two cops who beat you up are going to pay."

"You get money from dem?"

"No. Well, maybe later. But what I meant is, I'm going to see that they are brought to justice—that they are punished for what they did to you."

"Dat sound dang'rous, Mister Hiram. I no want you get hurt."

"That's for me to worry about. I just wanted to let you know that I'm going to do everything I can for you. I've got to go now. I'll be in touch with you later."

***

"The car is at A-Plus Towing and Salvage west of Lake Worth," Garbuncle said on his office phone. "It's a bit of a hike, half-way to Lion Country Safari. We need that mechanic expert to look at it."

The insurance agent said he would give the mechanic two days' notice, and they could meet Garbuncle at the junk lot in the afternoon.

***

The pair were waiting on a dilapidated couch used by customers who'd ordered parts when the attorney arrived at the salvage office. He took a space between the agent and the mechanic, and drew several eight-by-ten photos out of a manila envelope.

"What do you think that mark in the asphalt might have been caused by—and also the gouge in the dirt leading to the car?"

"I doubt it was the muffler dragging," the mechanic said, "'cause it's not that heavy, and—"

"Almost no chance it was the muffler," Garbuncle said. "I had a new one put on just a few weeks ago. It wouldn't have come loose."

"Unless somebody loosened it," said the mechanic. "But it still wouldn't

172

have been heavy enough to make those marks. And why would anybody loosen it? It couldn't cause any damage."

"Exactly," said Garbuncle. "I was thinking the gas tank."

"I think your thinking probably is right. A full tank, or mostly full, would be heavy enough—maybe eighty pounds—to dig into that freshly laid asphalt."

The desk clerk gave them directions to where the destroyed car was deposited, and they walked along a dusty path to the designated row of junk cars. Garbuncle recognized his.

The mechanic circled the car, and dropped on one knee to look underneath. "Not much I can tell from this. It's too severely burnt. Too bad they didn't recover the tank. I might be able to tell whether it came loose by itself. Not much I can tell just by looking at—"

"I was getting to that next," Garbuncle interrupted. "The sheriff's office called me this morning and said a guy who lives a couple doors from the explosion scene came in with a badly damaged part that looked like a tank to hold liquid. Said he'd spotted it in some thick shrubbery on the side of his house."

"Let's go take a look at it," said the agent.

The insurance agent and mechanical expert followed Garbuncle on the long drive east, then north, to the sheriff's office near the airport.

"We're here to see Lieutenant Casey," the attorney told the male desk clerk, who summoned the detective.

Garbuncle introduced the agent and mechanic, both of whom showed their credentials, and said they wanted to look at the gas tank.

"Sure, come back to the evidence room." They started back, and Casey stopped. "I've got something else for you, too."

He dragged the gas tank off a shelf. "I don't see how you're gonna learn anything from the tank. But you might find this interesting." He reached to the shelf and retrieved a cellophane bag containing a piece of metal.

"A bolt of some kind," said Garbuncle, inspecting the bag. "Where did it come from?"

"A guy who lives near where the explosion happened said his kid found it in the dirt next to the road while he was riding his bicycle. The dad apparently is a mechanic for a repair garage in Boynton Beach, and said he thought it might have been the bolt holding the gas tank in place. You can take it out of the bag. It's charred, of course, and the kid and his dad got their fingerprints all over it, so it won't hurt to handle it."

Garbuncle withdrew the bolt and handed it to the expert mechanic.

"Yeah. That's the adjusting bolt. It's obviously been tampered with. The piece it's attached to is from the gas tank, and there's about two inches of thread sticking out. That bolt is one of two that hold the tank in place. This indicates the bolt on one side wasn't tight against the tank, which would allow that side of the tank to come loose and drag on the road, causing the gash."

***

"Jacob Schmidt should be charged with murder," said Garbuncle. He sat at an oval table in a conference room at the Palm Beach County State Attorney's office. "And Granville police officers Larry Pickens and Pete Bullard should be arrested on suspicion of initiating this murder."

"Murder?" the young assistant state attorney said. "It's not murder unless Ms. Malone dies."

Garbuncle stared, struggling to maintain his composure. "She died yesterday," he said in a trembling voice.

"You sound upset about this. Did you know her?"

Garbuncle could only nod, and pulled a handkerchief from his pant pocket.

"I'm sorry," the prosecutor said. He paused while Garbuncle regained his composure.

"Well, this adds a whole new dimension."

Garbuncle handed him a manila envelope containing Schmidt's fingerprint file, along with a pen light that he withdrew from his pocket. He shined the light on the file.

The prosecutor bent over it. "Yes, I have to agree, that pretty clearly reads Jacob Schmidt under Harold McCann typed over it."

He turned to Garbuncle. "There had to be some collusion going on with the Hardinton Police Department."

Garbuncle finished dabbing his eyes, and returned the handkerchief to his pocket. He wore a wry smile. "Ya think?"

"I'm going to get with the chief about this, and I'm sure he'll assign an investigator."

"The chief? You mean your boss, the state attorney?"

"Oh, sorry, yes. I didn't mean the Hardinton police chief. He could be in cahoots with these guys."

"The agent for Donna Malone's insurance company is working on this. Shall I have him contact you?"

"Yes. We need to coordinate our efforts. But the first order of business is Jacob Schmidt. I think the chief will want to file a charge of murder against him."

"There's more," said Garbuncle.

The youthful prosecutor had begun to rise and extend his hand. He sat back down.

"That fiery explosion of a car west of town. You must have read about it or seen it on TV."

"Oh yeah, the one where the guy burned alive in his car. Horrible. What about it?"

"That was my car. My mechanic was driving it. That explosion was meant for me."

The prosecutor stared, mouth open. "Somebody was after you?"

"Same guys. I'm sure of it."

"So we've got *two* murders. What's going on here?"

"They're both connected to that resisting arrest case—where the guy got beat up by two cops during a traffic stop and the jury found him guilty. I was—am—the guy's attorney. He was totally innocent."

"Well, yes, of course that's what you're going to say, but—"

"I witnessed the incident. I know exactly what happened."

"So how are these murders connected with that case?"

"In the Donna Malone crash, she knew too much. And the two cops knew she and I were good friends, and they figured she'd tell me what she knew."

"Wow, this is complicated. I'll get with the chief. He'll want to put an investigator on the case, and you and the insurance agent can work with him."

CHAPTER EIGHTEEN

"The assistant told me the outlines of what happened and why he thinks an investigation is warranted," the investigator said. "I was a police detective in West Palm Beach for three years before I left for law school, so I'm no stranger to criminal operations, even though I've been at this job only a year. I understand you're a criminal attorney?"

"That's right—for decades."

"I'm glad to know that, because it makes my job easier."

Bart Sutherland was in his early thirties, on the tall side, and hefty. Nonetheless, the attorney had detected a wiriness in his step when he walked into the waiting room. He greeted Garbuncle with what the attorney perceived as aloofness, his rounded facial features revealing no emotion.

"Let's get down to the details. This car crash fatally injured a woman you knew—is that right?" Garbuncle nodded on the other side of the desk. "There also was a car crash and explosion that killed—was it your mechanic?" The attorney nodded again. "And you think they were linked. As I understand it, you were defending a black guy charged with resisting arrest with violence by two Granville police officers. Right?"

"You got it right—almost. He's black and Hispanic."

"I handled a few of those colored cases," the investigator said, Garbuncle noticing the smirk. "So who were the cops?" Sutherland took a pen from a plastic sheath in his shirt pocket, and grabbed a yellow legal pad from a drawer.

"Pete Bullard."

Sutherland asked him to spell it, and wrote it on the pad.

"Larry Pickens."

The investigator frowned, and spelled the name back to the attorney.

"Okay, now who's the guy you think caused the car incidents?"

"Jake Schmidt." Sutherland jerked his head up from his pad. "Give me that again."

"Schmidt. You know him?"

"Huh? Oh ... no, no. I'm just not sure how to spell it." He listened without writing as Garbuncle spelled Schmidt, then wrote it on the pad with no hesitation.

"Now fill me in on how you think this all came together. I've got to admit, it sounded a little far-fetched to me when the assistant explained it."

Garbuncle related that Schmidt's fingerprints were found on the tie rod of Donna Malone's car, and the gas tank on Garbuncle's car appeared to have been loosened. He explained how Pickens and Bullard learned the attorney was friendly with Donna, whom Jake had introduced to the two police officers on a date at a Ku Klux Klan meeting. Further, two Hardinton cops named Hank and Art, partners who slapped a DUI on Donna, were part of an operation that gambled on dog fights.

Sutherland stared at Garbuncle for a few seconds after he finished. "As an attorney, you must realize some of what you told me is circumstantial evidence. You've made the case for a motive in the loose tie rod, although a lot of that is conjecture. And the prints—the defense is going to argue that the letters aren't visible enough to show with certainty they spell Jacob Schmidt."

"It'll be my job to convince them. And I'll get a typewriter expert."

"You? You'll just be a witness. You sound like the prosecuting attorney."

"I'm going to volunteer to help the state attorney's office, pro bono."

"Pro bono?" Sutherland's thin voice rose an octave. "Why are you so gung ho about getting these guys? You that fond of the black guy?"

"I'm ..." Garbuncle's lips trembled. "I lost someone precious to me. And I like Alec."

Sutherland hesitated. "The whole thing sounds pretty iffy to me."

"You don't sound very excited about pursuing this case." Garbuncle wore a frown, and studied Sutherland with head lowered.

"No, no, that's not it. I just want to be sure that what we have is solid enough to win the case for us. What about the gasoline tank on your car? You have no proof that anybody disconnected it from its mooring. That expert's opinion won't cut it. In fact, we don't even know for sure the gas tank is what made the marks on the road and the shoulder. And since we don't know that, we can't be sure about what caused the explosion."

To Garbuncle, the investigator seemed to be fishing for reasons not to go forward with the prosecution.

"I think my persuasive powers will prevail."

"Well ..." The investigator bent forward, then leaned back in his swivel chair and looked up at the ceiling. "I'll get with the chief about this, and we'll see where we're going with it. I'll be in touch. My schedule is pretty full, so it may be a little while."

***

"Brad, what are you doing after work? Wanna meet at Johnny's?"

"Yeah, I can do that. I have to finish a story about a guy who got beat up when he told some jerk in a bar to lay off the smart-ass remarks to his girlfriend. The dipshit was some kind of sales manager, and apparently told the young gal he could help her sell her body and make big bucks. He'd drunk a lot, the bartender said. Hey, maybe I've got a client for you. The beat-up guy said he might sue the sales asshole. I can get there 6:30 or 7."

Garbuncle had downed a vodka tonic when Hitchens arrived. He ordered a Pabst and poured it into a glass. The attorney told his friend of the misgivings he harbored about investigator Bart Sutherland's attitude toward the case. "He seemed anything but enthusiastic."

"You think he might be reluctant to go after cops? They almost always get favored treatment from the state attorney's office and judges. It's hard to convict them of anything."

"That's exactly what I was thinking." Garbuncle paused, his jaw set, eyes riveted on the bar counter. "There may be more to it. I hope I'm not getting paranoid, but ..." He hesitated again.

"You think he might have an in with those cops?"

Garbuncle jerked his head to look at Hitchens. "We're on the same page. You're close, but I had somebody else in mind."

Hitchens stared at him, saying nothing, his forehead wrinkled.

Garbuncle peered left, then right, and said in a lowered voice, "Jake Schmidt."

"What makes you think so?"

"The way he reacted when I mentioned the name. I can read people well. He seemed almost startled."

"I suppose it's possible. Most law enforcement types have lived here for a long time—lots of them since they were born. Not very many Floridians grew up in Florida, or at least not in the same locale where they were born. So it seems like the natives often get to know each other. Especially the ones in business, 'cause they deal a lot with the public."

"Now you're thinking." Garbuncle smiled.

"I do a lot of that."

"I did grow up around here, so I know what you said is spot on. You've been here less than two decades, and you've picked up quite a bit."

"I ain't no slouch."

They clinked glasses.

"So what are you gonna do?" Hitchens asked.

"The first thing is pretty simple. I've got to research Bart Sutherland—find out if he grew up here, where he went to school, his family and relatives, everything I can learn about his background. It may be a wild goose chase, and my suspicions could be nothing but paranoia. But I've got to try."

"You'd better be careful he doesn't find out you're checking on him."

"Yeah. And after I dig up as much as possible, I probably need to keep tabs on him—play detective and tail him to see who he associates with."

"Sounds like a plan."

"I'm gonna need your help."

"I'm in. But the first thing you need to do is buy a reliable car, so you don't get stranded when you're running around getting the lowdown on this guy. 'Cause I won't be able to rescue you every time."

Chapter Nineteen

"You've lived here a long time, haven't you?" Garbuncle's secretary looked at him with a quizzical expression.

"Since I was three. Moved here from Georgia. Why?"

"Have you ever heard of a guy named Jake Schmidt? Or Bart Sutherland?"

She turned her head slowly. "Nooo, those names don't ring a bell."

"Okay, here's what I need. Get into your computer—you know I can hardly operate the thing. Do a search of Bart Sutherland. Do you know where to go for that?"

"Sure. Intelius.com."

"Great." He spelled the name for her. "Find out as much about him as you can. His background, family members, relatives, schooling—whatever comes up."

"Are you sure? There might be a fee. I'm not certain."

"Oh, yeah. Damn. Wait ... it's okay. I'll just bill the insurance."

"How soon do you need it?"

Garbuncle looked at his watch. "It's 9:30 now, and I've got a deposition at one. Should be back by 3. Is that enough time?"

"No problem."

"What did you learn?"

"Here." She handed Garbuncle two sheets of paper, stapled together, with information copied from the website and pasted.

"Wow. That's a lot of info." The attorney skimmed the pages as he walked to his desk and sat down. He read aloud: "Bart Sutherland. Six eighteen Endicott Lane, West Palm Beach. Age thirty-three. Investigator for State Attorney. Former officer West Palm Beach Police Department. Married to Jane, formerly Stoddard. Real estate agent. One child, Samantha, age seven."

Garbuncle continued reading, mumbling the words. "Oh Lord almighty," he almost shouted.

The secretary glanced over her shoulder at him from the computer. "Find something?"

"I sure did."

She waited. He didn't go any further, and she turned her back to the computer.

Garbuncle sat with his arms in his lap, staring at the blank screen of his own computer, which he used only as a word processor. He felt his face tighten.

After several minutes, he picked up the phone and dialed. "Hey Brad, I found out something important. Okay, it turns out ... let me tell you later. I haven't got time to talk. It's a big development. I need you to meet me at 4:30 at the state attorney's office. Yeah, that's before your quitting time, but oh geez, man, I really need ya. Yeah, 4:45 will prob'ly work. But any later might be too late. See you there. Park in the city parking garage."

He dialed again, and let it ring over and over. "Damn, he's not there. What the hell am I ... Oh, Earl, I almost gave up. Huh? I understand. That's called crappus interruptus. Never mind; it's Latin. Look, I need your help. I know, I know. What is it, Thursday? I swear on my mother's grave I'll have that mattress for you this weekend. Yes, I know I promised it last weekend. But I couldn't find what I wanted. I want to get a good one. All right, when do you go to your Walmart job? Not till 10? Great. I'm coming by your apartment at 4 to pick you up. That's a half-hour from now. Okay, see ya."

Garbuncle took a key from the middle desk drawer and unlocked the drawer on the bottom right. He withdrew his cellphone, a cheap affair that he used only for emergencies, and put it in the pocket of his suit coat.

"Oh shit," he mumbled. "That thing isn't charged." He grabbed the charging cable and stuffed it in his coat pocket.

"I'll be gone the rest of the day," he told the secretary while hustling out the door. He hopped in the rental car, inserted the cellphone charging cable into the dashboard outlet, and headed for Earl's apartment. The door was open, and Earl was tucking a soiled white T-shirt under his belt. He wore scruffy work shoes.

"Where we goin'? Do I need to change clothes?"

"Well, maybe ... no, this is perfect. We're headed to the state attorney's office, and my friend Brad is meeting us. Him and me are wearing coats and ties, and you'll look like a redneck client."

"Hey, I ain't no redneck. I don't think I like that."

"Oh, sorry. I didn't mean to insult you."

Garbuncle saw that Earl looked hurt, but the apartment tenant didn't reply.

"Have you got a baseball cap?"

Earl retreated to the closet and came out wearing a Budweiser cap.

"Perfect. It's a little too big, and covers part of your face."

"You telling me I'm ugly?"

Garbuncle broke into a broad grin. "No uglier'n me."

"Hell, I hope not."

"There's a certain guy, if he sees you, I don't want him to remember what you look like. You've got one of those brand-new cellphones that lets you record conversations, right? Like the one I bought for you to record the cops at the dog fight. You showed it to me once."

"Yeah."

"You pretty good with it?"

"Hell yes. I use it all the time." Earl sauntered over to his scarred, pine chest of drawers, and returned with the phone. "I charged it just last night. But why do you want it? You already got one."

"I don't want to take any chance of recording over or something like that. These recordings are gonna be super important. If we can pull this next one off, that is. You got any tape?"

"You mean like scotch tape?"

"Any kind."

"I got masking tape and duct tape."

"Great. Let's take the masking tape."

Earl went to a closet and came back with a roll of the cream-colored tape. "I don't know what you got in mind, but duct tape holds better."

"Yeah, but it's too hard to tear."

They drove to downtown West Palm Beach, parked, and entered the stately courthouse through a glass door set back of a row of square columns. They emptied their pockets onto the conveyor belt, and walked through the metal detector. Garbuncle and Earl put their articles back into their pockets. A smattering of people milled about the lobby. Garbuncle took Earl to a wooden bench back, and to the right, of the heavy wood office doors of the state attorney's office. Ten minutes later, Hitchens hurried in, and spotted the pair.

"Am I late?"

"It's okay."

"This better be good. I told the city editor I had to meet somebody for an interview."

"No problem. I'm waiting for an investigator named Bart Sutherland to come out of the office. He might see me, and that's okay. He'll just think Earl is a client and you're maybe another attorney. I want you both to get a good look at him, so you'll remember. But if he looks at us, don't look back. I don't want him to remember you."

"Huh?" said Earl. "You gonna get me into another spy deal?"

"Yeah, I think so."

"Oh, man ..."

"You're good at it, Earl. With a little more practice, you might be able to get a job doing this. Here's the situation: I found out Sutherland is a brother-in-law of Jake Schmidt. Sutherland's wife, Jane, and Schmidt are half-siblings. Schmidt is quite a bit older. His dad married Jane's mother, who was a lot younger. I now know why Sutherland tensed up when I mentioned him."

"Whoa. What the hell you talkin' about?" Earl said.

"All right, I'll fill you in. Sutherland is the investigator assigned to look into the two car accidents—which weren't accidents." Garbuncle, sitting between Hitchens and Earl, looked at his tenant. "I never told you about this before. Those two happenings were intended to keep me from defending Alec Monceau, the guy who those two cops beat up."

"Aw man, I ain't gonna help you get that nig… that colored guy outa trouble."

"How's your back feeling lately, Earl?" Garbuncle looked straight ahead with a deadpan expression.

"Look ... Okay, okay, dammit, what do I hafta do?"

"I told Sutherland late yesterday afternoon that I dug up this incriminating information about Jake Schmidt. He'll likely try to warn him as soon as possible. Schmidt hangs out in bars. I've got a hunch they'll meet at some joint after work. We're going to follow Sutherland."

Garbuncle explained his plan to Earl and Hitchens.

"What?" Hitchens retorted with a look of disdain. "Oh come on. That's a cockamamie idea. We could really bungle this."

"Yeah, we could. You got a better idea?"

Hitchens shrugged.

"Man, sounds like a wild goose chase to me," said Earl.

"It might be," said Garbuncle. "But it won't hurt to try."

"Well, I suppose it's a little like gambling on stock market options," said Hitchens. "If we lose, it won't be a lot, but we could win big."

"I don't like that analogy," said Garbuncle. "You trade options, and you keep losing. Uh-oh. Here he comes. Pull that cap down, Earl. Both of you look away, like you're talking to me, but watch him out of the corner of your eye."

Sutherland emerged, carrying a briefcase. He looked straight ahead, then glanced to his left in the direction of the trio of men, but turned back and headed for the doors at a brisk pace.

"Whew, that was close," said Garbuncle. "It didn't look like he saw me. Now you two follow him—not too close; don't want him to get suspicious. He's prob'ly parked in the garage. I'll follow farther back, so he won't see me. When he drives out of the garage, Brad, you two follow him in your car. I'll try to catch up. If I can't find y'all, I'll call you on your cellphone. I hope you've got it charged up. Mine's charging."

"Yeah, it's charged," Hitchens said. "Although I don't use it much, just like you."

"All right, let's move."

Hitchens and Earl saw Sutherland walking fast toward the parking garage a couple of blocks south. "We'd better hurry up," said Hitchens. "We're going to lose him."

They caught up to their prey, and saw him through a small window in the door, standing in front of the elevator. "Wait here," Hitchens said to Earl. "When he boards the elevator, go to the ticket machine and feed it." Hitchens handed him two dollars. "I'm going to go through the car entrance and run up to the second floor, where I'm parked. If the elevator keeps going, I'll run to the third floor. Hopefully he'll get off by then or I'm going to run out of breath. I'll watch him leave and jump in my car. Stand back of the ramp, next to the ticket machine, so he doesn't see you when he comes down, and keep your cap low."

Hitchens exercised regularly and was in good shape. He was puffing only a little when he saw the elevator go past on the second floor. He resumed running up the ramp, turned the corner, and continued up the next ramp, stopping below the top to look. Breathing hard, he saw Sutherland, with the elevator door closing behind him. Hitchens watched as the investigator hustled to a red Camry, a few years old.

Hitchens raced back down to the second floor and jumped into his Mazda. He waited as Sutherland's car drove down the ramp, and took off. Sutherland was feeding the exit pay machine. Hitchens opened the passenger door for Earl, and they headed for the exit as the Camry moved onto Dixie Highway. Earl looked left, and saw Garbuncle walking fast around the corner toward the garage entrance.

"He's not going to find us," Earl said.

"Nope," said Hitchens, "not unless he's prepaid and can drive out in a hurry. I think it's cheaper to prepay. Oh, yeah, he prepaid. But he drives awfully slow, even when he's in a hurry. He might have to call us."

It was rush hour, and the street was jammed with vehicles. "Good thing Sutherland's car is red—easier to see," said Hitchens. He spotted it two stoplights ahead, and had to stop for a red light.

"Damn, I think we're going to lose him," he said. Two lights farther, the Camry was just pulling from a stop at a light.

"There he is," Earl yelled. "We're okay."

They reached the southern edge of the downtown, and traffic moved at a steady pace for more than a mile.

"He's turning in to that bar, almost to Belvedere," Earl said. "I know the place. The Dixiecrat. A lot o' red… it's a watering hole for Southern good ol' boys."

"Well, I'll be damned. Looks like Ham might have called it right. Is it a popular spot?"

"Not so much. Average-sized crowd, I'd say. Not too many guys every time I've been there. 'Course, it mighta just looked that way 'cause the place is pretty big."

"That might be why Sutherland chose it. If he's meeting Schmidt, they need some privacy when they talk. Tell you what we're gonna do. I'll drop you off out front and go park in ... Woops, that must be Ham calling."

Hitchens pulled his cellphone out of his pocket. "Hello. Where are you? Don't worry about it, for cryin' out loud. Don't you know there's no law in Florida against talking on a cellphone while driving? Hell, there isn't even a law against texting. Just keep driving south on Dixie. We're at the Dixiecrat, just before Belvedere, right side. We're parked in the lot in back, waiting for you."

Earl went out to the sidewalk in front, and saw a blue Ford subcompact approaching. He stared, saw it was his landlord, and waved. Garbuncle drove to the back.

The three converged in the parking lot. "Here's what we do," said Garbuncle. "You two walk in and look around, and I'll stand just outside the door. Hopefully, he chose a table a ways away from the entrance. If you spot him, signal to me, and grab a table close to the entrance. I'll go back to the car and wait, 'cause I have to make sure he doesn't see me."

Earl pulled the heavy back door open, and he and Hitchens entered. They gazed across the room. Hitchens turned toward the open door with his right thumb up. Garbuncle stood to the right of the door. Hitchens let it swing shut, and walked to a table on the right, near the corner. Earl followed.

"Don't stare, but that's him," Hitchens said. "At that table in the center of the room. The guy in the suit. His tie is loosened. He's facing us—so he can see who comes in the door. We were blocking his view of Ham. Nobody sitting near him. He's by himself, so must be waiting for somebody, or he'd sit at the bar. He's probably waiting for Jake Schmidt."

The door opened, and a good-looking man with a thick mop of hair and a thin mustache entered. He hesitated, then walked toward Sutherland and sat.

"That's probably our man," said Hitchens. A young waitress went to the two, and Hitchens watched them order. She walked to the barmaid, spoke briefly, then headed toward Earl and Hitchens. They ordered—a Budweiser for Earl, cabernet for Hitchens.

The two looked away from the table with Sutherland and Schmidt so they wouldn't suspect anything, but Hitchens glanced at them when the waitress delivered their order: two draft beers. Earl took the cellphone and masking tape out of his pant pocket. With his broad back turned at an angle to block the view of what he was doing, Earl tore two long strips of tape off, and stuck them to both ends of the cellphone. He turned the recorder on, then reached under the table and pressed the tape against it to hold the phone in place.

Sutherland and Schmidt were taking swigs of beer.

"Ready?" said Hitchens.

"Yup. Here goes."

Earl rose and walked in the direction of the pair, peering up at the television behind the bar on his left. He reached the table and slammed against it. The glasses toppled over, beer sloshing over the table and onto the shirts and trousers of Schmidt and Sutherland. Schmidt, who was facing the wall, whirled and rose part way out of his chair. When he saw Earl, who was half a foot taller and much bulkier, he sat back down.

"Man, you need to look where you're going," said Sutherland, rising and holding his arms outward. "Look at us. We're soaked."

Schmidt got out of his chair and took a napkin to his pants.

"Aw geez, I'm awful sorry," said Earl. "Damn, that was clumsy of me. I was lookin' at the sports report on TV. Wow, this is a mess." He placed his arm around Sutherland's shoulders and said, "Come on, you guys go sit at me and my buddy's table. We were gonna go to the bar, anyway."

"No, we'll just—"

"I insist," said Earl. He nudged him toward the table near the front, and Schmidt followed.

"What the hell did you do?" Hitchens said, rising. He sounded and looked angry.

"I know, I know. I wasn't watchin' where I was goin'."

"You sure as hell weren't. Look what you did to these guys. Here, gentlemen, sit down. Let me get you each a beer. What were you drinking?"

"Miller regular—both of us. But that's all right. We'll order from the waitress."

"No, no, I won't hear it," said Hitchens. "Sit down, and we'll be right over with the beers."

Sutherland and Schmidt sat, and Hitchens and Earl went to the bar to order. Earl returned with the beers. "I feel real awful," he said.

"Aw, just forget it," Sutherland said.

Back at the bar, Earl said to Hitchens in a lowered voice, "Damned if it ain't workin'. So far."

"Yeah. I hope they don't stay forever. I'm not sure how long that masking tape will hold."

They pretended interest in the sports highlights flashing on the TV. Now and then, Earl pumped his fist in the air for authenticity. He looked toward the door when someone entered, and glanced at the men's table.

"Uh-oh. Don't look, but the phone has come loose at one end. It's dangling. The tape didn't hold. Holy shit. What if the phone comes loose and falls to the floor? They'll hear it?"

"Then the game is up. The whole plan is exposed. There's nothing we can do. We'll just have to hope and pray."

"I told Ham I wasn't sure that masking tape would stay stuck, but he wouldn't listen."

They sipped their beer and wine. Hitchens came down from his stool and bent over as if to tie his shoe. Rising back up, he looked at the table, and climbed onto the stool.

"I think we're in trouble," he said, looking at the TV. "The strip at the other end is coming loose. It won't hold long. We've got to think of something."

"We could ask to join 'em, and talk loud so they won't hear if the thing drops."

"Yeah, I think ..."

Earl glanced in their direction. "Wait. They're gettin' up to leave." He looked back to the TV.

Out of the corner of his eye, Hitchens saw them walk out the door. "Come on, let's go back to the table."

They sat, and looked at each other as a clattering sound erupted. Hitchens glanced around to see if anybody was looking, and bent under the table. He picked the phone off the floor, and felt under the tabletop.

"Some kind of oil. Somebody must have rubbed a greasy hand there. Didn't you feel it when you stuck the thing on?"

"I had to hurry. I didn't feel it."

They waited a couple of minutes and exited. Garbuncle was headed toward them. "I saw them get in their car and leave," he said.

Hitchens related the scare they had in the bar, and the three drove to Garbuncle's office.

Hitchens and Earl pulled up chairs from the waiting area and circled the attorney's desk.

"I can't believe you guys pulled that off," Garbuncle said, breaking into an admiring smile.

"This guy," Hitchens said, gesturing at Earl, "deserves an Oscar. That performance was a tour de force."

"Think I oughta move to Hollywood?" Earl deadpanned.

"Nope," said Garbuncle. "We may need you again."

"That's what I was afraid of. I ain't so sure I wanna do somethin' like this again. That'd be pushin' my luck."

Earl turned on the cellphone recorder.

"Stupid son-of-a-bitch ..." Earl paused the recorder.

"That's Sutherland," said Garbuncle.

Earl started the recorder again. "If we didn't have more important business, I'd have told that big clumsy clod we were sending him a laundry bill. Okay, so here's why I called you here. I'm not gonna mince words, 'cause this is serious, and your ass is grass if we don't take some kind of action. This attorney, Hiram

Garbuncle, is onto you. As you obviously know, he's the attorney for the black guy who was beat up by those two cops who are friends of yours, and he's found out you caused the accident with his girlfriend. He's sure you tried to bump him off, too."

The three men leaned in closer to hear over the hum of the recorder rolling.

"How'd you find all this out?"

"He laid all the cards on the table yesterday in my office. He's going after you."

"Shit. What am I gonna do?"

Several seconds of silence.

"Jane thinks the world of you. You were her big brother when she was a little girl. You defended her, got after the parents of kids who were mean to her at school, helped her with her school work. And you know how I love Jane. I could get into deep trouble, but ..." Silence. "I'm going to see if I can get you out of this."

"What can you do?"

"That's what I asked myself. I thought about it all last night. Couldn't sleep. I could only come up with one solution."

"What've you got in mind?"

Another break in the conversation.

"We've got to get that attorney off this case."

Garbuncle and Hitchens stared at each other. Earl looked at the floor.

"How the hell are we gonna do that?"

"I think we could've intimidated him if his girlfriend—Donna Malone, the one in the car crash—if she'd lived. Now, it looks to me like he's throwing caution to the winds. He's a man on a mission. There's no stopping him—unless ..."

Another moment of silence.

Schmidt's voice: "I think I know where you're going with this. Are you sure you want to get involved? If we're found out, it'll be the end of your career, of course, but a whole lot worse."

"I've gotta do it for my sis. If it was just for you ..."

"Oh, thanks a lot, buddy." They both laughed.

Schmidt: "What are we gonna do?"

"I don't know. I haven't thought that far yet. I'll try to come up with something. You need to give it a go yourself."

"Give me a call at the office if an idea hits you. I'll buzz you if I come up with a plan."

"Okay."

"Let's go."

They heard what sounded like chairs scraping the floor. The recorder rolled on for a half minute, and Garbuncle turned it off.

Hitchens and Earl looked at Garbuncle. "What're you gonna do?" Earl asked. "They might be plannin' to bump you off."

"You wanna be my bodyguard? I'll get you a top-of-the-line mattress." A grim smile.

"Oh wow. Thanks, but no thanks."

"You better be constantly looking over your shoulder," said Hitchens. "Maybe you oughta get your condo management to let you park your car in an area that's busy and well-lighted."

"Good ideas. And here's a better one." Garbuncle opened the middle drawer in his desk, and pulled out a .38-caliber Smith & Wesson Special Revolver.

Hitchens and Earl straightened. "Where the hell did you get that?" said Hitchens.

"I had a client who scared the shit out of me once. He was trying to beat a rap for armed robbery of a convenience store. He disagreed with me on my strategy, and I could tell he was about ready to explode. I told him we'd do it his way. Then I went to a gun show and got this baby. I always keep it loaded in my desk. I also got a concealed weapon license. I never told you that."

"Yeah, that's news to me," said Hitchens. "Come to think of it, you did tell me you used to do some hunting in your younger days. And you did two years in the Army, right? So I guess you know how to handle a gun."

"But my personal safety isn't the most complicated thing I'm up against," Garbuncle said. "How the hell am I going to prosecute these people? Where can I go with this information? I'm not about to report it to the state attorney. There's no way I can tell whether the people in that office can be trusted."

Nobody said anything. Hitchens looked intensely into space. "Damned if I know what we can do. You're in a pickle, Ham."

"Yeah, and I'm in a jam, too. Neither one goes well with ham." Garbuncle laughed in a fiendish way. His face sobered. "And I'm hamburger if these guys get me cornered."

"Pickles and hamburger go great together," Hitchens said, his lips twisting into a sardonic smile.

Earl roared with laughter.

"Let's sleep on it," said Garbuncle. "We'd better get going. Don't want to be out too late. It's getting toward dusk, and we don't know if Schmidt or Sutherland are spying on us. I'm sure they're aware of where my office is."

***

Earl walked with Garbuncle to his rental car at a metered space on the street, near his office.

"Keep a watch out for anything that might look suspicious," Garbuncle said.

They drove south down Dixie Highway out of downtown West Palm Beach. At Belvedere Road, Garbuncle turned right. Earl looked through the mirror on the passenger side. A half-block farther, Earl saw a black pickup truck also turn. He'd noticed it before, but there was nothing to cause suspicion. They reached Interstate 95 and entered the south ramp. The pickup followed from a short distance.

"Speed up," Earl said.

"What's your hurry? I don't want to get a ticket."

"Just speed up. I've got a reason."

Garbuncle tromped on the accelerator and moved onto I-95. Earl saw the pickup speed up, too.

"Okay, stay in the right lane and slow down."

"What the hell—?"

"Just do it."

Garbuncle slowed, and Earl looked in the mirror. He saw the pickup, in the same lane, slow rather than overtake their car.

"There's a pickup behind us that's been following us from downtown," said Earl. "Might be nothing, but he sped up when you did, and slowed down."

"That's not good," said Garbuncle. "Maybe I should exit at Forest Hill, and see if he exits too."

"Good idea."

"You're full of good ideas."

"Yeah, and I think even better when I sleep good."

"Okay, I can take a hint. You'll get a quality mattress."

"My back feels better already."

"After I exit, I'll keep in the outside lane of Forest Hill and drive slow. He'll have to pass on the inside lane 'stead o' followin' us, 'cause otherwise he'll know we're onto him. When he passes, look at his door and see if his business name is on it."

Garbuncle pulled a small notebook and pen from his shirt pocket, and handed them to Earl. "See if you can get his license."

They exited, and the truck followed, then moved into the empty right lane and hurried past. Earl jotted fast. "I got all but the last letter. Kind o' hard to read. The sun's gone down."

"A C—or an O, but I'm pretty sure it was a C," said Garbuncle.

"Okay, then we got it. Nothin' on the door, but there was somethin' on it before. It's been painted over in gray."

"I know. I got a glance. That's suspicious right there."

"Yeah. Real fishy. Quick, turn left here on Lake."

Garbuncle swung the wheel. "What was that for?"

"So he can't keep track of us. He ain't so far ahead that he can't see us in the rearview mirror."

"That mattress keeps getting firmer," said Garbuncle.

Garbuncle dropped Earl off at the apartment he rented from the attorney, who drove to his own. Floodlights rendered the area around the clubhouse and pool almost as bright as a baseball park during a night game. Garbuncle took a guest spot, and began trudging to his building a fair distance away. The narrow roads in the complex weren't well-lighted, but he figured walking them would be less risky than getting in his car in the morning if it were parked overnight in his regular, darkened spot, where someone could tamper with it with little likelihood of being noticed. Nonetheless, he took the .38 out of his inner suit-coat pocket and slid it into his pant pocket, keeping his grip on the handle.

He was going to be ready.

CHAPTER TWENTY

The bedroom in Garbuncle's first-floor condo apartment looked out onto a lawn that had a few brown, dead patches, but was otherwise well-kept. It divided his building from another parallel with it. In the center of the lawn was a small pond with a fountain in the center. It gushed water with a soft hissing sound during the day, mitigating ambient noise. But it didn't run at night, and at every unidentifiable sound—a loose shutter scraping in the breeze, a lizard scurrying in the patio—Garbuncle stiffened as he lay on his back in his queen-sized bed. His arm darted reflexively under the adjacent pillow, where he had tucked his gun.

Ideas about how to proceed with the Alec Monceau case flitted through his mind like minnows in a country creek. It was obvious he couldn't go to the state attorney's office with his new information. He'd have to present it in the discovery process for a new trial.

Sleep came in fits and starts, the occasional nocturnal sounds jerking him awake. In the morning, he readied for his day at the office. His right hand gripping the pistol on the left, inside pocket of his suit coat, he flung the door open and stood. Peering left down the hall, then right, he closed the door behind him, locked it, and headed for his car. It was daylight saving time, and the sun was low in the east, the cool air bracing to his sleep-deprived brain. He walked around the car, looking for anything untoward, and returned to the driver's side. Placing a handkerchief on the asphalt, he knelt to his knees and checked underneath. Nothing suspicious.

At the office, the attorney checked with his secretary, who had nothing on his calendar for the day. He pulled out the *Auto Trader* ad he'd placed in a desk drawer over a pint-sized flask of vodka. After taking two swigs, he walked to his rental car, which he'd parked at a meter. In the parking garage, someone could tamper with it. He drove to Stan's Sav-A-Lot Autos on Military Trail.

He sauntered through the lot, and found the car in the ad: a beige, 1999 Mercury Marquis. As he peered through a window, a salesman arrived.

"This one's a beauty," the tall, portly man boomed.

"Hello there," Garbuncle greeted.

"Only eighty-three-thousand miles in nine years on the road—a little over nine thousand a year. Owner kept it in great shape."

The salesman unlocked the driver-side door, and Garbuncle looked inside. He asked to look under the hood, and inspected the frame. Then he ran his fingers along the rubber molding surrounding the windshield, and closely checked the gap between each front door and the fenders. He pulled a handkerchief from a rear pants pocket, laid it on the asphalt, and stooped down to look underneath.

He rose, and brushed his hands together. "This car's been in an accident. It's been repainted, and there are several other signs."

The salesman differed with him, and he didn't respond.

"Let's go for a spin," he said.

Except for a slight vibration in the steering wheel, Garbuncle found nothing wrong. He asked the price, which the man quoted as nine thousand dollars. Garbuncle pulled the ad from his pocket, pointed to the eight thousand listing, and offered five thousand. They haggled, and Garbuncle walked away, getting twenty feet before the salesman called him back and agreed to his last offer of six thousand dollars.

***

The attorney noticed that his secretary was busy on the computer, and pulled his flask out of the drawer. He took a long gulp, replaced the now two-thirds-empty bottle in the drawer, and dialed the newspaper office.

"I just stuck it to those bastards trying to do me in."

"What are you talking about?" Brad Hitchens asked.

"I just bought a car, and they don't know what it is. I'm sure they've got the license of the Ford Focus. I threw them off my trail."

"Not necessarily, unless it's a different color. If it's a similar looking car, they still could spot you."

"No way. It's beige, for one thing, and for another, it looks totally different."

"What kind is it?"

"Mercury Marquis. Nineteen-ninety-nine."

"Oh no, not again!" Garbuncle pulled the phone from his ear. "Damn, I just woke up the newsroom. It's a slow day."

"I got a great deal."

"Yeah. Another gas guzzling behemoth that'll break down all the time, just like your other one. I can't believe you would repeat that mistake. Why the hell do you need such a big clunker? You don't need to tell me. You like the feeling of power. Ham, you're always spouting that psychobabble, so I'm going to throw some back at you. You've got a problem with your size." In a lower voice, "I don't mean your dick, but maybe that's part of it."

The vodka was taking effect, and Garbuncle said, "Thass got nothin' ta do with it. This car is safer'n those little bugs. I need a big vee-hicle in case those guys try to ram me with the pickup."

"Well, yeah, I guess you've got a point there."

"Whass more, I gotta have a big car to haul a new mattress for my tenant."

"All right, all right. What's next?"

"I wass thinkin' 'boutit all night. I've gotta get ready for the new trial. I hafta let Seward know the evidence I'm goin' to present at the trial, so I'll lay out to the judge what we found out."

"Don't you think you ought to take the evidence to the state attorney, so they can investigate?"

"I don't trust those guys. And b'sides, they prosecuted my client, and that case is the reason for what's been happenin' to me. It'd be like tryin' to get 'em to work contrary to their own interests. They'd be admittin' they were wrong. What happened to me is all part'v this here case."

"Yeah, I see what you're saying—that is, slurring."

CHAPTER TWENTY-ONE

"I need that mattress. Now."

Garbuncle heard anger in his tenant Earl's voice.

"No need to be upset, Earl." The attorney held the phone two inches from his ear. "Remember I told you I was planning to get you one this weekend. Are you free Sunday, or are you watching out for shoplifters at Walmart?"

"I've got Sunday off. Let's do it."

Garbuncle was hoping his tenant had to work, and buying the mattress could be delayed some more.

"So ... you're sure you'll be able to go with me?"

"Hell yes. Why not? Let's get it done finally—so I can get some good sleep."

"Okay, I'll look at the ads in the *Palm Beach Hawk* Sunday, and we'll go shopping. I've got a little left over from the insurance check for the car, and I'm gonna get you a quality mattress. Firm."

"I'm not holding my breath."

Full-page color ads by two mattress stores bore screaming headlines about their limited-time sales. "Top Quality Brands! Prices Slashed! Huge Savings! Sunday and Monday Only. Don't miss out!"

Earl pulled into a guest parking space at Garbuncle's condo building. They climbed into the low-slung Mercury and headed to Sleep Tight in a strip mall on west Okeechobee Boulevard in West Palm Beach. Garbuncle estimated the showroom was the size of a baseball diamond, with the beds arranged similarly in clean, geometric patterns. They strolled among them, noting the prices.

Earl flopped down on a light-blue one that struck his fancy.

"Hey, this feels real good. I could sleep like a slug on this baby."

Garbuncle glanced at the price sign at the foot of the mattress. "I'm not sure slugs sleep, but if they do, they don't spend $795 for the pleasure. Let's keep walking."

"That ain't so bad. I don't want no cheapo, now."

The landlord stopped at an off-white model with a price tag that read: "Close-out. $395. Was $595."

"Now this is more like it," he said, and sprawled out on it. "By golly, this one's a winner. Try it out."

"You want to get up first? No offense, but I got no hankering to get in bed with a lawyer."

A weary smile crossed Garbuncle's face as he pulled himself off the mattress.

Earl lay on his back and stared at the ceiling for several seconds. He dug his heels in and bounced lightly, then turned onto his ample belly, arms splayed.

"Whata ya think?"

Earl didn't reply. He turned onto his left side, legs almost straight, then curled into the fetal position.

"Not bad."

A salesman ambled up, and Earl asked if he could provide a pillow.

"Of course, sure, no problem," the man said, and hustled to another bed for the head support.

Earl propped his head on it and closed his eyes. "G'night, gentlemen."

"I think they charge rent for sleeping on the premises," Garbuncle quipped.

The nondescript salesman laughed. "Take your time."

"Don't encourage him."

The salesman chuckled with his head down, exposing his pate under thin, combed-back hair. Garbuncle detected nervousness.

"Come on, you big lout. We've got things to do. And so does this man."

"No rush."

But Garbuncle could tell the salesman was uncomfortable.

"Okay," Earl said, climbing off the bed. "Let's get it."

"Huh? I thought you didn't want to sleep with me. I'll get it, and you sleep on it."

The salesman wore a smile that Garbuncle thought was painful.

"Are you happy with it?" Garbuncle asked. Earl heard in the condescending tone a father addressing his child.

Garbuncle turned to the salesman. "We can't return it. Right?"

"That's correct. I'm afraid mattresses are not returnable—unless, of course, there's a defect. Nobody wants to buy a mattress somebody has slept on."

"I'm good to go," Earl confirmed.

"Just come with me, and we'll get squared away," the salesman said. He pulled a sales sheet out of a basket on his desk, and began writing. "Oh." He peered up from glasses lowered on his nose. "The delivery charge is sixty dollars."

"You can just omit that," Garbuncle said. "We'll be transporting it ourselves."

"Sure. Whatever you want to do. When will you be coming for it?"

"We're taking it now."

"Huh?" said Earl, looking bemused.

The salesman stared at Garbuncle with a quizzical expression.

"I've got some rope in the trunk. We'll just tie it on the roof. It's a big car. Strong enough to hold it."

"Well," the salesman said, rubbing his chin, "occasionally somebody will tie a single-sized mattress to the car. But I'm not sure ... Do you think a queen-size will work?"

"Yup. I've done it before."

"What about the box spring? Do you think maybe you better make two trips?"

"Nah. That Mercury will hold both of them just fine."

"Okay then." The salesman led the two men to a storage area in the back, and located the two bed pieces.

Garbuncle gripped one end of the box spring, and Earl the other end. The salesman rushed up to hold the door open. Earl walked backward as they carried it outside to the driver's side.

"Stand back," Earl said. He hoisted it to the roof, and let it flop into position.

"You lifted that like one of those rasslers you used to throw onto the mat," Garbuncle said. He noticed Earl's pleased look.

"Yeah ... 'cept I didn't let 'em down so easy. The roof woulda caved in if I'da manhandled that thing like one of my victims."

Garbuncle decided he never wanted to arouse his tenant's anger.

They went back inside the store and carried the mattress out, and Earl tossed it atop the box spring. Garbuncle took a spool of yellow nylon cord out of the trunk and opened the windows a few inches. He flung one end through the driver's side window to the other side, where Earl pulled it through the window and heaved it over the roof to Garbuncle. Earl came around and tied a slip knot.

"Learned that from my uncle who was in the Navy," he said. Garbuncle divined the pride in his face.

They repeated the procedure in the rear interior, and closed the back and front windows up to the cord.

Garbuncle pulled at a crawling pace out of the strip mall onto busy Okeechobee. He sped up to beat the traffic and make it to the other side for a U-turn. They drove east toward Military Trail, where Garbuncle stopped for a red light and waited for vehicles zooming south. At the same time, a black pickup left the mall and followed the same path.

Garbuncle turned onto Military and kept to the inside lane. The traffic was moving fast, and a beat-up old car with two young men in worker's attire honked. The attorney felt the pressure to drive faster, and wind built up in the wedge between the windshield and the load on top, lifting it.

"Holy shit," Earl shouted. "The damn thing's gonna blow off."

"I'll pull onto this side road coming up." The dilapidated car behind now was close to the Mercury's bumper. Garbuncle could see in the rear-view mirror that the two men had tattooed arms jutting out the windows with their middle fingers up. Garbuncle turned onto the road at a faster speed than he wanted to, and the load on top swung at an angle. He slowed, looking for a spot to pull over and stop. Junky cars and pickups littered the shoulder in front of shabby houses, and mail boxes stood just off the road.

"Here's a space," he said after driving a quarter-mile. They climbed out of the car, and saw that the rope had slackened, allowing the bed to twist askew. They stared at their cargo, assessing how to solve the problem.

"I'm afraid we're going to lose them," Garbuncle said. "We've got quite a ways to go, and I can't drive too slow and hold up traffic, or somebody will call the police."

"Yeah. This was a dumb idea. I thought you said you did this before."

"I did once, but only had to drive a short distance."

"Man, you are some cheap son-of-a-bitch. All this trouble just to save sixty bucks. You're tighter'n that place we just came from."

"Huh?"

"Sleep Tight. You don't just sleep tight; you live and breathe tight. And drink till you're tight."

Garbuncle ignored the insults. He knew they were true, and needed his tenant now more than ever.

"There's only one way to solve this, and you're not gonna like it," the landlord said.

"What'ya got in mind?"

"You'll have to ride on top of the mattress."

"What? Are you fuckin' crazy?"

A dog several houses up the road trotted to the edge of its driveway and barked in the pair's direction.

"I ain't goin' up there. No way."

Garbuncle held his arms out, palms up, a resigned look on his face. "Well, okay then," he said in a helpless tone. "The spring and mattress probably will blow off, and if that happens, the box spring won't be in any condition to hold a mattress—which likely will be torn up, anyway. I can't afford to buy you a new bed."

Earl stared at him. "Son-of-a-bitch," he muttered, and began untying the rope on the front. He slid it between the box spring and the mattress, and began tying it on the other side.

"What are you doing?"

"It'll hold better if we tie the spring and mattress separate."

"We can't do that. The rope is only eight yards long."

"You're shitting me. You mean you didn't buy enough rope?"

"It only came in twenty-four-foot and forty-eight-foot lengths. I figured twenty-four would be enough."

Earl threw up his hands, dropped them, and stared at the ground. "I got an idea. You ride on top, and I'll drive."

"Huh? I'm not heavy enough. It won't do much good. I'm only 155 pounds. You're about ... what, two-sixty?"

Earl gazed up the street, then turned to look behind him. He spotted a tree limb on the shoulder of the road, two houses away. Its leaves were turning brown, and he surmised it had been placed there for the trash haulers to remove. He was so intent on looking for a heavy object that he didn't notice the vehicle parked up the road, near the corner with Military Trail.

"Aha," he shouted. The dog in the other direction barked again, this time louder.

"Keep it down, will ya?" said Garbuncle. "That dog's awfully big. I don't want him coming after us."

Earl walked back to the tree limb, and began dragging it to the car.

"What the hell are you doing?"

Earl dropped the limb behind the car. "The weight of this limb and you together will be heavy enough to hold the load in place."

"You want me to ride up there with a hundred-pound tree limb on top of me? I'll be crushed. You'll have to find a new landlord, 'cause I'll be dead."

"Naw. You ain't thinkin'. You can lay on top of the limb."

"You're right. I didn't think of that—because it's the stupidest idea I ever heard of. My body would be banged up worse with me on top of the limb than on the bottom. Those twigs up and down the branch would stick me like a pitchfork."

"Hey, I've got an idea."

"You're full of ideas. And full of something else," Garbuncle said.

"Easter ain't too far away," Earl said. "We can celebrate the holiday by planting the limb in the courtyard of my condo complex, with you tied to it." Earl mimed the image of Garbuncle tied to the tree with his arms out.

"Very funny. Look, we've got to get going. The forecast called for rain late afternoon, and we might not make it to the condo in time. You'll just have to ride on top."

Earl looked sour as the big man pulled the rope from between the spring and mattress, but Garbuncle didn't respond. Earl repositioned the load, and climbed onto the car's trunk. Squatting like a rassler ready to grab his opponent, he leaped onto the mattress and rolled onto his back.

Garbuncle poked his head inside the car and inspected the roof. He withdrew.

"Man, you just about went through the roof. It looks okay. We're lucky."

"How in the name of Lucifer was I s'posed to get up here? You forgot to buy me some wings."

Garbuncle threw the loose end of the rope over the top and went around to the passenger side. He pulled hard on the rope.

"Holy Moses," Earl yelled.

The dog barked with a sound that Garbuncle detected as vicious. He turned to see the animal leave its owner's yard and trot a short distance up the road toward the hapless pair before stopping.

"What are you tryin' to do, strangle me? Loosen up and let me get that damned thing off my neck so I can stretch it over my chest."

Garbuncle released his hold on the rope. "Tell me when you're ready."

Earl pulled the rope down to his chest. "Okay, tighten it."

Garbuncle secured the rope and came around to the driver's side. He stood back and appraised the cargo. "Damn, you look all primed and ready for a pig roast."

"Screw you, Ham. Let's get this show on the road."

Garbuncle pulled the car onto the road at a snail's pace because the shoulder was uneven, and slowly accelerated. In the rear-view mirror, he could see through the part of the rear window not covered by the bed hanging over. A dark vehicle was approaching from behind. "No problem," he thought. "He can just go around me."

Earl heard the vehicle getting closer, and lifted his head to see. It was a black pickup with two men inside. He lowered his head, and a second later jerked it back up.

"Oh shit, Ham," he shouted, wiggling under the rope. "I think it's him."

"Who are you talkin' ...? Oh lordy." Garbuncle swerved off the road and scraped a mailbox before bouncing to a stop. The pickup gained speed, and Garbuncle slid down the seat to below the door window.

The truck slowed, and its passenger leaned out the window with a rifle. Bullets shattered both rear door windows, just below the upper frames, and another smashed the left headlight as the vehicle sped away.

"Dammit, get me down from here," Earl yelled as he squirmed. Garbuncle jumped out and loosed the knot on the other side. Earl wriggled out from under ropes and jumped to the ground.

"That's it. I've had it." His face was red. "I damn near got killed."

"Look what they did to my new car." Garbuncle inspected the rear windows where the shots exited.

"New? You call this piece of junk new? I'm lucky to be alive, and all you care about is your damned car?"

"Sorry Earl. That was a close call." They both fell silent.

"You know what I think?" said Garbuncle. "I don't think they were trying to kill us. Nobody is that bad a shot. They could have hit you up there if they wanted to. I think they were just trying to scare me."

"Well they sure as hell scared me."

"Now what are we gonna do?" said Garbuncle.

"I'll tell you what we're gonna do. You're gonna ride on top, and I'm gonna drive."

"But I'm not ..." Garbuncle began. He walked to the back. "Okay, help me up."

Earl pushed him up onto the trunk lid, and climbed up himself. Garbuncle placed a foot inside Earl's clasped hands, and Earl vaulted him onto the bed. The attorney lay face up on the mattress, and Earl tightened the ropes.

Earl drove to busy Haverhill Road, and stayed to the inside, as people in passing cars gawked. Three turns later, they arrived at Earl's apartment. They carried the mattress and box spring inside, and positioned them on the bed frame. Earl threw a pillow from a chair onto the mattress, and flopped onto his back, spread-eagled. He stared at the ceiling.

"And I thought rasslin' was dangerous." He closed his eyes.

Garbuncle marveled at how serene he looked, as though he were lying in a coffin. The bullet had missed by inches.

The landlord chased the thought from his mind, and stole out of the apartment.

CHAPTER TWENTY-TWO

Motion Filed in Resisting Case. The two-column headline appeared below the fold of the *Palm Beach Hawk*'s Local News section. The subhead read: New evidence exonerates, attorney says. The story read:

The attorney for a Hardinton man who faces a retrial on a charge of resisting arrest with violence has filed a motion to introduce new evidence that the lawyer called "shocking revelations" about the Granville police officers who arrested him.

Alec Monceau was treated for injuries sustained April 18 after Sgt. Peter Bullard and Officer Larry Pickens stopped his car for an inoperable taillight. In the trial July 7-11, a hung jury resulted when the members voted four to two to convict, and a mistrial was declared. They were four men and two women, all but two of them whites ranging in age from 30s to about 70. An elderly black woman and a middle-aged Hispanic man, the only minority members, voted not guilty.

Attorney Hiram Garbuncle argued that the policemen beat Monceau, who, the lawyer insisted, had done nothing to provoke the attack. He told the Hawk that his client's left shoulder was dislocated and he sustained severe facial bruises and deep gashes on his skull. The officers were uninjured.

The attorney said he had uncovered what he called "solid evidence" that the officers were motivated by racial animosity. Monceau, a computer salesman at the Computer Freak store on Lake Worth Road, is of black and Hispanic heritage, and sends part of his income to his family in Trinidad, Garbuncle said.

Asked if he thought the jury was racially biased, Garbuncle said, "I have an opinion, but do not think it prudent for me to reveal it."

Darrell Seward, the prosecuting attorney, denied that the officers were racist, but declined to comment further.

At the conclusion of the trial, Circuit Judge Jonathan Crabtree extended until the new trial the period of Monceau's freedom on his own recognizance. The retrial is set for Nov. 9.

***

"Hi Jake. Bart here." Sutherland leaned into his desk in the Palm Beach County State Attorney's office, elbow supporting his hand holding the phone.

"What's up?"

"Did you see today's *Hawk?*"

"Nah. I don't read that paper. Run by a bunch o' commies. Like all o' them papers."

"Sometimes it pays to know what's going on. We're in big trouble."

"You got my ear. Sock it to me."

"Looks like that pesky attorney in the Monceau case has got some more evidence on us."

"Oh shit. What other stuff ya think he's got?"

"I don't know, but I suspect it's damning. He must think he's got a reasonable chance of nailing your buddies on it. He must have something on Pete and Larry."

"What are we gonna do?"

"We'll just have to wait on Darrell Seward. He prosecuted the case for the state attorney's office. Garbuncle has to disclose the evidence he plans to introduce. He has to turn it over as part of the discovery process. The judge will schedule a hearing, where Seward will learn about the evidence. He'll want to talk to Bullard and Pickens."

***

Judge Crabtree emailed Garbuncle and Seward with a notice of the evidentiary hearing, to be held at 3 p.m. Sept. 21, 2008, in the judge's chambers in the Palm Beach County Courthouse, 205 N. Dixie Highway, West Palm Beach. "At that time, the claimed evidence will be examined, and I will entertain arguments from the attorney for the defendant and the prosecutor as to the legality and feasibility of allowing said evidence to be introduced at the trial."

***

"Mister Garbuncle, please present to us the evidence you claim to have discovered since July eleven, when a hung jury resulted in the mistrial of your client Alec Monceau, who was charged with resisting arrest with violence." Judge Crabtree sat at the head of a rectangular, oak table. Hiram Garbuncle and Darrell Seward flanked him on opposite sides.

"Certainly. To begin with, I have two recordings made on cellular phones at public venues." The attorney withdrew the recordings from his briefcase and laid one on the table in front of him and the other to his far side, both out of reach of Seward. "This recording"—he gestured toward the one nearest him—"is prima facie evidence that Jake Schmidt and Bart Sutherland conspired to murder me."

Seward had been leaning forward with his arms on the table. He jerked erect.

"This other recording—" Garbuncle paused and gestured toward the device—"it shows two officers from the Hardinton Police Department are the proprietors of a gambling enterprise centered on dog fighting. At a dog fight, an associate of mine, using subterfuge, got them to reveal that they knew Donna Malone and I were friends. She was fatally injured when that tie rod assembly—" he pointed to the auto part on the floor at the other end of the table—"came loose on her car and she crashed." Garbuncle's lips quivered.

He reached into his briefcase for the tape recorder he'd used to record Donna. "This recording is Ms. Malone telling me from her hospital bed that Jake Schmidt, Larry Pickens, and Pete Bullard were at a Ku Klux Klan meeting she attended with Schmidt. I think you can see the connection."

Garbuncle sauntered to the end of the table and lifted the tie rod mechanism. "This is what caused Donna's car to crash." He set it down, ambled to his seat, and took two manila envelopes from his case.

trailed off, and leaned forward, staring intensely at the tan-tiled floor.

"They must have had it hidden near the table," Seward said. "Any place they could have put it where it wouldn't be seen?"

"The table was in a corner, and I don't remember anything there but the walls and the bare floor. 'Course, I wasn't looking for anything."

"Maybe the tape recorder was on the floor under the table."

"Did you say tape recorder?"

"Oh, yes, I meant cellphone."

"Naw, our feet would have touched it on the floor. And they wouldn't take such a big chance we'd find it. This is really strange. I can't figure ..." Sutherland looked at Seward. "Wait a minute ... tape. I think that's it. They must have taped the cellphone to the underside of the table. That's why they wanted to get us moved there. The whole thing was staged."

"You know what? I think you're right." The two men stared at each other in wonderment.

"That attorney is a wily bastard," said Seward.

"Yeah, if he planned it. I don't know those two guys—never saw either one in my life. The big guy put on a hell of an act." He paused, and Seward could see something had occurred to him. "You don't suppose Garbuncle would have hired them?"

"I doubt it. He's too stingy. A couple of attorneys have told me he finagled it so his bill went on their tab when they had lunch in the courthouse café."

They went quiet.

"So is that it?" Sutherland said. "He show any other evidence."

"Yes. Another cellphone recording. A guy talking to two Hardinton cops at a dog fight—Hank and Art." Seward fumbled through papers in the briefcase sitting on the couch between him and Sutherland. "I've got their full names somewhere. Oh well, we don't need to know that now. Hank tells the guy—who happens to be Garbuncle's landlord—that he and Art arrested Garbuncle when he interfered with a traffic stop of a woman. Hank says to this guy that he tipped off either Pickens or Bullard—he didn't name which one, but it doesn't matter—he let whichever one it was know that he, Hank, had he'd seen her walk into the courtroom for their trial. So they figure Garbuncle and the woman have more than an attorney-client relationship. The woman, of course, was Donna Malone, the one killed when her car crashed.

"And that's where more evidence comes in. The attorney found out Jake's prints were on the tie rod that came loose on her car."

"Holy shit. This keeps getting worse."

"Hey, you know what? Something's been niggling on the edges of my mind—and it just hit me. The voice of that guy at the dog fight—it was like I'd heard it before. Now I know where I heard it—on the other tape. The big guy who slammed into the table in the bar is the same one who was at the dog fight. He's Garbuncle's condo tenant."

"Now things are adding up," said Sutherland.

"There's more. That accident where the car exploded and the driver was incinerated? He was Garbuncle's mechanic, and Garbuncle was supposed to be driving. He's got photos of marks in the road that an expert figured out were caused by the gas tank coming loose. They recovered the tank, and he's testifying it was tampered with."

Seward watched Sutherland take a deep breath, and let it out in a slow, resigned way.

"You weren't lying when you said it doesn't look good."

"Bart, what the hell did you do here? You've gotten yourself into a pile of trouble. It's a good thing we're friends, or I'd turn you in."

"I know," said Sutherland. "I can't believe how out of hand this thing has gotten." Seward saw the dejected look on his friend, who gazed at the floor.

"Look, I've known you for a long time. Your dad was a classmate of mine at Forest Hill High School, and he was one of the guys in a group of us who palled around. I lost touch with him when I went off to the University of Florida and then law school, but we still run into each other once in a while. He's a good man. I really hate for anything to happen to you."

"Darrell, you don't know how much I appreciate your concern."

"You and Jake and Bullard and Pickens will have to testify in the trial. I can argue that the tape recordings in the bar and at the dog fight were obtained without permission of the persons recorded. I'll have to research the law. I'm not sure it will fly. Seems to me permission isn't required if the recording is made in a public place. I think any judge would rule that a bar is a public place. The dog fight—well, they let the big guy in, so Garbuncle could argue it was at least partly open to the public. Even if it wasn't, it was an illegal operation, so Hank and Art wouldn't have much of an argument against allowing a recording to be admitted as evidence. Anything that happens at an illegal event likely would be regarded as admissible evidence.

"The tie rod could have come loose by itself. The expert testimony does not prove that it was tampered with, and this is circumstantial evidence. The problem with that is, they've got Jake's fingerprints. I can just hear Garbuncle's rebuttal: 'Did the great magician in the sky plant them there?' The jury would love that.

"The photos of the road likewise are circumstantial evidence. There is no proof that the marks were caused by the car's gas tank coming loose, or even that the tank was tampered with. But how is a jury going to look at it—in combination with the other stuff?"

Bart sat with his head hung.

"I'm sorry, Bart, but we have to be realistic. This is what we're faced with."

"Yeah, I hear you," Sutherland said, sighing. His elbow rested on the arm of the couch, fist supporting his jaw.

"That jury obviously was racially biased," Seward continued. "But if the new jury believes the evidence, Monceau will be exonerated, and this office will have no choice but to lay some very serious charges against all of you. I could recuse myself from continuing with the case, claiming I'm a friend of your father, but that won't do any of you any good. As you know, another assistant state attorney would be assigned. Maybe the boss himself would take over the case, since it's exploded into something so high-profile and it affects this office, you being an investigator.

"But the good thing is, the chief is a good ol' boy. Been living in these parts for a long time, like the rest of us. Grew up here when things were different. Didn't have this political correctness bullshit get in the way of things. Nonetheless—and I hate to say this—if you guys get convicted, you're going to spend a long time in prison. You know that."

"This whole thing makes me think of the quagmire we got into in Vietnam,"

Sutherland mused. He leaned back and looked away from Seward into space. "I wasn't quite born yet, of course, but we studied it in American History at Florida State. It started out with Eisenhower sending a group of advisers to help the South Vietnamese against a Communist takeover by North Vietnam. The South Vietnamese leadership was corrupt, but we supported them because we were afraid of the domino effect if South Vietnam fell into Communist hands. We figured Laos and Cambodia would be the next to topple."

"I remember it well," said Seward. "I was one of those hippies protesting the war." His wistful look metamorphosed into one of sadness. "I had ideals then."

Sutherland paused to allow Seward a moment of reflection.

Picking up where Sutherland had left off, Seward said, "Kennedy began the escalation in the early nineteen-sixties with a small number of troops. The troop level greatly increased under Lyndon Johnson. Then Nixon, who promised in nineteen-sixty-eight to end the war, expanded it to Cambodia and Laos, and we lost another twenty-two-thousand soldiers. We got out in nineteen-seventy-three, and two years later the war ended—in defeat for the United States and South Vietnam."

"I got a B-plus in that history course," Sutherland said, "but you'd have gotten an A."

"Oh, what a tangled web we weave when first we practice to deceive," Seward said, as if he hadn't heard the investigator. "We should never have gotten involved."

"I agree with you completely. I remember Professor Stanard's lecture. I jotted it down word for word: 'The so-called domino effect would have been minimal, but the war became one of our country's greatest tragedies, with scores of thousands of young people killed and even more maimed. And the South Vietnamese suffered immeasurably.' I don't think I'll ever forget that lecture."

Sutherland paused, staring at the floor. "Look at the mess we've gotten into here. If Jake had just let the law take its course with Pickens and Bullard, they likely would've ended up getting tossed from the force for belonging to the Ku Klux Klan. The two Hardinton cops would've been hit with felony charges for running an illegal dog fighting operation and gambling. Yeah, they might've seen a little jail time. But that stuff is a hell of a lot less serious than murder and attempted murder charges, which is what me and Jake are looking at—and maybe Pickens and Bullard as accomplices if Garbuncle can convince the jury they were complicit."

"Okay, now just hold on," said Seward. "It sounds like you're throwing in the towel with the fight barely underway. The opera ain't over till the fat lady sings. Yes, you guys are in a pickle. You've got a decision to make. You can take your chances with my legal skills, but I don't hold out a lot of hope I can win, especially against that shrewd bastard Garbuncle. Or ..." He brushed his lips with his forefinger.

"You just might already be in a hole too deep to crawl out of. If you see it that way, there's only one way out of this, in my estimation. You've got to stop the trial from going forward."

"That's easy to say," said Sutherland. "How?"

"One way would be for me to just drop the charge."

"So why don't you do it?"

"It's not that simple. There likely would be some bad repercussions. Suspicions would arise as to why we weren't pursuing it. The boss would wonder why. He'd quiz me about it. The media probably would raise the issue, and the public would wonder what was going on. A lot of people would ask questions. Reporters would do some digging. *Hawk* reporters would be abetted by their colleague Brad Hitchens, even though he's probably recused himself because he was a witness in the trial."

Sutherland threw his hands up and sighed. "What the hell are we gonna do?"

"I leave that to your own imaginations. I'll just say this: If Garbuncle could be persuaded to plea bargain for his client, and we could let Monceau off with a token sentence, maybe a couple years' probation—real light—we could be done with it. But we can't be too lenient, like clearing the charge from Monceau's record, or questions will be raised, and the media would start investigating. The legal community would buzz about it. But we could try to work something out. How do you get Garbuncle to plea bargain?" He lowered his hand to his side, and rubbed a thumb and two fingers together. He winked.

"I'll try to keep a lid on what's transpired," Seward continued. "I'll talk around it. The judge isn't going to press me. If Monceau was an important person, it'd be different. But I doubt he's going to be overly concerned about what happens to a guy from Jamaica or Haiti."

"Trinidad."

"Okay, one of those places nobody cares about. If that doesn't work ..." Seward looked hard at Sutherland. "It's up to you."

CHAPTER TWENTY-THREE

Bart Sutherland pulled up WhitePages.com on his office computer. He entered Hiram Garbuncle, West Palm Beach, Florida. Data danced across the screen, and became stationary.

White male. Age: 58. Last known address: 618 Sherwood Avenue, Apt. 113, Unincorporated, Palm Beach County, Florida.

Occupation: Attorney at Law.

Marital status: Divorced February 18, 2001, from Janet Garbuncle, formerly Slater.

Children: Liza Larson, Druid Hills, Georgia; Grace Chamberlain, Charlotte, North Carolina.

The report went on to list three previous addresses since 1992. It named seven people he "may know." Four, with the last name of Garbuncle, apparently were his relatives.

Arrest report

"Ah, now we're getting somewhere," Sutherland muttered.

Income tax evasion, 1997; nolle prosequi.

"Shifty SOB prob'ly talked the judge out of that one," the investigator said under his breath.

Failure to pay alimony, 2003. Adjudication withheld.

"So he made his back payments, and kept his record clean," he mumbled. "Shit, that's it."

He punched buttons on the phone. "Jake, it's me. I struck out. Nothing big enough to get him on. No leverage there."

***

Traffic was heavy on Garbuncle's way home from the office. He kept on the main arteries, in the middle lanes, feeling safer with vehicles surrounding his Mercury. But he had to get in the left turn lane of Forest Hill Boulevard to make the turn onto Sherwood. He stopped at the red light.

Always wary, he glanced at the Dodge Charger on his right and saw a figure hunkered low in the driver's seat, a Panama hat pulled down even with dark sunglasses. The window was down. Garbuncle saw a pistol appear at the bottom of the window. He slid down in his seat simultaneously with a pop that shattered the windows on both the passenger and driver's side. The bullet hole was inches above and in front of his nose. Glass splinters stung the left side of his face.

He slid down farther in the seat, threw the door open, and flung himself onto the median strip. Another shot pierced the hum of cars idling behind his. The bullet tore into the passenger side door just below the window.

The Charger whirled in front of Garbuncle's Mercury, its tires squealing, and did a U-turn against the red light. Garbuncle rolled into the narrow space between the median strip and his car. As the Charger sped away, he raised his head, and saw that traffic heading east was light. It was rush hour and most people were heading west from cities' business centers to their homes. The incident happened so fast, he realized, that no one would have gotten the Charger's license number.

***

"Holy shit," Brad Hitchens said, nervously twisting his glass of beer on its cardboard Heineken coaster. "I'm not sure it's safe hanging around with you." He did a half turn on the bar stool, surveying the room at Johnny's.

"We're okay here," said Garbuncle. "I've never seen those guys in this place."

"I've known quite a few cats—jazz hipsters who played saxophone, trumpet, piano. But you're one cat who doesn't have a lot of lives left in his repertoire. One of these times, your luck is gonna run out."

"Yeah, they definitely tried to do me in when my car exploded with Ed inside." The attorney took a swig of the vodka in his glass. "I was running all this through my head this afternoon after a client canceled an appointment and my secretary went home with an upset stomach. I was alone. This shooting and the other one— I'm not sure they wanted to kill me. It occurs to me they were trying to scare me. The bullets missed their mark, but maybe they were supposed to. They came pretty close, but I'll wager the shooter is a marksman, and he just wanted to make me think I was his target."

"Why would he be doing that?"

"They're prob'ly hoping I'll see if I can get the judge to let me back out of the case."

"Maybe it's time to get ahold of the FBI."

"I sure as hell have thought about it. But I'd be leaving Alec in the lurch, and he might get a stiff sentence. I can tell he's deathly afraid of going to jail. The FBI might nab Jake Schmidt and Bart Sutherland, but I'm not sure that would help Eric.

"I'd have to argue successfully for admission of the tape showing Schmidt and Sutherland planned to kill me. If it was admitted, the jury would have to be persuaded they were working on behalf of Larry Pickens and Pete Bullard. 'Cause that would be circumstantial evidence. So if either of those things failed, all we'd have left is hoping Schmidt or Sutherland, or both of them, rat on Pickens and Bullard as being Klan members.

"And what would happen to them? They'd prob'ly be kicked off the force for their Klan membership. They'd just wait awhile and get jobs with police departments in other towns. Maybe even in Palm Beach County. In any case, they'd just go on their merry way. Nothing would prevent them from continuing to make life miserable for innocent guys like Alec."

Hitchens said nothing, and Garbuncle noticed the troubled look on his face. "Yeah, I suppose you're right. Damn. I wish there was some way I could help you with this."

Garbuncle was staring hard at his glass of vodka, his lips tight, as if he didn't hear Hitchens.

"And there's another reason I need to keep fighting to get justice for Alec."

Hitchens turned his head toward his friend, who returned the look. His voice quavered: "Because Donna wanted me to."

"You're reminding me of a favorite song of mine."

"Which one?"

"From *A Chorus Line. What I Did for Love.*"

Chapter Twenty-four

"Hello. Mister Garbuncle?"

"Yes."

"My name's Jonah Feinberg. I'm an attorney ..."

"Feinberg, Feinberg. Did you say Jonah?"

"That would be me."

"Okay, yes, I know who you are. You're the one in Broward County, somewhere around Pompano Beach. Right?"

"You hit it on the button."

"You're famous—or notorious, I'm not sure which, probably both. You've represented some of the worst criminal cases to come down the pike."

"Well ... I'm a humble man, and I don't like to boast."

"Defending mobsters is your specialty, if I'm not mistaken. And you've got a pretty good success rate."

"As I said, I'm humble. But one thing I've never been known for is false modesty. My win record has been *damned* good. But I thank you just the same."

Garbuncle's reaction was mixed: He instantly liked the man for his candidness, but was turned off by his arrogance.

"I'm sure you're wondering what I called you about."

"I was just going to get to that."

"Indeed. It's about that resisting arrest case involving the black client of yours and the two police officers."

"I suspected that might be where you were going. Who are you representing?"

"I think it best that we not discuss this on the phone."

I think it best … The guy doesn't sound like he associates with mobsters. Too well-spoken. Years of experiences in a wide array of situations had taught Garbuncle to be on guard, and he was instinctively suspicious of the person on the other end.

"So how do you propose we communicate?"

"Why don't we arrange for a place to meet?"

"What do you have in mind?"

"I'm open to suggestions. Your place or mine?"

Garbuncle was certain the guy wanted to propose a deal, and relished toying with him.

"It's been a long time since I've heard that proposition. In fact, I may never have heard it. I was always the one making it. And she almost always offered another alternative: neither place."

Feinberg chuckled, but Garbuncle could tell it was a forced response and the guy wasn't amused.

"I guess we've all been in that situation. But seriously, where would you like to rendezvous?"

Rendezvous? This attorney is a smooth talker. Gotta be careful. "Give me a day to come up with a suitable location for both of us, and I'll get back to you."

"Fair enough. Let me give you my phone number."

"I've got it on my caller ID."

"Oh yes, of course. I'll await your call."

***

"Let's sit at a table," Hitchens said. He leaned toward his attorney friend, and lowered his voice. "Too many people at the bar to overhear us." He carried his draft Pabst to a secluded spot against the wall, with empty tables on both sides. Garbuncle followed with his ever-present companion, a glass of vodka. A waitress brought coasters.

"Are you going to meet this attorney alone?" Hitchens asked.

"Nope. You're coming with me."

"What?" Two men at the bar swiveled their bar stools sideways. Hitchens lowered his head. "Sorry. I'm attracting attention."

"You don't want to come?"

"Well, yeah, but ... Look, Ham, I hate violence, because I'm very religious."

Garbuncle gawked at his companion with a nonplussed look.

"I'm a devout coward."

Garbuncle threw his head back and cackled. A woman at the near end of the bar twisted her head to look at him with an amused smile. He smiled back.

"*Now* who's got people curious? We have to keep it down."

Garbuncle took a long swig.

"I didn't mean the booze." Hitchens paused. "Hey, you know what? I haven't seen you drunk in awhile."

"Excuse me. I don't get drunk."

"No? Then you put on a hell of an act."

"I imbibe excessively on occasion."

It was Hitchens' turn to laugh.

Nobody else in the bar reacted.

"I think they're getting used to us," said Hitchens.

Hitchens saw Garbuncle's face turn thoughtful and sad.

"Donna would want me to keep after ..." He paused, and his face brightened. "I just have to be alert. I may be paranoid, but that doesn't mean people aren't after me."

Hitchens squelched a laugh, and let out a soft chuckle.

"So you're not coming along," Garbuncle said, raising an eyebrow.

Hitchens sighed. "Okay, okay, I'll do it. But I don't carry a gun, you know."

"I do. And so does Earl. I'll get him to come."

"Good. Now let's figure this out. We need a location where there's a lot of people." Hitchens watched the foam bubbles pop on the top of his draft Pabst and the froth diminish. "So he and a crony who might be hanging around incognito won't have a chance to plug us. Johnny's wouldn't work. This place is usually less than packed, like today."

"Of course not. You're a reporter. You get around a lot more than I do. And you chase women more, too. You know the spots."

"Not so much. Just the jazz haunts and the dance halls."

Hitchens looked hard into space. His eyes grew large, and he jerked upright in his seat.

"I think I've got it. The Glitter 'n' Glide Ballroom in northeast Broward."

"Are you serious?"

"Dead ... ooh, bad term ... very serious. I go there all the time. You know that."

"Yep. That's how you earned the name Twinkle Toes."

"Yeah—from you. But I only go there Sundays. It has to be on a Sunday— after five o'clock or eight. They get four hundred, sometimes five hundred people." He rubbed his chin. "I think 7:45 would be perfect. Latin dancing— mainly salsa—goes till eight, and a lot of young, athletic guys come for that. Some of them stick around for the switch to regular ballroom at eight. Lot o' waltzes and fox trots. Earl told me once he was in this musical where he had to learn the cha cha and the fox trot, and we may need him to do some dancing. If Feinberg— or more likely, anybody with him who's hiding in the crowd—if they try any shenanigans, these young virile dudes will pounce on 'em. That's in case Feinberg's goons are too tough for Earl to handle."

"It's sure as hell not a conventional strategy. I've never been to the place, but it sounds like it might be just what we need. One thing: Do I have to dance?"

"I'll ask Feinberg to shoot you if you do. I'm gonna be scared, and I don't wanna be embarrassed besides."

***

"Hello, Mister Feinberg. I was just going to call you."

"Well, fancy that. So now you don't have to—not that you had to, anyway. I just meant—"

"It's okay. I understand what you meant."

"Then may I assume that you have come up with a suggestion for where we can meet?"

"Indeed I have. There's a large ballroom in your neighborhood. I think that would be the perfect spot."

A pause. "Did I hear you right? Did you say ballroom? What kind of ballroom? You mean a dance hall?"

"You got it. The Glitter 'n' Glide Ballroom. Great place. Are you familiar with it?"

"Seems to me I've heard of it, but ... wouldn't it be a little crowded?"

"Oh yes. Hundreds of people. But that's what we want."

"Mister Garbuncle, somehow I'm missing the point. We have important business to discuss. And we need to be clandestine about it."

Clandestine? I wonder if this guy talks to his mobster clientele like that.

"But don't you see? Everybody will be talking amongst themselves and dancing and having a good time. Nobody will pay any attention to us. If we were in some bar, there'd be a lot less noise, and people might overhear us. Or they'd wonder why we were huddling and talking in low tones. Besides, this is a serious issue, and I don't want to get depressed. I'd rather do this in an upbeat setting. Good music, a fun atmosphere. In fact, I may want to do a little dancing, although I'm not very good at it."

"Mister Garbuncle, I think it would be much better for us to meet in a secluded spot, where we can discuss the issue openly and not worry about being overheard."

"Your manner of speaking indicates that you are a man of refinement, Mister Feinberg. I'm sure you're familiar with Edgar Allan Poe. Am I right?"

"How could I not be? A nineteenth-century American literary giant."

"Then you might be acquainted with a famous short story that he penned, *The Purloined Letter.*"

"That rings a strong bell. Remind me what it's about."

"It's a detective story in which police search a hotel room for a stolen letter. They turn the place upside down, looking in every nook and cranny, and cannot find it. Poe's detective hero finds it—hidden in plain sight, in an open box hanging from the fireplace."

"Um, yes, I see where you're going with this."

"The way to bring attention to yourself is to appear as though you have something to hide. Nobody will suspect us of discussing anything secretive in a spot surrounded by people. We can go to a far corner, which won't arouse any suspicion because all the other tables probably will be occupied."

"I don't like the idea. It sounds like specious reasoning to me." His theretofore suave tone had a harshness. "There is a nightspot west of Boca Raton whose owner I know. He would make sure nobody would bother us."

"Well, Mister Feinberg, I'd like to be more accommodating, but I just don't find that suitable. Think about it, and if you'd like to meet me at the ballroom, you have my phone number."

"So you're not ... Well, I suppose I can subjugate my misgivings. Okay, we'll meet at the ballroom."

"Seven-thirty Sunday, then. Oh ... and of course you'll be alone."

"I might take an associate along to take notes and assist me in unforeseen ways."

"No sir, I'm afraid that wouldn't work. That would be a deal breaker."

"You drive a hard bargain, Mister Garbuncle."

"This shouldn't be that complicated. I'm sure you and I can reach an agreement by ourselves. It would be easier to negotiate without any outside interference."

"But I ... Very well, then. I'll see you there."

"We can meet at the front desk, just inside the entrance. I'm not very tall, and I'll be wearing a suit—sort of a blue-gray and tan mix—and a royal blue tie. Let me give you directions."

***

The huge parking lot for the Glitter 'n' Glide Ballroom and various other businesses was loaded, as usual, for the Sunday dance. Hitchens had to park the Mazda on a broad grassy stretch bordering the lot in the rear.

"Are all these cars for the ballroom?" Garbuncle gazed out at the sea of vehicles that filled the lot. "This looks more like a Miami Dolphins game than a dance."

"I told you hundreds of people come to this thing," Hitchens said. He turned toward the back seat. "Earl, hand me my shoes, will you?"

"I was wonderin' what was in that bag, but I didn't wanna be nosy," said Earl.

"What do you mean, shoes?" Garbuncle said. "You wear special shoes to dance?"

"Yeah. You got a problem with that?"

Garbuncle tittered.

"What's that for? If you knew how to dance, you'd want dance shoes too."

"You don't need to be touchy about it." Garbuncle's smile was teasing. "Do they have little twinkly lights around the edges?"

"Go screw yourself. If it was you, you'd need lights so your partner could keep from gettin' stepped on. Now listen up, Ham: The dance floor is surrounded on three sides with tables. After you meet Feinberg at the front desk, take him straight back to the rear corner on the right. Earl and I will enter a few minutes later, after you've paid the admission."

Garbuncle frowned.

"Earl and I'll look for you in the corner. If you can't find a table there, come back up to the front and check around. We'll watch for you. When you and Feinberg settle on a table, Earl and I will find one somewhere nearby, where we can keep an eye on what's going on."

Garbuncle walked up the aisle of cars leading straight to the entrance, glancing around for anyone who might look suspicious. Two women approached separately from the right. One, around forty, wore a loose, flowery dress. The other, thirty-ish, was sexy in a short, tight skirt and bejeweled heels. Both carried sizable bags.

A man with a thick mop of salt-and-pepper hair, a little taller than Garbuncle but of similar build, with a small paunch, approached from his left. The man stared at Garbuncle through wire-rimmed glasses.

"Are you perchance Hiram Garbuncle?" Garbuncle recognized the oily tone.

"Yes, I am. You must be Mister Feinberg."

"It would be hard to miss that tie. I like it."

They entered together, and Garbuncle pulled his wallet out.

"Put that away. It's on me."

"If you insist."

Garbuncle strained to see to the far corner on the right. "This place is very crowded, but I spot a table way in the back"—he pointed to the corner—"that looks like it might be empty. It's not surrounded by other tables."

"Hmmm ... yes, I see it. We should be able to converse there without much ambient conversation." They wove their way among the irregularly positioned, large round tables. Garbuncle led, nearly tripping twice as his splayed feet caught chairs jutting into the aisles where their occupants had left them to venture onto the dance floor. The round corner table was empty, though the pair spotted a man's and a woman's street shoes side by side on the carpet under the front perimeter of the table.

Garbuncle and Feinberg took adjacent seats on the wall side of the table, which afforded clear views of the entire ballroom.

"Looks like a couple are sitting there," Garbuncle noted. "They'll likely be back when they're finished dancing, but they'll be too wrapped up in themselves to pay any attention to us."

"I see they have a bar on the other side of the dance floor," Feinberg said. "Can I get you something to drink?"

"Yes, thanks, if you're having something yourself. A vodka on the rocks would be fine."

"Any brand?"

"Well, I usually drink Absolut."

"I'll be right back."

As Feinberg crossed the floor in front of the wide platform with the deejay booth, Garbuncle stood and looked toward the desk for his companions. Hitchens spotted him, and gave a quick salute.

Garbuncle saw Feinberg stop in front of the bar and look toward the wide opening of the kitchen to the rear of the floor. He's curious about the place, Garbuncle thought. Then he saw a nattily dressed man wearing a yellow ascot, standing in the walkway between the tables and the kitchen, and facing toward the bar. He was big—at least as tall and heavyset as Earl—and swarthy.

Feinberg nodded, and the man did likewise. The attorney carried the drinks back to the table, and Garbuncle noticed the guy with the ascot turning his head to follow Feinberg.

"Here we are. Absolut for you and Jack Daniel's for me." Garbuncle lowered his head, pretending to watch Feinberg set the drinks down, but looking peripherally at the man near the kitchen, who was watching them.

"Lots of beautiful women," said Feinberg. "I'm going to have trouble concentrating on the business at hand."

"Yes, me too. So what did you want to see me about?"

Feinberg took a sip of his drink. He fished in his coat pocket on the other side of Garbuncle, who jerked upright in his chair and reached into his inside pocket. He fingered his Smith & Wesson.

Feinberg withdrew two sheets of paper. "I've drawn up a simple contract protecting each of us. By signing it, we each swear to total silence about the conversation we're about to have. It precludes us from discussing anything that is raised here with anyone—except, of course, our associates. This meeting shall remain strictly confidential."

Garbuncle pored over the copy Feinberg handed him. "This paper repeats what you just told me. You have it virtually memorized."

"I called before coming here to see if there was a notary on the premises," Feinberg said. "The owner told me he was, and would be manning the desk, admitting customers. Let's go up and get this thing notarized."

The two maneuvered between the tables to the front. "Sir, you must be the one who told me over the phone you were a notary, is that correct?"

"Oh, sure, I remember." The middle-aged man, slight and mostly bald, stepped to the right side of the wide counter and drew a stamp from a drawer. Feinberg took a ballpoint pen and the document, plus a copy, out of his coat pocket. He signed both and handed the pen to Garbuncle, who did likewise. The proprietor stamped each one and applied his signature to make it official.

"Thank you, sir," said Feinberg. "With that business out of the way, we're ready to enjoy the entertainment on the floor."

"Don't you gentlemen dance?"

"No, we just enjoy watching," said Feinberg. "My friend here told me about this place and raved about the quality of the dancers."

"There are a lot of highly skilled people here, some of them professionals."

"We'll probably come again."

They sauntered back to their table in the far corner, where a couple had placed their drinks on the opposite side. Each man took a long swig of his drink.

"I understand that in the course of seeking a new trial for your client Alec Monceau, a series of mishaps has occurred and two friends of yours lost their lives. Is that correct?"

"That is correct."

"I'm most sorry for your losses."

Garbuncle's head was turned down. Feinberg glanced at him and detected a look of disdain.

"Both your lady friend and your car mechanic were killed in automobile incidents. Is that right?"

"Mister Feinberg, you and I both know what happened. Can we please dispense with the formalities and get to the point?"

"Certainly. But I need to present the issues first so we can discuss a remedy to a situation that seems to have gotten out of hand. Now, as I understand it, you did some detective work and captured two conversations on a recording device—one of them by my clients. I believe that what you did was illegal, but let's put that question aside."

"I don't think it was illegal. I researched the law."

"Then you apparently intend to introduce these recordings in the new trial that has been scheduled—if the judge allows it. You are too good an attorney to be dissuaded by any—"

"Excuse me, counselor. I have a sudden urge to urinate. The old prostate is beginning to act up on me. You're about my age. I'm sure you understand. If you don't, you will in time." Garbuncle smiled. "I'll be right back."

"Go right ahead. I'm not going anywhere."

Garbuncle took the long way to the restroom, meandering among the tables to the front before turning right down the narrow walkway between the kitchen and tables set back from the dance floor. He knew Feinberg would be watching, and didn't look for Hitchens and Earl as he took a right turn and continued past the bar to the restroom.

It was empty, and he stood before a urinal. A half-minute later, Hitchens entered, and pretended to pee in the urinal next to Garbuncle.

"There's a guy wearing a yellow ascot—I think he's sitting at one of those rear tables," Garbuncle said, his voice low. "I think he and Feinberg know each other. He's pretty big, about as hefty as Earl. Have Earl get a dance partner when he sees the guy with the ascot take to the floor. Get Earl to provoke a confrontation. He can bump the guy hard and make him mad. The floor is crowded, so it will look like an accident, but the guy will prob'ly get pissed and challenge Earl. Earl can invite the guy outside, and flatten him. Otherwise, I'm afraid that guy is going to come after us when we leave."

"Earl may not be able to do the dance if it's not a cha cha or fox trot."

"Hell, Earl is athletic. He can fake it. Tell him I'll replace that tattered armchair in his room."

They heard the door open, and Hitchens ducked into a stall. Garbuncle pretended to pull his zipper up, perfunctorily washed and dried his hands, and exited. Out of the corner of his eye, he saw the guy with the ascot sitting at the rear, watching the dancers, who were doing the American tango. Garbuncle looked straight ahead, but peripherally saw the guy turning his head toward him as he passed.

"That's a beautiful dance," Feinberg said when Garbuncle reached the table. "Smooth and sensual."

"Yes, I wish I could do that. Anyway, where were we?"

"I was commenting that you apparently plan to introduce those potentially damning recordings in the trial."

"I haven't mapped out my strategy yet, but yes, I foresee doing that."

Feinberg took a sip of his Jack Daniel's, and sighed. He stared out and above the heads of the dancers, and Garbuncle perceived tenseness in his face. To break the awkwardness of the silence, the defense attorney lifted his own drink to his lips, eyeing Feinberg sideways.

"This has to be terribly vexing for you, Mister Garbuncle."

Garbuncle took a sip, and lowered his glass to the table. "It is indeed, but probably not as stressful as it is for your clients."

"Well, I'm sure that no one is comfortable with the way things are heading. Before I proceed, let me remind you that you are sworn to silence over what we discuss here. Agreed?"

"So be it.'

"All right then. Let me ask you: What would it take for you to consider getting together with Darrell Seward, the prosecutor, to work out a plea bargain?"

Garbuncle had figured that was what his adversary would come up with. "Give me a few moments to reflect on that."

"Take your time."

"The deejay has changed the music."

"Yes, I think this is a cha cha, from what little I know of dance music."

"I think you're right. Two slower steps, when they swivel their hips, and then three quick ones. Fun to watch. Let's just take it in for a couple of minutes."

"Certainly. The night is young."

Garbuncle looked to the rear of the floor, and saw the guy with the ascot get up and ask a sexy looking woman a few tables away to dance. She complied, and Garbuncle could tell they were practiced dancers. He spotted Earl rise on the far side, move his ample form with agility through a network of tables, and bend toward a young, pretty woman who appeared to be Latino.

Garbuncle leaned back and took a furtive look at Feinberg, whom he saw eyeing his associate with the ascot. The defense attorney also knew that Feinberg was unaware of who Earl was, and didn't know Garbuncle had figured out that the guy with the ascot and Feinberg were connected.

Earl gracefully maneuvered his partner over the crowded floor to a small space near Mister Ascot, and saw the man gazing hungrily at the woman while holding one hand loosely and clasping her shoulder with the other as he led her through the steps. Earl positioned himself so that he would be facing away from the man when the two moved backward in opposite directions during the to and fro movements.

On the next sequence, Earl took shorter steps forward and long steps backward. He collided hard with the man, who staggered forward into his partner, nearly knocking her over.

The man recovered and whirled around to face Earl. "You clumsy idiot," he yelled.

"Me clumsy? You backed into me. You need to watch where you're goin'."

The man stepped toward Earl. "Why you fucking ..."

Earl held up both arms. "Wait a minute. You wanna get rough with me? We can fight here and both get thrown out of the place, or we can go outside."

"Come on, let's go."

"Did you see that?" Feinberg exclaimed.

"You mean those two guys in the middle of the floor? I didn't catch what happened, but I see they're both headed outside."

"That big lout slammed into, uh, the other guy and almost knocked him and his partner over."

"Geez, yeah. Looks like those two guys are planning to duke it out. But their partners look okay. They just walked off the floor."

Both men stalked toward the glass front door. The ascot-wearing man exited first, and swung the door hard on Earl. He caught the outside frame with extended hands.

"You like to play dirty, dontcha?" Earl said. "Wanted to take me out before I could defend myself. Now it's just you and me."

The guy swung a right-handed haymaker, and Earl ducked. He came up, and lunged at the guy. Throwing his right hip to the guy's side, Earl grabbed him around the shoulders and flipped him backward onto his back. He scrambled upright. While the man was still off-balance, Earl locked an arm around the man's neck and spun around to face the other direction. With a powerful thrust, Earl propelled the man in a somersault over the former wrestler's back onto the sidewalk. He landed with a thud, and lay there, unmoving.

"Had enough?"

The man didn't answer.

"You gonna make it?" Earl worried that he'd killed the guy.

"I think you broke my back."

"Yeah, well, maybe next time you'll think twice about who you pick a fight with. I eased up—coulda killed ya on this concrete. If we was in the ring, I woulda showed ya my body slam."

The man rose slowly, grimacing, and reached for the inside of his coat pocket.

Earl grabbed his gun out of his own sport coat, and pointed it at the man. "Don't even try it." Earl jammed the pistol into the guy's midsection, and fumbled in the guy's inside pocket with the other hand.

"I'll take that," Earl said, withdrawing a Ruger snub-nosed revolver and depositing it in his other coat pocket. "Cute little baby. I'll bet you was fixin' ta use that, huh podner?"

"What about you?" the man said, holding his lower back with both hands.

"I need ta pack heat. I'm always on the lookout for assholes like you. Now why don'tcha go back inside and behave yourself. I'll be watching."

The man adjusted his ascot, hobbled into the ballroom, and took his seat at a table at the rear of the floor. Earl ambled over to the table with Hitchens on the right side of the floor.

"See that?" said Garbuncle. "They both came back. The one guy is limping, but the other one looks fine. He must have gotten the better of the guy."

Garbuncle glanced at Feinberg, who looked stern as his eyes followed the man with the ascot.

"Well, no matter," said Feinberg. "I guess they settled it. Now where were we? You haven't answered my question."

"Ah yes. What would I need to enter into a plea bargain for my client? That's an interesting question."

Feinberg turned to look at him. Garbuncle returned the stare.

"I haven't even given it any thought. Hmmm. What would it take for Alec and I to try negotiating a deal with the prosecution?" He looked off into space, his eyes moving left and right. "I really don't know if there's anything that would work. But I can tell you what won't work."

Garbuncle returned his gaze toward Feinberg.

"Yes?"

"These scare tactics your clients have been using against me."

Garbuncle saw the puzzled look on Feinberg's face, and thought: *This guy may be good in the courtroom, but he'd be lousy onstage.*

"I don't understand what you're referring to."

"Mister Feinberg, you know full well what I'm referring to. But in case they haven't apprised you of everything, I'll review it for you."

The couple returned to their seats at the table, glanced at the men on the opposite side, and leaned into each other, talking in hushed tones. Garbuncle and Feinberg waited until the next dance began, an Argentine tango, whereupon the couple returned to the floor.

"At first," Garbuncle resumed, "they killed my girlfriend to keep her from talking. After that, they tried to kill me, but got my auto mechanic instead. By then, they realized that the state attorney's office and the judge were aware of what was going on, and killing me would very possibly implicate them. So they shot at me and my friend, and performed an encore on me. The shots came close both times, but missed. I don't think they intended to hit either of us, but hoped to intimidate me enough that I'd try to resolve the case."

"I think your imagination has run a little wild, Mister Garbuncle. But be that as it may, where are we now? You've told me what wouldn't make you compromise, but still haven't indicated if there were something that would induce you to work this thing out to the benefit of all."

"As I said, Mister Feinberg, I haven't given it a thought. But I'd be willing to bet my life's savings that you have."

"Of course. That's why I called this meeting." He gazed at someone on the dance floor, but Garbuncle could tell he wasn't seeing the person; he was wrestling internally with something. "I'm not sure how to put this so that you don't perceive it as a bribe. Because that's not the way it's intended. I just want to do what's best for all concerned."

"Why don't you just tell me what it is, and I'll decide how you intended it."

"All right. According to the information that came through in the trial of your client, Mister Monceau, he has been sending part of his earnings to help family members in Trinidad. Is that correct?"

"He has two children, young adults, one married with a child. They barely make ends meet."

"That is admirable of Mister Monceau. It's so unfortunate that he finds himself in this situation. I'm not going to defend nor condemn my clients over what transpired in the traffic stop. I'd just like to propose a solution that will make everybody happy. Would that be something you'd be willing to consider?"

"I don't know whether I'll consider it until I hear what it is. You haven't told me."

"Okay, let's put the cards on the table. My clients feel badly for Mister Monceau."

Garbuncle couldn't stifle a sarcastic smile, which Feinberg ignored.

"Before the trial, they regarded him as just an immigrant living off the fat of the land, someone who hadn't earned the right to partake of America's riches. They resented his being here."

"Do they show the same regard for white European immigrants?"

"Well, I ... I'm not really aware of how they feel on this issue."

"I doubt it, because they generally are better off and well connected. They're not as susceptible to bullying." Garbuncle's face registered surprise, as if he couldn't believe he'd just made that remark.

"Did you want to say something else?"

"Huh? Oh ... no, no, not at all."

"Excuse me then. You looked as though something had startled you."

"Let's continue."

"You may have a point, but I don't think we will accomplish anything by getting into a discussion about the sociological ramifications of race relations in this country."

"Then you shouldn't have brought it up."

Feinberg cleared his throat and shifted in his seat. "Perhaps not. Let's forget I mentioned it. What I'm trying to explain is that after they learned during the trial what a responsible and hard-working man Mister Monceau is, giving of himself to help support his family, they regretted the confrontation they had with him. Mind you, they're not admitting to any wrongdoing on their part, but they're willing to put the issue of who's to blame behind them and do what they can for Mister Monceau in his humanitarian effort on behalf of his family."

"Really big of them that they're willing to forget about who was to blame—since they were to blame."

"All right, all right, I didn't state that very well. Can we just move on and get to the crux of what we're here for?"

"I've been waiting quite some time for that. Please proceed. How do they propose to help Mister Monceau?"

Feinberg paused, and Garbuncle turned his head toward him. "They feel as though they'd like to make a donation to his family in Trinidad. Their hearts go out to these struggling folks."

Garbuncle coughed to cover an inadvertent laugh, and leaned forward while drawing a handkerchief from his rear pants pocket. He wiped his mouth, returned the hanky to the pocket, and took a sip of his vodka. "And what might the size of this offered donation be?"

"That could be negotiated."

"Negotiated? That doesn't strike me as much of a heartfelt gesture. Sounds more like a business transaction."

"Perhaps negotiated was a poor choice of words. What I meant to say was that ... uh ... the officers would like to contribute twenty-five-thousand dollars to Mister Monceau's family in order to make their lives easier. I believe that twenty-five-thousand would go a long way in Trinidad."

"That's fine, but I'm not at all certain it would adequately benefit Mister Monceau."

"I haven't finished, Mister Garbuncle. My clients also would like to reimburse you to the tune of twenty thousand dollars for the pro bono time and efforts you have put into Mister Monceau's defense." Feinberg's face lit up as he studied Garbuncle.

"That means Mister Monceau would receive forty-five-thousand dollars, because I would turn my share over to him. But it still doesn't address the issue. How far would the prosecutor be willing to go in a plea bargain that would set Alec Monceau free?"

"I'm afraid that's something I have no control over. I will assist you in any way I can, because it's to the benefit of my clients and I, as well as to you and Mister Monceau, for you to succeed. But in the end, you and Mr. Seward will determine the outcome. I must add that failure to reach an agreement would of course nullify our financial arrangement."

Garbuncle spotted Hitchens strolling past the kitchen on the way to the rest room.

"We interrupt this program to bring you this special announcement," Garbuncle deadpanned. "My bladder is demanding my attention again." He chuckled, and Feinberg smiled. "An older man's bladder is like a child: always nagging."

"Or a wife," said Feinberg.

Garbuncle laughed. "You got that right. Women ..." The image of Donna lying helpless in her hospital bed popped into his mind, and he sobered while rising. "I'll be right back."

"No rush." Feinberg eyed his ascot-wearing associate, who sat with head slumped into his chest, as though he were sleeping. A woman brushed him on the way to the dance floor, and his head jerked up. Feinberg noticed his sullen look.

"Damn him," Feinberg muttered. "He should be following that slippery attorney."

Hitchens was zipping up at a urinal when Garbuncle entered.

"Stay there," Garbuncle said. "I'm finishing with Feinberg. We've got to plot our exit."

The door swung open, and a young black male dancer entered. Brad Hitchens had watched the man sweep past him and a dance partner with consummate grace and athleticism, gliding down the floor in the newsman's favorite dance, the Viennese waltz. The man took the urinal at the far end, quickly completed his business, washed his hands, and left.

"Those young guys," Garbuncle said to Hitchens. "I envy 'em. Takes me three times as long. Sometimes longer, if I catch my cock in the zipper. You ever done that?"

"Yeah, and it hurts like hell. Come on, let's hurry up and talk while nobody's here."

"I figure that in five minutes, Earl should walk to the car. You wait another five minutes, and walk outside. Stand against the wall and look around as though you're waiting for somebody, just in case the guy Earl beat up comes after me."

"So what if he does? What am I supposed to do? You know how I hate violence 'cause of my religion."

"Huh?" Garbuncle looked bemused.

"I'm a devout coward, remember?"

Garbuncle lowered his head and laughed soundlessly. "Feinberg prob'ly will want to walk out with me, but I'll tell him I spotted a gal I met here once and want to talk to her. I'll wait a few minutes, and Feinberg should be gone by then."

"Gotcha," Hitchens said.

"Okay, let's get out of here, you first."

They returned to their seats. Feinberg took a swig of his whiskey. Garbuncle fingered his almost-empty glass of vodka.

"Well, I'll have to strategize on what would be best for my client," Garbuncle said. "I need a little time to figure things out."

"You won't be able to wait too long, because the judge will need enough time to clear the scheduled new trial from his docket."

"I'll go to work on it, and get back to you. Are we finished? I'd walk out with you, but there's a woman on the other side I know. Noticed her on my last trip to the restroom, and I want to stop and see her."

"All right. Until later, then."

Garbuncle took a last swig of his drink. He ambled across the dance floor in front of the deejay booth, did a half turn on the other side, and saw Feinberg walking past the front desk to the door. In case he would turn around, Garbuncle grabbed a seat at a mostly occupied table, and sat slumped in the chair so his adversary wouldn't see him. Feinberg stopped, looked around, and continued out the door.

Garbuncle saw the guy with the ascot rise from his seat in the rear, and limp out the door. After five minutes, the attorney walked around the rear of the ballroom and on to the door, and peered through the glass. He exited.

Hitchens leaned against the wall on the left. "The coast is clear," he said. "I saw Feinberg go to his car, and Mister Ascot follow him. Earl is waiting in the car."

The two sauntered through the by now half-empty lot to the Mazda on the grass.

"Mission accomplished," Garbuncle announced to Earl. "Tell me what happened with you."

"Nothin' happened with me. That guy in the ascot is another story. His ass is gonna be in a sling, not on a cot." Earl let out a guttural laugh. The other two joined him.

"Didn't know you were a punster," said Hitchens.

"I didn't either. 'Cause I don't know what the hell that is."

"It's somebody who makes puns," said Garbuncle.

"No shit. I already figured that out. So what the fuck is a pun?"

"A play on words," said Hitchens.

"Yeah ... well, I sure as hell didn't play with that dude. That was fun. I got my chops back. Maybe I'll climb into the ring again."

"Don't even think about it," said his landlord. "I need you off the mat."

"Brad here said you was gettin' me another chair if I did the cha cha."

"Yep. I'm going to see what they have at the Like New thrift this weekend." He looked back in time to see Earl roll his eyes. "Don't worry, they have good stuff at that store. It's down there on South Dixie in West Palm Beach. The furniture is top-notch. I'll get you something good."

Hitchens started the car, and they rolled off the grass and out of the plaza into the night.

Chapter Twenty-Five

"You know, we keep coming to Johnny's, and they're liable to track us down one of these nights. We prob'ly oughta change bars." Hitchens looked over his shoulder toward the entrance.

"The same, Joe," said Garbuncle. "Vodka on the rocks."

"Pabst," said Hitchens.

The bartender placed their drinks on the bar.

"I don't think they'll be bothering me for awhile. I'm sure Feinberg told them I'm considering his bribe offer, and they need to hold off till I get back to him. What he and they don't know is that I'm going to delay as long as possible before getting ahold of Seward about a plea bargain. I plan to leave them wondering. Meanwhile, they won't be coming after me. I should be safe for awhile. It's still seven weeks till the trial. They'll wait till no more than a couple weeks before if they plan on doing me in."

"Maybe so, but you damned well better keep your guard up. You don't know what these guys are gonna do. They may decide they don't like the idea of paying a bribe after all. In that case, there's only one other way to keep you from going through with the trial. Bye bye Ham. The curtains come down on a life of ... Well, I'll stop there." Hitchens broke into a wicked smile.

"Thanks for the warning—and the aborted accolade. I'm sure that's where you were going." Garbuncle's smile was sardonic.

***

For the next two weeks, Garbuncle carried his Smith & Wesson wherever he went. That meant he had to wear a suit coat or sports jacket, which he was accustomed to doing, even if these pieces of apparel were far less than natty. If he had to use the restroom in a public building such as a supermarket or restaurant, he entered a stall to urinate so he wouldn't be seen. In his office, he stashed the firearm—loaded—in the top desk drawer, where it was readily accessible. Before opening his car door, he always checked underneath for wires that would indicate an explosive device. In traffic, he continually peered into the vehicles on either side of his at stop signs or lights, and hunkered down in his seat if the windows were opaque. While walking on the street, he scrutinized every man within his vision, and often turned to check if anyone were following him.

He instructed his secretary to keep the office door locked at all times, and never let anyone in while he was away. She expressed alarm, but he told her it was just a precaution in the remote chance a particular client, who had a reputation for a bad temper, would lose control and come after him.

He found this constant vigilance wearing, but it also kept him from over-imbibing—a main reason he found it so taxing, even though he already had cut back on his vodka consumption out of a singlemindedness inspired by the memory of Donna. He figured that if he kept his wits about him, he could survive this ordeal and bring down the murdering band of outlaws out to do him in before he could get justice for Alec Monceau.

Even if he and Alec accepted a plea deal that involved no jail time for Alec, the attorney wouldn't be safe, he realized, because they would always be fearful that he might expose their deeds in some other way.

The phone rang, and his secretary answered. "Ham, a Mister Feinberg. Said he needs to speak with you."

"Uh-oh, I was afraid he'd call. It had to happen eventually. Tell him I must have stepped out for coffee, and ask if I can call him back. I need a little time to figure how to handle this."

He'll ask me if I've decided to try to negotiate with Seward. What will I tell him?

Garbuncle started for the front door of his office, then walked back to the coat tree, donned his suit coat, and took the revolver from his desk drawer. He resumed his journey to the door, peered through the glass, and stepped into the warm sunlight. It was a weekday afternoon, and traffic was light. An attractive young woman in a short, tight skirt and pump heels walked by on the other side of the street. He stared, desire overcoming his thought processes. He sighed, and walked back inside the office.

"Hello Mister Feinberg. Hiram Garbuncle returning your call."

"Yes, Hiram, thanks for getting back to me. It's been a while since we met at the ballroom and discussed a way to resolve the pesky problem involving your client. I haven't heard back from you on a decision whether to accept my offer."

"Ah yes. Well, my client Alec Monceau and I talked it over, and we concluded that, considering the physical injuries and immense turmoil inflicted upon him by the two police officers, forty-five-thousand dollars is a paltry sum. It is woefully insufficient."

"Because you hadn't gotten back to me, I suspected that might be the problem. I talked it over with my clients, and we felt the same as you. Forty-five thousand is inadequate. We are prepared to up the ante. How does ninety thousand sound to you? That's a doubling of the offer."

"I see. Well, that's certainly an improvement. I'll need to present it to Mister Monceau for his approval or disapproval, and we'll go from there. I'll get back to you."

"I understand. Let me remind you, however, that time is running out. We'll need to come to an agreement soon."

"Yes, you're right. I'll give the matter priority attention."

"I'm sure that you will, Hiram, and look forward to settling it and putting the whole unpleasant affair behind us."

***

"Is Alec Monceau working today? I bought a computer from him once, and his advice turned out to be good. I'm thinking of buying a printer, and want his input."

"Yes, he's here until 5 on Wednesdays. Shall I connect you?"

"Oh, no, thanks. I have some business in the area of the Computer Freak in a short while, and I'll just stop in."

Garbuncle drove to the store. He stopped inside the door, patted the inner left side of his suit coat, and turned to scan the parking lot. A conservatively dressed woman got out of her car and headed for the store. No one following the attorney. He looked back at the computer section and saw Alec standing over a small desk at the end of a row of shelves displaying desktop computers. Garbuncle sauntered up to him.

Alec looked up, and beamed. "Oh, mister Ham. I so happy see you."

"It's been a while. Have you been okay?"

"Yes, I do my job. I try no worry."

"I wanted to talk with you about a recent development—uh, something that has happened."

"Oh, dat no sound good." Alec's face sobered.

"No, no, everything is okay. I just wanted to update you on the progress we're making on your case."

"Oh, I breate good again." He laughed softly.

"The reason I came on a weekday morning was that I figured there would not be many customers in the store. I'll keep my voice low anyhow, so nobody can hear me."

"Yes, dat good."

Garbuncle did a slow, panoramic gaze of the store. A nondescript man in blue jeans was checking out office chairs in the furniture department. The attorney surmised that he was oblivious of his surroundings. The woman who'd followed him into the store had gone straight to the stationery section, and was inspecting a packet of something he couldn't ascertain.

"The two police officers and two other men—one is a friend of the cops, and the other is a family member of his—they're trying to get me to plea bargain to avoid the new trial."

Alec's jaw dropped. "What dat mean?

"It means they want to make an agreement to let you off with a light sentence.

They're probably thinking about no jail time or a fine, maybe just a short probationary period."

Alec frowned.

"Don't worry. I'm not going to let them succeed. You would still have a felony on your record, and that would jeopardize your immigration status and your employment possibilities. You wouldn't be able to get a bank loan. It would be bad in a lot of ways."

Alec looked blank.

"Now I'm going to tell you something, but I don't want it to worry you. These people are desperate."

"Pardon, Mister Ham. Des ..."

"It means they're scared, and they're doing extreme, reckless things to protect themselves. They shot at me and my friend twice. The shots almost hit us, but I don't think they intended to kill us. They were trying to scare us. They think I will back out of a new trial."

"Oh, Mister Ham, dis too dang'rous. You no should do dis for me. Maybe we no do trial, judge give me easy sentence."

"That's what they're hoping for. They want to bribe us. That means they will give us money if we don't go to trial—if we plea bargain. But they might—I don't think it's likely—but it's possible the prosecutor would insist you have to return to Trinidad. I don't want to accept that deal."

Garbuncle saw the eager look on Alec's face. "How much ...?" He paused, and the attorney saw the look become sheepish. "What dey want give?"

"Fifty-five thousand dollars to you and thirty-five thousand to me."

Alec gasped.

"It's no good, Alec. These men have to be brought to justice. They are bad men. They have committed two murders, and if they are allowed to get by with it, they might want to try it again. I wouldn't feel safe with them remaining free, and you would be in danger as well. They might decide to kill you so you could never talk about what they did to you."

"Maybe we should take chance." Alec's guilty expression didn't escape his attorney.

"No, Alec. I don't think it would work. They would always be worried that I might bring murder charges against them, and prob'ly would find a way to get rid of me—and you too. We would never be safe." He paused to let that sink in.

"The trial isn't far off. I'm going to keep stalling them. I'll be in touch with you. Don't worry. We're going to get your conviction overturned. And you can keep making money for your family in Trinidad."

***

"Earl, your landlord here." Garbuncle heard the gravelly "hello" by his tenant on the other end of the phone. "You sound drowsy. I woke you? Oh, I'm sorry. You don't usually do the graveyard shift at Walmart. Go back to sleep, and give me a call when you're up. Couldn't understand you. Oh, okay, here's why I'm calling. I went to the Like New place yesterday ... yes, they're open till 2 on Sunday ... and I bought you a chair you're gonna love. When do you wanna pick it up?"

Garbuncle held the phone from his ear. "Now don't get all up in arms." He paused. "You can get up in arms after we get the chair. What am I talkin' about? You don't get it? You're the punster, remember? Now it's my turn. Arms. Chair. Armchair. You can get your arms up on it." Garbuncle cackled.

"Come again? No, I don't drink much these days. You can't insult me about my boozin'. I'm an unrepentant alcoholic." He pressed the phone against his ear. "How? We're gonna tie it on top of the car, like we did the mattress. No, no, you won't have to sit up there. We'll lay it on its side, and it'll be plenty secure. The store closes at 6, and I'll leave my office a little early to pick you up around 5."

***

Earl was waiting at his apartment. He boarded the Mercury, pulled the lever on the side of the passenger seat, and slid it backward.

"What are you doing that for?"

"'Cause if anybody starts shootin', I'm goin' horizontal."

"Nah, nobody's coming after me. Not yet, anyway. They're counting on me trying to get the judge to let Alec off easy if we don't go through with the new trial."

The Mercury meandered through the streets on the way to South Dixie Highway on the near-south side of West Palm Beach.

"Man, if somebody did wanna shoot at us, he'd have an easy target. You drive slower'n a turtle."

"Turtles don't drive, unless there's a species I don't know about." Garbuncle grinned.

"Wise ass."

They arrived at 5:40, and an employee was rolling up an Oriental runner that was displayed on the carpet.

"We're here to pick up a chair I bought yesterday."

"Oh yes," the smiling woman behind the register said. "It's over here."

They walked to a far corner.

"What'dya think?" a beaming Garbuncle said.

Earl stared at the chair, frowning.

"You look like you don't like it."

"It's kinda old, ain't it?"

"Of course it is, man. That's what makes it so valuable. It's a Queen Victoria chair—an antique. It's just got a couple little scratches on it. But that was too much for the owner. She was some rich Palm Beacher. Right?" Garbuncle looked over at the sales lady, who nodded. He noted her strained expression.

"Neurotic, obviously," Garbuncle said. "But her silliness is our gain."

"What'd you pay for it?"

"I got a real bargain."

"You sure did," the lady confirmed. "We dropped the price eighty percent from its original. It wasn't moving, and we needed to make room for other merchandise."

"Them curves up on the back, and the little legs," Earl observed. "Looks girly."

"Geez, you don't know when you got a good thing. If you don't want it, I'll take it and give you the one in my place."

"That beat-up piece o' junk? No thanks."

"Then let's load it up and go. This lady wants to close. You'll get used to it, and you're gonna love it."

***

"Mister Feinberg on the phone, Ham."

Garbuncle sighed. "I knew he'd call. Tell him I'll be there in a minute."

"Mister Feinberg? Mister Garbuncle will be with you shortly."

He already knew what he would say, but wanted to rehearse it in his head.

"Yes, hello Jonah. How have you been?"

"Very well, Ham. And you?"

"Not bad at all. Haven't done any dancing lately, but I plan to take a few lessons, so I can feel more confident when I ask women onto the floor. Not private lessons. I figure I can learn enough to make my way around the floor with group lessons." Garbuncle was going off-script, but was pleased with his conversational way of handling it. Feinberg likely would think he was being spontaneous. It might dispel any notion that he was being duplicitous.

Feinberg laughed—a little too hard, Garbuncle thought. He heard the phoniness in it.

"I know what you're calling about, so let me tell you where I am with this. At the moment, I'm tied up with motions and depositions on two cases I have going. But I've put it on my calendar to contact Darrell Seward."

"When is that going to happen?"

"In two days—Wednesday. Any agreement we come up with has to go before the judge, anyway, and he's too occupied to see us for a little while. He had a murder trial set to begin—a feud by a couple of young black guys over a drug deal."

"So you're going to see about working out a deal with Assistant State Attorney Seward to avoid the trial?"

"Yes. It depends on what terms we can negotiate—whether I can get a light enough sentence for Alec."

"We're getting down to the wire. The trial is less than three weeks away. Isn't there any way you can speed things up?"

"Well ..." Garbuncle paused. "I have a responsibility to my other clients. I'm getting to it as fast as I can.

"Perhaps I can motivate you to try. That is, to give it all you've got."

"What do you have in mind?"

"Let's just say that with my final offer, you won't have to anguish over whether to take private dance lessons or group. You'll be able to take all the private lessons your feet will allow."

"Let's hear it."

"My clients are willing to donate two-hundred-thousand dollars if we can plea bargain out of this. You can split the amount with Mister Monceau in any way you choose."

"Hmmm. I have to concede, that is indeed a lot of money."

"And it would go a long way in Trinidad, if Alec decides to return."

"I can't deny that."

"Mister Monceau wouldn't have to worry anymore about taking care of his family. You could help him invest most of the money prudently, so he would have enough steady income to provide financial security for himself and his family for the rest of their lives. That's if you insist in turning over the entire amount to him. Personally, I think you deserve to keep at least half of it, and the Monceaus still would be in a very good position. They might have to continue working, but we all have to do that."

The two went silent for several seconds.

"I'll see what I can do," said Garbuncle.

"Get back to me as soon as possible."

Garbuncle slowly placed the phone on its cradle. He folded his hands in his lap, and lowered his head into his chest. The wheels in his head turned this way and that. It was more money than he'd ever had at one time. He really needed to think about this.

***

"What's happenin'?" Garbuncle was in an ebullient mood. He hadn't seen his friend Brad in almost a week.

"That's what I wanna know. I was just about to call you. What's cookin'?"

"Well, a couple of steaks, if you're up to it. I'll even buy the steaks—and some asparagus."

"Man, I can't pass that up. A rare offer. Oh, that's right, you like yours medium."

"Huh? Oh ... rare, med—"

"I got nothin' goin' tonight. Hang up the phone, hop over to the store, and get on over here. I've got stuff for a salad. Uh ... leave the gangsters behind."

"It's fall. Getting dark earlier. I doubt if anybody'll pick up my trail. Seven-thirty okay?"

"Yup. See ya then."

The salad was ready when Garbuncle arrived. He and Hitchens chatted about sports, a client of Garbuncle's who wanted to sue his wife for divorce and avoid alimony payments because he discovered her cheating, and a breaking newspaper story about the sheriff's fudging the numbers to get bigger funding for his department.

Their salad devoured, Hitchens went to the kitchen, placed asparagus spears in a sauté pan with some coconut oil, and turned the burner on medium-low. He laid the two strip steaks on a wire rack, slid it into the broiler oven, and returned to the dining table.

"What's the latest with the Monceau case? Something important must be in the works, or you wouldn't be so generous with the victuals."

"I'm in a bit of a dilemma. Feinberg has made an incredible offer in order to stop the trial. I told Alec about that previous offer, and he acted like he might want to take the money and run. I had to talk him out of it."

"So what's the problem?"

"I feel like I'm obliged to tell Alec about this last offer, and he's going to be sorely tempted. In fact, I'm having second thoughts myself."

"How much is it?"

"Hold onto your chair."

"Go ahead."

"Two hundred grand."

Hitchens let out a high-pitched whistle that held for a moment before descending like a waterfall. "That's a lot o' guacamole."

"Yeah, and I'll have a tough time persuading him we shouldn't accept it. I'm not even sure about it myself."

The savory scent of browning asparagus wafted into the dining room, and Hitchens rushed to the kitchen. He returned with a plate of the vegetable and the two steaks.

"You might want yours done more, but it's healthier if you undercook it."

Garbuncle sliced into his steak. "It's pretty damned red, all right. What the hell, I'll be adventurous." He cut a piece off and chewed on it. "Oh wow, this is juicy. Okay, I'm sold."

"Ahh, I got the asparagus stalks just right—a little crunchy, but not too firm," said Hitchens.

Garbuncle took a bite. "I have to hand it to ya. You've got a good touch."

"Now where were we?" said Hitchens. "Oh yeah. Here's the thing: If you accept the offer, and can't plea bargain Alec's way out of this, what then?"

"Then we don't get the money, and we go to trial. Alec seemed inclined to try it with the last offer. That was ninety thousand. Feinberg suggested fifty thousand for Alec and forty thousand for me, although I'd only take thirty-five. Two hundred this time—that would be about eighty for me, one-hundred-twenty for Alec. Hard for both of us to pass up."

"But Alec would still have a record, and that would hurt him in a lot of ways."

"I know. But if he wants to do it anyway, and maybe return to Trinidad ..."

A pregnant pause. "This beef is delish," said Hitchens. "You made a good selection."

"I ain't no slouch."

"You're in a tempting situation, Ham. I wouldn't want to be there. But it seems to me that you have to take yourself out of the equation, and decide which route is better for Alec. It would be easy to decide that taking the money would be in his best interest. And I'm not saying accepting the offer wouldn't be the right thing to do. But if you're honest with yourself, you'll look deep inside to see whether you're rationalizing. You're right about facing a dilemma—a moral dilemma."

The two men fell silent while they polished off their meal, and carried their dishes to the kitchen.

"I'll sleep on it."

Chapter Twenty-Six

Six days later, Garbuncle left his law office and drove to the Computer Freak. It was mid-morning, and he knew few customers would occupy the store. Parking in a front corner of the nearly empty lot offered a panoramic view. A car was just leaving, but none was coming, so he patted the holster in his inside suit pocket and headed for the store, looking around as he walked.

Alec was advising a customer at his computer station, so the attorney pretended to inspect the printer cartridges in a row next to the computers, where Alec could see him. The matronly lady left, and Garbuncle approached. They shook hands.

"I'll be quick, before you have to help another customer."

"It okay. Quiet day."

"The attorney for your opponents ..."

"What that mean? I no know dat word. Oppon..."

"The two cops and their friends."

"Ah, yes."

"Their lawyer has made me another offer. It's huge. Try not to get excited."

"I be calm."

"They want to give us two-hundred-thousand dollars to join them in working out a deal with the judge by which you wouldn't go to jail, and the trial wouldn't be held."

Garbuncle saw Alec's eyes grow as large as eggs. He clasped a hand over his mouth to stifle a gasp.

"You would get one-hundred-twenty thousand, and I would get eighty thousand. They know they're in a lot of trouble. Feinberg is a good attorney, and he wouldn't have them come up with that much money if he wasn't pretty sure his clients would be convicted and get very severe punishment. Maybe even the death penalty. I don't know where they would get that kind of cash. They might have a usurious loan in mind."

"Us ..."

"Oh, sorry. That's a loan at a very high interest rate. The person might charge so much because he thinks the loan is risky. He might not get paid back."

"Oh. Okay."

Garbuncle could tell he didn't understand. "You don't need to worry about that."

"What you tink we do, Mister Ham?"

"I'm having an awful hard time deciding, Alec. Nothing has changed as far as the risk I told you about if we accept the money. But you'll have to decide whether you want to take your chances."

"But Mister Ham, you say you have danger too, no?"

"Well, yes, probably more than you. But let me worry about that. I want to do what's best for you."

"I must tink."

"All right—but it's getting close to the trial date. I'll need to know within a couple of days."

"Okay. Friday I call you at office. I have number."

"Talk to you then."

***

"Hello Mister Ham." Garbuncle recognized the voice on the phone right away, and the greeting—Mister Ham. "I am Alec."

"Hi Alec. Everything okay?"

"Yes, I good."

The attorney detected a somber tone.

"Did you think about what you want to do?"

"Yes, but ... I no can decide. I want you decide."

Garbuncle sighed and leaned back in his swivel chair. "I think it would be better if we discussed this in person. What time do you get off work today, 5 o'clock?"

"Yes. Maybe few minutes later if I have customer."

"Can you meet me at—let me see—how about Hap's Corner on Military Trail? You know where that is?"

"Yes, I see it coming to work."

"Good. I'll meet you there at 5:30. We can sit outside and talk."

***

"Hi Alec. Sorry I'm late." Garbuncle looked around as he sat. They were on the edge of the patio. "You chose a good spot, away from other people."

"Yes, I know we must be alone."

Garbuncle looked back at the entrance road to the rear parking lot. He saw no one.

"What do you want to drink?" he asked, studying the menu that a waitress had placed on the table. "It won't cost you ..." Garbuncle paused. "Get what you want. I'm buying."

"I no drink alcohol, Mister Ham. I just have Coca."

Garbuncle handed the menu back to the waitress. "A Coke for Alec and ... I'll have one too."

"How'd it go today? Business good at the Freak?"

"Not much customer. Easy day."

"Alec, that offer from the attorney—it's a lot of money. For both of us. I agonized for days over this. The money can't be the only consideration. You need to have your record cleared. We talked about it before. With a criminal record, you will be harmed in many ways. I'd have to work out an agreement that would keep the charge of resisting arrest with violence off your record. I don't know if the prosecutor would be willing to go that far. If we go to trial, I'm pretty sure I'd win for you, what with the awfully damaging evidence I've got against the cops. I would let Judge Crabtree try the case this time instead of a jury. He surprised me by allowing me to testify. But if for some reason I didn't win, I think the judge might give you a jail term."

"How long you tink?"

"He could sentence you to as much as a year behind bars. Judge Crabtree has a reputation for being tough."

Alec's eyes widened.

"I don't think he'd give you that long, but I've been surprised before. Six months is well within the realm of possibility. I wish I could read the judge's mind, but I can't."

"I very scared jail."

"I know you are. And to be honest, it's not a pleasant experience. I've never been ... Well, there was that ... I've had a lot of clients who were in the county jail, and from what they've told me, I can tell you that I wouldn't want to spend much time there. A few of the people who end up in jail are like you. They're either innocent, or they just had some bad luck. Some are just guys who aren't very responsible and aren't motivated to do much with their lives. They commit petty crimes to cut corners—to avoid the inconvenience of following schedules and obeying the rules that society imposes on all of us."

"I obey rules. I try be good cit ... citizen. I make appointment fix back light."

"I'm aware of all of that, Alec. The jails don't hold many people like you. But it happens now and then. Justice goes awry."

Alec looked down, and Garbuncle saw the glum look.

"And then there are the predators—the ones who don't belong in civilized society. They ... Thank you, ma'am. Put both on my bill."

They took swigs of Coca Cola. Garbuncle wiped his mouth with a napkin.

"These men are angry at everybody, and have the attitude that the rules aren't meant for them. They want to do as they please, regardless of the effect it has on others. If anybody opposes them, they retaliate with violence. It's all about them. They have no concept of fairness, of getting along with others. These people are the dangerous ones. They're predators. Sometimes they sexually attack people who they think are weak and can't defend themselves."

"Mister Ham, I no want—"

"Hold on for a second, Alec. The possibility of going to jail is only one consideration, though not a big one. A second one is the danger I mentioned before. Even if we plea bargain your way out of this, these men are always going to worry that we might turn them in to law enforcement for what they did. They might decide that they'd be safer if one or both of us were dead. You could go back to Trinidad, but they might come after you and force you to give the money back."

Alec looked up at the ceiling and raised his arms as if imploring God to help him. "Why dis happen me? I no hurt nobody." Garbuncle heard the pleading in his voice, and saw that he was on the verge of crying.

Two young men in worker clothes took an adjacent table, facing away from Garbuncle and Alec.

The attorney lowered his voice. "Life is often unfair, Alec. You have no choice but to deal with it. I know it's awfully hard. But we'll get through it. "

"You good to me, Mister Ham." Garbuncle saw him perk up.

"Now let me make my third point. It simply wouldn't be right to let these men get by with what they did. You think you're being treated unjustly—and you are. But these men caused the deaths of two innocent people. One was a lady I ..." Garbuncle gulped.

"I know, Mister Ham. I sorry."

Garbuncle took a deep breath. "These are the reasons I think we should pass up their offer. But if you want to accept it, I'll go along with you, and we'll try to bargain for a light sentence—nothing more than probation—and skip the trial."

Alec looked over the heads of the workmen, and Garbuncle could see him wrestling internally.

"No. You make good decision. I okay."

"Are you sure? Because I don't want to make up your mind for you."

"I sure. It no problem."

"Fine. Now here's what I plan to do. There's only nine days before the trial. I'm set to meet with Darrell Seward tomorrow and see what kind of deal he's willing to make. It's just to delay these guys, because he can't be too lenient. He knows the media and important people would start asking questions. He's not going to expunge the felony from you record. Feinberg is going to realize that I've been stalling him and have no intention of making a deal. I'm afraid his clients might come after me. So I'm going to leave town day after tomorrow. I'll be back in six days." He pulled a pen from his shirt pocket, and wrote a number on a napkin.

"Here's my cellphone number. Call me if you need to. But be ready to appear in court for the trial."

***

Garbuncle dialed Darrell Seward.

"Oh, hello Mister Garbuncle. I was just about to call you, but you beat me to it."

"Perhaps we had the same thing in mind. I'm wondering if you might want to meet to try and plea bargain the Alec Monceau case."

"That's exactly what I had in mind. Let's do it—the sooner the better."

"Do you have tomorrow morning open—say, 10:30?"

"I don't have anything on my calendar before a staff meeting at 1 o'clock. It shouldn't take us long."

"Good. I'll be at your office half past 10."

***

"Sit down." Seward gestured toward an office chair in front of his desk. "Let's get right to it."

"Okay. What kind of terms are you willing to offer?"

Seward leaned forward, drummed his fingers on the desk, and fell back in his high-backed office chair. "Mister Monceau has a fine reputation. He has never had so much as a traffic ticket. This incident with law enforcement is the only blot on a clean record, and ..."

"I'm sorry I must disagree with you, Mister Seward. The felony he is charged with is not a blot, because he didn't do it."

"Of course you will say that, because you're his attorney, but—"

"I would say it regardless of what my position was, because I witnessed it with my own eyes."

"Fine. However, I don't think we're here to argue Mister Monceau's guilt or innocence. Both of us would like to reach a compromise. As I was about to say, Alec Monceau apparently is considered a valued employee at the Computer Freak. He is frugal, and selflessly sends money to help support his family in Trinidad. I'd like to propose that we eliminate jail time for Mister Monceau."

"That's a big step forward. So far, so good."

"Of course, I cannot simply drop the charge. But what I would like to propose is a sentence of five years' probation, the only condition being that he commit no crimes during that time. Is that something you would be amenable to?"

"I'm afraid not, Mister Seward. That is far too onerous."

"What did you have in mind?"

"I wouldn't want my client to agree to anything more than one year probation—and even that is too much. He still would have a felony on his record, and that would have numerous adverse effects on his life going forward—such things as obtaining a home mortgage— you know what I'm talking about."

"Hmmm. Well, I suppose I could reduce the probationary period to two years."

Garbuncle knew he would accept nothing less than having the felony expunged from Alec's record. But he had to delay the desperate villains long enough for the trial to proceed. He knew that the evidence he had against the four conspirators was so damning that Alec would be declared not guilty, and the attorney then could pursue an array of charges against the officers and their friends, including murder and attempted murder.

"You've sweetened the pot. I'll have to get with my client to see if I can persuade him that it has enough honey. I'll be in contact with you."

CHAPTER TWENTY-SEVEN

"Hey Nick. How's everything?" Garbuncle could hear his younger brother's teenage children chattering and laughing in the background.

"Oh, hi Ham. Same ol' same ol'." Nick spoke into the wall phone in the kitchen of his Clewiston home.

"Agnes okay?"

"Yeah, she's good. We had a little argument the other day, but neither of us holds a grudge, so everything's hunky-dory."

"How's business at the store?"

"Oh, you know, pretty much the same. Planting time for the crops, so the farmers are gearing up. I've been busy inventorying the tools, and got some on order. Good time of the year to be in the hardware business. What's up with you? You recovering from that tragedy with your girlfriend? I'm sorry for you, Ham."

"Yes, I'm gradually adjusting to the loss of Donna. It's not easy." Garbuncle cut off a choke and took a deep breath.

"I shouldn't have brought it up."

"No, no, thanks for asking me. Shows I've got a brother who cares."

The two fell into an awkward silence.

"I didn't mean to get maudlin. I need to ask a favor of you."

"Shoot it to me. What's up?"

"Well, I'm in a dicey predicament at the moment."

"Uh-oh. That doesn't sound good."

"It isn't. This situation that caused Donna's death has intensified. The guys involved in her death have taken pot shots at me'n Earl. You know, my tenant."

"Yeah, sure, I know Earl. Holy crap, you're in big danger."

"It sure looked like it the couple of times when it happened. But I figured it out. I think they were trying to scare me. And they sure as hell did. But I'm still alive, and still going forward with the case."

"I remember you said you got a mistrial. You mean they were trying to get you to drop it?"

"You got it. I've come up with some really incriminating evidence against them."

"Where do you go from here?"

"They're trying to bribe me into plea bargaining. I've been stalling them. But the trial is now only eight days away. They're going to figure out real soon what I've been doing. The only way they can stop the trial is to do away with me. I have to get out o' town till the trial date."

"Oh man, I see where you're goin' with this. Get on over here, pronto. The spare bedroom is waiting."

"Fantastic. I'll postpone some stuff I've got scheduled at the office. Let's see ... Clewiston is about fifty-five miles. I have to go through that bottleneck in Belle Glade where the highways come together. You think it'll be very busy at about 6 in the morning?"

"Nah. Hardly any traffic."

"I think I should start out before dawn to make sure nobody is following me. So it'll take only an hour, hour-and-a-half, I figure."

"Take your time. I'll be at the store, but Agnes will be here."

***

"Is Alec Monceau in today?"

"Yes, till 5 o'clock."

"Thank you. I've talked to him in the past about my computer, and I think I'm in the market for a new one. I'll just stop by."

Jonah Feinberg entered the Computer Freak, scanned the store, and sauntered up to the computer department. Alec Monceau was attaching a price tag to a shelf in front of a Hewlett-Packard desktop computer. He finished, and looked up.

"May I help you?"

"Yes, thank you. I believe you must be Alec Monceau." Feinberg wore a smile that Alec perceived as patronizing.

"I am Alec. How you know my name?"

"Let's just say that we both know the same person."

"I no know who you mean."

"Hiram Garbuncle."

Alec stared at the attorney, not knowing how to respond.

"Am I right?" said Feinberg.

"I know him. How you know him?"

"I'm Jonah Feinberg." He smiled and extended his hand.

Alec hesitated, then slowly raised his right hand and clasped Feinberg's lightly, looking at him with eyes wide.

"There's nothing to be worried about, Alec. I'm here to see if I can help you out of a bad situation."

"I no need help."

"But you do. You could be put in prison. Have you ever been inside a prison?"

"No. I see television prison show."

"Uh-huh. And those are vicious men. They beat and stab and kill their fellow inmates. It's a terrible place to be. You probably wouldn't make it out alive."

Alec's heart raced, and he stared at Feinberg, trying to hide his fear.

"I can make sure you don't go to prison. Not only that, but I can make you rich, so your family won't have to struggle anymore to put food on the table and pay the rent, and will have enough money to see the doctor when they need to."

"I ... I no know what ..." He squeezed his eyes shut and screwed up his face, as if in pain. Feinberg thought he was going to cry, and squelched a smile.

"I'll tell you what we should do. Let's go to dinner at a nice restaurant and talk it over. Once you get some good food in your stomach, you'll be able to think more clearly. Is that okay?"

"Where we go?"

"Let me think a moment." Feinberg rubbed his chin and looked into space. A nattily dressed customer stopped at a computer at the far end of the aisle. He read the information tag while Feinberg eyed him, then sauntered over to the stationery section.

"I know. There's a wonderful restaurant on South Dixie Highway in West Palm Beach. Vitello's. You like Italian food?"

"I no eat res'rant. No have money."

"But it's on me. I'm paying. It's about time you learned something about fine dining. This is gourmet Northern Italian cuisine, prepared by a chef who worked at a famous restaurant in Italy and one in New York. You're going to think you died and went to heaven."

"I sure food good," Alec said.

Feinberg looked at his watch. "I see it's a couple minutes after 5. Shall we go?"

Alec wrung his hands, then rubbed the pockets of his pants. He looked down. "I no should go."

"Alec, there is nothing to worry about. I just think we should talk in a relaxed setting. You don't have to feel any pressure. It can't hurt for you to come with me and enjoy a delicious meal."

Alec sighed. "Okay. I come in my car. I follow."

"But I'm afraid we might get separated, and you wouldn't be able to find it."

"I follow close."

It was Feinberg's turn to sigh. "All right, if you insist. I want you to feel comfortable."

The two cars cut east through the rush-hour traffic, which wasn't as bad as it was going west, where more of the population lived. Feinberg slowed twice when cars managed to squeeze between his and Alec's cars. Arriving at Vitello's, Feinberg pulled up to the awning-covered valet drive-through adjacent to the paved entryway fed by a sidewalk extending around the building from the rear parking lot, where the hoi polloi self-parked. He got out of his car and looked back just as Alec drove into the entrance. Feinberg waved Alec forward as the valet raced the attorney's black BMW into the lot away from the building.

Feinberg extended his hand for Alec's keys, and turned them over to another parker. The pair entered the masonry building, light-green with red trim, through thick, wood-and-glass double doors. Yellow drapes adorned windows on one side. The attorney fixed his gaze on a single man at a small table against a window, and nodded almost imperceptibly when he returned the stare.

In the back of the room, a wide rack of wines stretched four feet from the floor almost to the ten-foot ceiling. White table coverings contrasted well with the red leather cushions of ornate, Renaissance-styled chairs. Atop the tables, white napkins stood like pyramids next to small bread plates graced with gleaming silverware. Booths with high wood backs and leather seats matching the table chairs lined the side that was partitioned from a bar.

The voluptuous hostess in a low-cut blouse and tight skirt escorted the pair to a booth, rather than a table, at Feinberg's request. It was near the front of the room, and Feinberg took the side facing the rear, glancing at the man by the window farther down on the other side. Alec gazed across the room with eyes opened wide.

"I no see nutin like this before. It very fancy."

"Yes, it's nice—my favorite restaurant in West Palm Beach."

"You ... from ..."—he swept his hands in a circular motion—"here?"

"No, but I have several high-end clients in this area. I come here fairly often."

A waiter in a black vest and pants, white shirt, and black bow tie handed them menus.

"I no can read dis," said Alec.

Feinberg chuckled. "Of course not. It's in Italian. Don't worry, I'll help you." He studied his menu.

"Tell you what. I'm going to order two different appetizers that I think you'll like, and we can share them. I've had both. They're great. See where it says Antipasti?"

Feinberg saw Alec's confused look, and leaned forward with his menu, pointing at the section.

"Ah, yes, I see."

"Underneath, see the Carpaccio di Manzo?"

"I see."

"It's beef that's ... well, it looks pretty red, but I think you'll find it delicious."

"I try."

"Then, below that, see the Calamari Fritti? You might know that better as squid."

Alec's face brightened. "Yes, yes, I eat squid. We have in Trinidad. It very good."

"Tastiest tomato sauce I've ever had. Okay, we'll start out with those two appetizers. And I'm going to order two entrees: the Agnolotti alla Panna. Ravioli filled with spinach and ricotta cheese, in a cream sauce. It's my favorite. You'll drool over it. See it? Under Primi."

Alec looked up and down the menu, frowning. "Yes, I find, I tink. I know spinach, cheese."

While Alec searched the menu, Feinberg looked peripherally at the man against the window, who glanced at the attorney while raising a glass of white wine to his lips. Feinberg returned to the menu.

"And for the second entrée, let's have the Quaglie Ripiene—two roasted boneless quails stuffed with Italian sausage and sage. One for you and one for me. It'll be new to both of us. I've always wanted to try it, and I'm sure it'll be good. Everything this place serves is delizioso."

"I see prices. Very 'spensive."

"Just enjoy it, Alec. I'm paying for everything. And let's have a bottle of Beaujolais—the Bouchard Pere & Fils Beaujolais Villages. It should go well with the quail and the carpaccio and everything else. And for dessert—you like chocolate?"

"Oh yes, I like very much."

"Okay, I'm ordering the Mousse Cake for you and the Espresso Panacotta for me."

The young waiter with dark hair combed back arrived and took the order.

"Excuse me, Alec. I need to use the restroom."

Feinberg crossed between the tables to the aisle on the other side, and the man by the window looked up without raising his head. In the restroom, the attorney stooped to look under the stall doors. No one there. Facing a urinal, he unzipped, and pulled his cellphone from a pocket of his suit coat, watching the door. He dialed, and spoke in a low tone.

"Angelo, you saw where we're sitting, right? Good. If I don't call you back after we're finished, everything worked out. Otherwise, I'll call you when he leaves. He drove his own car. It's a Geo Prizm, royal blue, late nineties, I'd say. Looks just like a Toyota. Follow him, and take him out."

Feinberg returned to the booth. The waiter arrived, uncorked the Beaujolais, and poured a small amount in Feinberg's glass. He swirled the wine in his mouth, swallowed it, and said, "Perfezionare. I made the right choice." The waiter smiled broadly, and poured both glasses half full. "Godere di."

Alec stared at Feinberg.

"He told us to enjoy the wine." Feinberg raised his glass, and waited for Alec to copy him. They clinked glasses.

"To a happy and prosperous life for you, Alec, as we put this unpleasant matter behind us."

Alec frowned. "How we do dat?"

The waiter passed by, and Feinberg raised his hand. "Could you bring us each a sharing plate, please?"

Feinberg lowered his head. With eyelids half closed, he smiled in a way that made Alec think of an alligator getting ready to devour its prey. A nature lover, he'd driven one Sunday afternoon into the back roads of Loxahatchee, and seen an alligator creep up on an unsuspecting rabbit on a canal bank and clamp its jaws on the furry animal. The rabbit wriggled and yelped, then went limp. Feinberg frightened him.

"Oh, here comes the waiter with our antipasti." Feinberg directed him to set the ravioli and carpaccio in the center of the table, and place a sharing plate in front of himself and Alec. Feinberg slid part of each on his plate, and exchanged it for Alec's empty plate.

"Try the beef," he said. Alec cut a piece off with his knife and chewed.

"Oh, it soft like butter. Dis good."

"I knew you'd like it. You'll like the ravioli just as much."

They both went silent while indulging in the gourmet dishes. Alec made mewling sounds. "I never have food so good."

"Well, Alec, you'll be able to eat food like this on a regular basis after you accept the offer I'm going to make. Are you ready for this?"

Alec had cleared his plate, and looked up. "I listen."

"If you will take a flight back to Trinidad the day after tomorrow, without telling anybody you're going, I'm prepared to hand you a small case with 2,500 one-hundred-dollar bills. That's two-hundred-fifty-thousand dollars. A quarter of a million."

Alec stared at him with mouth open. "Two hun... you tell joke, no?"

"I'm dead serious, Alec."

"I no know what say. I must tink."

"Take your time. It's an important decision that will determine how well you live from now on. Have another bite of that carpaccio, and down another ravioli. Let your taste buds guide your thoughts. That's the kind of food you and your family could dine on for the rest of your lives."

Both men ate in silence while Feinberg sneaked glances at Alec to gauge his thoughts by his facial expressions. He had a pinched look.

"I sense that you're bothered by something. Care to tell me what it is?"

"How I know police no come Trinidad, take me back?"

"You have nothing to worry about there. I strongly doubt that the state attorney's office will want to get you back for a trial. And the courts are so busy that they'd love to have this off their dockets. It's not worthwhile for them to invest a lot of time and money into a case of such little importance. As long as you don't return to the United States, they're not going to bother you."

"Mister Ham tell me no take money. He say maybe you come Trinidad, take money back."

"Alec, he's just trying to scare you. He wants to win this case. It would be a feather in his cap. He's thinking of himself, not—"

"What you mean, feader in cap?"

Feinberg leaned back, smiling from ear to ear. "That's just an expression. It means that winning the case would give him good publicity and help his law practice."

Alec looked down for several seconds. He straightened, and breathed deeply. "Okay, I agree. Give me money. I go home to Trinidad."

The waiter returned, and poured wine into their depleted glasses. Both sipped.

"You have made the right decision, Alec. A quarter-million dollars is probably more than you could make at the Computer Freak in ten or twelve years. And in Trinidad, that money would go far. Your living costs would be only a fraction of what they are here. You and your family would be financially secure for the rest of your lives."

Feinberg noticed peace come over Alec as he fell back in the booth.

"Now, I have to tell you that the money comes with a caveat."

"What is cav… you give me jewel?"

"No, no, I'm afraid not. A caveat is a warning."

"Oh. dat not good."

"I didn't mean to scare you. Everything will be fine as long as you abide by one condition. You can't tell Mister Garbuncle that I made you this offer and you're leaving. You must leave without contacting him. I'm sorry, but that's the way it has to be. Otherwise ..."

"Mister Ham good to me. What you do if I talk him?"

"I know he is your friend, and you don't want any harm to come to him. For that reason, you must promise to have no contact with him. Is that understood?"

Feinberg watched Alec's face sober and his lips quiver. His eyes moistened.

"Okay. I no talk him."

"Good. Now here's what we're going to do. Tomorrow, after you get off from work, we need to meet someplace."

The waiter arrived with the desserts just as the two men polished off their entrees. They devoured them without talking.

"Dis best choc'late I ever eat."

He hesitated. "We go my 'partment, yes?"

"Uh ... no. I don't mean to insult you, Alec, but I wouldn't feel safe in that neighborhood. My skin is not the right color."

"I no tink it dang'rous for you."

"Maybe not, but I have a better idea. There's a sports bar not far from the

Computer Freak. It's called the Stop Inn, on Military Trail, two or three blocks north of Lake Worth Road. We can meet there."

"Dat dang'rous for me. Many redneck on dat road."

"If you went in alone, yes, it might be a little dicey. But in the company of a white guy, you'll be okay. I'll get there a few minutes early, and wait for you in my car. We'll walk in together."

***

Feinberg parked his BMW over the line dividing two spaces in the Stop Inn parking lot, and waited as the lot began filling up with workers getting off work. He stood outside his car waiting for Alec, and waved to him as his Geo Prizm pulled up. The attorney jumped in his BMW and moved it over to make room for Alec to park next to it.

Workers filed into the bar—tradesmen, construction workers, wanna-be cowboys with the boots and wide-brimmed hats. The two took a seat in a corner. Three men at the bar who had been talking loudly to each other about how they despised their construction boss looked back at the newcomers. They stopped their conversation and stared.

"Men at bar no look friendly," said Alec.

"Don't worry," Feinberg said. "They cause any trouble and they're in for a big surprise." He slowly patted the breast pocket of his suit coat while returning the stares.

"Why you touch coat?"

"I have a gun in there. I represent some scary clients. I always have to be ready."

He knew they had gotten his hint when they turned back to the bar.

The thin, scraggly haired waitress arrived, and Feinberg ordered a glass of white house wine for both.

"I no drink alcohol," Alec told the waitress. "I have Coca."

"Do you work Saturday or Sunday?" Feinberg asked.

"No. Dis week no."

"That's good, because tomorrow is Friday, and your boss won't start looking for you until Monday. You'll of course want to pack a couple of suitcases with your clothes and anything else you can fit in them that's valuable to you. We have to do something with your car."

Feinberg looked up. "Thank you, Miss."

Feinberg clinked his glass with Alec's bottle. "Here's to a great life in Trinidad."

Alec was noncommittal.

"Yes. What I do wid car?"

"I've already got that figured out. Do you have your title to the car?"

"I keep in ... what you call, little closet in car?"

"Huh?" Feinberg frowned, then brightened. "Oh, you mean the glove compartment."

"Yes, yes, dat it."

"We will meet at the tax office in downtown West Palm Beach at 1 p.m. tomorrow. I'll write the directions down for you."

"What reason I tell boss leave early?"

"Oh yes, that's right, you'll need an excuse. Let me see ..." He looked down and stroked his chin. "I know. Tell him you have to be at a law office to give a deposition for your upcoming trial—which won't be upcoming, of course."

"Dat good idea."

"You will transfer the title to me. I will add ten thousand dollars to the quarter-million. It's probably worth half that much, but that's okay."

"You take car tomorrow? Where I leave it?"

"There is an empty lot coated with broken asphalt. It's just northwest of the courthouse. A few people park there for short periods rather than pay the fee in the parking garage. It's on the edge of a seedy area, so it's a little risky leaving a car there for very long. But I'll have someone I know pick it up after I take you to the airport."

"You take me?"

"Yes. I'll have your ticket ready. After we transfer the title, we'll go and sit in my car, and I'll count the money for you. Then I'll drive you to the West Palm Beach airport. The flight is at 4:30. It arrives at Port of Spain Airport in Trinidad at 8:15."

"I call family. Dey come airport."

Feinberg pulled a pen and pad from a coat pocket, and wrote the directions to the tax office and the nearby vacant lot.

"You'd better leave the Computer Freak at 12:15. Park in the lot, and I'll see you in the tax office. It's on the first floor. Just ask a uniformed officer if you can't find it. Be sure to take your passport with you."

Chapter Twenty-eight

Alec drove down back streets on the way to his small apartment south of Lake Worth Road and west of Military Trail. Since his arrest, he always avoided the thoroughfares, which the police patrolled. He'd grown fearful of them, even though he'd made sure everything on his car was working properly and complied with the law, so they would have no excuse for stopping him. He knew they could still pull him over and accuse him of a driving infraction, regardless of whether he was guilty. Even worse, they might beat him. They would lie about it in court, and the judge would believe them. He knew that, if he removed his Obama bumper sticker, the police would be much less likely to stop him again. He considered doing so, but wanted desperately to cling to his childhood belief in the United States as a land of freedom, where one could express political views without fear of reprisal.

Warring emotions swirled through him as he weaved through the streets. Elation over the prospect of greeting his family members with the news that they were suddenly rich gave way to fears that something would go wrong and he wouldn't get to Trinidad. Maybe Feinberg would shoot him with that gun in his coat pocket and dump his body someplace on the way to the airport. Or maybe Mister Ham was right: The men would come to Trinidad and take the money back from him. Maybe they would kill him there. And what if the police from Palm Beach County came to arrest him? Or they might ex… exdite … make Trinidad send him back.

As he drove into the shabby neighborhood where he lived, the streets were almost dark in the waning twilight. The county spent money on street lights along the main streets only. Returning to his apartment at night, he always had to watch carefully for the entrance to the small complex, which he'd missed several times shortly after moving in a few years earlier.

He was glad to see his allotted parking space was empty, so he wouldn't have to find a guest spot and walk farther in the dark to his apartment. Reaching it, he looked around to make sure no one was waiting in the shadows to attack him. An unarmed young man had tried that once, but the athletic, medium-sized Alec had surprised him with a blow to the face, whereupon the man fled.

Inside the rental apartment, he switched on the living room light. The cramped quarters had a tiny kitchen, a bedroom that could not fit much more than a single bed and a dresser, an adjoining bathroom, and the main room, furnished with a three-by-five-foot table, a narrow flowery couch, and an armchair with gray suede fabric. He'd bought the items from a thrift store. He stored his meager possessions in a miniature closet off the bedroom. He kept the apartment clean and fresh-looking.

Alec turned on his seventeen-inch television to hear the news while he set about packing his clothes and few other belongings in an old, frayed leather suitcase. The outpouring of bad news from the TV took his mind off the foreboding thoughts of what was to come the next day.

He set the suitcase near the door, and went to the kitchen. Uh-oh. He'd forgotten to have the power turned off. When he called Mister Ham the next day, he'd ask the attorney to take care of it. He made a ham sandwich and watched an old movie, *Dead on Arrival*, starring Edmond O'Brien. Before retiring, he secured the dead bolt in the door, mindful that several burglaries had occurred in the complex.

He lay on his back, staring into darkness relieved only by a sliver of light from the lone light pole in the small complex, seeping through a crack in the shade. Sleep wouldn't come. He turned onto his left side.

From the airport, he would use his cellphone to call Mister Ham, and thank him for what he'd done. Alec would send the attorney ninety thousand dollars from Trinidad.

The events of the previous few months began playing in his head. Mister Ham had been so good to him, representing him without charging a fee, just because he had serviced the attorney's computer for free a couple of times. Even after the policemen caused accidents that killed Mister Ham's lady friend and his auto mechanic so the cops wouldn't lose in court, the attorney never stopped working for justice.

Ninety thousand wasn't enough for the attorney. But if Alec didn't accept the offer, Mister Ham would get nothing. On the other hand, the attorney's life would be in danger. He knew bad things about the policemen, and they might kill him. Oh my goodness, that's right. He could die.

Alec jerked upright. What was he doing? He sat for several minutes. This was insane. He couldn't go through with it. Mister Ham was right: Alec should not accept the money. He should stay and see this thing through to the end. That's what he would do. In the morning, he would call Mister Ham and tell him about the plan.

The pent-up tension in Alec washed away like an ocean wave receding after crescendoing on the shore. The turmoil over his quandary over, he lay back and turned onto his favored side. A profound calm came over him, and he drifted into slumber.

The alarm wakened him from a dream in which an attractive woman customer from the morning before invited him to a fancy restaurant, where she offered him a large sum of money to cancel his trip to Trinidad and come to her home to help set up her new computer. He sat up on the edge of the bed, rubbed his eyes, and went through the ritual of brushing his teeth, using the toilet, and showering.

Refreshed, he donned the pair of shorts hanging on a clothes tree, and walked to the phone in the kitchen. It was 6:30. He dug into his wallet, retrieved Garbuncle's cell number, and dialed. Alec heard the grogginess in the "Hello."

"Mister Ham, I am Alec. I sorry call you early."

"Huh? Oh, Alec, hi. It's okay. I've been getting to bed early here, so it was time I got up. Is everything all right?"

"No, Mister Ham, not all right. I tell you what happen." He related the restaurant rendezvous with Feinberg, and his offer if Alec would return to

BLOOD ON THEIR HANDS

Trinidad. "I tell him I take money, he buy airplane ticket. He tell me meet him tax office, give him my car. He say he pay me, take me to airport. He tell me no call you—warn me you die. I plan call you at airport, say I send you ninety-tousand dollars from Trinidad. Last night, I no can sleep. I tink. I know I make big mistake. Mister Ham, I so sorry. I very scared."

"Stay calm, Alec. We'll figure out what do to. What time are you supposed to meet him?"

"One o'clock. Courthouse in West Palm Beach."

"What time is it? Let me switch on the light so I can look at my watch. Six forty-five. Good. I'll leave at 7:30. Meet me at my office at 9:30. You remember where it is?"

"Yes, Mister Ham. I be dere."

Garbuncle hustled out of bed and readied himself for breakfast. His brother's wife was frying eggs and bacon, and cooking grits.

"Hey, you're up a little early," his brother said.

"Just got a phone call. Alec may be in trouble. He was taking off for his home in Trinidad, but changed his mind. I have to meet him."

"Well sit down and eat up first. You can't get anything done on an empty stomach."

Garbuncle wolfed down the food set before him, thanked his hosts, and schlepped the few clothes he'd carried in a hanging luggage bag to the car. He drove down the familiar roads, which were heavily trafficked on this Friday in early November with people heading for their workplaces in the towns along the route. Strategies for dealing with the new development played out in his head. He missed the turn at the convoluted highway interchange in Belle Glade, and had to circle around and make the correction.

His secretary was snacking on Fritos Corn Chips as he walked in the door at 9:15. He noted her surprised look. "I thought you wouldn't be back in the office till the Alec Monceau trial on Monday."

"A crisis has come up. Alec called me. He's meeting me here in a little while. Anything happen while I was gone?" Garbuncle hung his coat on the rack.

"No, nothing unusual ... except maybe something a little strange on Wednesday afternoon. Two men walked slowly past the office, and peered through the window. I thought nothing of it, but an hour or so later, they returned from the other direction. One tried to open the door, but I'd locked it. He stood looking for a second, and then they walked away."

"What did they look like?"

"One was wearing a suit and tie. Young, tall, stocky—professional looking. The other one wore worker clothes, middle-aged, good-looking, thick hair, thin mustache."

Garbuncle stared into space, and muttered: "I'll bet I know who they were. The bigger guy sounds like Bart Sutherland, and the worker fit the description Donna gave me of Jake Schmidt."

"I couldn't hear you," the secretary said. "Anybody important?"

"Huh? Uh, no ... yes. I think—"

The door opened, and Alec stood in the doorway. "Alec, come on in."

"Hello, Mister Ham. I sorry for—"

"There's no need to apologize, Alec. Come on back to my desk. We'll work this out." Alec sat in front of the desk in the cheap chair of the kind seen in hotel conference rooms.

"I need some coffee," the attorney said. "I'm going to walk down the block a little ways to the Dunkin Donuts." He started for the coat rack, and turned around. "Want a couple donuts, Alec—and a coffee?"

"Tank you. Yes, I hungry. Too much in hurry cook breakfast." He took his wallet from a back pants pocket.

Garbuncle hesitated. "Put that away, Alec. It's on me. What do you want in your coffee?"

"Cream, sugar, please. Tank you. I want pay." He fished in his wallet.

"No, no, don't worry about it. I got it. And the cream will be real, not that low-fat or fake stuff. My buddy Brad Hitchens—you know him—he preaches to me that low-fat milk is junk. He studies this stuff, and says saturated fat is healthy.

"I never hear dat."

"No, and you probably never will, because ... Okay, no more nutrition today. We're looking at something a lot more dangerous than low-fat milk."

Alec still had his wallet out. "I pay tip." He fumbled for a bill.

"Absolutely not." Garbuncle's voice was raised. "It pisses me off when you're standing in line, and they have a tip jar. All they're doing is taking your order and handing it to you. That's not service. It's what they're paid to do. If they're not paid enough, raise the prices, but don't make beggars out of them. Every place you go these days, somebody wants a hand-out. It's enough to drive a guy to bankruptcy. And don't get me started on women." He chortled, but quickly sobered and grew quiet. "Except Donna. She never asked for anything, and gave a lot—of love."

He paused, reflecting, then grabbed his coat from the rack. He returned to his desk, and took his revolver from the drawer. Alec's eyes grew big.

"What you do wid gun?"

Garbuncle patted it, and Alec noticed his sly smile. "I'm always on the lookout for these guys. They've shot at me more than once, and if they try it again, they're in for a surprise." He jammed it into his inner coat pocket.

"I never shoot gun."

"I've never shot anyone, and hope I don't have to. I'll be back in a few minutes."

The secretary walked up to Alec and handed him a copy of *Time*.

"Tank you."

He'd leafed through the magazine, and was struggling to read a story about the soon-to-be-held presidential election when Garbuncle returned. He handed the donuts and coffee to Alec, who poured the condiments into the beverage and stirred.

Garbuncle did the same with his, and took a sip. "So tell me what happened."

"Mister Feinberg come Computer Freak, say he take me 'spensive res'rant. I 'fraid what he do if I no go. I eat very good food, drink much wine. He say he give me two-hundred-fifty-tousand dollar if I go back Trinidad. Everyting be okay, nobody come get me, he say. I say okay. He say we meet next day, he give me ten-tousand dollar for car. I must meet him 1 o'clock. We change title, he give me money take on airplane. He count money in car, put in little box, take me to airport. He have airplane ticket."

"Oohh, my ..." Garbuncle shook his head. "I should have known that bastard would come up with something sinister. Look, what you did might have saved you. If you'd have refused his deal, he might've had you killed so the retrial couldn't go forward. So don't regret accepting the money. It probably will turn out to have been the right thing."

"You make me feel better, Mister Ham. I no deserve."

"Forget it. You're supposed to meet him at 1 o'clock at the courthouse and turn the title over to him, right?"

"Yes, Mister Ham. Mister Feinberg say leave car in parking lot near courthouse. Almost nobody in dat lot, he say. He park dere too."

"And you said he's going to count out the money for you, and put it in a packet that you can carry on the plane, and drive you to the airport."

"Dat right."

"Do you have any idea where these guys came up with a quarter-million dollars in such a short time?"

"I never tink."

"They're not wealthy. I can almost guarantee you that money is counterfeit."

Alec's jaw dropped.

"Feinberg is an attorney for mobsters. He has sources. I'd bet real money that he found someone who's an expert in printing fake money."

Alec's eyes widened. "Mister Ham, you so smart. I tink you right."

"And how was he going to pack the money so it would get through the x-ray inspections at the airport?"

"He say put lead 'round it. X-ray no can see trough."

"I suppose that's possible—but an X-ray wouldn't be able tell if it was counterfeit. Now here's what we're gonna do. Tell Feinberg you changed your mind about the car, and decided to give it to me. Tell him you put the keys with a letter in an envelope and mailed it to me, then took a bus downtown. If he asks where you were living, say he doesn't need to know that. If he keeps pushing you to tell, ask if he plans to steal it. I'm sure he'll back off."

"I give you keys."

"Where did you park?"

"Fern Street, two block west from Olive Avenue. Sout side."

"Good. Easy walking distance if I have to move it for some reason."

"Yes. I walk here five minutes."

"Is your luggage in the car?"

"Yes. I have big suitcase, hanging bag."

"Oh, thank God for the hanging bag, because you can carry that on the plane. You'd have to check the suitcase in, and it would go to Trinidad. We need to transfer as many things as possible from the suitcase to the bag, so it'll look bulky and Feinberg will think those are all of the belongings valuable enough to take with you. Go get your car and park right out in front."

"I no want lose space. I walk here wid suitcase and bag."

"Are you sure? Aren't they heavy?"

"No heavy. I strong."

Alec set out for his car. Fifteen minutes later, he walked into Garbuncle's office with the bags.

"That was really fast. And you're not even out of breath."

"It easy." He handed the keys to Garbuncle.

The attorney escorted him to an open space in the back of the office, where a shabby couch that he occasionally napped on sat near a side wall. Alec laid the hanging bag on the floor, and opened the suitcase. He withdrew several pairs of pants and a half-dozen shirts, and laid them atop a sport coat, a light winter jacket, and three pairs of walking shorts. He also took from the suitcase a pair of athletic shoes, one of street shoes, and a leather bag of toiletries. These he stuffed into the wide zipper pockets at the bottom of the hanging bag on both sides. The front side already held his underwear, socks, and two ties. One of the pockets had more room, which he would need later. He zipped all of the openings shut, and held the bag up.

"Perfect," said Garbuncle. "It's hulky, and it's feasible to surmise that all of your possessions are inside."

"Feas ... dat okay?"

"It just means that it makes sense."

"Oh. What sur ...?"

"Surmise just means to assume, or believe."

"Tank you. I want know new words."

"I will drive you to a couple of blocks from the courthouse. You will walk to the entrance. You'll have to go through the screening. Just lay your bag on the conveyor. There's nothing in it that will set off an alarm. If the attendant asks you what's in it, just tell him you're going from there to the airport for a trip."

"I can do."

"Wait on a bench just inside the screening area so you can see Feinberg when he enters. Tell him you're giving the car to me. You already called the tax office, and they said you could transfer the title by mail."

"Dat smart."

"He will have you walk with him to his car in the nearby lot, and count the money. You will put the packet of money in the pocket of your hanging bag. He'll drive you to the airport, and likely will want to escort you to the gate. If the packet of money doesn't cause any trouble getting the bag past the security checkpoint, you will go to the boarding area and wait. Feinberg probably will want to wait with you, and that's allowed. When the agent calls for passengers to board, you will shake Feinberg's hand and say goodbye. You'll show your boarding pass and passport to the checker, and walk up the ramp to the plane."

Garbuncle saw the alarm in Alec's face. "I no want get on plane. Why I go up ramp?"

"Because Feinberg might—in fact, he probably will—he'll be waiting to make sure you get on the plane. Don't come back off the ramp before the plane takes off. So what you will do is stand aside at the end of the ramp, allowing the passengers to walk past you. When they've all boarded, the agent will ask you why you're not getting on. Tell her or him you forgot something important, but don't want the person who took you to the airport to know that you didn't board. When the plane leaves the ramp, you will walk back inside the airport."

"What happen Mister Feinberg still dere?"

"Then we're screwed." Garbuncle chuckled, but he saw the concern in Alec's face. "I'm sorry, Alec. I know this is no laughing matter for you. It isn't for me, either. If Feinberg hasn't left, you need to become a thespian. Excuse me, that means an actor. I know you're a very honest person, but you'll have to tell a big fat lie. Say you left something very important in your apartment—a locket of hair from your deceased wife. You'll have to go back and get it, and take a later flight. Go with him to the desk to check on later flights. If that's the only one leaving today, let him book one for tomorrow. It'll cost him more money, but he won't mind. He's not paying for any of this. They're paying him."

"Who dey?"

"I just mean the two cops, Larry Pickens and Pete Bullard. And their scummy friend Jake. And Bart Sutherland."

Garbuncle looked at his watch. "It's only 10:45. Did you put money in the parking meter?"

"Yes. But meter say park only two hour."

"Okay, let's go and move it. I know a place farther west where there's no time limit and it's free. It's near a run-down old hotel."

Alec carried his now-empty suitcase, and they walked the short distance to the garage where Garbuncle had parked, figuring he wouldn't be there long. He scanned the streets and the garage for anything suspicious. They drove to Alec's car. Garbuncle returned the keys, and Alec followed Garbuncle to the remote spot, whereupon they returned to the attorney's office. Garbuncle parked a block away, and fed the meter.

"Why don't you go sit on the couch, Alec? I have a little business to take care of."

Garbuncle asked his secretary for the phone numbers of the insurance agent for the company Donna's car was insured with, and the one for Giovanni, the art restoration expert. The attorney called the agent to get confirmation that the certified mechanic was set to testify Monday or Tuesday. Garbuncle then called Giovanni, and left a message reminding him of the court date.

The attorney got on his computer, looked up the airline flying to Trinidad, and dialed. The agent told him the flight was on schedule, departing at 4:30.

"It's a little after 12 noon, Alec. Let's get going." They walked down the street to Garbuncle's car, and he drove to within two blocks of the courthouse, scurrying into a spot that a car had just pulled out of. It was a balmy, sun-drenched day, and he pushed the buttons on the Mercury's doors that rolled the windows down.

"Here's what I think you should do after you come back inside the airport from the ramp. Stay in the waiting area for fifteen minutes. That will be enough time for Feinberg to get to his car, unless he stopped in a bar or restaurant at the airport. Then go to the baggage office on the first floor, and wait for me." Garbuncle looked at his watch. "Okay, I think you'd better walk over to the courthouse now."

"I scared, Mister Ham."

"Just take a deep breath. I'm going to park near that lot where Feinberg is leaving his car, and I'll watch when you two come out of the courthouse and walk to the car. When he drives away to drop you off at the airport, I'll follow at a distance. Don't worry. This is going to work out."

Alec pulled his garment bag from the back seat, and walked stiffly to the courthouse, where he passed the stone structures serving as both art and barriers to vehicular attacks. Inside the brass-plated doors, a uniformed officer greeted him with an order to place his bag on the conveyor belt along with his wallet, belt, watch, and pocket change. He passed through the scanner, and recovered his belongings at the end of the conveyor.

He looked around, saw only a few people walking down the halls at the end of the atrium. He took a seat on a wooden bench against a wall, and waited, studying the people trickling in: professional types in suits and ties, or knee-length skirts or dresses in plain, businesslike colors; men and women casually dressed for jobs in commerce or government; and elderly folks in street attire. The big majority were white, and Alec envied them, knowing their chances of facing a crisis with the law of the kind threatening him were remote, and they were free of the fear that had been instilled in him.

Feinberg entered, carrying a manila envelope, and passed through the electronic surveillance. Alec held his hand up, and the attorney approached him. Alec stood, and accepted Feinberg's outstretched hand.

"Where did you park? It's not in the lot where I told you to leave it." Alec heard the aggravation in Feinberg's voice, and saw the pinched expression. He felt unnerved, but determined that he would summon the courage to be resolute.

"I change mind," he said without flinching. "Mister Ham good to me. I want him have car."

"So where did you leave it?"

"I leave it at 'partment. I put keys in envelope wid letter, mail him. I take bus here."

Feinberg stared, and Alec could tell the attorney was debating with himself whether to believe the explanation. Alec stared back, and Feinberg perceived that he was undaunted.

"Didn't you bring a suitcase?" He gestured toward the bag. "Is that all you're taking to Trinidad?"

"It all I need. I tell Mister Ham in note, give tings in 'partment to homeless or charity store."

"Well, then we won't have to transfer the title. Let's go to my car, and I'll give you the money." They exited the courthouse and headed for the nearly abandoned lot, where Feinberg's black BMW was parked. The radiant blue sky was mostly clear, and the car glistened in the sun's rays. The few cumulus clouds seemed to avoid them, Alec thought, like dogs staying clear of a porcupine in his native Trinidad.

The BMW's interior was hot, and Feinberg turned on the motor and set the air conditioning on high. He reached into the back seat and withdrew a travel bag from the floor. He pulled a zipper back. Inside was a smaller bag. The attorney unzipped it and withdrew an eight-inch cubic box made of lead, the sides held firm by glue. The top was loose, and he dumped two thick wads of bills onto the seat.

Alec's eyes grew large. A twinge of regret that he wouldn't be getting that money swept through him. Then he remembered Garbuncle's warning: It likely was counterfeit.

Feinberg reached into the back seat and lifted a piece of plywood measuring three foot by one foot into the front seat. He laid it across their laps.

"This is going to take a while," Feinberg said. "There are 2,500 of these hundred-dollar bills. I'm going to count out twenty-five stacks of them.

As Feinberg thumbed through the bills, he handed each stack to Alec, who positioned them side-by-side on the board. Alec lost track of the counting, but knew it didn't matter.

"It's all there," Feinberg said. "Did you count with me?"

"Yes, you count right."

Feinberg inserted the stacks into the lead box in two piles, and put the lid on. He wrapped two tight elastic bands around it, and placed it in the small, zippered bag, which he handed to Alec. He opened the back door on the passenger side, and placed the bag in the pocket of his hanging bag,

"Are you happy?" Feinberg asked.

Alec remembered Garbuncle's admonition to summon whatever thespian talent he had. His mouth opened into a bright, toothy smile that Feinberg interpreted as greed. "Oh yes. I very happy."

"I guess we're ready to go then," said Feinberg. He drove down Dixie Highway two miles to Belvedere Road, then west a shorter distance to the airport. He took a spot in the parking garage across the entrance road from the row of various airline departure fronts, and fed the meter. The pair went straight to the escalator leading to the second floor gates, Feinberg explaining that he'd already retrieved the boarding pass from his computer.

At the gate, Alec remembered that he had to remove his shoes. He laid them with his bag, wallet, wrist watch, and pocket change on the conveyor belt. Feinberg was right behind him, and did the same with his possessions. The agent instructed Alec to remove the bulky package in the bag.

He did so.

"What's in that heavy box?" the agent asked.

Feinberg had instructed him what to say. "I sell house. Give money family in Trinidad."

"I'm his attorney, sir." Feinberg handed his business card to the agent. "I negotiated the sale of his house. I helped him locate a strong container to keep the money secure. I'm seeing him off."

The agent studied Alec's impassive face, frowning. Alec's heart pounded, and he was afraid the agent could hear it. The agent looked at Feinberg, who gave a reassuring smile.

"How long has he lived in this country?"

Feinberg had prepared for this. "Twelve years. He's very frugal, and was able to buy a house on a short sale for a great price. He just sold it for a good profit, and wants to rejoin his family in Trinidad to help them financially. His daughter is in ill health."

The agent's frown disappeared, and he waved them on. They found their way to the United Airlines gate for the Trinidad flight.

It was 2:30 p.m., two hours before departure. Feinberg confirmed with the desk agent that it was on time.

"Nothing to do but wait," he said. "We can just relax and watch television—catch up on the news. They've got it on CNN."

"You no need wait, Mister Feinberg. I be fine."

"No, no, I'm going to wait with you, just in case something goes awry."

"Awry. What dat word? I jus know bread."

"Huh?" The attorney's brow wrinkled, and he stared at Alec. "Bread?" His expression changed, and he laughed heartily. "I get it—rye bread. Awry means to go wrong—in case something happens that we didn't anticipate."

"I learn more new word."

Feinberg lost interest in the television news, and repositioned himself on a couch facing out at the planes taxiing. He stretched Alec's garment bag across the top of the vinyl couch back, and rested his head on it. Alec, sitting on a couch facing away, was still a little nervous. He rose and ambled down the wide hall, peering into the shops. On his return, he stopped in the restroom. Emerging, he saw Feinberg standing in the aisle, looking in his direction.

"You had me worried," he said when Alec made it back to the gate waiting area. "Where did you go?"

"I no go far. I tired sitting, go look in windows at tings." He sat on the couch and watched the TV. Soon the desk agent spoke into the microphone: "Passengers for flight six-sixteen to Trinidad may begin boarding. This is the first call."

"Okay, it's time for you to go."

"I like wait few minute. No like sit long time on airplane."

"All right. There's no rush."

They chatted about the weather. Feinberg had checked, and it was mostly sunny and eight or ten degrees warmer in the island country than in South Florida.

The agent issued a second call, and Alec rose to go. Feinberg extended his hand, and wished him well.

"Tank you for money," Alec said, faking a smile. He walked to the ramp and showed his papers to the boarding agent, who checked them and waved him on. Alec strolled to the end of the ramp, stopped, and leaned against the wall on the left, where it would be harder for the greeting flight attendant to see him. A stream of passengers passed him, and then he was alone. But another group approached after the third and final call was made. When all were inside, a male attendant stepped onto the ramp.

"Is everything okay? It's time to board."

Alec's pulse quickened. "I no can fly. I forget important ting. Must go back. Get flight later."

"Oh, I'm sorry. I have to ask you to go back inside the airport."

"Please allow me wait. Somebody inside I no want see. I want wait till plane leave."

The attendant frowned. "Who's waiting inside?"

"Man who tink I go Trinidad. He bad man. I no want him know I no go."

"Well ... you have to go back inside after the plane rolls toward the runway. Can you agree to that?"

"Yes, dat no problem. Tank you so much."

The attendant returned to the plane, and pulled the door shut. Several minutes elapsed, and Alec heard the plane engine rev up. He waited several more minutes, and walked slowly to within a dozen feet of the ramp entrance. The agent had left, and he waited a little longer, then took slow, deliberate steps to the inside. He stood and glanced to his left. No Feinberg. He walked to the nearest lounge chair and sat. Through the windows, he saw the back of the plane as it disappeared on its journey to the runway, and exhaled.

His watch showed 4:40 p.m. He would stay till 5, then go to the luggage desk on the first floor, where Garbuncle would be waiting. He glanced alternately out the window and down the hall, wary that Feinberg might return. An American song he'd heard on the radio in Trinidad many years before popped into his head: *The Man Who Never Returned*. The Kingston Trio. As a young man, he'd loved to hear the leader, Bob Shane, sing along with the vibrant strumming of the banjo in the background.

He hoped Feinberg wouldn't return, but felt uncomfortable. Into view, through the windows, a plane rolled slowly in the direction of the gate. Alec jerked upright. It was a United plane, and looked just like the one to Trinidad.

Down the hall, he made out the figure of Feinberg headed his way, staring out the windows as he walked. Alec jumped off the couch, grabbed his garment bag, and marched away in the opposite direction. He knew that Feinberg would be at the gate in seconds, inquiring as to what happened. He had to get out of the hall—fast. But where could he go?

The bookstore was directly on the other side, but crossing to it would put him in full view of his nemesis. The restrooms were fifteen feet away, but he couldn't take a chance; Feinberg might use the men's room.

Walking with head down, almost running, Alec darted into the entrance for the ladies' room, stopping behind the partition blocking a view of the room. A late-middle-aged lady in a dress reaching inches below her knees emerged. She threw her hands up, and yelped.

"Please ma'am, I no hurt you. I hide from man want hurt *me*. I leave soon." She slid past him, shrinking against the wall, and hurried into the hall. Alec held his breath, but no other women entered or departed. After a minute, he peeked into the hall, and saw Feinberg standing in the middle, staring at the entrance to the ramp. Alec knew he was waiting to see if anyone might get off the plane. Feinberg walked toward the waiting area on the other side of the gate, and Alec figured he wanted to look out the windows to see if the ramp were reconnected with the plane.

Alec hurried to the waiting area on the opposite side of the gate, and sat next to the windows. He held his bag in front of him and fiddled with a zipper, as if searching for something inside. But he was looking furtively beyond the bag.

With Feinberg nowhere in sight, he scrambled to his feet and, head lowered, stepped briskly down the hall toward the escalator. He heard an agent over the intercom: "Attention everyone. Flight six-sixteen to Trinidad has returned to the gate for a maintenance check. We expect that the problem will be corrected in a half-hour to an hour. We do not think passengers will need to deplane during the wait, but they will be allowed to if they wish. Thank you for your patience."

Good, Alec thought. Feinberg probably would wait to see if anyone got off the plane to be sure Alec hadn't taken the opportunity to change his mind.

Feinberg walked to the check-in desk. "What seems to be the problem, ma'am?"

"Oh, it's minor. The crew discovered that the cabin door failed to close securely."

With the bag slung over his back and head lowered, the computer salesman made it to the escalator. But he knew he could get to the first floor faster via the stairs, which he descended two at a time. He half-ran to the luggage office at the end of the baggage area. Garbuncle sat inside on a stiff-backed chair.

"It took you a while," he said, smiling. "I was getting a little worried."

"We must leave quick. Mister Feinberg still in airport."

"Holy crap. How do you know?"

"I see him, but I tink he no see me. I do trick. I go ladies resroom."

Garbuncle laughed. "Good thinking. Yeah, let's vamoose." They hurried to the Mercury parked in the garage across from the terminal building. Garbuncle drove down the arteries leading to his office on the edge of downtown, and found a nearby parking spot.

"You need to take your bag to my office so we can inspect that money."

They went to the couch in the back, and Alec withdrew the lead box from his bag. Garbuncle took the elastic bands off and emptied the contents onto the couch. He withdrew a bill, taking care not to put his fingerprints on the other bills, and held it to the ceiling light.

"Uh-huh. I was right. This money is fake."

"Yes? How you know?"

"See that picture? That's Ben Franklin, one of the great people of American history."

"Yes, I see. What wrong?"

"Hold it to the light. See that other picture to the right of Franklin, faintly visible, sort of in the background? That's called the watermark and it's Abraham Lincoln."

"I know Abraham Lincoln."

"Yes. He's on the five-dollar bill. That watermark is supposed to be Benjamin Franklin, same as the main picture."

Garbuncle took the bill and held it to the light again. "There's supposed to be a narrow, vertical bar on the left. It's called the security strip. No strip to be seen."

Alec stared at Garbuncle, agape. "Mister Ham, you so smart. Mister Feinberg try cheat me. I so glad you tell me no go Trinidad."

"I'll take the box with the so-called money to the courtroom Monday," said Garbuncle. "Be at my office at 8:30 a.m."

A devilish smile crossed his face as he muttered, "The shit is about to hit the fan."

CHAPTER TWENTY-NINE

"So you're back. How's it going with Alec?" Brad Hitchens cradled the phone on his shoulder while he continued typing on the computer.

"I'll tell you all about it later. You don't have to fill in at the *Hawk* Sunday, do you?"

"No," Hitchens answered. "Everything's been pretty quiet around here. Slow news days."

"Good, because I'm in a good mood with Alec's problems with the law about to end, I think. I've been getting my apartment in order today—somewhat. At least I don't have stuff lying all over the floor. I'm looking forward to the Dolphins game tomorrow. It's the Sunday night football game on NBC. They're playing the Patriots. Big challenge. Miami is doing great this year. Looks like they're headed for the playoffs."

"Yeah, amazing comeback after that disastrous season last year."

"Why don't you come over? I'll rustle up dinner."

"Sounds good—except for you doing the cooking. I got a better idea. Why don't you order a pizza or two—a good one, not one of those cardboard specimens from the supermarket? Maybe Cucina Pizzeria, or one of those brick-oven places. That'll make it easier for you. Oh, and you can spend the cooking time cleaning your pad, instead."

"Well, okay, my pad's not so bad now, but whatever."

"Everything is relative."

"I'm having Earl over, too."

"All right. And I'll bring the beer. Oh, that's right. You only drink vodka."

"No, beer is fine. I've been lightening up on the booze lately."

"You know, I noticed that. Good. I'll be over there about—what, 8?"

"Yeah, maybe 8:15. The game starts at 8:30, and I've gotta get the pizza first. Don't wanna pick it up too early, or it'll be cold by game time."

***

"Feinberg told me Alec Monceau is gone," Bart Sutherland said. "He boarded a plane for Trinidad. Feinberg gave him the counterfeit, and away he went into the wild blue yonder. So that problem is solved."

"Fuckin' A, that's great," Jake Schmidt shouted. He sat at a table in Sutherland's office. It was Saturday, and no other state attorney's personnel were there.

"Don't get too excited," the investigator said. "That was only one part of the equation. The opera ain't over till the fat lady sings. I'm just afraid that little attorney is gonna sing. No way he'll just forget about what happened."

Sutherland saw the looks of elation evaporate from the faces of Schmidt, Larry Pickens, and Pete Bullard. "As long as Garbuncle is around, we'll never be able to rest easy."

"I get your message," said Pickens.

"Loud and clear," Bullard joined in. "So what're we gonna do? We have to act fast. There's only two days left before the trial."

"Well," said Sutherland, "Alec Monceau obviously is not going to be there. But Garbuncle will, and he'll be explaining everything to the judge. Feinberg couldn't get him to accept our offer, but he'll tell the judge that we made it— that we attempted to bribe him. That won't go down well."

"That's an understatement," said Pickens.

"The only solution to this is to prevent Garbuncle from meeting with the judge," Sutherland said. "I think you know what that means. It's our only hope."

Schmidt and his two friends, the police officers, looked down at the floor in Sutherland's office. Their glum looks did not escape Sutherland.

Pickens looked up. "We've already got a lot o' blood on our hands. A little more's not gonna change things. We gotta do what we gotta do. We've got nothin' to lose."

***

The temperature was seventy-five degrees, and Garbuncle wasn't headed to a social or business event on this balmy Sunday evening, but he donned his sport coat. He needed it to hold his Smith & Wesson.

He walked out of his condo building, looked around, and continued to a guest parking space half a football field's distance away. His designated space was empty so that anyone looking for his car would be thwarted, or at least the job would be more difficult. As always, he checked for any loose wires under his car.

He arrived at Romeo's Coal-Fired Pizza at 7:40 p.m. The two pizzas, a large and a medium, weren't quite ready. Ten minutes later, he headed back to the condo, the piping hot Italian pies warming his car. He turned off the air conditioning to keep them hot.

Somebody had taken the guest spot he'd left, so he parked in a different guest space. He had told Hitchens to park in his designated spot in front of the condo, but a different car than the Mazda was there.

"Inconsiderate people," he mumbled while entering the condo building.

He inserted his key into the lock on the door, twisted it, and turned the handle. The door didn't budge. "What the hell?" he said aloud. "I just locked it." *I must have left it unlocked. How could I be so careless?*

He unlocked the door, and entered. He switched on the light next to the door, and turned around. He let out a cry, and almost dropped the boxes of pizza.

"Hello Mister Garbuncle. I see that you've brought dinner for us. How nice of you."

Garbuncle reached into his coat pocket. The man who'd addressed him grabbed the pistol lying on the small table next to the chair he sat in, and pointed it at the attorney.

"Don't even think about it," the man said. Another man sat in the rickety chair in front of Garbuncle's computer desk. The attorney recognized him immediately as

Sergeant Pete Bullard. The man with the gun approached slowly, reached out to take the pizza, and laid it on the floor to the left. Garbuncle was speechless with fear. He turned to run for the door, and the man swung the pistol, catching Garbuncle on the back of the head. A gash opened, and blood flowed, matting his salt-and-pepper hair. He staggered, and almost fell. The man grabbed him by the arm and held him up.

"I don't think we've met. I'm Jake Schmidt." He pulled Garbuncle's coat off and dropped it on the floor next to the wall.

Garbuncle looked up, and got a peripheral view of a man standing farther away to the right, near the kitchen entrance. He knew it was Officer Larry Pickens.

"Gentlemen, I'm sure we can settle this without further violence," Garbuncle said in a quavery voice. His adversaries heard the pleading.

Pickens strode up to him, bowed at the knees, and Garbuncle remembered thinking in the courtroom that the cop walked as though he had a poker up his ass.

"Don't worry," Pickens said. "There won't be any more violence—as long as you do what you're told."

"Anything," Garbuncle said. Pickens thought the attorney was going to cry, and the officer felt his penis harden.

"I'm sure you will. Haven't you had a bath in a while? You smell pretty ripe."

"I just took a bath yesterday."

"Well, I think you need another one. Don't you think so, guys?"

Schmidt and Bullard nodded.

"Is that your bathroom, on the right there, in the little hallway next to the bedroom?"

"Yes, but I don't think I need to take a bath."

"Thank you for your opinion, but it doesn't count. You need to clean that blood out of your hair. Now let's go to the bathroom."

Garbuncle was on the verge of going to the bathroom in his pants. He hobbled up to it.

"What I need for you to do is fill the tub with water. Go ahead. Pull the drain shut and turn on the faucet."

Garbuncle obeyed, and Bullard came to the little hall and stood outside the bathroom to watch.

"Why did you have to go and make things difficult for yourself?" Pickens said. "Was that nigger worth all this trouble?"

"I'm a defense attorney. I was just doing my job."

"But you did it pro bono. You didn't have to do that."

"Attorneys are required to do a certain amount of pro bono work."

"You chose the wrong person to help."

"What are you going to do?"

"What do you think we should do?"

"I think we ought to forget all of this ever happened. I'll meet with Darrell Seward tomorrow and tell him we want to plea bargain."

"It's a little late for that," Bullard said. "You've gotten us all too deep in doo-doo." The water was a foot high in the tub.

"Okay," said Pickens. "Time to take your clothes off and climb in."

"I'd rather not. I'm a little shy."

Pickens laughed, and Garbuncle could tell it was mockery, not humor. "Come now. I'm sure you have a wonderful body."

"But—"

"Hey dude, off with the clothes." Garbuncle heard the curtness in Pickens' tone. The attorney removed his shoes and socks, and began undressing—first his shirt, then his pants and underwear.

Pickens dipped a hand into the water. "Perfect. You're gonna get real relaxed and feel great. Now go on in."

Garbuncle stepped in, and lowered himself to a sitting position, his legs stretched forward.

"How's that feel?" said Pickens. "Good? Just lay back and relax. Slide down lower. To really feel good, you need that warm water on your chest. Reach your legs to the end, and put a foot on the drain plug. This tub's kind o' old, and you don't want the water to leak out. We want you to be as comfortable as possible."

He turned and called, "Jake, we need you."

Jake walked up, carrying an old, marred radio. He was wearing rubber gloves. "We thought you might want to hear a little music while you're taking your bath."

Garbuncle froze with fear. "Where'd you get that radio?"

"Oh, just something I had laying around the house." Schmidt plugged the radio cord into a socket above the sink, next to the bathtub.

The men heard the apartment door open.

"Hey. Ham. I'm here holding this cold beer. Where are you?"

Bullard came charging into the living room. Hitchens dropped the six-packs and ran back out the door, Bullard in pursuit. Earl had just come up the hallway, and crashed into Bullard. Earl twisted the gun out of the sergeant's hand, and grasped his arm while flipping his own back into the policeman's chest. With a mighty downward thrust, Earl catapulted Bullard into a somersault. The hefty sergeant landed on his back on the tile floor with a whump. Hitchens grabbed the gun from the floor and hustled to the left side of the door, flattening himself against the wall.

Pickens rushed into the hallway, his gun drawn. He pointed it at Earl.

"You forgot about Brad," said Earl. "He's standing right behind you and about to shoot if you don't drop the gun."

"He's right," Hitchens barked in a tremulous voice, the gun shaking in his hand. "Just lay it down gently."

Pickens started to turn his head, thought better of it, and complied.

Schmidt heard the commotion and figured his cohorts needed help. It was time to bid Garbuncle goodbye. He tossed the radio toward the tub and ran for the door. Garbuncle flipped onto his left side and kicked the radio away in mid-air with his right foot. The decrepit appliance landed on the floor, away from the water.

He leaped out of the tub, ran around the corner into the living room, and snatched his gun out of his jacket by the wall. He ran to the door, and saw Schmidt just outside the doorway, pointing his gun at Hitchens, who still held Bullard's gun with a violently shaking hand.

"Drop it," Schmidt ordered. Hitchens complied.

"Now it's your turn to drop it," Garbuncle said in a voice so calm he couldn't believe himself. Water dripped off his naked body onto the carpet.

"Do it," said Bullard from his position on the hallway floor. "They've got us."

"I'm counting to two, and on three you're a dead man," Garbuncle said. "One ..."

Schmidt hesitated, then dropped the gun. Hitchens pounced on Schmidt's and Bullard's pistols. Earl pulled Bullard upright and marched him, hobbling and holding his back, to the door. Hitchens handed Earl one of the guns.

"Come on inside, gentlemen," said Garbuncle. "Just take a seat on the couch there. I've got a phone call to make." He dialed 911, and reported his address and the situation. Then he darted into the bathroom and fetched his clothes while Earl held a gun on the men. Hitchens held the other gun by his side.

Four sheriff's deputies arrived in two squad cars.

"I live here, and these two men are my friends," Garbuncle said, gesturing toward Earl and Hitchens. "But these three fellows on the couch are intruders. I'm not sure which one is the expert lock picker, but suspect it's Mister Schmidt here. He seems to have a mechanical aptitude, which he used to disconnect the tie rods on my girlfriend's car. I should say my *late* girlfriend. She was killed."

The sergeant in charge asked a few questions, and the four officers handcuffed Pickens, Schmidt, and Bullard. The lawmen led the three into the glare of flashing red lights, deposited their cargo, and drove off.

"Earl, what did you do to that cop?" said Garbuncle. "He was hardly able to walk. I think you oughta go back in the ring. You've gotten a lot of practice lately."

"Looks like I'm more valuable outside the ring."

"You sure as hell are—and you know what?"

"I'm waiting," said Earl.

"You're gonna get a new carpet that'll knock your socks off. I'm talkin' plush."

"Wow. I can't say no to that. Always did prefer to go bare-footed."

"Anybody hungry for pizza?" said Garbuncle. "The game's already underway."

"Yeah," said Hitchens. "And a couple o' beers. I need to stop shaking. Good thing those guys didn't know I'd never handled a gun before."

CHAPTER THIRTY

The Miami Dolphins game went into overtime with the score tied at seventeen, and it was after 11:30 p.m. Garbuncle had a big day coming up, and knew he should clear his guests out and shut off the TV, but the game was exciting, and it helped the three relax after their ordeal. It ended with Miami losing by a field goal. But the attorney was too elated that he was still alive to feel down.

He was at the sheriff's office at 8 a.m., and asked the receptionist for a copy of the police report from the incident of the night before. Then he drove to the state attorney's office. Assistant State Attorney Darrell Seward was just heading out the door.

"Good morning, Mister Seward. I'm glad I caught you before you reached the courtroom. There was a little excitement last night, and I think you'll want to know the outcome." He handed him the police report. "Here's evidence of what's in the report," Garbuncle said, placing a hand over a large bandage on the back of his head and bending forward.

Seward looked at the patch of white tape holding gauze in place. He set his briefcase down, and read. Garbuncle watched his face become crestfallen.

"I'll see you in the courtroom," Seward said tersely. He walked out of his office and over to the adjacent courthouse.

Garbuncle drove to his office.

"Sorry I'm late, Alec. Let's go. We only have ten minutes. The trial begins at 9."

Seward was already seated at the prosecutor's table when Garbuncle and Alec entered and sat at the defense table. A smattering of people sat on benches in the gallery.

299

"All rise," the bailiff instructed. Everyone stood. "Court is now in session. The Honorable Jonathan Crabtree presiding. All please sit down."

The judge entered the courtroom and took his place at the bench.

"State of Florida."

Seward rose. "Your honor, I would like permission for the attorney for the defendant and myself to meet with you."

"Request granted. Please come forward."

The two attorneys walked to the bench. Seward asked if they could meet in the judge's chambers. Crabtree beckoned them to the door at the rear of the platform.

"Your honor, I will not be able to produce witnesses for this case. They are being held in the county jail following an incident that occurred last night." He handed the judge the copy of the police report. Crabtree read it and looked up.

"In light of this new development, the state would like to move that the charge against Alec Monceau be dismissed," Seward said.

"Are you in agreement with this request, counselor?" Crabtree said to Garbuncle.

"Yes, your honor, I am."

"Very well." The three returned to the courtroom.

"Mister Monceau, please rise."

He looked at Garbuncle, who smiled.

"I hereby dismiss the case against you. You are free to go."

Alec beamed. Garbuncle rose and embraced him.

"Come on. Let's get out of here."

When they reached the hallway, Garbuncle asked Alec to take a seat on the bench against the opposite wall while the attorney visited the restroom. He headed down the hall and around the corner to the men's room opposite the elevators, a jauntiness in his splayed stride. As he was about to enter the restroom, an elevator door opened, and he glanced sideways. He stopped in his tracks.

"Mister Feinberg, hello there. Aren't you a little late? The court is adjourned."

"There was a bad accident on I-95. What did I miss?"

"Not a lot. Let's walk over to the courtroom, and I'll fill you in. Somebody you know is there, and I'm sure he'd like to see you."

Garbuncle saw the skeptical look on the attorney's face.

"Come on, I'll lead you to him."

They went around the corner, and Garbuncle asked Feinberg about the accident to keep him distracted from what was ahead. They reached the courtroom. Without turning his head, Garbuncle motioned with his left arm for Alec to rise. Feinberg was looking at the courtroom door, and Garbuncle pointed to the other side of the hallway.

"The person you know is right over there."

Feinberg stared.

Garbuncle caught him as he staggered backward, his face much paler than the ghost he saw before him.

"You missed today's event, Mister Feinberg, but not to worry. Another trial will be coming up, and you'll be one of the featured participants. Along with a few of your friends: Larry Pickens, Pete Bullard, Jake Schmidt, and Bart Sutherland. That will be quite a menagerie. At least I think that's the right word: a collection of wild animals. You know—the predatory kind."

"I didn't do anything wrong."

"I guess that'll be up to the jury to decide, sir. After they learn about your fingerprints on 2,500 pieces of fake paper currency in the hundred-dollar denomination."

Feinberg spun around and hurried down the hallway.

"I'm sorry you couldn't get that money, Alec. It would have made your and your family's lives much less difficult."

"Dat okay, Mister Ham. I so happy you end trouble for me. I no know how tank you."

"You don't have to, Alec. You're going to be in the courtroom a couple more times, criminal and civil cases. But unlike before, you'll enjoy it. And so will I. We're going to collect that money after all. *Real* money. Tell your family in Trinidad you'll be coming home soon—for good."

The End